HUNTER'S DAWN

WHITE HAVEN HUNTERS BOOK FOUR

TJ GREEN

Hunter's Dawn
Mountolive Publishing

©2022 TJ Green

eBook ISBN: 978-1-99-004739-8

Paperback ISBN: 978-1-99-004740-4

Cover Design by Fiona Jayde Media

Editing by Missed Period Editing

This is a work of fiction. Names, characters, businesses, places, events, locales, and incidents are either the products of the author's imagination or used in a fictitious manner. Any resemblance to actual persons, living or dead, or actual events is purely coincidental.

All rights reserved.

No portion of this book may be reproduced in any form without written permission from the publisher or author, except as permitted by U.S. copyright law.

CONTENTS

1. One — 1
2. Two — 10
3. Three — 21
4. Four — 29
5. Five — 41
6. Six — 49
7. Seven — 58
8. Eight — 68
9. Nine — 82
10. Ten — 93
11. Eleven — 104
12. Twelve — 116
13. Thirteen — 123
14. Fourteen — 134
15. Fifteen — 145
16. Sixteen — 154

17.	Seventeen	166
18.	Eighteen	175
19.	Nineteen	184
20.	Twenty	193
21.	Twenty-One	202
22.	Twenty-Two	212
23.	Twenty-Three	223
24.	Twenty-Four	237
25.	Twenty-Five	249
26.	Twenty-Six	262
27.	Twenty-Seven	273
28.	Twenty-Eight	286
29.	Twenty-Nine	301
Author's Note		313
About the Author		316
Other Titles by TJ Green		319

ONE

"Well," Shadow said, looking around at the reinforced doors and security system cameras, "this is impressive."

Jackson smiled as he led them along the corridor. "Hazards of the Paranormal Division—and I guess government intelligence agencies in general. They have to be prepared for attack."

Gabe's eyes narrowed as he examined their surroundings. "I guess they do. It feels like a warren down here."

Harlan was walking alongside Shadow, and he nodded. "I think I'm lost already."

"I felt like that the first time I was here," Jackson admitted, "but I've got used to it."

Shadow exchanged a look with Harlan. As suspected, Jackson was very familiar with this place, and as usual, he'd underplayed his hand.

It was Wednesday morning in early July, a couple of weeks after the events with the Dark Star Astrolabe in France, and Jackson had invited Shadow, Gabe, and Harlan to the government's Paranormal Division headquarters. It was situated in the basement of the MI5 building and accessed via a rear entrance on Thornley Street. They had passed through the plain front rooms to a well-manned security checkpoint where they had been searched and scanned, and annoyingly, Shadow had to leave her weapons in the screening area—even the ones she tried to conceal.

Once through security, they used the lift to descend two floors down from street level, and found themselves in a low-ceilinged space with narrow corridors and small rooms. It felt cramped and neglected.

Harlan huffed. "It feels like you're out of sight, out of mind down here."

"That's exactly how they treat the PD, and it suits us," Jackson admitted, not looking concerned in the slightest. "The bigwigs don't really like to acknowledge what we do here. Hence the rear entrance. But there are a couple of labs here, a back entrance that leads to our own morgue, and even a few cells which we can use for a limited time. They have another entrance, too."

"I presume," Gabe said, prowling like a caged cat, "they are well guarded?"

"Of course." Jackson grinned as he stopped outside a closed door. "Anyway, time to meet our director, Waylen Adams."

Our? Shadow had a feeling they were being recruited, whether they wanted to be or not.

Jackson swung the door open into a very unusual office. The entire back wall was glass, and as they progressed into the room, Shadow could see that the vast window looked onto a couple of labs staffed with a handful of black-clad scientists. There appeared to be one old-fashioned laboratory, complete with alembic jars, glass jars, flasks, crucibles, and other equipment, and another one kitted out with state-of-the-art machinery and modern technology.

She inwardly groaned. *More alchemy and magic.* She'd pretty much had her fill of it with Black Cronos and JD, but knew it wasn't going away. However, she had very little time to take in the details, as a man rose from behind the desk and limped around to greet them as Jackson made the introductions.

ONE

Waylen was a very average man who Shadow estimated to be in his forties. Average height, average build, wearing an average suit, and with sensibly cut hair, but his eyes were a pale brown, the colour of honey, and it felt like they looked right through her.

"Good to meet you all," Waylen said, shaking their hands. "Jackson has explained how helpful you've been regarding Black Cronos." He ushered them into seats around a large, wooden table. "Your fighting skills are impressive."

"Er, not mine," Harlan said, shooting Jackson a nervous glance. "Are you sure you want me here?"

Waylen smiled, his sharp eyes narrowing. "Oh yes. You work with JD."

"Unfortunately, yes, I do. What's that got to do with anything?"

"I'll get to that." Waylen turned back to Gabe and Shadow, studying them with interest. "Not many could have killed so many of Black Cronos's...*soldiers*."

Gabe gave him a grim smile. "As I'm sure Jackson has told you, we have a few extra skills that others don't."

Waylen nodded. "Advanced fighting ability, wings, and," his gaze slid to Shadow, "fey magic."

Shadow bristled under his stare. "I presume we're here because you want our help."

"With Black Cronos, yes. We're trying to find where Toto Dax and The Silencer of Souls have fled to, but so far are having limited success. They've covered their tracks well. But," he stood and walked over to the window to look at the labs, "in the last twenty-four hours we have identified one lead that seems to be current. I'm just waiting on an update."

Gabe nodded. "And you want our help to find them?"

"Exactly." Waylen leaned against the glass and folded his arms across his chest as he stared at them. "I had originally thought to keep our search within this division, but I have to be realistic. We need your help. What I want to do now is secure your agreement. You have brothers, I understand, and a witch who helped you in France."

Herne's horns. Shadow knew she'd have to put up with more time around Estelle, but it still grated on her.

Gabe said, "Six brothers, but not all are free to help all the time. I organise their availability." He glanced over at Harlan. "We also work with The Orphic Guild, in addition to doing a few other things."

Waylen shrugged. "That's fine. I trust you to organise who you need and when. Just be aware that you may have to move quickly."

"We can do that—for a price. I presume you offer good rates?"

"We're competitive."

Shadow butted in before anyone else could answer. "You'll have to be *very* competitive. Black Cronos is dangerous. That means hazard pay. Or no deal."

"And," Gabe added, "we want real details, not just some sketchy, scant amount of information you're happy to tell us. If we're risking our lives, it's the least you can do."

"Agreed." Waylen limped back to the table and Shadow wondered what had caused his injury. If Waylen noticed her interest, he didn't explain himself, instead saying, "I want you to be successful, so of course I'll share what we have."

Gabe leaned forward, arms resting on the table. "Are we expected to catch them or kill them?"

"That really depends on the circumstances, I guess." Waylen glanced at Jackson, who was watching the exchange. "Jackson will liaise with you."

"And where do I come into this?" Harlan asked, looking very suspicious.

"I need you to keep tabs on JD, and make sure he doesn't get in the way."

Harlan snorted. "You've got to be kidding! You want me to watch that sneaky son of a bitch? I hardly ever see him. And in case Jackson didn't tell you," he gave Jackson a long sideways glance, "we're not exactly on good terms right now."

Waylen smiled. "I understand. JD is a tricky character. Has he recovered from his experience in France?"

"Being kidnapped by Toto Dax? I think his pride was more injured. It's Mason who was affected more. He's grieving for Smythe. In fact," Harlan shuffled in his seat, "it would be fair to say he wants revenge. He's furious."

Waylen's hands steepled together, elbows on his desk, and he leaned on them, his eyes hooded. "Yes, I understand that. They've been responsible for many deaths in their time. How is Caldwell Fleet? I gather his colleague was killed, too."

"As well as can be expected," Harlan told him. "Especially considering the manner of his friend's death."

"Aubrey Cavendish," Gabe said, his voice hard, "was killed by The Silencer of Souls. You wouldn't happen to know how she kills with her lips, would you?"

Waylen sighed. "I'm afraid not. But I would dearly like to."

Gabe muttered under his breath, "Of course you don't."

Shadow knew that Gabe had been more disturbed than he'd like to admit when he was attacked by The Silencer of Souls. Not many things unnerved him, but she did. However, Waylen ignored Gabe's sarcasm and opened a slim folder, extracting several sheets of paper. He slid them across the table, one for Shadow and Gabe, and one for Harlan.

"Our contract. It outlines our terms and pay. I need your answer now, though obviously I'll give you a few minutes to go through it." He headed to the door. "I'll be back soon."

In seconds he'd gone, leaving them alone, and Shadow leapt from her chair to study the labs beyond the glass wall. Jackson joined her. "Don't you want to read the contract?"

"I'll read it in a minute. I'm more interested in those." She nodded to the men carrying out their investigations. "You obviously come here a lot. Do you know what they're doing?"

Jackson gave a lopsided grin and ruffled his shaggy hair. The last time she'd seen him he'd looked tired, exhausted from the chase. He looked better now, flushed with success. "I'm not privy to everything that happens here, you know."

Shadow stared at his mischievous expression. "Liar! You're a dark horse, Jackson Strange."

He just laughed. "It's the name of the game." His eyes travelled across her face and then back to the labs. "I know some things, but am not privy to all. Some of the scientists are trying to recreate Toto's experiments. Not on humans, you understand!"

Shadow stifled a snort. "No, of course not!"

"I'm serious. It's more the alchemical process they're interested in."

"For now." Shadow knew how these things worked. The Paranormal Division were at a disadvantage, and they didn't like it. That's why they needed them. "They've been trying for years though, right? And failing."

"But the documents we found weeks ago have changed things."

Shadow turned to look at him. "Caldwell allowed you access to his papers?"

"Of course. That was the deal that allowed the order to have access to the Dark Star Temple." Jackson pointed to a far wall where a series of objects were laid out. "A few things we retrieved. But so far, all that they prove is that Toto—or someone—is a genius. And of course, he escaped with some of the research."

"It's early days though, isn't it?"

"Very."

"And you have the bodies?"

Jackson nodded. "Yes, and the remains of those who had been dead in that temple for years. They're being examined, too."

Images of blood tests and autopsies flooded Shadow's mind. *What a fate*. Another thought struck her. "What about Stefan Hope-Robbins? Has he said much?"

"Ah! No." Jackson rubbed his jaw, his eyes brooding. "But I haven't seen him for a few days. Our security team continues to question him, though."

That sounded suitably ominous.

"Have you found the order's mole yet?" They all knew someone had betrayed Caldwell and Aubrey, despite their protestations. Shadow just hoped Caldwell wouldn't become a victim, too. He was an odd man, but she liked him.

"No. Things have been very quiet there, but we're watching and waiting."

"And this new lead?"

"Looks good."

Before she could ask any more questions, Gabe called her over. "Have a look at this, Shadow."

She walked to his side and lifted the contract, skimming through it. "I'm happy with it. I'm sure your brothers will be, too."

He nodded. "At least we retain discretion as to how we organise ourselves."

Harlan's eyes narrowed as he put his contract down. "Standard waffle," he drawled, "and the money is okay, but I earn more not having to babysit that awkward bastard, JD."

Gabe looked at him, clearly amused. "You must get paid way more than us, then. I thought the rates were pretty good."

"Maybe you're risking death more than I am and your rates are better," Harlan answered, his hand raking through his hair. "I'm just risking my sanity."

Jackson was still at the window, and he called over, "You don't mind spying on your boss, then?"

"I'm not exactly comfortable with it, but if it keeps us all a little safer, I can deal with it." He signed his contact with a flourish. "JD is borderline nuts...a loose cannon. I guess that's what immortality does to you. Gives you a damn God complex. I'll do what I can to keep an eye on him. Hell, I try anyway! I may as well get paid for it now."

"I don't envy you," Shadow confessed, sinking into her seat again.

The last time they'd seen JD was in France, and he'd left early to go to the Paris branch, leaving the rest of them in peace at the *château*. Days of bliss, in which Shadow had only reluctantly left Gabe's bed. She only wished she hadn't hesitated for so long. She glanced at him now, noting his hard jaw, firm mouth, and dark olive skin. The sun was kind to him, and he looked good.

"Seriously, though," Harlan continued, addressing Jackson. "How the hell *am I* supposed to keep tabs on that man? He does what he likes when he likes, and I've barely seen him since France. And Mason is tight-lipped about him. There may even be a rift between them."

"Perhaps," Gabe suggested, also signing their contract and passing it to Shadow, "he blames him for Smythe's death."

"Yeah. I think there's a fair bit of that."

Despite the fact that Gabe and the others had saved JD and Mason, JD had barely given them thanks. Instead he was preoccupied with the papers that Caldwell had retrieved from the Minotaur's tomb. *Ungrateful bastard*. But Shadow reminded herself that she wasn't doing this for gratitude, but for the money, and JD was unlikely to ever show gratitude for anything.

"I think," Jackson mused, "that once JD knows we have a lead, he will suddenly make himself *very* available to you. Just make sure you keep him updated."

The door swung wide as Waylen re-entered, a broad smile on his face. "I hope you're happy with your contracts, because our lead has been confirmed. Can you travel today?"

"Today!" Gabe's voice rose with surprise. "Sure. But I need to get the team together. Where are we going?"

"Scotland. A remote abbey, in fact. We'll have to fly you there. We can provide weapons, but..."

Shadow interrupted him. "We prefer our own. Are you sending a team, too?"

Waylen's smile disappeared. "There'll be an extraction team like the last time for anyone you catch. Or kill. But you go in alone."

"And we attack tonight?" Gabe asked. "My preference is to do this in darkness."

"Absolutely."

"And some of my brothers will need flights from Cornwall."

Waylen didn't hesitate. "Not a problem. I just need names." He nodded to Jackson. "Liaise with him. He will organise it all."

"And me?" Harlan asked, alarmed. "Do I need to be there?"

Gabe answered immediately. "No. It's too dangerous. But we'll let you know what we find so you can update JD."

Harlan looked relieved as a wicked grin crossed his face. "Sure. I'd like to rattle him."

"In that case," Waylen said, skimming the signed contacts and adding his own, "here are your copies. Can you be ready by late afternoon?"

"No problem," Shadow said, already eager to be out of there. "But we need details. Background."

"Of course." Waylen settled himself at the table again. "I'll tell you what we know so far. But I warn you, it's not much."

TWO

Nahum ended the call with Gabe, his mind whirring with necessary preparations, and went in search of Niel, who was in the barn fighting with Ash.

The clash of metal and thumps carried across the courtyard, and he could see them easily as he approached. The weather was hot, and the barn doors were thrown wide open, revealing the dusty, straw-strewn interior. Ash was of a slimmer build than Niel, and more agile. Niel was ridiculously strong and brawny, so it was an interesting fight, and well matched for all their differences.

However, Nahum hadn't got time to indulge them. "Guys! We're flying to Scotland in a couple of hours. We need to pack and get to the airport."

Ash wiped a hand across his sweat-beaded brow and walked to his side. "Scotland? Are you kidding?"

"What for?" Niel asked, cricking his neck as he grabbed a towel and wiped himself down.

Both men were shirtless, their olive-toned bodies ripped with muscles. Niel had many tattoos, but Ash had tattoos only on his arms. Both had their hair tied up in top knots, revealing corded neck muscles.

TWO

"The Paranormal Division has got a lead on Black Cronos," Nahum told them, hoping neither had changed their mind about the pursuit of their alchemically-enhanced enemies. "It's just us going in."

A gleam of pleasure lit Niel's eyes. "Excellent. I take it negotiations went well?"

They all knew Gabe and Shadow had gone to meet Waylen Adams. "Good rates and no interference was pretty much all Gabe said. Even so, I think he was surprised we're involved so quickly."

"Are we taking Barak?" Niel asked.

"Gabe wants him," Nahum admitted. Barak was at Caspian's warehouse, flirting with Estelle no doubt. "Caspian has been good to us lately. I'm wondering how far we can abuse his generosity, though. It doesn't seem fair to keep pulling out and leaving him short-staffed."

Ash frowned. "It depends on what we find when we get to Scotland. If there are just a couple of them, it's not an issue, but if it's some kind of barracks, we'll need him. What *is* the situation?"

"Information is scant. But, they have tracked businesses and places owned by Toto Dax—tricky, it seems. Shell corporations and other such weird stuff. A lot of their leads proved to be old and useless. But then they traced an old Scottish abbey to Toto. They've been keeping a discreet eye on it, and Toto has been spotted in the area."

"Is *she* with him?" Niel asked.

Nahum knew exactly who he meant. *The Silencer of Souls*. "Yes, it seems so."

Ash groaned and started to collect some of the weapons in the barn. "Of course she is. I better head to the shower and start getting ready then." He gestured to the swords and daggers. "Can we get these on a flight?"

"You can with the permission of the government," Nahum said, glad there were some perks. "We'll need our protective vests, too. And Shadow wants her armour."

Niel smirked. "We need to go through her clothes?"

Nahum glared at him, thinking Niel might want to prank Shadow, which would be a very bad thing. "Leave that with me. Gabe is calling Caspian, so with luck Barak will be back within the hour."

He left them to prepare and headed to Shadow's room, thinking he should call Eli and Zee with an update, too. *At least leaving them behind wouldn't be a worry this time.* And they hadn't been bored while they were away, having helped the witches with their own problems.

For the next hour, Nahum kept busy packing their things, and was surprised when he heard Barak's shout and his footfalls along the hall. He appeared at the living room door, grinning with pleasure when he found Nahum packing up the large case of weapons.

"He let you go, then?" Nahum asked with a smile.

Barak headed to his side, idly picking up his own sword and running his palm along the flat of the blade. "Sounds like negotiations are up for us to be finished with Caspian in the next month or so. Just enough time for him to get more staff."

"I'm sort of sorry to hear that." Nahum took Barak's sword from him and placed it next to Shadow's armour, hoping he hadn't missed anything. "It's been steady work. Safe."

"It has, but this is better." His grin broadened, revealing white, even teeth that gleamed against his dark skin. "And Estelle is coming. She'll meet us at the airport."

"Good. We need a witch. I'm not sure you need the distraction, though."

Barak laughed. "I can concentrate."

"Really? You spend a lot of time checking her out."

"I like to show a woman that I appreciate her assets."

"I'm not entirely sure Estelle's that type of woman." The last thing Nahum and his brothers needed to deal with was a horny Gabe and Barak. "Go and pack your gear, because we need to be out of here in an hour." That wasn't strictly true, but Barak had a shower addiction and time pressure helped.

TWO

He nodded, already backing out the door. "And where are we staying?"

"No idea. It will be a surprise. Although, we might only be there for a night!"

Barak grunted and disappeared, leaving Nahum alone with his preparations, and wondering what they may face that night.

Harlan arrived at The Orphic Guild to the unfamiliar sight of Eloise Ward coming down the stairs.

She paused as she reached the bottom, greeting Harlan with a shy smile. "Hi, Harlan. Sorry, I know you only just got back, but Mason wanted to see you as soon as you arrived."

Eloise had taken over as Mason's secretary, and from all he could gather, she was having a hard time, mainly because she wasn't Smythe. She'd previously worked within the admin team, and was young and competent, and Harlan was pleased she got a promotion. She was always far more polite than Smythe when Harlan considered how he'd often greeted him with his supercilious attitude.

Pushing his uncharitable thought aside, he asked, "Is he cranky again?"

She nodded, and her blunt, dark bob fell around her flushed cheeks. *Grumpy bastard.*

"It will get easier...I hope. He's like that with all of us."

She nodded and straightened her shoulders. "I know. He's grieving, but we all are." A hand flew to her cheek. "It's not often a colleague dies under such circumstances, is it?"

"No. Let's hope it's the last time, too." He started for the stairs, and added, "I'll go and see him now."

"Thank you." She gave him a smile of utter relief and hurried onwards, and Harlan was suddenly glad he wasn't in his twenties and so unsure of himself anymore. *Although, maybe a little less cynicism wouldn't go amiss.*

Because it was Eloise who'd asked so nicely, he went straight to Mason's office, took a deep breath, knocked, and went in.

Mason scowled as he looked up. "Oh, it's you."

"I thought you wanted to see me?"

"You are quicker than I expected. Have a seat."

Clenching his fists and wishing he'd stopped for a shot of caffeine on the way, Harlan forced himself to be polite. "How can I help?"

"Black Cronos. Have you heard anything?"

For a moment, Harlan's fear that he was being spied on returned, and then he shook it off. This was a regular question from Mason, but the timing was uncanny. He lied, having decided that until there was definite news, he'd say nothing. "No. There have been tentative leads, but nothing certain."

Mason banged his fist on the table. "That's not good enough! They have got away with murder!"

"You've met them, Mason. They are well organised, heavily funded, and clever. It was never going to be easy. But Jackson assures me they are searching. The government is not without its own extensive resources."

"You're keeping in touch with him, then?"

"You know I am! But that isn't my job. I hunt occult objects, remember? I have cases that keep me busy."

"This is Smythe we're talking about! One of our own!" He shot off his chair and started pacing. "He deserved a better death, and JD is giving me nothing!"

"I'm sure he knows nothing. But you see him more than I do."

"He's holed up in Mortlake Estate right now, so I have no idea what he's doing. Messing with his bloody experiments, I presume."

Yep. There was definitely a rift. "Coming up with a way to find Black Cronos, no doubt."

"Or to turn himself into some sort of superhuman!"

Harlan blinked. "You think JD wants to do that? He's old!"

Mason smacked his chest over his heart. "It doesn't stop how you feel! And he felt very frustrated at being thwarted by Toto and that bloody woman and his team of aberrations!"

Fuck. He hadn't even considered that. "Toto has years of research on superhumans, and as ambitious as JD is, I'm sure he's not anywhere close to that." He hesitated, wondering if Mason knew something he didn't. "Is he?"

"I have no idea what he cooks up in his bloody laboratory." Mason marched to his cupboard, pulled his whiskey bottle out, and poured a hefty shot, downing it in one go. "I just want justice."

No wonder Eloise looked strained. Mason was having a very bad day.

Mason hadn't finished his rant. "Do me a favour, and keep an eye on JD."

"What?" *This day was getting weirder.* "You want me to spy on him?" He almost added 'too,' but quickly clamped his mouth shut.

"Did I say spy? No! Just keep an eye on him, and let me know if he does anything sneaky."

"That's called spying." Harlan wondered why he was complaining. He'd been given permission to spy on JD, and was getting paid to do it, too. The Gods were messing with him. "Seeing as he's not here, and I'm pretty sure you've noticed that we clash—badly, how do you suggest I do that?"

"I've got some papers I need him to sign. I want you to take them to him and see what he's up to."

"What kind of papers?"

"Does it matter? Just do it. I'll get them ready, and you can go tomorrow."

Harlan knew his mouth was hanging open and that he looked like an imbecile, so he cleared his throat and composed himself. And besides, this suited him perfectly. "Absolutely. Tomorrow. See you then."

And without giving him a chance to change his mind, he left Mason stewing and went to make himself a coffee. A strong one.

Despite the undoubtedly hard night ahead, Gabe was looking forward to visiting Scotland. It was another opportunity to see more of their new world, and it was even better that someone else was paying for it.

As the plane circled over Glasgow Airport, he noted the huge, sprawling city and the water beyond it, but of more interest was the endless green of Loch Lomond and The Trossachs National Park. Somewhere in there was Arklet Abbey and Toto Dax.

Shadow nudged his arm and looked past him to peer through the tiny window. "So much green!"

He nodded, breathing in her musky scent as her face pressed close to his. "And so rugged. It's very different to Cornwall."

"Wild. Untamed." She turned her head and stared at him. "Anything could happen tonight."

"Like that worries you!"

She gave her feral grin. "I'm looking forward to killing The Silencer of Souls." Her eyes narrowed. "Unless you want to."

"I don't care who kills her. But as much as I admire your enthusiasm and skills, that won't be easy—if she's even there!"

"I know. A girl can hope." Shadow leaned back, readying herself for descent. "When do the others arrive?"

"Half hour after us."

"Good. And Jackson?"

"I'm not sure. He just said he'd be in touch when he landed." He thought back to their last conversation before they boarded the plane. "I think the extraction team was holding him up. They'll be travelling in a private plane."

"Lucky for them!" Shadow arched an eyebrow.

He laughed. "So will Nahum and the others. That's the only way they get to bring all the weapons."

"Typical. And we go commercial!"

"But we get to travel unsupervised. I have a feeling Jackson will join us just to make sure we don't screw up."

She snorted, "As if!" and then fell into silence, no doubt like him, mulling on what they may find in Arklet Abbey.

When the plane landed, they threaded through the disembarking passengers to the rental cars and picked up the keys to the two SUV's that Jackson had arranged, and had only a short wait after that to collect the rest of the team. Gabe spotted Niel first, striding easily through the crowd, a good foot taller than most people, his blond Viking-like appearance drawing stares that he was oblivious to. However, his other brothers were just as tall, all drawing looks too, as they walked purposefully through the crowd, watchful eyes darting everywhere. Estelle was with them, and although she was much shorter, her appearance was just as commanding. Gabe just hoped she and Shadow would remain civil.

Niel raised a hand when he saw Gabe and Shadow, grinning when he reached their side. "Brother! Shadow. Another interesting night ahead."

"The Gods hate us to be bored." Gabe greeted his brothers and looked at the bags they carried. "You have the weapons?"

"Right here," Barak said, pointing to a large case. "And there." He nodded to one that Nahum carried.

"We better get on." Gabe turned to lead them to the car park. "I'd like to go over our plans before we head out there later."

"Where are we staying?"

"An old house the government keeps on standby. One of many, I gather, from what Jackson said. It's close to Loch Lomond."

"And our target?" Nahum asked, falling into step next to him.

"Arklet Abbey, not far from the shores of Loch Arklet. Isolated. One road in and out."

"So, we fly in then?"

Gabe grinned. "Absolutely."

Niel studied the map spread out on the table in front of them, marvelling at the many lochs, waterways, mountains, and endless greenery that surrounded the area.

"I see what you mean by remote, Gabe," he said, studying Loch Arklet in particular. "There aren't many roads around there at all."

Ash nodded. "Perfect for Toto's purposes."

"Perfect for ours, too," Gabe said. "Not many people around to see us fly."

They had all arrived at the large stone house on the edge of Loch Lomond about an hour before, and had quickly organised rooms and weapons. It was close to seven in the evening, and they had a few hours before darkness descended. Plenty of time to plan their attack. They were all gathered around the scrubbed wooden table situated at one end of a rustic kitchen. A huge picture window was next to them, offering a stunning view of the loch, but most of them were focussed only on the map.

"I feel I've missed the details," Estelle said, leaning back in her chair and picking up her coffee. "Tell me about this abbey."

Gabe nodded. "Arklet Abbey is privately owned, sold by the Church in the last century, and the ruins of the old abbey are still there.

One of the buildings was converted into a house." He dug out a couple of photos from under the map. "This is it. Toto has owned it for about thirty years, but there are very few records on it. It's at the end of a drive that lies off the road running alongside the north of the loch."

Barak was sitting next to Estelle and examined the photos with her. "So, it's just a private retreat?"

Gabe shrugged. "Perhaps. Various Paranormal Division scouts have been looking out for any sign of Black Cronos since France. They've investigated any buildings or businesses that belong to them—but it's been hard. Toto covers his tracks well. The one sighting they had of him yesterday is the only one anyone has had yet. We have to hope he's still there."

Niel felt disappointed. "I thought this was going to be a bunker where some of his soldiers were holed up."

"It might be, idiot!" Shadow said scathingly. "We don't know!"

Niel glared at her. "Yes, I gather that. Thank you for your sarcasm. So," he turned back to Gabe, "what's the plan?"

"I think a couple of us should circle the place first. It's not far from here. We can assess it properly, and then all of us can head over."

"Too risky," Barak said immediately. "I think we should all go and surround the place—move in slowly. If we're spotted overhead, they could leave."

Gabe's jaw tightened. "You were shot and poisoned the last time we went in blind. I'd like to avoid that."

"I know. But whether we have two trips or one, the risks are the same."

Nahum, always Gabe's right-hand man, sided surprisingly with Barak. "He's right, Gabe. The element of surprise is all we've got. I know you want to be safe, but Barak's idea is better."

"Agreed," Shadow said, taking the photos from Estelle to study them. "We have no idea what surveillance systems are there. Once in and out is easiest."

Niel was pleased her relationship with Gabe meant she still held her own opinions, and she was good at strategising. He knew Gabe liked independent thinking, too. Gabe's gaze dropped to the map, and the others exchanged speculative glances. Niel appreciated safety, but this was no time to be slow, and everyone knew it.

Finally, Gabe said, "You're all happy to go in sight unseen? That map and old photos are all we have. The layout could have changed."

Ash spoke for them. "Toto and Black Cronos are slippery. We strike once—hard."

"What about the extraction team?" Nahum asked. "Where are they?"

Gabe shrugged. "Arriving later with Jackson. We move without them. They have to catch up—Jackson's instructions."

"And Jackson?" Barak asked.

"Will be with them, well out of our way." Gabe rolled his broad shoulders, his expression still tight, and Niel knew he wasn't happy. Gabe was a planner, and this was sketchy. "Preferably we want Toto alive, and anyone else with him, but we all know that's unlikely. If your lives are at risk, their death is the only option. With luck, however, we'll find something of use in the house or grounds. But we clear it first!" He stared around the table. "Let's split into groups. Me and Shadow will take the front of the house. Barak and Estelle, you can take the rear. Nahum, Ash, and Niel, the abbey's remains."

Niel nodded, pleased. Black Cronos felt like unfinished business, and he was keen to put an end to their dangerous experiments. "Good. Now for some food," he said, rising to his feet. "I can't fight on an empty stomach."

THREE

Shadow slipped from Gabe's grip on the outskirts of a bare garden under the shadows of a huge tree, and watched the old, stone-built building on Arklet Abbey's grounds.

The abbey was situated at the head of a small valley, the hills rippling around them. It was a well-protected area, nestled in its spot that would probably be sheltered from wind. There was no sign of the loch from here, but she'd had a good view of it as they flew overhead. Fortunately for their safety, it was a cloudy night with little moonlight, and the air was cool and damp.

Their initial scan of the area had shown no movement, but they hadn't lingered, sweeping in low instead, the others doing the same. The building was more mansion than house, the ornate, gothic arched windows adding a chill to its appearance. Beyond were the remnants of the abbey, its huge, ruined buttresses rearing into the night sky.

Gabe leaned close to her ear. "That building over there looks to be a garage."

"No lights anywhere, though. It's a big place."

They stood for a moment more, trying to discern any noises disturbing the night, but there was only utter silence. If she hadn't known about the rest of their team, Shadow would have assumed they were alone.

"Come on," Gabe said, drawing his sword. "Let's take this slowly."

Keeping to the border of the poorly maintained lawn, they edged their way to the drive and garage. Shadow felt naked without her bow. She was looking for a new one, but so far, nothing she'd seen suited her. Instead, she pulled both swords free and followed Gabe, keeping watch while he looked inside the garage, converted from an outbuilding.

Moments later, he returned. "One car inside, but that's all. Let's hope that means Toto is here."

They prowled around the front of the house inspecting all the windows and doors, but everything was sealed tight. Shadow looked up to the floors above, and on the second floor spotted a partially open window. She nudged Gabe and pointed. In seconds he had extended his wings and holding her tightly, soared upwards. She opened the window wider, and Gabe set her on the sill. After assessing the darkened room, she dropped inside, Gabe quickly following.

They were in a bedroom, in the centre of which was a four-poster bed draped with heavy material. Evidence of female clothes and toiletries were strewn around, and Shadow saw Gabe's eyes light up.

Someone was here—perhaps The Silencer of Souls.

Again they waited, breath held, but still hearing nothing they passed into the corridor. A low light burned at the end, but it was an inner corridor, with no windows to reveal the glow. Gabe headed left and she went right, easing open doors to peer inside the rooms, but the whole house was unnervingly silent.

They congregated on the landing, and together they progressed downward. They would search floor by floor, and room by room. Toto had to be here somewhere.

Barak grimaced. "It's too quiet."

"Did you think they'd be having a party?" Estelle looked at him, amused.

"What the hell else would you do around here? Oh, wait." A big grin spread across his face. "I can think of something."

"Your mind is in the gutter again. *Focus.*"

She turned away, but she was smiling, and Barak knew she liked his flirting. *Good. He wasn't planning on stopping.* He was in this for the long game, and so far she'd kept him at arm's length, but he sensed her resolve weakening as she began to trust him. Estelle was wary of men and relationships, and he didn't know if it was because of a bad experience, or just her normal defensiveness. Whatever it was, he was prepared to wait.

But she was also right. He needed to focus. The rear of the house was a walled kitchen garden, and once no doubt it would have been magnificent. A glasshouse lay to one side, but now most of its windows were broken, and the garden beds had run to weeds. It was also huge, and at one point it had probably fed the entire abbey.

Estelle however was focussing on the house, and she pointed at a ground floor window where a chink of light was visible. She put her finger to her lips, and they crept across the grounds, keeping to the shadows. But once outside the window there was no sound from within. Barak edged to the back door and turned the handle. It was open, and he felt both excited and wary. He had a horrible feeling that they'd been spotted and were walking into a trap.

Nevertheless, he pushed the door open and stepped inside, Estelle on his heels.

"Another building consecrated to a God who doesn't care," Ash said, shaking his head as he stepped beneath the ruined arches. "What a waste. All that time spent worshipping when they could have been doing something more useful."

Niel snorted so softly he sounded like a horse snickering. "It soothed their soul, you heathen."

"Heathen yourself," Ash shot back, and the damp air swallowed his words.

"Will you both shut up?" Nahum hissed. "We're supposed to be finding Black Cronos."

Ash stepped into the deep shadows and studied the remnants of old walls lost within long grass, the silence settling around them. "No one's been here for a long time, brother. It's too eerie. Look at the grass—no footprints. Untended grounds. Slabs broken into rubble with weeds and time."

"This place may be for the ghosts, but the house is intact," Nahum pointed out. "Let's pan out in a line and sweep our way towards the house. Step carefully in case there are traps."

"I'm not a novice," Niel complained.

"Then get on with it!" Nahum said.

Ash subdued a smile and walked to the far corner to begin his sweep, but his foot caught on something, and he stumbled. Crouching, he saw an iron ring sticking out of a stone slab, only the edges covered by grass. "Nahum!"

Nahum spun around, his eyes widening as he focussed on the spot, and he summoned Niel, all three of them examining the ground together.

"There's no sign of footprints around this, either," Ash noted.

"But," Nahum said, poking the turf, "the grass isn't embedded in the stone."

Niel nodded. "As if it's been partially maintained." He lifted his gaze. "And it's in the corner of the grounds. Easy to get into the woods from here."

Nahum's eyes gleamed in the darkness as he studied the treeline only a short distance away. "An escape route, perhaps." A smile spread. "Keep watch, Ash, and we'll head to the house."

Ash looked up at the ruined walls and shells of window frames, and high above him saw the perfect spot. A ledge within the curve of the ruined gothic arch. "I'll be up there. Happy hunting."

Within moments he was settled on the cold stone, the window edge at his back, the abbey remains spread below him, and placing the crossbow on his knees, he settled in to wait and watch.

Gabe scanned the dark kitchen, his excellent night vision easily seeing used pots and pans stacked on the side. *Someone was definitely here, but where were they now?*

As he and Shadow progressed through the house, they had found another bedroom in use, and once on the ground floor, increasing evidence of people living there. Newspapers left in a darkened lounge, the remnants of a fire, boots and coats in the hall. The silence, however, was unnerving.

Gripping his sword tightly, Gabe stepped back into the hall where Shadow was standing, virtually invisible in the darkness. A sound up ahead startled both of them, and as they progressed down the long corridor, a chink of light came through a partially closed door, and then the murmur of voices.

Gabe raised his sword and flung the door open. It banged against the wall, sounding like a gunshot in the silence, and he leapt through, sword raised, only to come to a skidding halt as he faced Barak's sword and Estelle with fire balling in her palms.

"Herne's bloody horns!" he exclaimed. "I thought you were Toto!"

Barak sheathed his weapon with a sheepish grin. "Sorry, brother. I thought *you* were!"

Gabe panned around the room, taking in the well-stocked bookshelves and desk laden with papers. "A library." He frowned at Barak. "Why did you put the light on?"

"We didn't," Estelle answered in her usual sharp tone, and once again Gabe wondered what Barak saw in her. "It was the only room with a light on. We found the back door open and searched the entire ground floor, but there's no sign of anyone here."

Shadow hadn't sheathed her weapons, and instead stood just inside the room looking back into the darkened corridor. "We found the same upstairs. But two bedrooms show signs of occupation. They must have heard us arrive...or were warned." She swung her gaze back to the room. "But why is this light on?"

"And why is the car in the garage?" Gabe asked as he headed to the desk and shuffled through the papers on it. "It's not rusty or dusty. I think it arrived here recently."

Barak grimaced. "They're hiding. They must be. On the grounds, perhaps?"

Gabe shook his head. "In the ruins? I doubt it. The others must have had time to search by now, and we would have surely heard something if they'd found anyone." A sudden image of his brothers lying dead in the ruins had him swinging around. "I'm going to look outside. Keep searching in here, Barak. These papers may give us a clue as to where they've gone."

"I'll come with you," Shadow said.

In moments they stood at the threshold of the back door, but before they could step outside, they heard Nahum's soft call. "It's us, brother." He stepped out of the shadows of the far wall, Niel with him, and headed to their side.

"Where's Ash?" Gabe asked, looking behind them.

"Watching the grounds from above," Niel said, "and what may be a possible escape route. That's all we found. You?"

Gabe explained what they'd discovered, adding, "It's freakishly quiet, and I don't like it." An uncomfortable prickle crept along his skin as he considered their options, still feeling like there was a trap waiting to be sprung. "I don't understand why this door was left open, when everything else is locked tight."

"It's a walled garden. Secure," Shadow pointed out as she studied the space. "They could just feel safe here…or, it's a lure."

Unable to shake off his worry, Gabe said, "Come inside, and we'll talk in there."

When they returned to the library, Estelle was examining shelves and pulling out books, and Barak was searching the desk. Both looked relieved to see Niel and Nahum.

"Tell us about the escape route," Gabe said immediately.

"Ash found a stone slab in the earth with a ring set into it," Nahum explained. "It's big enough that someone could get through it, and it's in the far corner of the ruins. It seemed suspicious."

Shadow nodded. "It's likely that an old abbey would have passages or cellars beneath it."

"And perhaps access from here," Barak said, pausing in his search. "Perhaps there's a hidden door in this room."

Niel nodded. "It would explain why this has the only light on. Maybe it's their after-dinner activity."

"An underground lab?" Gabe asked. "That might mean more people are down there, but I doubt it. It's too quiet, and there are not enough cars parked." His gaze swept around the room again, and he noted Shadow had joined the search, pulling books out and tapping the panelling while Niel and Nahum looked at him expectantly. "You want to lift the slab, don't you?"

Niel grinned. "Of course. We need to flush them out. *If* they're there!"

"They're here somewhere, I know it! And I'd rather *them* be on the end of a trap than us. Which it could be!" He rubbed his jaw. "Okay. Niel, you and Ash lift that slab, and if there's something under there, head inside—carefully. We either flush them out to here, or if we find an entrance, we pincer them in. Nahum, go with Niel just to see what they find, and then report back."

As they left the room, Estelle said, "I could try a finding spell, it's one of my specialties, but I'd need something of theirs. Something very personal."

"There'd be something in the bedrooms," Shadow suggested, clearly eager to get on with it.

"Let's focus on searching this room thoroughly first," Gabe said, finally sheathing his sword. "Anything interesting in the papers, Barak?"

"Nothing much. Alchemical documents, books on ancient civilisations—all too varied to narrow them down..." Barak was crouching as he searched through the drawers and he paused, his lips tightening. "I can feel something."

Everyone stopped and stared as a small click broke the silence, and a section of the bookcase opened a few inches. Estelle was closest and she pulled it open carefully, revealing a hollow wall behind it and dark stairs leading downwards.

FOUR

Ash had been walking through the deserted passages beneath the abbey for several minutes when something snarled in the darkness, and then flew at him.

It landed on his chest, throwing him to the ground as jaws snapped at his face, drool splattering everywhere. His sword clattered out of his right hand, and he fumbled for it, while his left hand pushed against the beast's neck, suspending it above him. It was a dog, hugely muscled, with an enormous head and jaw, and glowing red eyes.

He yelled, "Niel! *Help!*"

Niel came running from a side passage, and within seconds, the animal was dead as his sword pierced its side. "What the fuck, brother?"

But Ash didn't have a chance to answer, as the clattering of claws on stone announced more. He had barely thrust the dead body off him when a second one leapt from the darkness. Ash fumbled for his sword, angling it upwards so that as the dog leapt, it landed on his upturned blade, again pinning him to the ground.

Niel leapt over him, axe swinging as he faced the others racing towards them. Ash scrambled from under the weight of the beast, cursing profusely, and trying to maintain a tight grip on his sword, the pommel now slick with blood. He managed to find his feet as another dog leapt from a side passage behind him. *What was this place? A kennel for demon dogs?*

"Are you with me?" Niel yelled, the crunch of his axe sounding brutal as it bit into another dog.

"Yes! Keep moving!"

Back-to-back, they battled down the passage, gore splattering, bodies strewn in their wake, trying not to stumble over the dead animals. The sharp smell of blood and confined beasts was strong, and their snarling filled the air with menace, but a startled yelp heralded the last of them as they entered a long, low room.

Finally able to draw breath, Ash scanned the space, noting the open cages down each side and a camera in the corner. "Niel. Up there. There must be other cameras we missed. They would have seen us enter."

Niel groaned. "Fuckers. There's a control room somewhere."

"Has to be down here...unless it's hidden in the house."

Niel grunted as he headed to the corner, looked into the camera, and roared, "I'm coming for you!" He smashed the camera and marched to the next exit. "Onwards, brother. There's more killing to do."

Barak had barely progressed down the first passage beneath the house when he felt something click beneath his feet.

He threw himself backwards, crashing into Gabe behind him as he yelled, "Everyone down!"

They dived to the ground as sharp metal spikes catapulted out of the walls ahead, zinging across the passage and thudding into the other side. No one moved as they waited for something else to happen, Estelle and Shadow also crouching in anticipation.

FOUR   31

But when silence fell, Barak struggled to his feet and pulled Gabe up. "It's a bloody death trap! Sorry, brother."

"I'd rather be squashed than you impaled."

Estelle threw a couple of witch-lights down the stone corridor, illuminating the long spikes embedded in the opposite wall, all at head and chest height.

He exchanged a wary glance with Estelle, and she pointed at the rectangular stone on the floor that Barak had stepped on, now a couple of inches below the others it was set into. "This whole place could be booby trapped, and it doesn't look that different from the rest of the floor."

Shadow had been at the rear, but she shouldered her way forward. "Let me. I'm lighter on my feet."

"But not weightless!" Gabe protested.

"I have an idea," Estelle said. "Let's see if I can trigger anything else. Let's face it, if they're down here, they'll know we're here by now."

Conjuring balls of energy into her palms, she launched them down the corridor, using them like cannon balls, and as they ricocheted off the walls and ground, spikes flew from hidden recesses and pits opened up the whole way down. At the end was a wooden door.

"They really want to keep us out of here," Shadow said, almost sounding impressed.

Barak still wanted revenge for the injury that had almost killed him, and he gripped his sword even tighter. "Well, they won't. Nice job, Estelle. Let's get this over with."

Estelle laid a hand on his arm. "Hold on. Why don't I open the door from here?"

She hurled more balls of energy directly at the door, her lips moving with a noiseless spell, and it blew off its hinges with a splintering crash. A deeper boom came from beyond it, and flames shot through the doorway. *Another booby trap.* While dust and debris billowed out, Barak used it as cover for his approach. He stepped carefully but confidently across sprung traps and around the spikes, finally pausing at the doorway and the ruins within, the others right behind him.

It was a control room, a handful of screens on the wall, all of which had been destroyed. Only one door lay on the other side, and it opened onto another corridor.

"Damn it," Gabe said. "They're on the move. Estelle, want to do the honours again?"

She didn't answer, instead just stepping up and hurling her cannon balls of energy down the next corridor. Nothing was triggered, but they saw multiple passages opening, and the slam of a door echoed from the far end.

Barak gave chase, the others on his heels.

"Shit!" Niel exclaimed as a boom echoed down the corridor, the ground rumbling beneath their feet, and Ash echoed his sentiment.

They were progressing slowly through the few empty rooms they found beyond the kennels, deciding to stick together for safety, but all they found were the detritus of desks and research stations. It seemed that although the dogs had been fed and looked after, the rest of the place had fallen into disuse.

Now they picked up the pace, Niel's thoughts with his brothers approaching from the other end.

They entered the next corridor and soon found their way blocked by a reinforced gate with heavy steel beams, another passage on the far side. He studied the rock that the gate was set into. It looked solid, and there were no obvious signs of a mechanism to open it.

"Think we can move this?" he asked Ash.

Ash ran his hands around it, frowning. "Odd. There has to be a way to open it."

FOUR 33

"I'm happy to try brute force," Niel said, putting his axe down and gripping the bars.

Ash joined him, and together they pulled, muscles straining with the effort, but nothing budged.

And then footsteps sounded, and light bloomed on the other side, illuminating Toto Dax and The Silencer of Souls running towards them. Both carried bulky bags and were breathing heavily. Toto barely glanced at them, skidding to his left, and disappearing down another passage, but the woman paused, and a smile spread across her face.

She pulled an object from her pocket and pointed it at them, and Niel felt himself being yanked back by Ash before an explosion ripped through the air, throwing them backwards as rock rained down on them.

The explosion knocked Shadow and her companions off their feet, but she rolled with it, and in seconds had vaulted over the others and raced down the corridor.

They had cornered their enemies, and Shadow was not about to lose them, even when she careened into a well-lit room covered with maps and images of stone tablets. She gave it barely a glance and raced onwards, the passage beyond snaking away.

Shadow reached a section filled with dust, and hesitated for a second before seeing a clear passage on her left, and she ran again. If they were ahead of her, then the route must be safe. She was vaguely aware of Gabe calling from behind her, but she ignored him, rounding a corner before finally skidding to a halt. The Silencer of Souls was a short distance away, waiting for them. A bag rested at her feet, and she clutched something in her hand.

Shadow studied the ground, wondering what new level of Hell was between them. The corridor was plain stonework, floor and walls smooth and unadorned. Still Shadow waited, her eyes locked with The Silencer of Souls, who wore an enigmatic smile. Shadow itched to wipe it off her face, and she clenched her swords.

But something was wrong.

Gabe arrived, breathless, at her side. "What's..."

The Silencer of Souls smiled as she lifted her hand. Shadow felt a searing pain in her chest as she flew backwards. A boom filled the air, and then utter darkness fell.

Nahum hovered over the abbey grounds, the dull booms below him making him more and more worried, especially when a wall crumbled before his eyes, masonry thudding to the ground. The booms were powerful. *What was going on down there?*

He kept a close eye on the dark hole that had been revealed when they moved the stone slab, but no one emerged. Nahum suddenly made up his mind. He couldn't wait any longer.

He dropped to the ground and descended the stone staircase, very quickly stumbling across dead dogs in the dust-filled air. With increasing panic, he raced onwards, barely noticing the rooms he ran through, and finally saw Ash pulling Niel out from under a pile of rubble.

Nahum raced to help, lifting chunks of rock and hauling them out of the way. "What happened?"

"Toto and The Silent Bitch. Who else?" Ash said bitterly, coughing as he spoke. "The whole damn place is booby trapped."

"Stop yakking and get me out of here," Niel complained, struggling to get one arm clear.

FOUR 35

As Nahum moved another chunk of rock, Ash grunted and finally pulled Niel free. He was covered in cuts and dust, but his eyes were furious as he staggered to his feet, his right arm limp at his side.

Niel's voice was a growl as he asked, "Where is she?"

"Gone, brother," Ash answered.

Niel groaned and coughed, hacking up dusty spit as he leaned his left hand on his knee. He peered up at Nahum. "Tell me you found them."

"I came looking for *you*!"

"Nahum, find me that bitch right now!"

There was a dangerous glint in Niel's eyes. A berserker glint he'd seen before, and the end was never pretty. "What are you going to do?"

"Move this rubble and get through."

"No, you're not. The search is over on this end. You move that and it will all come down on your heads. *Again*. Ash, make him see sense! I need to check on the others."

Ash nodded, and Nahum ran for the exit, hearing Niel yell, "I am not stopping now!"

Gabe saw the blast hit Shadow, and an explosion of fury ripped through him.

As she flew past him, he raced forward, and he saw the shock in The Silencer's eyes as she retreated. She thought she'd take them both out. He was happy to prove her wrong.

She turned her weapon on him, but he was too quick, and he threw himself at her. Unfortunately, the bag that was on the ground tripped him up, and his momentum wasn't as great as he'd planned. Instead of tackling her around the waist, he caught her legs instead.

They both landed with a thud, but she kicked her way out of his grasp, her boot striking his jaw. Gabe's head snapped back, and blood filled his mouth. He staggered to his feet, whipping his sword from his scabbard. But she had gained precious seconds.

Her weapon—something small and metallic—had skidded across the ground, and with lightning-quick reflexes, she rolled and grabbed the weapon in one slick move, shooting at Gabe. He dived out of the way, and he saw her eyes dart to the bag. But he was between her and it, and leaping to his feet again, he charged at her.

She turned and ran, firing multiple shots behind her. One struck the roof of the passage, and with a thunderous roar, it collapsed, dust billowing out. Once again Gabe found himself on his back. He blinked several times and brushed dust from his eyes and face, desperate to see his surroundings. But when the air cleared, he saw that the way ahead was completely blocked. The Silencer of Souls had gone.

He regained his feet, slower this time. Everything ached, and his head pounded. He studied the other direction, and to his horror saw that Shadow was motionless. "Shadow!" His voice sounded muffled in his ears, as if he was deep underwater. The explosion had deafened him.

He skidded to Shadow's side, but she didn't move. She'd hit the wall and was lying in a crumpled heap, a huge dent in her breast plate. His heart almost stopped when he saw blood trickling from Shadow's slack mouth. He'd always thought of her as indestructible. She was such a force of nature. But right now... Lifting Shadow as carefully as he could, he limped back down the corridor to the main chamber where he'd left Barak and Estelle.

Barak met him just beyond the entrance, words dying on his lips as he took in the sight of Shadow in his arms. "In here, on the table." He ran before him, sweeping everything onto the floor so Gabe could lie her down.

FOUR

In the light of the bare bulbs hanging from the ceiling, he could see Shadow's injuries more clearly. The massive dent in her fey armour ended in a sharp point, but it hadn't broken. Blood smeared her forehead from where rubble had struck it, and her breathing was shallow. He quickly loosened her breastplate, cursing his shaking fingers. Gabe could barely think straight. Or hear. His ears were still ringing, and everything sounded muffled around him.

"Let me," Estelle said, resting her hand on his. He saw her mouth the words rather than heard them, and he blinked the dust from his eyes and stepped back.

She was deft as she commanded Barak to help her, freeing the fastening that secured the armour and quickly stripping it away to reveal Shadow's supple leather jacket beneath it. Estelle also unzipped that, just enough to see a huge bruise already spreading across Shadow's chest. Estelle laid a hand on bare skin and said a spell, and Shadow took a sharp intake of breath. Estelle nodded to herself, and then did a quick sweep of Shadow's other injuries, magic swirling across her skin.

Satisfied, she turned to Gabe who stood stupefied, wishing he could think straight. He was used to keeping a clear head in battle, and wasn't sure if the blast had addled his brain, or if it was his worry about Shadow. Whichever, it infuriated him. Estelle forced him into a chair and laid hands on either side of his head. Barak watched, arms folded across his chest. Gabe's eyes idly travelled around the room as he felt her magic wash over him like a cool breeze. The underground chamber had a couple of large tables, chairs, and work benches around the edges, as well as drawings and maps on the walls. It looked as if things had been evacuated hurriedly. There were bare patches in places, and papers scattered across the floor, but several images caught his attention—photos of a stone tablet. He tried to rise to his feet, but Estelle forced him back with a frown.

"Just wait! Bloody men," she muttered under her breath, and he subdued a smile as he realised his hearing was returning.

Barak wagged a finger at him and winked.

"Can you do me a favour, Barak?" Gabe asked, suddenly realising he'd abandoned their weapons and the bag. "Can you find our swords and her bag? Head to the left once—"

Barak interrupted him, already walking to the door. "No problem. Stay put!"

After another few moments, during which his hearing improved, Estelle straightened and lowered her hands. "There you go. That's as much as I can manage right now."

He smiled at her. "You're a miracle worker. I feel much better. What about Shadow?"

"She's a stubborn, hardy madam," Estelle said, returning to her side. "I'll work on her head now, since you're fixed and she's breathing."

Gabe headed to the images that had caught his attention, but knew he needed to thank Estelle properly. "Look, Estelle, I know we don't always see eye to eye, but you've been fantastic tonight. The way you triggered those traps, and then healing us…"

She met his eyes, her expression sincere. "Thank you for letting me join you. You've given me a lifeline I didn't know I needed." And with that enigmatic statement, she turned her attention back to Shadow.

Gabe stared at her a moment longer and decided not to pursue it, instead studying the photos of the stone tablet. They were taken from various angles, but one in particular showed how big it was. The writing on it was tiny cuneiform, and he strained to read it. A few words, however, caught his attention immediately, and he groaned with dismay. *The Igigi. What did Black Cronos want with them?*

Nahum spent a good while flying over the abbey grounds and surrounding area, his keen eyes investigating every moving branch, twitching shadow, and swaying grassy patch. But there was no sign of Toto or The Silencer of Souls.

He checked the garage a couple of times and made sure the car was still there, but eventually had to conclude they'd either holed up underground, or had an escape route that led them far from the abbey.

Anxious to check on his brothers, he finally returned to the passageway, finding that Niel and Ash had cleared the way, and had used the huge, metal-barred gate to wedge into the weakened roof. *Clever.* Casting a wary glance at it as he passed beneath, Nahum pressed onwards, finally hearing Niel's strident boom.

"The bloody *Igigi*? You have got to be kidding me!"

A glow of light up ahead illuminated Barak standing by a door, armed with two swords and a grim expression, and Nahum shouted, "It's just me!"

His posture relaxed. "Good hunting, brother?"

"No. You?"

Barak stepped aside, allowing him to enter the room. "Nothing but images and papers they abandoned after a concerted attempt to kill us all. We did manage to get her bag, though." He gestured to a holdall that was half unpacked on a table, papers spewing out of it.

Everyone was clustered around a series of photos. All except for Shadow, who was sitting in a chair, a mixture of pain and fury on her face, and Nahum asked, "Did I hear the Igigi mentioned?"

Barak rolled his eyes and nodded to the photos. "Yes. It seems that tablet provides a way to find them."

Disbelief rolled through Nahum. "Impossible."

"See for yourself. I've had my fill for now, and just want to get out of here." He lowered his voice, but there was no chance of anyone hearing him anyway over the heated debate. "Gabe is not himself."

Nahum nodded at his warning, and not feeling ready to argue with Gabe right now, crouched next to Shadow, noting her damaged armour on the floor. "What happened to you?"

Her violet eyes that were normally so teasing were now hard, pain lurking behind them. "Guess."

Nahum exhaled. "Anyone else injured?"

"Gabe, Niel, Ash—all less than me, fortunately."

Maybe it was because Nahum had only just entered the chambers and the others were used to them, or maybe it was because he hadn't got swept up in the Igigi talk, he wasn't sure, but he knew they needed to leave. He suddenly wished he hadn't left the entrances unguarded.

He stood abruptly. "Gabe. Now isn't the time. We need to take what you need and get out of here." Gabe turned to him, startled, a huge bruise darkening his cheek and blood staining his lips. He looked feral. The raised voices died as the others faced him, too. Under the bright lights, Nahum could see Niel holding his right arm awkwardly, he and Ash splattered with blood, cuts, and grime, and Gabe didn't look much better. Only Estelle and Barak were unharmed. Most of his brothers seemed to have been possessed by some collective madness. "What is the matter with you all? I can't find Black Cronos, and for all I know they'll be back with reinforcements. The last thing we need is to be trapped down here like cornered rats." He clicked his fingers angrily. "Focus!"

Reason returned to Gabe's eyes. "Of course. You're right."

"I'm going to sweep above the house and grounds, and I'll see you back at our rental in fifteen minutes. Agreed?"

Gabe nodded, and as Nahum turned on his heel and left, he said to Barak, "Get them moving."

FIVE

Ash called Jackson, relieved when he answered the phone. He left the group in the kitchen and wandered onto the slabbed patio, glad of the peace and the night breeze that kept away the midges.

"Where are you, Jackson?"

"In a van on our way to the abbey, why?"

"I suggest you come here instead." He quickly summarised the events of the night.

Jackson's normally confident tone faltered. "They've escaped? *Again?*"

"Honestly, we're not sure where they are. They're either circling back, or have a well-planned escape route."

"Did you get anything?"

Ash sighed as he remembered the scant items they'd been able to salvage. "Look, come here and we can explain better. Preferably without your team."

He listened to the mumble of voices while Jackson conferred, and then he said, "I'll be with you soon."

Ash turned to watch the drama playing out in the kitchen, the bright yellow lights showing the tableau of activity. Niel was doing what he always did when faced with a crisis—he cooked. Right now he was cooking up a storm, a very apt word for it too, because the crash of pans was like thunder. Gabe was having a heated debate with Nahum, both of them wearing stern expressions, both gesturing at the papers they'd rescued that were placed on the table and the images now secured to the kitchen walls. Barak was leaning on the counter, arms folded across his mammoth chest as he watched and listened, the quiet centre of the space. Estelle and Shadow were elsewhere in the house, Estelle tending Shadow's wounds. *Yet another worry.*

In the cool of the garden, unseen, he studied the images of the stone tablet, pondering on the references to the Igigi. They were their contemporaries a lifetime ago—half man, half beast. Some of whom could fly. *No wonder Black Cronos was interested in these hybrid creatures.* They were created by the Sumerian Gods, the Anunnaki, for labour, and were treated as slaves. Monstrously strong, considered demons by some, they eventually fought back and fled across the desert, before vanishing without a trace. At the time, rumours were varied. Some said they were dead, their bodies buried where no one would find them. Others said they had made a new life for themselves. Even if they had survived, in theory they would have died later in the flood.

Taking another deep breath, Ash returned to the kitchen, took a seat at the table, and pulled the papers towards him, hoping not to get dragged into the argument.

Too late.

"Ash! You're the scholar amongst us!" Gabe said, his expression tight. "What do you think this passage means?"

"I've barely looked at it, so I can't say right now. Maybe when I've had a chance to read it properly..."

"Read it now! It's legible!"

Ash's gaze slid to Nahum, whose eyes held a warning, and then back to Gabe. "It's a large amount of text. We'd be unwise to jump to conclusions."

"But if Black Cronos know where they are..."

"*Were*," Nahum corrected him. "They still have to find the place, and that won't be easy!"

Gabe rounded on him. "But they could have been studying that text for months!"

"Or mere days," Ash said calmly. "Obviously they thought the stone tablet important enough to hide within a booby-trapped bunker, but it doesn't mean they've found anything."

"If anything," Barak added, "it means they're only just starting to translate it. Look at it! The photos are clear, but the writing is tiny. Certain words are weathered and damaged. Even we who translate easily would have to make calculated guesses to interpret it properly."

Ash shot Barak a grateful glance. They had all been shaken by mention of the Igigi, but he was glad to see that most of his brothers were calming down now. "Exactly. We need to take these home and study them properly. What I'd like to know is where that stone tablet is."

Nahum nodded. "I'd like to see the original too, but that would seem impossible right now."

A knock at the door disturbed them, and Ash stood. "That will be Jackson. I'll get it."

Barak waved him down. "Let me."

Instead of sitting again, Ash left Nahum to reason with Gabe, and headed to the fridge to get a beer. He wished he could go to bed, but knew they needed to talk a few things through before then. Their nerves were all on edge after the night they'd had. He was aching from the earlier explosion, and grimy with dust and dirt. He grabbed several bottles, placing one on the counter next to Niel. "Are you okay?"

Niel grunted as he flipped the steaks using his left hand, his right arm now in a sling. "I'm more annoyed that we got bested by that bloody woman than the Igigi."

"How's your arm?"

"Sore, but I can feel it getting better already. Muscle damage to my shoulder—not a break."

Ash nodded. One of their abilities was understanding their bodies' injuries, as well as healing them quickly. "Good. We'll come across her again, there's no doubt about that. You'll get your revenge. We all will."

As he crossed the kitchen to the table with the other beers, Barak returned with Jackson, Estelle, and Shadow. Whatever healing magic Estelle had used on Shadow had worked. She looked to be her normal feisty, self—well, almost.

Shadow turned down Ash's offered beer, instead heading for the fridge. "Gin for me."

"Me too, please!" Estelle called after her as she sat at the table. She and Shadow still didn't seem that comfortable together, but at least their blatant animosity had waned.

Shadow nodded and prepared their drinks, but Jackson paused at the door to the kitchen, his sharp eyes sweeping over them. "If you don't mind me saying so, tensions seem to be high tonight, and many of you look injured. What happened?"

Ash tapped the chair next to him. "Take a seat. This will take a while."

"You all need to sit," Niel's commanding voice said. "Food is ready. We can talk while we eat."

Jackson laughed. "Steak and chips at three in the morning! I haven't done that since my student years. Is there enough for me?"

Ash laughed too, glad to feel the atmosphere brightening as they all found a seat. "You've clearly never experienced Niel's cooking before. He prepares enough for a small army."

Between them they summarised the night's events, and Jackson made notes on a pad he pulled from his pocket, jotting down points while he ate, and asking the odd question as they went. When they finished, he exhaled heavily. "Potentially, every place of theirs that we might find could have similar traps. That's worrying."

Gabe pushed his empty plate away. "I'm not sure the abbey is safe, even now. There are a few corridors we didn't explore. I'm not sure it's okay for your men."

"Agreed," Nahum said. "They could be planning to return, too."

"Nevertheless, we have to search it." Jackson's gaze swung to the images of the tablet. "Are those everything you found?"

Ash shook his head. "No, we just took the essentials. There are more papers down there, abandoned rooms, dead dogs, and of course Toto escaped with a bag."

"Dangerous or not, we have to go, but we'll proceed carefully," Jackson said, sipping his beer. "However, what I'm more interested in right now is the Igigi. What's the big deal with them?"

"I'd like to know that, too," Shadow said, staring at the Nephilim accusingly, especially Gabe. "You're all very cagey, and I want to know why!"

Ash felt sorry for her. Shadow hated to be left out of the loop, and her injury had side-lined her for a short while. "Because," he told her, "they are superhumans. Well, half human, half beast. Made by the Sumerian Gods for labour."

"And what are Sumerians?" she asked, eyes narrowing.

"An ancient Mesopotamian people who lived in the south of the region—now the Middle East. It was a collection of city states more than anything else. But they were clever, inventive people, highly respected. They invented the concept of time—literally the way the day is structured, and the concepts of cities and farming. And," Ash added, staring at the tablet, "they invented writing. Cuneiform, it's called now."

Nahum gave a dry laugh. "Yes. The world literally changed around us. And as we lived for a long time, we saw how those changes civilised everyone."

Jackson leaned back in his chair, tapping his notebook. "The Sumerians were undiscovered until the nineteenth century. They were lost to time until then."

All of the Nephilim were shocked at that, their heads jerking around to stare at Jackson.

"Are you serious?" Gabe asked, confusion clouding his features. "They were a powerhouse. It seems impossible that they would have disappeared."

"Really, brother?" Niel said sceptically. "Many civilisations are buried beneath deserts, jungles, and modern cities. What remains is paltry. The British Museum, and I'm sure many like it, prove that. Mere fragments remain."

Ash hated this talk as much as he loved it. To think of their own time utterly destroyed was unnerving and fascinating.

Jackson continued, "Their existence was discovered by scholars who were anxious to prove the Bible's stories. What they found challenged everything. It proved the Bible wrong, for one thing. It pushed history back...or I should say, civilisations. A place referenced in the Bible—Shinar—puzzled scholars for years. It turned out to be Sumer."

"Because *that* book is full of stories," Estelle said, amused. "Interesting for the light they shed on a certain time and place, but that's all."

Ash watched Jackson, intrigued. He had paused in his note taking, and was leaning forward, studying them all intently. Ash voiced his thoughts. "You seem well-informed on this topic, Jackson. How come?"

"I'm a collector, like Harlan and Olivia. I like knowing about old things. Sumer is one of the more fascinating places. It has its own flood history, too. It was documented in the Epic of Gilgamesh, which I admit to having only a passing knowledge of."

Ash was familiar with it. "I've done much reading on the flood since our return. It seems the Sumerian Gods colluded with our own God in wanting to rid the world of humans. One of their men was able to build an ark, as well." He looked at his brothers. "Either way, it wiped us out."

"A universal flood myth?" Shadow asked, intrigued.

"It appears in many histories," Ash told her. "Time and time again. We weren't the only civilisation at the time. But as we've said before, I doubt it was a worldwide flood. Maybe just most of the Mediterranean and the Middle East. How would we know, though? It killed us." Ash's last memory surfaced of him standing on a hill watching a gigantic wave roll in, smashing everything in its path. He had considered taking flight, but he was far from the mountains. He had waited with the others besides him, resigned to his fate, and feeling like he had deserved it for some of his activities. He, like his brothers, now felt their time on Earth was a chance to rectify past behaviours. A type of atonement.

Shadow was single-minded, however, her questions dragging him from his reverie. "And the Igigi? Where do they fit in?"

"The Sumerians," Niel said, "had their own Gods, like many civilisations did. Each of their city states had one. The Gods created the Igigi to build their cities and do the heavy work. That's why they were so powerful. They could work tirelessly for hours."

Nahum cut in, "Until they decided they didn't want to. They rebelled."

"And," Gabe added, "our own God became twitchy at their rebellion. Some of us were sent to subdue them. We failed, and they disappeared."

Ash had not been part of that, but knew why Gabe was so troubled. He, Niel, Zee, and Nahum had fought them, and it had been hard and dangerous. Some of the Nephilim had died. Barak, like Ash and Eli, had not been involved.

Estelle asked, "Their own Gods couldn't subdue them?"

"It seemed not," Gabe answered bleakly. "And we never found them once they escaped."

"But that tablet," she pointed beyond his ear to the wall, "points the way?"

They all turned to stare at it as Gabe's low voice rumbled around the room. "It seems to tell the remnants of their history, and yes, suggests a resting place. But that's just my initial interpretation."

"A resting place that Black Cronos is searching for?" Shadow asked.

"It appears so." Gabe gave a dry laugh. "They're powerful enough already, without recruiting the Igigi to their side."

"You think they're still alive?" Estelle asked, alarmed.

"I sincerely hope not," Niel said, "but equally I wouldn't rule it out." He glanced at his brothers as he started to collect the empty plates together. "I doubt, however, that they could have kept their existence so quiet over so many millennia. They must be dead."

"Agreed," Barak rumbled.

Jackson folded his notebook and put it in his pocket. "It's maybe just their bones that Toto wants. We have no idea how they fit into his plans. Yet. But we do need to stop him." He looked around the table, weighing them up one by one. "Are you interested in helping?"

Gabe didn't even consider their opinion when he answered, and Ash knew why. It was unfinished business. All of it.

"Of course, we will."

SIX

Harlan set out early on Thursday morning, eager to get his visit with JD over with.

He wasn't particularly pleased to be Mason's messenger boy, but it suited his needs, and to be honest, he was intrigued by Mason's attitude. Once again, he felt on shifting ground, and wished he could have seen Olivia. He valued her opinion, and besides, she let him complain without judgement, usually adding her own complaints, too. It was a general bitching session that suited both of them. With luck, he'd catch up with her later.

Once at JD's Tudor mansion, Anna, JD's assistant, met him at the door, a frown on her face. "I'm not sure this is a good time, Harlan. He's very busy."

He waved the papers secured in an envelope at her. "He's got to sign these. Mason's instructions."

She let him in, edging the door open with obvious reluctance. "Doesn't he have admin staff for that kind of thing?"

He smiled and lied. "I'm down this way on business. It was convenient. Didn't Mason warn you I was coming?"

"Of course." Her voice was brusque. "He knows he must. JD is a busy man." She waved him into a comfortably old-fashioned reception room with French doors that looked onto the garden. "Let me see if he's ready to see you."

She didn't give him a chance to argue his case. He wanted to see where JD was working and what he was up to, but he also believed Anna wouldn't have the slightest problem throwing him out if he didn't behave, so instead he walked to the open doors and stepped on to the patio to admire the garden. He presumed JD had a gardener. The garden was a riot of summer colour. An elaborate Elizabethan knot garden was in front of him, and from here he could see what looked to be a well-planned herb garden in the distance. Harlan smiled. It seemed JD still liked to surround himself with things from his youth.

Fortunately, he didn't have to wait long. Anna returned after a few minutes, saying, "He'll see you downstairs. He's in the middle of something and he said it's tricky timing."

Intrigued, Harlan followed her down the hall to where a door lay open, previously disguised in the panelling. Wall lights illuminated steps descending beneath the house, and she directed, "Down there. Don't touch anything!"

With her words ringing in his ears like he was some kind of wayward child, he went cautiously, emerging onto a small landing with a heavy door. Pushing his way inside, he gasped with surprise. It was a long, low-ceilinged laboratory, lined with bottles, jars, Bunsen burners, and lots of equipment he didn't even recognise, as well as some more modern technology in one corner.

There was no natural light at all. Instead, electric bulbs illuminated the space well. It was also extremely clean—clinical, even. Cupboards and shelves lined one wall, and if it wasn't for some of the more modern items and the lighting, Harlan would have thought he'd stepped back in time. He was in an alchemist's laboratory.

JD was oblivious to his arrival, watching a series of jars linked with tubes, some stacked above each other, all filled with bubbling liquids of various colours, while making notes on a large pad of paper. As Harlan walked closer, he realised the paper was illegible to him, filled with odd symbols and tiny handwriting.

"I'll be with you in a moment," JD said, not taking his eyes from one jar whose contents were bubbling down to a solid lump of...*something*. After another few seconds he whipped the jar off the heat and placed it on the counter to cool. He finally looked at Harlan, his eyes narrowing and his lips puckering with distaste. "I can spare a few moments only. I would have thought Mason would have sent someone else."

"I was down this way on business," Harlan said, repeating his earlier lie and not bothering with pleasantries. If JD couldn't be bothered, why should he? "I have some papers..."

"Yes, yes, yes." He thrust his hand out. "Let's get this over with."

Harlan's fury suddenly bubbled over. "Hey, JD! Stop being a dick. I'm doing you a favour!" He slapped the envelope on the counter rather than in JD's hand. "You should work on your manners!"

JD froze, eyes locked with Harlan's, then he snorted, grabbed the envelope, and ripped it open. "As I suspected. This could have waited. Stupid contracts. Have you been sent to spy on me?"

Harlan folded his arms across his chest. "It seems that I am caught between your and Mason's stupid feud! I don't care for it. Sign the damn paper so I can go. I couldn't give a shit what has happened between you two. All I know is that your behaviour a few weeks ago was infantile and dangerous. You and Mason could have been killed! And I felt compelled to try to help—risking my life, too!"

JD drew himself fully upright, shoulders back. "Liar. You couldn't wait to get out there and see what was happening."

"You're right. I was interested, but I was worried about Mason. He's not good in the field, and you took him with you! If you wanted help, you should have asked me. It's what I'm good at. Mason is traumatised, and Smythe—not only his secretary, but his good friend—is dead! He's very upset right now."

"Which is not my fault!" JD jabbed him in the chest with his finger. "Black Cronos killed him, not me."

Harlan grabbed JD's hand, squeezing it within his own. "Don't you ever touch me again." He stared into JD's eyes and had the feeling he was talking to a sociopath. "If this is what immortality does to you, I want none of it. You're a monster, JD. Mason is supposed to be your friend. I fully realise you are not mine, and I'm more than happy with that if this is how you treat them."

JD clenched his jaw, and he stepped back, wrenching his hand free. "I had a good reason for finding Toto Dax. What he's doing is against all the principles of alchemy. He's subverting it, sullying it. It is meant for finer things. I want to stop him."

"We all want to stop him, but getting your friends killed in the process is not the way." Harlan studied the jars currently bubbling away. "Seeing as how you disapprove of Toto's actions, I take it you are not trying to become superhuman yourself?"

"Are you insane? Of course not!"

"Then what are you doing? You've been keeping your head down, which means everyone's making assumptions. Especially knowing you were looking at the research found in the Dark Star Temple."

"What do you mean, *everyone*?"

"The Paranormal Division, Jackson, the Nephilim, me!" He decided to leave Mason out of it. "Your attitude isn't instilling confidence."

JD looked incredulous. "I am trying to find an antidote, you imbecile!"

Harlan was so astonished, he forgot to be angry about being called an imbecile. "You're doing *what*?"

"An. Antidote." He said it slowly and loudly, as if Harlan was deaf.

"An antidote to their superhuman abilities?"

"Of course!"

"Is that even possible?" Harlan's gaze swept across the array of jars. "Is that what this is?"

"These are the early stages of my experiments, yes." JD wiped a hand across his brow and closed his eyes for a moment, before fixing Harlan with an impatient stare. "As to whether it's possible, I have no idea. If I don't try, I won't know."

Harlan's annoyance evaporated, and he sat on the closest stool. "That's amazing."

"Nothing is amazing yet. I've barely begun."

"Why haven't you told anyone? The Paranormal Division, for example. They'd want to know. I know you know them."

"I don't like to share my experiments until I know I'm making progress, and so far, I'm making none."

Harlan fell into silence while JD continued to tinker with the Bunsen burners and his jars. He'd turned his back as if Harlan wasn't even there, and for a few moments, Harlan watched, fascinated, thinking through what he knew about Black Cronos. "But JD, Toto or whoever was before him have been doing these experiments for years. Why have you only just started to look for an antidote now? I know you were involved in the search for them during the war."

He shook his head and muttered under his breath, "You have been sent to try my patience."

"I'm genuinely curious."

"Of course I've tried before...multiple times. But until I saw them recently—actually saw them," he swung around to look at Harlan, "I had no idea what they'd achieved. I'm horrified. It's so much more than I'd imagined. And..." He stopped and seemed to summon his courage. "And I have to admit that I thought I was brilliant, but I confess that I find myself impressed by their achievements."

Ah. So that was it. JD, for all of his brilliance, couldn't work out how they'd done it.

"But you didn't have any of this old research before," Harlan said.

"And I have mere fragments of it now. This will be no easy task." He gestured towards a row of metals on the bench, small and large chunks of what Harlan recognised as iron, silver, copper, and gold, and others he didn't know. His fingers ran across his lip as he stared at them. "It's some ingenious use of these. Some way of fusing them..." His voice trailed off.

"How would the antidote work? I mean, how would we administer it?"

"Too soon to say. Far too soon."

"Working with the Paranormal Division might help. They have labs—"

JD cut him off. "They're not alchemists. They will have no idea."

"They're scientists. That's what alchemists are, right?"

"We are so much more than that." He grabbed his pen and signed the papers Harlan had given him, and then thrust them back. "There you go. How is Mason?"

"Angry. You should call him."

JD didn't respond, instead returning to his work, and Harlan left him to it, happy to leave feeling at least slightly victorious. At least he knew what JD was up to now.

Shadow woke late on Thursday morning, cocooned next to Gabe's sprawling body in their bedroom in the Scottish house. His arm lay across her back, and she rolled over, trying not to disturb him.

She immediately winced as she felt the pain within her chest, and lifting the duvet, saw the dark purple bruise that started on her sternum and spread across her breasts and down to her abdomen. *Shit.* If not for her fey armour, she'd likely be dead.

Gabe heard her stir, and still sleepy, pulled her close.

"Not so tight," she murmured.

His eyes flew wide open at that. "Are you okay?"

"Hideously bruised. Maybe a cracked rib or two." She snuggled into him despite her discomfort, and showered kisses along his jaw. "I haven't been so badly injured for a long time."

He propped himself up on his elbow and pulled the duvet back, his eyes widening with horror at her bruise. "That's worse than last night."

"It's to be expected. Estelle did something to draw the bruise out. It eased my breathing, whatever she did." She pulled the duvet back and studied his face. "What about you? How's your head?"

"Fine. Just scratches and minor bruises now. They've almost healed already." He grunted. "And my pride, of course."

"I don't know why. The Silencer of Souls is a worthy opponent. I just wish I knew what weapon she was using."

"Do you admire her?"

"To an extent. She's fast, strong, clever... What's not to admire?" She teased him. "Not as fast as me, though. I am fey."

"She might not be as fast as you, but she got first strike last night."

"Her weapon gave her an advantage. Something handheld." Shadow tried to remember if she'd seen anything within her clenched fist. "It was metal, I think. Small, whatever it was."

"And deadly. At least she didn't kiss you."

Gabe's eyes always took on a faraway, glazed expression when he thought of that almost deadly embrace, and she knew it wasn't from lust. She had genuinely unnerved him, and not much did. In fact, Black Cronos had unnerved all of them. Which reminded her of the stone tablet. "Tell me about the Igigi. You were holding something back last night."

"Not really." He sank back on to the pillows, pulling her gently against his chest, and she rested her hand on him, feeling the soft rise and fall of his chest. "Honestly, we fought so many campaigns, sometimes it's hard to distinguish them. But no doubt *they* were different. I suppose thinking about it now, the Minotaur we encountered at the temple was of a similar height and build. Some of the Igigi had the legs of horses, some the heads of lions, others the strength of apes. Some had the trunk of an elephant on a human face and elephantine feet. Some had wings and the upper bodies of eagles. Some were intelligent, though most were not, bred only for slavery. It was the intelligent ones who led the revolt, of course."

"Against the Gods?"

"Enlil, to be precise. The God of air, wind, earth and storms, and most senior of all of the Sumerian Gods."

Shadow thought her own world had too many Gods, but Earth's past seemed to have thousands. "He rivalled your God."

He looked at her and raised his eyebrow, amused. "*My* God? No. I worshiped none, even though he was the leader and father of the angels, even the Fallen."

"Which makes him your grandfather."

"Ha!" Gabe's laugh rumbled deep within his chest. "I've never thought of him like that before. But he wasn't, not really. Not in the true sense of the word."

"Why didn't the angels battle the Igigi?"

"They couldn't walk on Earth, not properly. When they fell, the Fallen had to take different forms that were not sustainable. To look upon the true face of an angel would cause madness or death. And they certainly couldn't mate with a human woman without taking a human shape."

Shadow was more confused than ever. "Then why fall in the first place, if they couldn't live on Earth?"

"To encourage descension, distrust, meddle, or, as they saw it, spread enlightenment. We were their servants, bred to do their dirty work as the Igigi were bred to do their Gods' work."

"But you said they were called demons."

"For their appearance, more than their actions, at least initially."

"And this stone tablet? What did you really read?"

He looked down at her. "I need to study it properly. My brothers were right. It is barely legible in places, but what I can read talks of a final resting place. Anyway," he sat up, easing away from her, "we have a plane to catch, and plenty of homework to do."

"We're going to find them, right?"

"Of course we are." He grinned. "We need to beat Black Cronos at their own game."

SEVEN

When Harlan returned to London, the first thing he did once he'd dropped the contract off with administration was find Olivia and take her to the closest pub. He was putting off speaking to Mason.

She was looking at him now, eyes wide. "JD is doing *what*? I can't get my head around any of it!"

"I know! I mean, he had all these jars bubbling away. What do they call it? Distilling stuff? Precipitating things?" He waved his hands ineffectually. "I don't know. And there were these modern, scientific instruments on one bench, too."

Olivia sipped her wine and stared at him over the rim of her glass. "But it's a lifetime's work...more than a lifetime, really. Do you think Toto is immortal, or has at least lengthened his own lifespan?"

"Possibly. Either that or they have some kind of alchemical apprenticeship where one picks up the work of another, always adding and building. That makes sense, right?"

"Sure. So, what's next for you?"

"Good question. I heard from Gabe earlier. They had a rough night." He filled her in on their brief conversation. "I'm hoping to hear more from him later, but what do you know about the Sumerians?"

"They were fascinating. Clever. There's some very interesting information on them in the British Museum, but obviously there's more elsewhere...Berlin, America. During the Gulf War thousands of ancient objects were stolen from the Iraq Museum in Baghdad. It was heart-breaking. Most have never been found."

"So maybe this tablet came from that collection."

"Possibly. I'm sure there are many private collections that have swelled from those thefts." Olivia leaned forward. "You say they only have images?"

He nodded. "Yes. Reasonably good quality, but they'd rather see the actual tablet."

"Good luck with that!"

"Any suggestions?"

She laughed, incredulous. "Whoever has anything looted from Iraq won't be advertising it."

"But have any of your clients got an interest in that era?"

Her eyes narrowed and she tapped her glass. "A couple. But the tablet could be anywhere in the world. There's a huge interest in that subject."

"Anything you can find will be useful. I'll ask Aiden, too. If I ever see him." Aiden was the third collector for The Orphic Guild, but of the three of them, he travelled the most. "Any idea where he is?"

"Cumbria. On the trail of an illuminated manuscript."

"Maybe I should call him, then."

Olivia smiled. "You don't think you're being followed anymore?"

He looked over his shoulder, and then dropped his voice, teasing her. "I don't think so, but I'll book right back into The Oriental if I suspect anything."

"You just like flash hotels."

"Who doesn't?"

They paused while a waiter delivered their food, and then Olivia said, "I'm sorry to hear that Mason and JD aren't getting on, but I'm not surprised. Mason is furious about Robert's death. He's dealing with it very badly."

"He blames JD."

Olivia shook her head. "He blames himself. He trusted Robert with everything, and everyone knew that." She picked at her food, distracted. "I was in the office with him the other day, talking about my new case, actually, and he could barely concentrate. I asked him if he was okay, and he nearly snapped my head off. Then he apologised, all tearful, and said he hasn't been sleeping." She speared a piece of tomato off her salad. "I tried to console him when he opened up a little, but he won't forgive himself."

"And we had one lead, but now they've disappeared again," Harlan said, thinking of the fight in Scotland. "What if we never get another one? What if that's it, for years?"

"But you said the Paranormal Division had got that professor guy, right? And you thought the order had a mole."

Harlan was so startled he almost dropped his fork. He'd forgotten he told Olivia about the Paranormal Division. He'd blurted it out after a few bourbons when he was telling her about France. "You're right. I should ask Jackson if they've made progress with that."

"Jackson?"

Harlan froze.

Olivia sniggered. "Oh, you should see your face. You'd be a terrible spy."

"Shit. I should have kept that quiet. I should really have kept it all quiet."

"Too late now." She patted his hand. "It's lucky you can trust me. Consider me impressed that you're involved in all of this cloak and dagger stuff."

"It's not all it's cracked up to be. I'm paranoid most of the time now."

"You'll get used to it. I must admit, Jackson's involvement intrigues me." She had another mouthful of her chicken salad. "I always knew there was more going on with him. At least you haven't managed to upset Sam from The Alley Cat. I'm still trying to get back into his good books."

Harlan laughed. "Of course. Your little problem with Caspian and Newton when they tried to trap Harry."

Olivia looked sheepish. "It didn't go as smoothly as we planned."

"He'll forgive you. Eventually." Harlan finished off his burger, wondering how Olivia survived on just salads. "Anyway, I'd better call Jackson and let him know what JD is up to. I feel like my life's gotten very complicated."

She winked. "Just stay off the bourbon. I don't think it's your friend when you have secrets. And by the way, I don't blame you for spying on JD. I know it seems like he's acting for the best, but I still don't trust him."

"No. Strangely enough, neither do I."

Gabe surveyed his brothers, Estelle, and Shadow, who were gathered in the living room of the farmhouse, trying to gauge the mood.

They had arrived back from Scotland a few hours earlier, and Eli and Zee had returned from work. A few of them were playing video games to relax, and he could understand that. It had been an intense twenty-four hours. Niel and Ash had recovered from their injuries, and although Shadow still winced sometimes, she seemed much better. She visited Briar as soon as they'd returned home, and as usual, the earth witch had used her magic to heal Shadow's injuries.

She was now examining her dented breastplate under the light, her lips pursed, and he knew she was planning on visiting Dante, the blacksmith, with El. She hoped he could repair it. They all laughed at her when she extolled the virtues of her armour, but not anymore, and Gabe was never more grateful for it. In the small amount of time they'd been together, his feelings for her had multiplied beyond his expectations. The thought of her dying was too much to bear.

He was more surprised that Estelle had joined them again after a quick visit to her home in Harecombe. She was sitting on the sofa watching Barak play on the console against Niel, amused by their good-natured banter. Although Barak had offered her the controller a few times, she'd declined, but Gabe was pretty sure she'd relent at some point. He wasn't quite sure what was happening between her and Barak, but it seemed to be suiting her. She'd lost her pinched expression—well, mostly—and she and Shadow seemed to have reached a truce, which was something.

They were all killing time, he knew, waiting for the discussion to begin, so he raised his voice to be heard over the game. "Hey, guys! Let's talk about the tablet."

"One minute," Barak complained as a volley of grunts and loud music filled the room, "while I smash Niel's head in!"

Gabe rolled his eyes and turned to look at the images of the tablet pinned to the back wall. Ash was already studying them. "What do you think of it?" Gabe asked him. "Is it genuine?"

"It's hard to know from the photo, but I'd say so just from the fact that Toto has it. He strikes me as a man who does his homework."

Gabe nodded in agreement. "I've been thinking about how we find it, and I keep coming back to the mole."

Ash's head whipped around. "From The Order of the Midnight Sun?"

"We both know they have one, and although Jackson hasn't mentioned them..."

"He must have been following it up," Ash said, finishing his sentence. He smiled broadly, his white teeth looking even whiter against his tanned skin. "We must call him."

"I figure he'll be calling us first," Gabe said, nodding at the tablet. "We've all got unfinished business."

A whoop and a roar of laughter ripped around the room, and Gabe gathered that the game had finished. He looked around, amused to see Barak punching the air, as Niel's character lay bloodied on the screen.

Niel was already complaining. "I demand another game."

Gabe interrupted them. "Later. I need your brains on this." They shuffled around to look at the back wall of the room, and when they'd quieted, he said, "As you know, we found this last night in Scotland, at Arklet Abbey—Toto's place. This was in a bag they were trying to escape with."

"One bit of luck, then," Zee said as he stared at the image.

"Not luck," Gabe replied. "Hard won. It almost killed us. The whole place was a bloody boobytrap."

"And the bitch blew us up!" Niel added, grimacing.

"Have you had a chance to look at these?" Gabe gestured to the images of the tablet.

Eli shrugged. "I had a quick glance at it. But what's the interest? It speaks of things we've long known, and that history talks of. The flight of the Igigi."

Ash tapped a section of the writing. "The first part does. But then it mentions a place that I've never heard associated with them before—Izalla. Have you?"

All of the Nephilim shook their heads, but Estelle asked, "Can you do me a favour and translate it? I know you've talked about it, but you haven't really explained what it says."

"I'll summarise it, because it's wordy," Ash said. "It essentially outlines the revolt the Igigi had against the Anunnaki, their Gods. It tells of a terrible battle in which cities were laid to waste as they tried to escape, and that armies were sent against them." Ash raised an eyebrow. "That would include us."

Gabe added, "We caused quite a bit of trouble, because we had been ordered in by our fathers, and it clashed with the Anunnaki's plans. They wanted their slaves back. We were trying to kill them, and banish them for good. It got messy."

Nahum was perched on the arm of the chair, and he grunted. "It always did."

"Anyway," Ash said, continuing, "the tablet obviously skips details, but says the Igigi gathered together and fled Sumer for the borders, seeking a place to call their own. And they finally found it, according to this. A place where they could live their long life free from persecution...a place close to Izalla. In our time, this city was on a trade route through to Mesopotamia, in the north of the country. It was on a hill overlooking the Tigris and Mesopotamian planes. Anyway, this is where it gets interesting. It speaks of a city of giants in an oasis in the desert. There the Igigi built castles, waterways, and canals, grew vegetables, and bred their children."

Estelle sat cross-legged in her jeans, her arms resting on her knees. "They made a sanctuary? How wonderful."

Barak nodded. "I guess it is. They built cities for the Anunnaki. Why not use that knowledge to build their own?"

"Indeed," Ash said. He paused, as if summoning his courage, and then looked at Gabe as he tapped the image again. "I couldn't work out what was bothering me about the wording on this last night, but I've studied it all day, and I now think this account is written by them. It's their own history."

Gabe's mouth gaped as he stared at Ash. "*What*? You didn't mention this earlier!"

He flashed him an apologetic smile. "Sorry. I've been second-guessing myself. I thought I was imagining it, but..."

"Holy shit!" Niel exclaimed, almost upending his beer. "That means this tablet could have come from that city!"

"Not could have," Ash said. "*Must* have! They would have had a records library of some sort. Or a commemoration of the city being built."

Gabe's mind was whirling with ideas, and he tried to keep things in perspective. "Hold on! Say you're right, Ash, and they founded their own city. That is amazing news. But grave robbers and archaeologists have been raiding such sites for years. Someone could have found this centuries ago and stripped whatever remains were there." He looked around at his brothers, their expressions a mix of excitement, puzzlement, or worry. "It does not mean there's anything to find *now*. And surely, the Igigi are long dead."

"Perhaps the flood swept them away, like it did everything," Eli reminded them.

That immediately sobered everyone. Well, everyone except Shadow. "The very fact that Toto was studying it and tried to hide it means *something* survived. Maybe the city, or at least remnants of it. Their cemeteries or memorials."

"If they buried their dead," Estelle pointed out to her. She addressed the Nephilim in general. "What did Sumerians do with their dead?"

Zee confirmed the suggestion. "They buried them, wrapped in baskets, usually. Children were sometimes placed in jars. They did not mummify them."

"Which," Eli said, "means their bones are probably dust by now. What possible use can the ruins of a city be to Toto?"

A light kindled deep within Ash's eyes as he stared at Eli. "Because it's not just any city. It's the *Igigi's* city. Supernatural, hybrid creatures are what Black Cronos is obsessed with. Toto is interested. *Very* interested. Perhaps he has information that suggests there is something useful there! Like Shadow said, he tried to hide this from us. No doubt he's furious right now that he failed."

The books and notes that were in the bag they'd retrieved were on the coffee table, and Niel leaned forward and shuffled through them. "These are books on Sumerian history, religion, and their myths, and there are multiple notes that look like translations of the tablet's text. But no maps or suggestions of where the city could be."

"I've given them a cursory read," Ash said, "and there are a few notes in the margins of some books that bear further examination."

"Okay," Nahum said, stirring into action. "If Black Cronos is interested, that means we are, too. Our main lead is that they built a city near Izalla. I remember the place well. It sat on a slope, buildings rising on top of one another. I bet that's long gone, too."

"But it isn't," Ash said, fairly humming with excitement now, unusual for the normally reserved Greek. "It still exists. It's called Mardin now, and it's in Turkey. Just across the border from Syria and Iraq." He shrugged at their puzzled faces. "Google is a wonderful thing."

"Have you looked at the terrain?" Gabe asked, always impressed with Ash's research.

"Briefly, on the internet."

"Let me," Nahum said, standing and stretching before heading to the bookshelf where they kept several maps and history tomes.

"What are you proposing, Gabe?" Barak asked, looking amused. "Another plane trip?"

Gabe didn't answer for a moment, instead studying the words and phrases of the tablet, his curiosity piqued. He finally turned back to him. "I think if we can find more clues as to where their city was, it might be worth it."

Shadow cleared her throat. "While I hate to smother everyone's excitement, I think I should remind you that you're talking about a city that disappeared thousands of years ago—along with all mention of the Igigi. How can you hope to find it when archaeologists only discovered Sumer recently?"

SEVEN

Estelle cast her a sidelong glance. "Shadow is right. And you're up against Black Cronos. They must have a lead, and they'll move quickly now that we have this information."

"All excellent points," Gabe admitted. "But Black Cronos still has a mole in The Midnight Sun. I suggest we find him and haul him in for questioning."

"I'd forgotten about him," Niel mused, looking impressed. "But I like that plan. If we know who it is."

Gabe had already made his mind up. "I'm going to speak to Jackson. They must have discovered who it is by now. Maybe they're watching him."

Ash shrugged. "We all want leads. And I'm sure Waylen Adams would fund us, too."

"You'd come to Turkey?"

"Try to stop me."

Nahum called them over to the coffee table where he'd spread the map. "I've found it." He jabbed his finger on the page. *Mardin*. "And it's still surrounded by desert."

Eli was scrolling through his phone. "It's a beautiful place. The old town is a UNESCO World Heritage Site."

Estelle had leaned forward to look at the map. "You're lucky it's in Turkey. Any further south and you'd have been searching a war zone."

Gabe walked over to stare at the map, noting the close borders of Syria and Iraq. "Very lucky. But that's a big expanse of desert."

"But a lot of small towns, too," Nahum pointed out. "And a couple of National Forests. That means a good water supply."

Niel grinned. "Old oases. Excellent."

Gabe was fired up now. "It's better than nothing, but it still leaves us a lot to do to get there before Toto. And to be honest, we can't afford to fail."

EIGHT

Harlan stared at Barnaby Armstrong's flat, and remembering how he'd been chased by Black Cronos soldiers only weeks before from this spot, turned to Jackson. "This might not be a good idea."

Jackson was leaning against a wall, his coat collar pulled up around his ears, looking like an old-fashioned gumshoe in his well-worn trench coat as he surveyed Armstrong's building. "This is the best bet. We go in quietly. He knows me, so he should let us in."

"He was being watched by Black Cronos the last time I was here. They nearly caught me!"

"An agent has been watching all day. He got home from the order an hour ago, unescorted. No one's guarding him." He winked. "And we've got the door code, too."

It was twilight on Thursday evening, and Jackson had called Harlan a couple of hours before asking for his help. According to their investigations, their initial suspicions had been proven correct. Barnaby was the mole. Large sums of money were regularly deposited in his account, and his hacked emails revealed he had been sending information about the order's alchemy research to an account belonging to someone named Beautiful Mother.

"You know he'll deny everything," Harlan said. "And he may be armed."

Jackson shook his head. "He's a pencil pusher and a sneak. He won't be dangerous." He straightened up, gesturing to the black van parked on the kerb. "We'll stick him in the back and take him to headquarters."

"Why aren't you using some kind of covert operative to do this?'

Jackson laughed. "We are the covert operatives, you pillock."

"That was not in the contract I signed! That was only to spy on JD!"

Jackson grinned. "Yeah, but this is fun, right?"

"That is yet to be determined. What am I supposed to do?"

"Let me do the talking and block the exit. Come on."

Harlan should have known Jackson was going to drag him into everything, and although he wasn't sure that it was fun, it *was* different. Jackson was already striding across the street, so he caught up with him, and together they walked up the path to the flat's front door and Jackson entered the code into the keypad. The door clicked open, and he led them upstairs and knocked on the door to the first floor flat.

When the door swung open, a short man with thinning, dark hair stood before them. He wore corduroy trousers and a knitted vest over his shirt, and Harlan thought he looked like the most unlikely spy ever. Barnaby looked at them with surprise, and then recognition. "Jackson? What are you doing here?"

Ever affable, Jackson said, "Sorry to swing by so late, but I have a question about a sensitive issue, and thought you could help?"

"Me?" Barnaby looked puzzled, and then suspicious. "Well, er, I suppose I could, but couldn't it wait?"

"It's really quite urgent. I've found some documents and really need your assistance with them. I was in the area, you see..."

"And this is?" He stared at Harlan.

"Harlan Beckett, with The Orphic Guild. I don't think you've met."

Harlan shook his hand as Barnaby said, "Ah! Harlan. I've heard of you. You helped us immensely only a few weeks ago. Of course, come in."

For all of his politeness, Barnaby looked flustered, but he ushered them in and down the hall to a richly furnished living room lined with books. The flat might not look ostentatious from the outside, but the inside was filled with high-end antiques and a few first editions, from what Harlan could see of the books.

"Fantastic books," Harlan murmured, pausing to inspect them so that he was close to the door. "May I?"

"Of course, just be gentle with them. Please, take a seat, Jackson." Jackson sat in a leather armchair while Barnaby headed to a side table where he had a few bottles of spirits and mixers lined up, and wiggled the bottle of gin. "Would you like one?"

Both declined, but they waited patiently while Barnaby finished fixing his drink and sat down.

Jackson pulled some papers from his pocket, and passed them to Barnaby. "These are the papers I want your opinion on. I wondered if you could tell me who the recipient of your email is. You seem to have been passing them some very interesting information."

Barnaby was so startled that he leapt to his feet, upending the side table next to him, and sending his drink crashing to the floor. Jackson was still waving the papers at him. "Don't you want to look?"

"How have you accessed my emails?"

Jackson's arm dropped and he leaned back in the chair, the papers resting on his lap. "I have my ways. Why don't you sit, and we can talk civilly?"

"I have nothing to talk about. I suggest you leave."

His eyes darted to the door, but Harlan stepped in front of it, arms folded across his chest, feeling like Jackson's enforcer.

Jackson continued, "I can't leave. You see, we suspect that you are working with Black Cronos, and they are a very dangerous organisation. That makes you dangerous, too."

"Me? Don't be ridiculous. I'm the secretary for the order and a middle-grade alchemist. I have nothing to do with Black whoever-they-are."

"You are a Senior Adept with The Order of the Midnight Sun, privy to the Inner Temple and all of their most secret plans, and that makes you very knowledgeable." Jackson's voice hardened. "I'm not an idiot, Barnaby, although admittedly you fooled us for a long time—and Caldwell, of course. Sit down."

Barnaby's eyes darted around the room, his lips twitching, and then he finally sat again. "You have no proof of anything. This is all ridiculous conjecture. I shall phone my solicitor first thing in the morning."

"How do you explain the large sums of money deposited in your account?"

"I do private consultancy work."

"Then please write down who you consult for, and we can confirm your story. It doesn't completely explain the emails, though. You advised Beautiful Mother that the Dark Star Astrolabe had been found, where it was stored, and the best time to steal it. Need I say more?" Jackson looked around the luxurious flat. "Some very nice goods here. Your betrayal certainly earns you an enviable lifestyle. Tell me, do you feel any guilt at all about Aubrey Cavendish's death?"

Barnaby clenched his hands into fists. "I had nothing to do with that."

Jackson leaned forward. "Of course you did. If Black Cronos hadn't been at the Dark Star Temple, he'd still be alive. They were there because you leaked the information about the Dark Star Astrolabe. The thief was killed, did you know? Blaze. A young man with much to live for."

Barnaby was silent for a moment, and then his eyes adopted a calculating expression. "Who do *you* work for? I thought you were an occult collector."

"I am. But like you, I have a side-line. I'm not a killer, though. You could receive a lot of jail time for your crimes. You might never see your flat again. Or any of that lovely money in your bank account."

"What if I cooperated fully?"

Jackson smiled and leaned back. "That's more like it. Who's your contact in Black Cronos, and more importantly, where is he? Or she?"

"I have no idea! It makes it safer that way. I was just given an email contact."

"But you must have met someone. This can't all have been done over the phone or through email. We're talking about a deadly organisation that certain areas of the government are very interested in."

Barnaby froze, and then a victorious light lit up his eyes. "It was Stefan Hope-Robbins. He kept in touch with me after he left. I agreed with his principles, but didn't leave with him."

"That does go back a long way. But unfortunately, that's not who your contact is, because Stefan has been in our custody for quite a while with zero access to email, and yet you are still sending them and receiving answers."

Barnaby's lips tightened. "Stefan is much higher up than I am. He is far more valuable, and has more information about this. You don't need me."

"You seem to think you can wriggle your way out of this." Jackson leaned in, staring at Barnaby. "You can't. We will track down Toto Dax and his enhanced soldiers, and you will help us. Time to go." He stood, shoving the printed emails back in his pocket. "Let's do this quietly so you can maintain some dignity, shall we?"

Barnaby looked between Harlan and Jackson, and must have fancied his chances. "I don't think so. You have no authority to detain me, and you're not the police! I have no idea who you work for or where you're going to take me. I'm not a fool. You could be working for another organisation that wants to kill me." He stood too, shoulders back, staring Jackson down. "You need to leave." He pulled his phone from his pocket. "Or I will call for help."

Jackson reached into his pocket, withdrawing an envelope with an official seal, and passed it to Barnaby. Even from across the room, Harlan could see the gilding on it, flashing in the light. "That letter is a warrant for your arrest, and it details my authority to do it."

Barnaby eyed it suspiciously and then snatched it from Jackson's hand. Harlan was almost as surprised as Barnaby. Jackson had kept that quiet, too. However, it did make him feel they had insurance in their actions. He was starting to feel like a kidnapper.

Barnaby's hands had a tremor when he passed the letter back to Jackson, and his voice shook as he said, "You'll find you are quite mistaken, but of course I shall assist your investigations. May I get my coat?"

He was already turning to take his jacket from the back of a chair positioned next to his desk, and in one swift movement had put it on, reached into the pocket, and then pulled out something silver. In a split second, it turned into a short, silver, rapier-like blade that glistened like molten metal, and he thrust it at Jackson. Jackson leapt back, stumbling over the chair and falling to the floor. He grabbed a statue on a side table and flung it at Barnaby, catching his arm, and spinning him around. Simultaneously, Harlan darted across the room, tackling Barnaby to the ground. They caught the edge of the side table, and Harlan felt the corner scrape his ribs as he slid to the floor, pinning Barnaby beneath him.

He was still clutching the narrow blade, and he twisted his hand, trying to thrust it in Harlan's face. Harlan punched his arm again and again, and Barnaby lost his grip. Jackson was back on his feet, and kicking the blade away, stood on Barnaby's outstretched arm while Harlan used his weight to keep Barnaby down.

Jackson met Harlan's eyes as he picked up the unusual weapon that had now become a small silver ball again. "Clever things, these. I'm glad we have one to analyse." He crouched down, bringing his face close to Barnaby's. "If you have one of these weapons, you are clearly very important to Black Cronos. You can be sure that we will strip this place and find every secret you have ever harboured."

He whipped a pair of handcuffs out of his pocket, and in another ugly few seconds of furious struggling, helped Harlan keep him secure while he pulled Barnaby's arms behind his back and cuffed him. Barnaby had fallen silent, fury behind his eyes.

Harlan hauled him to his feet and carefully searched his pockets. "I can't find any other weapons. We should get him out of here—just in case he has backup." He studied the comfortable flat and hoped there were no hidden cameras or recording devices around.

"Don't worry," Jackson said, and between them they frogmarched Barnaby to the door and down the corridor to the van. "The team will be searching this place as soon as we've left."

Shadow raced across the fields surrounding the farmhouse, crouched low against Kailen's back.

When she awoke on Friday morning, it was to a cloudy, overcast day, heavy with impending rain, but she didn't care. Her meeting with Dante and El was all arranged, and she was going to ride, regardless of the weather—and her bruises.

She could feel the dull ache in her chest even now, despite Briar's magic and Eli's poultices. As she adjusted her position on Kailen's back, she felt the twinge in her ribs but ignored it, instead relishing the feeling of freedom that being on horseback gave her. The long grass that swayed in the light breeze looked like pewter in the light, and she hoped it would thunder. The weather matched her mood.

The fury she'd been feeling at having her armour damaged had been growing ever since Scotland. And she was still angry that her bow had been broken. Black Cronos, and especially The Silencer of Souls, were proving more and more dangerous every time they met. But she hadn't been lying to Gabe. She couldn't help but admire the woman's skills. And she was determined to find out more about her.

As Dante's Forge came into view, she slowed and finally stopped on the other side of the wall bordering Dante's car park. El was already there, her old, battered Land Rover parked at the side. Shadow dismounted, tying Kailen to the wall and allowing him to graze, before heading inside the forge with her armour. The heat hit her immediately as she inhaled the familiar, pleasant smell of metal, oil, steam, and fire. Skirting around the iron, she joined El and Dante where they stood next to the long bench examining a sword. Dante's powerful arms were revealed by his sleeveless t-shirt, and sweat glistened on his dark skin. His dreadlocks were bound up on his head in a colourful bandanna.

He winked as he greeted her. "Getting into trouble again, Shadow?"

"You could say that. Thanks for agreeing to help me."

El hugged her. "You know we'll try."

"I'm intrigued," Dante said, eyeing the bag with a twinkle in his eye. "I can't wait to see your *special* armour."

He didn't know Shadow was fey, but she had a feeling she might have to reveal it when he examined the metal. She extracted it and placed it under the light cast from the bare bulb. "I better not keep you in suspense, then."

Both El and Dante gasped when they saw the dent in the breastplate. It was dead centre, the bullseye narrowed to a point, the rest of the dent shallower as it radiated outward. It had damaged most of the breastplate, including the engraving in the centre.

El's eyes widened as she stared at it. "What did this?"

"Good question. We're not entirely sure. My opponent pulled something from her pocket, something small, and pointed it at me. All I know is that a wave of *something* struck me. My arm guards have a few dents in them, too. I'd appreciate you fixing all of it."

Dante ran his hand across the surface of the breastplate. "The weapon was invisible?"

She exchanged a nervous glance with El. "Essentially, yes. I should also say that I have used this armour many times, and it is rarely ever damaged. It's made of a particularly strong metal." *Dragonium, predominantly, but she wasn't about to tell Dante that.* Dragonium was a metal only available in the Otherworld, sourced from dragons, and the metal was imbued by the fey blacksmiths with special protection, too.

Dante lifted it and frowned. "It's incredibly light for something so strong. What metal?"

"It's special to the area I come from."

His lips twisted into a wry smile. "I get it. Well, whatever it is, it should respond to the usual treatment." He headed to the fire, Shadow watching him warily. If it shattered or couldn't be fixed, she'd be devastated.

El took her by the arm and led her outside to the fresh air. "Come on. Let's give him some space. Tell me more about the weapon."

El was, as usual, dressed in skinny black jeans and a t-shirt, and her makeup was bold and immaculate. The faint scent of musk and patchouli emanated from her as they sat next to each other on the wall.

"I don't know what to say," Shadow confessed. "As I said, it looked like a small silver device, but it happened so fast, and it was in her hand, so it's hard to be certain. But the wave of power from it was huge."

"Magic?"

"I'm not sure. If it was, it wasn't familiar to me. As you know I'm sensitive to magic and can usually feel it, even in small amounts."

"And these are the alchemists, right, who have been doing experiments on people?"

"Making superhumans, yes, and superweapons. It seems they've been using planets and their correspondences, among other things, but..." she shrugged. "That's as much as I understand."

El frowned. "They must have harnessed power much like we did when we put spells in bottles and other objects for Ghost Ops. I wouldn't imagine it could reproduce it like a gun, but who knows? They're inventive."

"Unfortunately, yes."

"I'm worried about you." El shuffled around to look at her properly. "I know how strong and quick you all are, but against Black Cronos..."

Shadow smiled. "We've met our match, that's for sure, but I think we're frustrating them just as much. And we think we know where Toto is heading next." She updated her on the Igigi.

"Wow! This keeps getting worse and worse. But it's also intriguing. Do you really think these creatures might still exist?"

"Surely not. But," Shadow added, finally voicing what was really worrying her, "Gabe is being cagey about the Igigi. I think there's something he's not telling me."

"He's probably trying to protect you."

"As gallant as that sounds, I don't think so. He knows better. I think he's ashamed of something, or more likely, worried." She shrugged and sighed. "I'll find out eventually. I'll just have to wear down his defences."

El giggled. "I won't ask how. But I am glad you two have got together. Now, tell me about Estelle!"

For a while they gossiped and laughed until Dante emerged from the forge, wiping sweat from his brow with the back of his hand. "That's some unusual metal, Shadow!"

Shadow's heart faltered. "You can't repair it?"

"I can, but I'm having to heat it to a very high temperature. I'll need it for a day or so to finish, okay?"

As much as she hated having to leave it with him, she had no choice. "Of course. Thank you. I'll pay, of course."

"No need. I have a feeling I'll learn something from this metal. If you ever feel like sharing, I'm all ears." And with an enigmatic smile, he headed back inside.

Niel studied the large map pinned to the wall, the photos of the tablet they'd stolen from The Silencer of Souls next to it. Or *salvaged*, as he liked to call it. His lips twisted with annoyance just thinking about her. *Damn woman*.

Ash was next to him, and he tapped the map. "I can feel your anger radiating off you. Focus on finding this place, and then you can get your revenge."

"I want to wring her neck and see the life drain from her eyes."

"Your ego is dented, that's all." Ash couldn't disguise his amusement, and it annoyed Niel even more.

"Yours should be dented, too. We both got flattened in that blast!"

"But I saw it coming." Ash turned to him with a smug smile. "I dragged you back."

"I was seething about the damn demon dogs!"

"Which distracted you. We can't afford to be distracted by their toys."

"Hardly bloody toys," Niel grumbled under his breath. But Ash was right. He did need to focus. He stared at the map that detailed the area around Mardin and exhaled. "Surely the forested areas are more likely...they fit with the story of the oasis."

"Perhaps. But landscapes change dramatically over the years. Places that we knew as very fertile valleys are now deserts. And I bet they're not heavily wooded forests, either. We *have* to find a way to narrow the search, or it will take us years."

Niel sat on the edge of the table behind him. "Then we should get out there soon. There's no other way." A feeling of excitement, but also worry, settled over him. "I'm not sure how I feel about going back to the Middle East. It will have changed beyond recognition. Right now I have my memories of places and people, but those will be shattered once we return."

Ash nodded, wariness entering his eyes. "I've considered that too, brother. I want to see Greece again, but fear I'll be disappointed by what I see. All the places I knew will have turned to dust or ruins. And there'll be places that will have sprung up after we left, and they'll be ruins, too. Whereas here," he gestured around him, "it's all new. There's nothing to compare."

"That's the best thing about Western Europe," Niel admitted. "We never came here. I feel we're beginning afresh. New life, new place. And my memories of the Igigi are bloody..." He trailed off as images flooded his thoughts. "They were worthy opponents. Strong."

"But not all were disciplined," Ash reminded him. "They weren't trained to fight like us."

"Is it a terrible thing to say that I felt guilty about attacking them? I wanted them to have their freedom."

"Of course it isn't terrible. But I'd still like to know how they disappeared so quickly and completely."

He was right. The battle had moved outside the cities and had broken into skirmishes. After a particularly vicious campaign, the Nephilim had withdrawn to regroup, and that's when the Igigi vanished.

"Perhaps," Niel mused, "someone had scouted a place and sent word out."

"But we scoured the plains and hills from the skies—for miles! They must have gone underground."

"An underground city? That's new!"

Ash shook his head and pointed at the map. "Not particularly. Cappadocia and Derinkuyu in Turkey—what was called Anatolia—are known for its cave dwellings. In fact, the authorities think the Phrygians excavated some. It could be something similar. I'll do some more reading. Old myths from after our time may reference hidden cities. What if," he turned away from the map to stare at Niel, "whoever had or still has the tablet had more information on the Igigi's city? That would help us narrow it down, too."

"But we have no idea who that is! And you said there's nothing in that handful of papers we found except endless histories of the Sumerians."

Ash nodded. "True. But the very fact they were taking them must mean something useful is in there. I must study them more closely."

Niel grunted. He liked action and movement, not endless research and speculation. "Better you than me." His thoughts returned to when he'd visited the museum with Nahum. "I wonder if it's worth returning to the British Museum. They have an extensive collection of Mesopotamian objects, including huge stone reliefs."

"I'd love to see them, but I doubt they'll offer much on this subject. Surely, hidden cities and clues to the Igigi would have been mentioned in the display notes?"

Deflating, Niel nodded. "I guess so. I certainly didn't read anything about them, but I was overwhelmed, if I'm honest. Although," he brightened as he thought of how huge the museum was, "I didn't see all of it—not by a long shot."

Ash slapped his shoulder. "Let me see how I get on, but perhaps you're right. A trip to the museum could be useful. And it might explain the photographs. Even Black Cronos would have their work cut out to steal from there." He virtually pushed Niel out the door. "Leave me in peace. I need to concentrate."

NINE

Jackson studied Barnaby Armstrong through the two-way mirror. He fidgeted and fussed, adjusting his cuffs and the collar of his now rumpled shirt as he waited to be interviewed, and the longer he waited, the more nervous he appeared—which was exactly what Jackson wanted.

He turned to Waylen Adams. "He's not looking quite as assured as he did last night."

"You did well to get him. Any injuries?"

"Some bruising from where I fell, that's all." He shrugged it off. "I think Harlan was worse. He hit the table as they went down."

"Was it a good idea to involve him?"

Jackson nodded, knowing Waylen was always wary. But his caution had served him well, and made him the director of the Paranormal Division. "Absolutely. I've known Harlan for a long time. He knows when to bend the rules and when not to. He's got good connections, and he likes the intrigue."

"How does he get on with JD?"

"Same as everyone. He drives him mad, but we all learn to tolerate him, don't we? He's brilliant, and that means we have to. JD trusts him, as much as he does anyone."

Waylen turned back to Barnaby. "What have you got planned for him?"

Jackson grinned. "I'm going to play him off against Stefan Hope-Robbins...just a little."

It wasn't normally Jackson's job to interview prisoners; they had a small team of security staff who did that. They would continue to interrogate him once he finished today. But right now, Jackson wanted information about the Igigi tablet, and Waylen had been happy to indulge him. In all of the weeks that they'd had Hope-Robbins in custody, he had kept infuriatingly mute, no doubt holding out for a rescue that wouldn't happen.

However, they were running out of time. The PD had special authority to question and detain, but only for a limited period. Soon they would have to process Stefan Hope-Robbins through the court and then he, and Barnaby when his time came, would be lost to them—or at least not available for regular access.

Jackson asked, "I presume this is being recorded?"

"Of course. There's a camera in the corner."

Jackson headed inside and sat on the plain chair opposite Barnaby, a wooden table between them. Barnaby's ankles were cuffed and chained, so even if he lunged at Jackson, he couldn't reach him properly.

"Barnaby, I hope you understand how much trouble you're in. Toto's protection is gone now. You're best to cooperate, and try to reduce your sentence."

Barnaby looked scornful. "A sentence based on *what*? Sharing the secrets of an arcane society? That's hardly breaking any laws. You have no grounds to keep me here."

"Actually, it's the fact that you're working with a corrupt, terroristic organisation that kidnaps people, commits experiments on their bodies, and attacks law-abiding societies and tries to kill them. And of course, theft of private property. You colluded with that. And the kidnapping of two individuals in France, and a full-on armed assault against others."

Barnaby paled, but still blustered. "I had nothing to do with that."

"But you do work for them. Stefan Hope-Robbins says you are a key figure in their organisation."

"He's lying!"

"Is he? He says he's known you for years, ever since he was a member of The Midnight Sun, and that you agreed to stay and spy for him." Jackson leaned forward. "And you did, as you worked your way into the Senior Adepts, gaining access to their occult knowledge. Hope-Robbins said you contacted him several months ago with news of the Dark Star Astrolabe and helped arrange it all."

Barnaby's eyes darted around the room before finally settling on Jackson again. "They threatened me...and you've seen how dangerous they are. I couldn't say no."

"Bullshit. I've seen your emails, remember? You contacted them and asked what they could provide for that information. I've seen the expensive furniture in your flat and your bank balance. It will be sad that it all has to be sold off. Unless you can help us. You may get a reduced sentence."

"I don't know anything."

"All I need to know is where Toto is going next."

"No one knows what Toto is doing! He tells no one except *her*!"

"The Silencer of Souls?"

Barnaby swallowed nervously. "Yes."

"Who is she?" Jackson was genuinely curious.

"I have no idea. All I know is that she is trusted and indispensable. And deadly."

"She was with him in Scotland. When they ran, we managed to obtain information about a stone tablet. Photos. We think they're going to the Middle East next."

Barnaby shuffled in his seat. "So, you don't need me, then."

"Where *is* the stone tablet? We'd like to see it properly."

"As I'm sure you can see from my emails, I know nothing about it!"

That was true, Jackson reflected. There were only emails about the astrolabe and the order's plans to go to France. He tried another tack. "But there were phone calls, too, to untraceable numbers. And our team found lots of research in your flat into Sumerian myths and the Igigi. I doubt that's a coincidence."

"I'm interested in myths and legends. There's nothing wrong with that."

"But it isn't a coincidence that Toto is now chasing after some Igigi legend recorded on a stone tablet."

Barnaby snorted again. "He's always searching after anything like that! Mythical creatures that blend human and animal or supernatural strengths are his obsession. He sees them as the supreme, ideal creation. Pre-natural abilities. He even was interested in vampires for a while, until he realised that they were utterly feral and uncontrollable. Above all else, Toto demands control. He coveted the ability of shifters, too."

Jackson was surprised. He didn't think Barnaby would be so well-informed about the paranormal world's creatures, despite his interest in the occult. There was something homely about him, but clearly those looks were deceiving. "You know about them?"

"I know they exist, but I don't know any personally. He's taken some of them, too."

Jackson hadn't even considered that. *What if Black Cronos had been experimenting with all sorts of creatures?* The thought made his blood run cold. "It seems you do know him quite well!"

"Only what Stefan has told me! He was his righthand man for years."

"How did they meet?"

"University, I think. He didn't elaborate."

"Toto is the head of Black Cronos?"

Barnaby's flowing chat suddenly ceased, and he sat back in his chair. "I doubt that."

"Why?"

"I don't know, actually. It's just a feeling."

"Stefan said something, didn't he?"

Barnaby sighed and closed his eyes, as if wishing everything would stop. When he opened them again, he looked resigned. "He just said something about how Toto's ambitions could push someone's nose out of joint. It made me think there was a hierarchy, and Toto wasn't at the top of it."

Jackson tried not to appear too excited. "Can you remember a name?"

"No. It was odd."

"Okay." Jackson took a breath and leaned back in his chair, mirroring Barnaby. "Thank you. You've been very helpful. If you think of a name, please tell us. Remember, it will help your own cause."

Barnaby shook his head. "It's not worth leaving here. My life is forfeit now that I've been caught. The little I know is enough to sign my death warrant." He met Jackson's eyes. "My achievements are over. So are Stefan's."

Jackson felt suddenly sorry for him. Barnaby wasn't old, nor was Stefan. Both were clever men—brilliant in their way, and now their academic lives were finished. "We were friends, of a sort, once. I don't want to be your enemy, but I don't get why you'd want to support such an endeavour."

Barnaby's eyes glazed as he stared at the desk. "It seemed like a dream to create hybrids and clever weapons. To manipulate flesh and matter. The pinnacle of alchemy and magic. Stefan told me what they'd achieved—years after he'd left the Order, of course. I was fascinated. I wanted to help them go further. Now, after hearing about France and poor Aubrey, it seems sullied."

"The reality is more dangerous than you thought?"

"I suppose so. I honestly didn't expect that anyone would die, but the attack on the order's London office did surprise me." His fingers worried his bottom lip as he talked. "Toto seems to control them now, but what if his soldiers rebel? What then?"

Barnaby's night in the cell, and maybe Aubrey's death, seemed to have chastened him. Jackson appealed to his conscience. "Then help us. The paranormal world is weird and dangerous enough without adding some magically-enhanced hybrids employed as someone's private army. In fact, I'm struggling to understand what Toto could want next. He seems to have achieved the perfect balance. His men and women are formidable."

"But they don't fly."

"What?" Jackson thought he'd misheard him.

"It's Black Cronos's next big step, but so far, it's proving impossible. His soldiers don't shift. Ever. They're strong and fast, yes, but he wants more. Always more. The Igigi had wings—some of them, anyway—and he's investigated other creatures that have wings. And then he saw *your* guys." His eyes widened, impressed. "Caldwell told me about the men he'd employed through Harlan. The huge men with wings—Nephilim. Now that Toto knows they exist, he wants to achieve that even more."

Jackson felt a horrible certainty spread over him, and he wondered why he hadn't thought of this before. "He wants to create his own Nephilim?"

"I believe so, but he knows that's virtually impossible...at the moment. But the Igigi are the first step."

Jackson's voice hardened. "Where did they find the tablet?"

"A private collection. That's all I know."

"Here? Abroad? London? *Where*?"

There was another long pause as Barnaby's eyes narrowed in thought. "A few weeks ago, before you caught Stefan, he mentioned something about a visit to Wales. He said Toto had finally found an intriguing clue to the missing Igigi. He was enigmatic. Smug, even. But that was Stefan all over."

"Just Wales? You can't narrow it down?"

He shook his head and fell silent. Jackson knew occult dealers and collectors all over the country, and there were a few in Wales. He might be able to find the right one—with Harlan's help.

"Thank you, Barnaby." He stood abruptly, pushing back his chair and gesturing to the interview room. "I'm sorry about all this."

Barnaby gave a short, barking laugh. "No, you're not. Does Caldwell know I'm here?"

"Not yet, but I'll see him today. Why?"

"Tell him I'm sorry...especially for Aubrey." He shrugged. "He'll never forgive me, but say it anyway."

And then he folded his arms across his chest and stared at the desk, and Jackson left him to his thoughts.

Harlan was in his office studying the files of his recent cases when Jackson called to update him on the interview. He was going to interview Stefan Hope-Robbins, and had asked Harlan to start the search, promising to liaise again in a couple of hours.

Harlan was happy to help. He had a comprehensive list of dealers of occult items, and that included those who bought historically significant objects, too. Many things that weren't strictly considered occult still had interest to the paranormal world, and that included ancient objects that didn't have any magical powers. Professional scholars and amateurs alike were always looking for hidden gems of knowledge, buried by history, and just waiting to be unearthed again to reveal secrets.

He opened up his files on the computer and then decided a fresh coffee would help. He winced as he moved, and gingerly felt his ribs. He was sure he'd cracked some during the fight, but was glad Armstrong had decided to talk. Harlan had volunteered to tell Caldwell the news about Barnaby's betrayal; he felt it was his case and his responsibility, and was planning to head over there soon.

Coffee made, he sat at his desk again, and started to search his database—an admittedly small one when it came to Wales, but three dealers immediately caught his attention. Although perhaps *dealers* was the wrong word. They were collectors, really, with extensive personal treasure troves of Egyptian, Assyrian, Mesopotamian, and European artifacts—all of which should belong in a museum, but didn't. And that meant they were wealthy, too.

He knew Silas Morgan from a deal a few years back. Collectors could be famously cagey about their acquisitions, but hopefully Silas would be reasonably forthcoming. However, five minutes later after a friendly, chatty conversation, Harlan had to rule him out, and with trepidation turned to the next one on his list. An octogenarian called Harry Gibson, who lived in the north of Wales and was famously cranky. As expected, the conversation was short and brutal and he was sent off with a flea in his ear, but also a flat denial. That left Countess Catarina Edevane, a formidable woman who had married the notorious Earl of Breconshire, sharing his passion for history and his collection of illicitly-obtained goods. He was older than her by some years, and in his youth he, like his father before him, had travelled extensively, essentially looting places before that became frowned upon in these enlightened times. Now it just happened in more devious ways. Although the earl was still alive, he was so frail that Harlan knew the countess dealt with the collection now.

The earl's ancestral home was in the Black Mountains, a wild area in the south of Wales, and suitably brooding for such an unusual family. And, from the little Harlan knew of British peerages, it was an old title.

He exhaled heavily as he stared at the photos of the stately home. It was small compared to some, craggy and piled with towers and turrets and crenelated walls, but with extensive private grounds.

Harlan had never worked for them, but knew that other Orphic Guild employees had a few years before. Hoping that alone would stand him in good credit, he summoned his courage and dialled the number on their records. A superior voice answered—a secretary, not surprisingly—and he was put on hold before being sent to someone who was impossibly brisk and annoying.

"You cannot possibly be put through to the countess because she is extremely busy."

"Is there anyone else I can speak to?" Harlan asked in his most diplomatic tone. "I just need to ask a question about the collection of Mesopotamian objects that belong to the earl."

The voice cut in, "There are no such things! I have no idea who is giving you such information, but you are sadly misinformed and—"

"Wait!" Harlan interrupted him, fearing the uptight man who reminded him of Smythe was about to hang up on him. "I'm from The Orphic Guild. We have helped acquire such items before, and have worked with the earl in the past."

A loud, commanding voice sounded on the other end. It dripped with impatience, and Harlan fell silent, struggling to hear what was being said. In seconds a woman was on the phone.

"Who is this?" Her voice was silky but with a core of steel, her accent plummy.

His heart pounding, Harlan thought he might be speaking to the countess herself, and he quickly explained who he was and what he wanted. He'd barely finished his sentence when she said, "I wondered if someone else would call."

"You did? Why?"

She huffed, and he heard shuffling, as if she was moving. "A rather annoying, obsequious man visited a few weeks ago with a gorgeous creature who smacked of violence. A Mr Plumley. If I'd have known quite how untrustworthy he was, I might have refused the visit. Perhaps I had a sixth sense, though." She was talking as if to herself. "I sense a refusal wouldn't have gone down well."

"I think I know who you're referring to," Harlan said cautiously, afraid she might slam the phone down on him if he said the wrong thing. "Does he have white-blond hair? And was his companion a woman with long, black hair?"

"Yes, that's them. He struck me as being very devious."

Harlan wondered what Toto had done to cause such umbrage. *Surely it was more than just his manner?* "You're right. He is not to be trusted. Can I confirm that he wanted to see a stone tablet describing the flight of the Igigi?"

"You can indeed. I have no idea how he found that it was in our possession. No doubt records published years ago when the previous earl was a garrulous, bragging fool. My father-in-law, you understand."

Harlan wasn't sure what to say to that. To agree would seem rude. Instead, he just said "Oh, well, yes, your visitor is known for his extensive research. And to be honest, your father-in-law's and your husband's discoveries were renowned at the time."

"Your name, again?"

"Harlan Beckett, a collector with The Orphic Guild, based in Eaton Place." He dropped the location, knowing it carried weight and credibility.

"Ah, yes, that name is vaguely familiar. What do you want, Mr Beckett? Spit it out!"

Harlan took the plunge. "My associates and I would like to see that tablet, too. We believe that it is vitally important."

"Do you intend to search for the location—the lost city it references?"

Suspecting that lying to her would be a mistake, he said, "I believe so, yes."

"Can you be here by tonight?"

Harlan checked his watch. It was late morning, so there was plenty of time. "In Wales? Of course."

"Good. But there are conditions. If you search for it, then I must come with you."

Harlan stuttered, thinking he'd misheard. "You want to come with us?"

"Yes. It is my condition for you to see this tablet. Yes or no? It's quite simple."

"Yes, of course."

"Good. How many should I expect? You said *associates*—emphasis on the plural."

Quickly calculating who should come, he decided Gabe, Shadow, and Ash would want to be there, as well as Jackson. "Five—if that's okay?"

"Perfectly. I can accommodate you all overnight. You'll have to stay after such a journey, and we have acres of rooms here. You're all in London?"

"Some are in Cornwall."

"Even worse! Such a long drive. And besides, we need to plan. See you this evening—and dress for dinner."

Without any goodbyes, she hung up, leaving Harlan's head reeling.

TEN

Gabe ended the call with Harlan and glared at his brothers and Shadow, who were clustered in the kitchen for lunch.

"What the hell does 'dress for dinner' mean? Does he suppose I'd go naked?"

Shadow's appreciative gaze ran down him, sending shivers along his spine, and he mentally gave himself a cold shower as she said, "That would be nice."

Niel mimed vomiting. "Ugh. No, thanks. I don't need to see Gabe's bare ass as I'm eating." He frowned at Shadow. "Seriously, keep those thoughts between you two."

She raised her eyebrows and grinned. "Are you a prude? Does the fact that we're having sex—a lot of sex—disturb you?"

Gabe leaned his elbow on the table and his cheek in his hand, closing his eyes in disbelief. *Not this again.* Since they'd started their relationship, that admittedly did involve lots of sex, Shadow had decided to embrace acknowledging their relationship, and now she constantly teased his brothers about it. Fortunately, they tolerated it in good humour—most of the time. Gabe, however, wished she'd shut up. She didn't hear the relentless ribbing he got when she wasn't there.

Niel glowered at her. "No, it doesn't disturb me. I'm a grown man who's had plenty of sex, thank you. But I don't need to hear about *your* sex life constantly."

She pouted. "Poor Niel. Does it remind you of what you're not getting?"

"I could have sex if I wanted to."

"With your hand?"

Nahum, Ash, and Zee almost choked on their burgers as Niel yelled, "*With a woman*! I have my charms."

She raised her eyebrows over her teasing, violet eyes. "I'm sure you do. Certainly, all this cooking would mean you'd make a fine wife."

Gabe intervened before Niel reached for his axe. "Shadow! Please stop, for the love of Herne."

"There is no love between me and Herne, but of course, *darling*. Whatever you say." She reached for her own burger with a chaste expression, although she couldn't resist shooting Niel a cheeky smirk.

"I ask again," Gabe said, trying not to laugh, because Niel was glaring daggers at Shadow, "what does 'dress for dinner' mean?"

Nahum swallowed his food, and said, "It means to wear a suit, or a tux, or something smart. Not jeans and t-shirt."

"A tux? As in, *tuxedo*? Why the hell should I dress up to eat food?"

"Perhaps," Ash said calmly, "you should explain the phone call, so we have some context?"

"Oh, that probably would help," he said, realising he'd been so flustered by the news from Harlan that he hadn't told them anything. He quickly summarised their plans. "So, my beloved one, and Ash, that means you also have to dress for dinner."

Ash's eyes widened. "I'm coming, too?"

"Yes. You're our scholar. I need your brain. So does Harlan, by the sound of it."

Shadow looked relaxed about it. "No problem. I have that black dress I borrowed from El. And the shoes. She told me I could keep them—a gift. And besides, Nahum said I looked sexy as hell in them."

Gabe glared at Nahum. "You said *what*?"

"It was merely a compliment! And well before you two were a thing!" Nahum wagged his finger at Shadow. "And you, stop shit-stirring!"

She sniggered, clearly in one of her more playful moods.

Gabe turned his attention to the most pressing matter at hand. "Well, we haven't got tuxes, but we do have smart suits, so that's something. Not that I've worn one for a while. I guess I should make sure it has no creases." He gave Shadow a knowing wink, aimed more at teasing Niel. "Perhaps I'll like dressing for dinner. And then undressing you afterwards."

"Oh, funny man!" Niel said, standing up to clear the plates. "I won't miss either of you. Stay away as long as you like!"

Ash laughed and checked his watch. "What time do we need to leave?"

Nahum was already searching his phone. "You need to allow five hours for the journey, possibly more for traffic."

Gabe nodded. "Right. We'd better get a move on. Let's pack weapons and enough clothes for a couple of days, just in case. As civilized as this sounds, I do not intend to go in empty-handed."

Barak was in the main security room at Caspian's warehouse, having just supervised the shift changeover, when Caspian entered the office.

He stood to put the kettle on as he greeted him. He hadn't seen him for a couple of weeks, and like Estelle, he seemed different, like he'd shed a weight.

"Have you recovered from your stab wound?" Barak asked him.

Caspian smiled and patted his side. "I have. Briar's magic and a lot of rest have worked wonders. It helps that we've bound the witches' powers, the ones who were behind the attacks. I sleep more easily because of it."

"Estelle told me what happened at Litha," Barak said as he prepared the mugs, presuming Caspian would want a drink. "It sounds like a sad business."

Caspian nodded as he stood in front of the monitors, absently watching the activities around the warehouse. "I hated doing it...we all did. But that's not what I wanted to talk to you about." He looked at him, a smile playing around his lips as he spoke. "I think you're the one responsible for Estelle's recent change in mood—for the better, I should add."

"I'm relieved to hear that. I'd hate to think I'd pissed her off! She can be mean when she wants to be."

Caspian gave a short laugh. "I'm well aware of that! She's asked to do less hours here. It seems she enjoyed the last job she worked on with you guys."

Barak leaned against the counter, hoping Caspian wasn't about to say it was impossible. "She was great—well, more than great. I think we already see her as part of the team. I mean, I know she can't work with us all the time..."

Caspian interrupted him as he sank into a chair. "It's fine, Barak. My own thoughts on our business are conflicted, too. It was a surprise to me to know that Estelle was so unhappy here. I suspect she's been unhappy for years, and didn't even know why."

Barak silently prepared the coffee and placed it in front of Caspian, scared of breaking a conversation that had the ring of a confession. While there was no doubt that he and Estelle had chemistry, nothing had happened beyond him flirting and Estelle tolerating it. *But she didn't rebuff him, either.* It was a dance; one he wasn't sure he knew the steps to.

Caspian continued, "All we have ever been brought up to do was to take over the business. It's been in our family for generations, and frankly, not being involved in it was unacceptable. My father was a hard taskmaster. Unforgiving. I suppose at least he was modern, and was as happy for Estelle to be involved in the business, too. I know my grandfather didn't think that way about women in the workplace." He met Barak's eyes and laughed. "Maybe she'd have preferred it!"

"I doubt it. Better to be involved than not."

"True. Anyway, neither of us has had time for anything beyond Kernow Shipping, and I think that only now are we beginning to see that as a mistake. Now the office feels like a chain."

"I get that, but what can you do? You're the CEO."

"I'm asking my cousins to pick up more of my work, and Estelle's. And we have some excellent staff who can be promoted. I will never leave the business completely, of course, and neither will Estelle. But we can arrange things so that our lives are less bound by it." He sipped his coffee and frowned at Barak. "I suppose I just wanted to ensure that using Estelle wasn't a short-term thing for you. I don't want to see her hurt."

Barak grinned. "Are you asking if my intentions towards your sister are good?"

Caspian laughed. "I trust that they are, and besides, what's between you two is your business. It's more the work. She enjoys it, despite the danger. Not that we've discussed it in depth, but I can tell."

"At the moment, there aren't enough jobs for all of us, but her magic is an asset, so she has a place. Which I guess brings us to me and Niel, and our work here..."

"Already organised. You can finish at the end of this month, if you want. If you guys have enough money."

Relief swept through Barak. "We've got enough, and I've got to be honest, I can't wait. As good as this place has been for us, especially when we really needed it, I want more."

"And you deserve it. You're too good for this role. So, you think you'll have a couple of jobs on the go at once?"

"Potentially. It's hard to say, but there's a market for our services, and the money's good, which means we don't need to work constantly, either. Are you saying *you* want to work with us?"

He shook his head. "No. I would crowd Estelle. This should be her thing. I was just curious. And who knows, I may wish to employ you in a different capacity. Sometimes we have need of more specialised services."

"You'll get good rates, I promise."

Caspian rose to his feet with his coffee. "I'll take this next door. I need to see Dean."

"Sure." Barak eased back in his seat, looking forward to telling Gabe the good news, but Caspian paused in the doorway.

"Thanks for Estelle, anyway. She looks happier...much happier. I hope things works out." And with an enigmatic smile, he left the room.

Harlan accepted a ride with Jackson to Wales, preferring to be a passenger for the long drive, rather than having to concentrate on the road. They'd had a diversion when Jackson announced he wanted JD to have the weapon they'd found, but Harlan had waited in the car while he dropped it off.

"I figure," Jackson said, navigating onto the M4 motorway that led to Wales, "that seeing as he's trying to find an antidote to their powers, the weapon might help. And besides we are baffled."

TEN

"You're kidding! Your science experts can't help?"

"It seems not, but there's a lot of magic involved in what Black Cronos does, and our scientists don't really understand that. I'm hoping JD's brain will unlock the secret."

"If he could, he might even be able to manufacture them."

Jackson laughed. "Tucking away a futuristic weapon in my coat pocket is tempting. And I imagine the military would be very interested in such a thing...should they ever find out."

"You're trying to keep it a secret?"

"Until we understand it more, yes. But Black Cronos is already making waves."

"With other government departments, you mean?"

"Not yet. Just within our own. The thing is," Jackson said, glancing over at him, "that for all the years we've been hunting Black Cronos, this is the most information we've ever found in such a short time. In the past, we discovered bits of information scattered around—fragments, that as soon as you had a lead on just seemed to evaporate. Now we feel like we have a real chance."

"Because of the Nephilim?"

"Partly. There's no doubt that their unique abilities—and Shadow's—have helped give us an advantage. But also partly because Toto seems to be the driving force that has decided to push ahead, whatever the cost. His supreme confidence suggests that he feels he will always be one step ahead."

Harlan angled himself in his seat so he could see Jackson better. "Tell me about your grandfather in the war."

Jackson gave a short laugh. "I wish I could, but I actually don't know that much. As I told you in your flat, he was sent into France after the Allied Forces were told about another faction that was operating in France. The Resistance were everywhere at the time, constantly communicating with Britain. It became clear that something else was happening, besides the German invasion. The Resistance were in the hills and countryside and privy to seeing certain things. Some men and women disappeared, and they knew it wasn't the Germans who had taken them. They always made a big deal about displaying the captured Resistance fighters. These guys were *never* seen again. My grandfather was sent in with a special team. They went missing, too."

"I'm so sorry. That must have been terrible for your grandmother and family."

"No more terrible than for anyone else at that time."

"I guess you're right. My grandfather fought too, but he came home. But why did you say that the PD runs in your family?"

"My great-uncle worked for the division, too. He survived the war, and well, I guess considering the nature of the job, the PD likes to keep their circle small. Obviously, we have new members, but if family members want to join and have the aptitude, that makes life easier. I was brought up knowing about the occult and paranormal creatures, although my parents didn't join. I think my father was bitter about my grandfather—understandable, really."

"Any other family members in the PD?"

"No. My older sister isn't interested, so it's just me."

"And of course, you know about JD. Does everyone in the PD know?" Harlan still felt a fool about that. He thought he'd been privy to a great secret, and yet Layla Gould, Waylen Adams, and Jackson knew about him, too.

"Absolutely not! JD insists we keep that information close. He's cagey, not surprisingly."

"He's a pain in the ass! He and Mason aren't talking right now... Although, I think that's Mason's doing. JD seemed oblivious."

Jackson glanced at him. "How is Mason?"

"Pissed off and grieving. But he'll come around."

"Good. So, tell me about this place we're going to."

Harlan laughed. "Breconshire House. Countess Catarina Edevane, the Countess of Breconshire, sounds crazy. I've never met her, but her husband's family is responsible for looting many ancient sites over the years. Especially between the wars, when it was all the rage. I understand the house is filled with ancient Mediterranean and Middle Eastern objects. You know what I mean."

"Stone columns, figures, reliefs, etc, etc..."

"Yep. Back when it was acceptable to have that stuff and you weren't accused of cultural theft. I think that's why the family keeps quiet about it now. They certainly don't want to give it all back."

"So, why did you speak to her and not the earl?"

"Because he's in his eighties now, and she's the one we were engaged by a few years ago."

"Not an alchemist?" Jackson asked.

"Hard to say, but I doubt it. She restored the ancestral home, too."

"They don't live in London?"

"They have a house there, but I'm not sure how often she's there. We only have Breconshire House listed to contact."

"As long as the bloody place isn't booby-trapped, it's fine," Jackson said. "Arklet Abbey was a bloody nightmare."

"I wish I could have been there," Harlan admitted. "Sounds fascinating."

"Gruesome, more like." Jackson shuddered, his hands tightening on the wheel.

"Did you find anything of use?"

"To be honest, not really. The house was full of stuff—furniture and the like—but nothing personal. The study was full of books, but nothing that could provide any clues about Black Cronos. Not obviously, anyway," he conceded. "No personal information like bank accounts, either. It could have been owned by anyone!"

"Except, of course, for the cellar of horrors."

"Yes, that. But everything was stripped bare, apart from the one room and the dogs. They must have virtually wound up their operation there."

"Someone must have been looking after the dogs."

"Well, they haven't been back since. We're still watching the place. But Toto will have warned anyone off now."

"They must have been local if they weren't living there," Harlan mused. "Or they left when Toto arrived."

"Maybe." Jackson shrugged, frustrated. "Anyway, do we know when Black Cronos took the photos of the stone tablet?"

"A couple of months ago. Well before the Dark Star Temple." Harlan considered the countess's tone. "She was unnerved enough by the visit that she expected there'd be more."

"She sounds smart." Jackson gave Harlan a knowing look. "And what else did she want?"

"What makes you ask that?" Harlan hadn't told anyone what he'd promised her, not even Gabe, although he was planning to tell him when they met at their rendezvous point.

"Because people like that—the entitled—think they can get extras."

"She does own the damn thing, and she is letting us see it!"

"Go on."

"She wants to go with the team when they try to find the city."

"I knew it! And?"

"I said yes."

"You said *what*? Ha!" Jackson threw his head back and laughed, almost swerving as he drove. "Gabe will kill you!"

"Tough shit. I made the deal. Without me, none of us would be seeing this thing."

"True. You know, I'm surprised they didn't hurt her or try to steal it."

"She's royalty...or something of the sort." Harlan was always confused by the titles of the nobility. "I would guess that must give her some life insurance. Killing a countess would get a lot of attention, and even Toto wouldn't risk that. And I'm sure she has security. I must admit, I can't wait to see the place. And her. I'm very intrigued."

"As long as you've packed a suit," Jackson said with a grin.

"Of course!" Harlan had a horrible thought. "Please tell me you have one. I never see you in anything but the scruffy shit you're wearing now." He gestured at the old trench coat, t-shirt, jeans, and sneakers that Jackson was wearing.

"Of course I do! A very nice one, too."

Harlan imagined that it was years old with moth holes, smelling of camphor. "Is it double-breasted with a kipper tie?"

"Cheeky bastard," Jackson said good naturedly. "Although, it is nylon."

"You're kidding, right?"

"If I'm not bothered, why should you be?"

Harlan wouldn't be surprised in the least. Jackson seemed like he couldn't give a crap about what he wore or what people thought of him. It was probably months since he'd last had a haircut.

"You're right," Harlan admitted. "But don't blame me if I laugh when I see it."

"And where are we meeting the team?"

"A country pub in Llanthony, on the way. We'll sort out the details then. Has Toto and The Silencer of Souls shown up yet?"

Jackson shook his head, his mouth settling into a tight line. "No. It was like they disappeared into thin air."

Harlan leaned back and looked out of the window. "Sneaky bastards."

"I'm not worrying about that right now. One step at a time. They'll show up again. Especially now that we know about the tablet."

"As long as they don't show up tonight, though I'm sure that's unlikely. I bet Toto and that woman have already left the country."

Feeling more relaxed than he had in days, Harlan settled back to enjoy the ride.

ELEVEN

Shadow sipped her gin and tonic as Jackson and Harlan settled into seats next to Ash and Gabe.

They were in the Black Dog pub having a private catch-up before heading to Breconshire House, and Shadow was glad to stretch her legs. The journey to south Wales had been long, and not helped by endless Friday traffic.

"How much further is the house?" Ash asked, looking relaxed as he leaned back and surveyed the room. Shadow knew his stance was misleading. His eyes were watchful, and he would leap into action as quickly as she and Gabe, should the need arise.

"About another mile or two up a winding country lane," Harlan said before sipping his pint. "Fortunately. That felt like a long drive! I have to warn you though, I'm not exactly sure what to expect."

"If we're staying overnight," Shadow said, "I'd at least like to think it's safe. The countess hasn't invited us to a trap, I hope." As she spoke, she absently played with the knives strapped to her thighs—hidden by her magic, of course. It wasn't the done thing to stride around with them on display, especially in quaint country pubs.

Harlan looked amused. "I'm pretty certain it's not a trap—unless she's a very good liar. She genuinely sounded put out by Toto's visit.

And, in case I didn't mention it earlier, we've worked with her before... Well, not me personally, you understand."

"Tell me about her," Gabe said. "I want to know what we're walking into. And how you found her." He stared at Jackson. "Are you sure Barnaby isn't setting us up?"

Jackson nodded as he brushed the head from his Guinness off his top lip. "Fairly certain. He was rattled last night, tried to get away, and pulled one of their weird weapons on us. But today he seemed resigned to his fate. Troubled, even. I think Aubrey's death has pricked his conscience. He even sent his apologies to Caldwell."

Harlan snorted. "Which were not accepted. I went to see him, and he's furious. And he feels like a fool. He was utterly shocked when I told him."

"Poor guy," Ash said thoughtfully. "He'll be second-guessing everything now. Every conversation, every plan..."

"He's already amending their plans to return to France," Harlan said. "Although, Toto has what he wants from there, I guess. I'm sure he'll have the copies of the old documents that Caldwell took from the temple, too. Barnaby will have shared them."

"Of course! I'd forgot about them," Shadow confessed, remembering that the manuscripts had been split between Toto and Caldwell in the mad scramble as the Minotaur attacked them.

"The countess," Gabe reminded Harlan. "What's she like?"

"From what I can gather, she married the Earl of Breconshire when she was eighteen, and he was in his forties. It was sort of an arranged, nobility marriage. Her father is an earl, too. I doubt it was a love match, but who knows?"

He shook his head, perplexed, and Shadow thought she couldn't imagine anything worse than being married to someone she didn't love. Especially someone so much older. In fact, she hated the thought of marriage in general.

"Anyway," Harlan continued, "it seems she became as interested in the family's acquisitions as her husband. They used to travel extensively. Now, of course, the earl is in his late seventies, and from what I can gather has been unwell for years after having a stroke. She's still fit and in her forties." He cleared his throat and looked sheepish. "Which brings me to the next thing. A condition of us seeing this tablet is that if we search for the city, she comes with us. I have already agreed."

"*What*!" Gabe's voice boomed across the quiet pub, and everyone stared. His face flushed with anger, and he forced himself to lower his voice. "What the fuck were you thinking?"

Jackson retreated behind his pint, but Harlan wasn't fazed in the slightest. "We wouldn't be seeing this tablet without her permission. She gave me little choice. Besides, when she knows what's involved, she may change her mind."

"Which requires us to tell her what's involved!" Gabe looked astounded. "Do we really want to tell our business to *everyone*?"

"She's hardly everyone," Ash put in, trying to calm Gabe down.

"She's a countess! And doubtless will have a million requirements!"

Shadow inwardly rolled her eyes. *Gabe was such a drama queen sometimes*. He was obsessively private, and liked to keep his team small. To be fair, every case they had seemed to balloon, and while part of her understood his frustration, she just rolled with it.

Harlan placed his glass down. "Gabe, can we just meet her first and go from there? She may not be as bad as we think! Think of the goal!"

"That's true," Ash said. "And her family found the damn thing. That must mean they have a more accurate location than we do right now." He raised his pint to Harlan. "I'm impressed you tracked it down in such a short time."

"Barnaby's intel helped. There are only a few places in Wales it could have been. I guess there was always the possibility that it was an unknown, but sometimes the Gods smile on you!"

"But more often," Shadow said, thinking of her own experiences, "they like to screw with you."

Ash leaned forward, excitement flaring in his eyes. "I confess, I can't wait to see the tablet. To think the Igigi found a place for themselves so close to where we were looking all those years ago…it's unbelievable."

"But Ash," Gabe said, seemingly now resigned to Harlan's news about the countess, "what if they *are* still alive somehow? They were our enemies. We were supposed to kill them. I'm not feeling good about doing that anymore."

Shadow felt sorry for him, knowing he'd had sleepless nights ever since the news. Despite all of Gabe's aggression and training, he was always fair.

"Me neither," Ash agreed. "And they certainly don't deserve to be kidnapped by Black Cronos for experimentation. But they surely won't be alive. They'll be dust."

"I damn well hope they're dead," Harlan said with feeling.

Gabe leaned back and rubbed his stubble. "I'm sure they are, but if they're not, I can't see Toto being able to kidnap any Igigi. They're too strong, even for his soldiers. We should help them. Or at least save their remains from being stolen. Anyway," he shrugged, "let's not get ahead of ourselves. We need to see the tablet first. The actual thing may give us more clues."

Shadow looked at Jackson. "I hear you interviewed Stefan after Barnaby. Did he tell you anything?"

"Not a thing." Jackson's jaw tightened. "He's been mute for weeks. It's uncanny. I thought that maybe with Barnaby in custody he would talk." He shook his head in frustration. "Nothing!"

"Surely he's too valuable to Toto to leave there," Shadow said. "He's waiting to be rescued."

"I'll be impressed if they get him. He's in a very secure place. But," Jackson paused, his pint halfway to his mouth, "I guess when he's transferred to court that will be the vulnerable moment. Our special holding powers only last so long before he has to enter the regular system."

Gabe grunted with worry. "Then I suggest you have very good security on hand."

"Come on, guys," Harlan said, draining his pint. "We have a dinner to get to. Best not be late."

Ash nodded. "Agreed. But one last question. If it is a trap, what's the plan?"

"Fight, kill, and see the tablet regardless," Shadow said, relishing the chance to get her own back on Black Cronos. Her chest continued to ache, and her armour was still being repaired. "And steal the tablet, if necessary. Easy."

As they drove higher and higher into the Black Mountains, Ash found himself falling in love with the rolling hills and brooding landscape. Up here, the summer air had become colder, and long shadows stretched across the ground. It felt as if they had left the modern world behind.

Ash had done plenty of reading about British history, and knew about the wars and skirmishes that had taken place here. The fights over the border between England and Wales, the feudal kings, the castles that littered the landscape. It was intoxicating. He could almost taste the past. Looking beyond the winding roads, he could imagine the men riding into battle, the attempts to tame the wilderness, introduce farming, build homesteads. The whole place seemed untouched by time. It might not be his past, but he loved it nonetheless. Ash had been fascinated by the past even in his own time, and the civilisations that had preceded him.

He was sitting in the back seat of Gabe's SUV, happy to let Shadow and Gabe chat up front. Although, they had all fallen silent now as Gabe followed Jackson's battered Volvo off the lane and through huge, wrought iron gates with an ornate design, and what looked to be a family crest: a boar and a hawk placed on either side of a shield. The rest of the elaborate design was lost to him as they swept past it. They wound up a long drive edged by thick foliage that was interspersed with topiary designs. He saw a dragon, an elephant, an eagle, and a unicorn, among others. The gardener was clearly skilful.

The drive led them past a gatehouse and then split in two in front of an archway in a thick stone wall with battlements overhead. One road snaked to the side, which Ash presumed led to more outbuildings, and the other, the one Jackson followed, led through the archway. Suddenly, Breconshire House was in front of them, across a huge, paved courtyard.

"Herne's horns," he murmured, unable to hide his surprise and admiration. "What a building!"

Shadow sounded breathless. "It's like a fey castle! It's magnificent."

"It's a bloody mess!" Gabe exclaimed.

To be fair, Gabe was right. The building was a jumble of styles, evidence that the house had been added to over the years. There were towers of a variety of shapes and sizes, crenelated walls, narrow windows, arched windows, three wings, one clearly Tudor in origin, and an enormous, studded wooden door marked the entrance. Virginia creeper scrambled up some of the walls, and enormous pots of topiary flanked the doorway.

Ash exited the car, his eyes sweeping everywhere. It was hard to decide if the place was welcoming or intimidating. Before anyone could speak, the huge door swung open to reveal a woman with long, chestnut hair and huge, dark eyes, dressed in a figure-hugging, calf-length, dark red dress. She strode forward to meet them, hand outstretched, and Harlan stepped up to greet her.

"Welcome! You found us, then!" She shook Harlan's hand vigorously.

"Countess Edevane," Harlan started, but she waved him off.

"Catarina, for God's sake. You must be Harlan with that American accent."

He nodded, looking amused by her strident welcome, and he quickly made the introductions.

When Catarina shook Ash's hand, she looked up at him, and he found himself caught in her gaze. He had expected her to be older, more severe, but she looked younger than her years, her figure trim, her eyes mischievous.

"Follow me," she instructed as she released his hand and walked back to the house. "I wanted to welcome you myself rather than have Bryn do it." She flashed them a warm smile as they stepped into the cavernous hall. The floor was constructed of huge slabs of grey stone, and the walls were covered in dark, wooden panelling with a fireplace halfway down. "We don't stand on ceremony here—not too much, anyway. I can't be bothered with it!"

"Except the required dressing for dinner, of course," Harlan said, holding up his suit in its bag. "We have all come prepared."

"Excellent!" A challenge was in her gaze as she studied them. "One must have some pleasures, and eating good food and drinking fine wine is best appreciated when one has dressed appropriately."

"I couldn't agree more," Ash said, deciding she was impossible to dislike, and already doubting that they were walking into a trap. There was something decidedly upfront and honest about her that he respected. "You're very generous to invite us to stay."

She laughed. "You might not say that when you experience our rooms with dodgy heating. But at least it's summer. Although, sometimes it's hard to tell up here when the mists roll in. I can almost hear the shriek of past battles when that happens." She turned and shouted, "Bryn! Our guests are here."

An older man with grey hair and a paunch, but wearing a smart suit, stepped out of a room to the right and nodded. "The drinks are ready, ma'am."

"Excellent. Bryn will show you to your rooms, and when you have freshened up and changed, you can join me in there." She nodded to the room Bryn had vacated. "Drinks, dinner, and then business!"

Bryn walked to the stairs that led to the upper floors in a huge sweep. "Please follow me."

Bags in hand, they trooped after Bryn, and Ash couldn't help but think that the evening ahead was going to be a very entertaining one.

There was no doubt that the countess provided an excellent dinner, Harlan thought, as he finished the main course of perfectly cooked roast lamb with all the trimmings and picked up his glass of red wine. *And it was the perfect setting, too.*

Their pre-dinner drinks had been served in the drawing room where they had talked idly about the journey and where they had travelled from, Catarina peppering them with questions all the while. But then she had led them up to the first-floor dining room that had a breath-taking view of the garden and mountains. The room was lined with blue silk and tapestries, candles glinted everywhere, and the table was covered in a snowy white tablecloth, silverware, and sparkling glasses.

Harlan had been taken aback when they entered the dining room, suddenly very glad they had dressed for dinner. To eat in such surroundings wearing a t-shirt and jeans seemed very wrong. Now, half-listening to the conversation about the history of the area, he looked out of the window at the thickening twilight and the garden washed in shadows. The room looked over the rear gardens, and a series of terraces filled with plants led down to a lawn edged with borders. On the far side was a stone pavilion, not as old as the main house, with columns lining an outer terrace. Large windows showed glimpses of the interior, but it was too far to see inside. He could also see other buildings around the grounds, and the topiary continued. A long, high hedge had been trimmed to look like a serpent, and there were also large, clipped balls, pyramids, and even a ziggurat, once favoured by the Sumerians.

The gardens were devoted to the passions of the owners, a curious mix of styles. Classic English gardens set against a wild Welsh backdrop, and notes of the ancient Middle East and Greece. Curiously, it all worked well together. *And its owner was also a mix of styles*, he realised, as he turned back to Catarina. She was a beauty, and probably had blended ancestry. Her dark eyes and slightly olive skin suggested Italian or maybe Spanish roots, but that shouldn't be a surprise, considering her name.

And with increasing certainty, Harlan was sure she was lonely. Her chatter suggested someone who loved company but was starved of it. He took advantage of a natural break in the conversation and asked, "Catarina, forgive my curiosity, but this is a big place. Do only you and your husband live here? And your staff, of course."

She smiled, a little sadly. "Yes, just us and half a dozen staff, gardeners, and there are nursing personnel, too. A team of four who look after my husband night and day. He suffered a severe stroke several years ago and is now bedbound. A terrible tragedy for someone who loved life and travel as much as he did."

"And a tragedy for you, too."

She was matter of fact when she answered him. "It changed our lives completely. I could return to London, but that would mean leaving him, and I won't do that—except for short periods. And he will not move. He wishes to die here, in his ancestral home. Our children visit from time to time. We have three. My son, Arthur—although he likes to be called *Art*—will inherit this place then. I hope he doesn't change it too much. I haven't decided what I will do at that point. I love it here, even though it's quiet."

"You're still young," Jackson said, who, despite Harlan's worries about his suit, looked very smart. "You could do anything you want."

"I could." She smiled at him gratefully. "Still young enough to travel."

"I love it here, too," Shadow announced. "It reminds me of home."

"And where is that?" Catarina asked. "Other than Cornwall. I'm sure you are not originally from there."

"A long way from here. It's also wild and free, full of quirks and secrets. I'm sure there are many here."

The countess laughed. "Secrets? Perhaps there are."

Ash leaned forward, looking ridiculously handsome in his suit, his hair tied in a top knot revealing his strong Greek features, his eyes golden in the candlelight. "You aren't entirely English, are you? Your eyes and skin. Italian?"

She nodded, clearly delighted. "My grandmother. I was named after her. And you are Greek, I think?" At his nod, she said, "I love Greece. A wonderful country with a rich history. I shall visit again, one day. And I think you," she looked at Gabe, "are from the Middle East. I guess that brings us to the reason for you being here. Our tablet."

Harlan's pulse quickened now that they had finally arrived at the subject they had all been dancing around, politely waiting for the countess to bring it up. "I must admit," he said, his gaze taking in his companions, "we cannot wait to see it."

"It will be worth it." She gestured behind her. "It's in another wing, with several other pieces."

"Can you give us some context?" Harlan asked. "Like where it was found, and when?"

She held her hand up to pause him and rang a bell, and within seconds, Bryn appeared. "You can clear the plates and bring dessert."

He nodded, and after silently collecting the plates, he disappeared, shutting the door behind him.

"There." She smiled. "That will give us more privacy, although I'm sure he knows all of this already. My father-in-law, Jasper, participated in many digs in the Middle East, and found this particular tablet, along with a handful of statues, to the east of Mardin. It was in the 1950s, when my husband was a teenager. Anyway, Jasper immediately knew the significance of the find, but they discovered nothing else." Her eyes clouded for a moment. "My husband doesn't talk about it much. He just says that they had to cut their search short."

Gabe exchanged a worried glance with Ash, who asked, "Does he think it was looted from elsewhere and dumped for some reason?"

"He thought it unlikely. It was found with related objects. You'll see," she replied enigmatically. "It certainly excited that unpleasant man the other month."

"Toto," Harlan said, feeling dread at the mention of just his name. "Was it just him and the woman who came?"

"Yes. They certainly didn't stay here." She shuddered. "I know of you and the guild, Harlan, but from the very first phone conversation I didn't like him."

Shadow's eyebrows shot up. "Why did you show him the tablet, then?"

Catarina stared at her glass, holding the deep red wine up to the candlelight before looking back at Shadow. "It was the way he asked. He *knew* I had it. It wasn't really a request. It was a demand, couched in polite terms. I could have said no, of course, but I sensed that would be a mistake." She gestured outside the windows where night had now fallen. "This place is secure. The walls are high, and the alarm system is excellent, but I just knew he was a man not to be crossed. I played nice, ushered them in and out, answered questions, played dumb about some things, and then celebrated when they left."

Gabe smiled. "What did you play dumb about?"

"The maps." She met his smile with her own, and her eyes twinkled with mischief as she looked at her guests. "We had a fire years ago in one of the oldest parts of the house. We have photos that I showed to Toto. The damage was extensive at the time, although it's all been repaired now. I lied and said all the old documents went with it. But they didn't. I have the maps. I have everything."

Jackson raised his glass in salute. "Smart! I'm hoping you'll share those with us."

"In return for confirming my earlier request. You're going to search for the lost city, and I want to come."

Harlan turned to Gabe to see his response, as did everyone. Despite Jackson's involvement and his representation of the Paranormal Division, and Harlan's own negotiations, everyone knew that Gabe was the leader of their group. He met her gaze with his own steady one. "It will be dangerous. They'll be searching, too, and they don't play nice. And when the fighting starts, neither do we. There's a lot at stake with this tablet...this city. Are you sure you want to come?"

"I am dying here as surely as my husband is. I need to get out. I need to smell hot, dust-filled air, feel harsh sand beneath my feet, and taste authentic Turkish food again. I have to come, and I promise you won't have to look after me."

"You could die. We all could."

"I'm prepared to risk it."

Her plea was sincere, and Harlan found that he liked her, and felt sorry for her. She shouldn't be cooped up here, even it was of her own volition. He hoped Gabe thought so, too. Surely, he couldn't back out now.

Gabe was quiet as he visibly considered her words, the room silent in anticipation. And then he nodded. "It's a deal, then."

TWELVE

As soon as Gabe stepped into the long room that stretched the width of the wing, windows on either side, he saw the tablet. It was unmissable, despite the fact that the room was filled with other ancient objects.

The tablet was huge and exuded a hypnotic power. It was at least ten feet high and six feet across, the surface pitted and eroded, the cuneiform text missing in places, and the corners crumbling. It was mounted on a stone plinth and spot lit, casting the cuneiform into faint relief.

Ignoring all the other objects, he strode towards it, aware of the others flanking him. Up close he could see the cracks in the surface that indicated where it had broken into pieces and had been reconstructed.

Gabe was speechless at its size, and clearly so was Ash, because he murmured in Greek, "*Apó tous Theoús. Eínai ypérocho.*"

By the Gods. It's magnificent.

Harlan gave a dry laugh. "No wonder he didn't steal it. I had no idea it was so big!"

"The photos are deceptive," Shadow agreed as she walked around it.

Catarina stood back, allowing them space, her arms folded across her chest as she studied it and them. "It's stunning, isn't it? I come in here most days, and have to remind myself not to touch it and risk further damage."

Gabe half-listened, concentrating on the text, and a sudden vision of the past swept over him.

The fight with the Igigi had lasted for weeks but felt longer. It had moved from the cities to the desert, where the Igigi had the advantage. Although the Nephilim were certainly accustomed to the heat and deprivations of battle, the Igigi were far more comfortable in the dry, arid conditions. Despite their size, they were able to blend in with their surroundings. Men called them demons because of it.

Jackson leaned in closer and frowned. "There looks to be more text here than in the photos."

"That's because there is," Ash agreed. "We obviously only found some of the images. Toto and the Silencer must have split them between them." He cocked his head at Gabe. "Clever. It means we only had half the information."

"There are images on the back, too," Shadow said from the other side.

Gabe joined her, frowning as he took in the three figures with horns, wings, and eagle heads with a human body. "Not surprising that the eagle-headed Igigi should be carved here. They were the most intelligent of them."

"Why do you say that?" Catarina asked sharply. "I don't remember reading that anywhere."

Startled, Gabe recovered quickly. "I must have read it somewhere—I forget the source."

"What does the rest of the text say?" Jackson asked Ash, watching as he crouched and leaned forward. The stone may have been large, but the text was tiny.

"Well, the first part is what we have photos of—the story of their flight and the founding of their city near Izalla. Some sections are missing, unfortunately, either through erosion or because of the cracks, but this latter half adds to those details." He glanced up at Jackson and then across to Gabe, a smile illuminating his face. "I was right. It is a personal history. The tone makes it clear. It speaks of Zu, who led them beneath the earth and into a great cave."

"Zu!" Gabe hurried to his side. "It mentions names?"

Ash pointed to a section. "Right there. He was one of their leaders, if I remember correctly." And then as if remembering Catarina, he hurriedly added, "In that text we found. And there is Urbarra's name."

Gabe remembered Urbarra well. He had a wolf's head and legs, as well as their cunning, speed, and strength. Gabe had got close to him in battle only once, before he made his escape and vanished into the dunes like a djinn. He nodded absently. "He survived...not surprisingly." He scanned the broken text. "It says that although many died, hundreds still survived to build their city."

Catarina sat on the floor with her legs tucked to the side, close to Ash, and studied the text, too. "You seem to translate it easily. You're a scholar?"

"I guess you could say that."

She looked up at Gabe and then back at Ash, her eyes narrowing, but there was also amusement there. "I think you're downplaying your skills for some reason, but I won't pry—yet."

"What about you?" Ash asked. "Can you read cuneiform?"

"No. It was my husband who could, but it took him a while. Nothing like as quick as you. And what about the rest of you?"

Jackson, Harlan, and Shadow all shook their heads as Harlan said, "Go on, Ash. What else does it say?"

"It speaks of the pleasure of building a place for themselves. 'We hid from the Watchers deep beneath the desert, and out of darkness came light, water, peace, and prosperity. The Watchers will not pass our defences, nor shall the Anunnaki enslave us again. Should they try, our response will be swift and bloody.'"

Shadow asked, "Who are the Watchers?"

Gabe caught himself in time, about to say *us*, instead explaining, "The Nephilim. They were often called 'Watchers' because of the responsibilities given to them by their fallen fathers."

Catarina nodded. "To watch over mankind. To herd them like cattle."

Gabe bristled at her tone. It made him feel like a slave master, but then he had to admit, that was one of the things they were created for. "Amongst other things," he murmured.

"The important thing is," Shadow said in her usual, impatient tone and with her hands on her hips, "does it give more clues to where the city is?"

"I need to study it more closely," Ash said, taking his phone out to snap some photos. "The language is ornate, cryptic, which was typical of the time. Even the Igigi were prone to embellishing their achievements. They caught the habit from the Anunnaki."

Jackson was studying the image. "Behind the three eagle-headed men, there looks to be fainter carvings. Steps, perhaps? Columns?"

"Are there?" Gabe asked, annoyed with himself for not seeing that before, but realising he'd been captivated by the text. When he examined the tablet again, he saw what Jackson meant. A fainter carving in the background did show what looked like steps descending to a cavern. "You're right." He turned to Catarina. "Did your husband or father-in-law ever search for the city again?"

She shook her head. "Not to my knowledge."

"Did Toto say anything?" Jackson asked.

"Whatever conclusions he came to, he kept them to himself."

"And said nothing about his plans?"

"No. His excuse for being here was that he was writing a paper on the Sumerian Gods and that he wanted access to as much material as possible. Apparently, he'd found records of Jasper's find in old library newspaper records. We certainly don't advertise this collection publicly anymore."

Harlan smiled. "You don't want to give it back?"

"Absolutely not." Catarina looked sheepish. "Is that terrible?"

"If I thought that was terrible, I would need a new job."

"I console myself," she said, walking around her collection, "by knowing that if they were still in Iraq, they would have been looted anyway during the war."

Gabe tore his gaze away from the tablet for the first time since entering the room and took in the rest of the collection, which was arranged much like a museum. Objects were displayed on plinths and lit with spotlights. Some were encased in glass, and descriptions on small cards were next to them. The objects were a mix of small and large, stone and metal, figures, bowls, jars, ritual items, and reliefs. They weren't just Mesopotamian, either; some were Greek. All were displayed perfectly on the highly polished wooden floor. Mounted on the walls and on long cabinets down the sides were smaller objects, and what looked to be manuscripts and photographs.

Spotting a man-sized statue of a hawk-headed creature carrying a sword in one hand and a spear in the other, Gabe hurried over to examine it. It was damaged, the features blurred by time, the sword broken. He couldn't resist running his hand across the surface. "Hurin Igigi. One of the fiercest in battle—*reputedly*," he quickly added, cursing his slip.

"It's magnificent, isn't it?" Catarina said, gesturing to a few more objects. "These were found with the tablet, too."

There were half a dozen full size statues, plus numerous small ones, as well as the remains of stone columns, drinking vessels, and bowls.

Harlan was already staring at the photographs, and he asked, "Are these from Jasper's digs?"

She smiled and walked to his side. "Yes. Look at all the men. Jasper was an enthusiastic amateur, so he hired an archaeologist, who supplemented his own knowledge. I forget his name. All the excavation work was carried out by hired locals. They spent months in the desert.

I know he missed it when he had to return here." She gestured at the room. "This was the old ballroom. We certainly don't throw those anymore."

She walked over to one of the cabinets and opened a door, pulling out a collection of maps and laying them out on a table in the corner. "I removed these before Toto arrived, and it was fortunate I did. He searched all the cupboards." She sniffed. "He was avaricious, and she was just odd. I'm curious to hear how you know about them?"

Jackson just grunted. "Unfortunately, we have met several times for different reasons, and none of them have been pleasant." He stared at the maps she had spread out, and Gabe and the others clustered around them.

They were years old, heavily annotated, and Catarina laid her finger on one. "These maps are from a variety of different digs in many places, but this one is of the area around Mardin. It's riddled with caves and old monasteries cut into the rocky hillsides, and it was to the east, as I mentioned earlier, where they found the tablet...but I'm not sure exactly where. My husband was always vague about it."

"It sounds like your husband was vague about a lot of things relating to that dig," Gabe said, feeling uneasy. *Someone is keeping secrets.* "It's a shame. I was hoping for better directions. How soon can you travel?"

Catarina lifted her dark eyes to his. "I can leave at any time. But surely you need to assemble a team? Men to dig? Secure a permit, even?"

Gabe shook his head impatiently. "We haven't got time for that, and with luck, no one will find out what we're doing. This is unofficial, and we have our own means." *Even if that meant digging it out with his bare hands.* But he had a feeling that wouldn't be the case. "I'll get Nahum to make the arrangements."

"Then I," Ash said, returning to the tablet, "will spend the next few hours here, working on the text."

Gabe nodded, eyes sweeping over the photographs and documents. "Good. And we'll try to glean any clues we can from these."

Catarina nodded. "In that case, I'll get Bryn to bring us more coffee and drinks here. It could be a long night."

THIRTEEN

Nahum ended the call with Gabe and stared at the map on the wall in the living room, his finger tracing the area to the east of Mardin.

They would need a hotel, somewhere small and unassuming where no one would notice their odd hours...unless they could camp in the desert.

"Well?" Niel asked, pausing his game with Zee as they ended a fight scene. "How are they getting on?"

Nahum sat on the sofa and reached for his beer. "Catarina has been very helpful, and we now know we need to search to the east of the city. I need to find us a base."

"It wasn't a trap, then?" Zee asked, putting the controller down and turning his back on the TV. "That's a relief."

"She sounds like an interesting woman," Nahum admitted, "but Gabe couldn't really talk properly. It sounded as if they were all together and have a long night ahead. The countess kept information back from Toto, so we might even have a head start."

"I guess that's something," Niel said. "But it's still a long shot. The city must be rubble by now."

"Maybe not. The tablet survived, and so have several other relics."

"And," Zee added, "the dry desert conditions can help preserve things."

A gleam of intrigue kindled in Niel's eyes. "I'm willing to search, anyway—despite my reservations about going there."

A troubled looked crossed Zee's face. "I'm worried that nothing will be the same. In fact, it's likely to be unrecognisable."

"I've considered that," Niel said, placing his long legs on the coffee table and reclining in his chair, "but it's like an itch I have to scratch."

"Even if it destroys our memories?" Nahum asked, interested in the fact that all of them were worried about returning, switching between excitement and trepidation. Interesting though their new life was, his thoughts often returned to their old one, especially at night when sleep refused to come. Whilst some memories were painful, others were comforting.

"Memories," Niel said abruptly, "cannot be destroyed! They're still up here." He tapped his head. "I have many that I return to...and many I shouldn't."

"Lilith?" Nahum asked, knowing how he still thought of her.

Niel huffed and nodded. "Yes. Lilith." Her name came out as a sigh.

Nahum had loved a few women in his lifetime, some with a passion he thought would never die, but he wasn't sure he had loved as deeply as Niel. Her death burned him, even now.

"Perhaps," Zee said gently, "it is time to put those memories aside, brother."

Niel stared at his beer glass. "Easier said than done. Maybe that's why I need the desert. Perhaps I can forget her there."

"It made no difference at the time," Nahum reminded him, cursing himself for mentioning her name. He could see where this was going, and so did Zee, from the concerned glance he shot Nahum. They needed to snap Niel out of it. "Let's focus on the present and stopping Toto."

"And killing The Silencer of Souls," Zee put in. "You have a score to settle, remember?"

"Like I'd forget," Niel said, rousing himself.

"And perhaps," Nahum ventured, "you need another woman to take your mind off Lilith."

Niel met his eyes with a baleful stare. "That never worked before."

"But it might work now. The trouble," Nahum said, thinking of Gabe and Shadow, "is that some of our brothers are moving on with their lives, while some of us are not. Gabe, Eli, and Barak are doing just fine."

Zee rolled his eyes. "Because they've found a woman—or *women,* in Eli's case…"

"Nothing new there," Niel pointed out. "Lover boy has always preferred a harem."

"But my point is that I'm doing just fine," Zee continued, "woman or not! It's about mindset!" He looked at Nahum with a frown. "And you're okay, too! Niel, seriously," he glared at his brother, "stop it! You get into these maudlin moments and reminisce about the good times. But they weren't all good with Lilith. Far from it!"

Nahum froze. *Zee was actually going there.*

"What does that mean?" Niel asked, a dangerous edge to his voice as he sat up.

Zee held his gaze. "You know what it means. You argued and fought. You were incensed when she started to practise magic! You said she meddled with the Gods' powers, and it would end badly. Then she abandoned you for months when she retreated to the hills with the local magi to enhance her skills. She drove you insane!"

Niel leapt to his feet, fists clenched. "That is not true."

Zee refused to stand. Instead, he leaned back in his chair, regarding Niel coolly. "You know it is. I also know you loved her and forgave her. But she wasn't perfect. No one is. What I'm saying is, keep things in perspective."

"I am." Niel's voice was almost a growl.

"You're not. You never do with her. You've always put her on a pedestal. Until you take her off it, you'll never love again."

Nahum hoped he wouldn't have to leap up to stop Niel from lunging for Zee. *Not that Zee needed his help.* He looked up at Niel defiantly, refusing to back down.

After what seemed like endless minutes of tension, but was in fact mere seconds, Niel said, "Screw you, Zee," before marching out of the room, slamming the door behind him.

"For fuck's sake," Nahum said, glaring at Zee. "What were you thinking?"

Zee grunted. "What we all think. Did you disagree?"

Nahum buried his head in his hands. "No. She's his blind spot. Always has been."

"We do him no favours by not addressing it. I decided it was time."

"He may never speak to you again."

"Of course he will. Eventually." Zee picked up the game's controller and turned back to the TV. "Want to play?"

"No. I need my bed. But I don't want to run into Niel upstairs."

Zee grinned broadly and threw him the other controller. "Then give him some space."

Shadow surveyed her companions over breakfast on Saturday morning, wondering if they would be spending all day searching through the relics and photos again. While it was interesting for a few hours, she really couldn't get as excited over them as Gabe and Ash.

They were both preoccupied even now, Ash poring over the notes he'd made that were propped next to his plate. Catarina was next to

THIRTEEN

him, asking questions and nodding to his answers. Gabe was obviously only half-listening, lost in his own thoughts. He'd had a restless night. Harlan and Jackson were seated opposite them, also chatting quietly, heads together. Sighing, Shadow looked out of the window at the mist-filled landscape outside. Perhaps she'd go exploring. The Black Mountains' brooding wildness called to her. *If only she had Kailen with her...*

Her thoughts were interrupted when Harlan said, "Hey, Shadow. I heard from JD this morning. He wants to know if you can spare him some time today."

She frowned, automatically suspicious. "Why? I don't trust that funny little man."

Harlan smirked. "Neither do I, but he's been examining one of Black Cronos's weapons, and has a theory he wants you to test."

"Weapons? Now *that* sounds more interesting. Why me and not them?" She jerked her head at Gabe and Ash.

He lowered his voice and leaned close so Catarina couldn't hear. "Your fey magic intrigues him."

"As it should," she acknowledged breezily. "But what does he want me to actually do?"

"He didn't exactly spell it out, Shadow! You know JD! We're both leaving soon. There's nothing else me and Jackson can do here. Do you want to come? Weapons are your favourite hobby, right?"

Shadow studied his amused expression. "You just want to know what JD is up to."

"Of course! Don't you? But then, if studying old stones all day are your thing..."

She quickly made her up her mind. "No, it is not! But how will I get back home?"

"I'll drive you there if necessary. Coming?"

"Hold on." She nudged Gabe, who hadn't been listening. "Are you planning on staying here all day?"

He looked bewildered as he focussed on her question. "Er, yes, I think so. Or at least for the next few hours. There's a lot more I want to study before we leave."

"In that case, I'm leaving with Harlan. JD wants to see me. When are we flying to Turkey?"

"It depends on what Nahum has managed to organise. Tomorrow, maybe? Or Monday?"

Jackson intervened with his opinion. "We can't wait much longer than that."

"You want to come, too?" Gabe asked, alarmed. "I'm not sure that's a good idea."

"Of course I'm coming! I'm the ears and eyes of the PD."

"I thought that was our job now?" Gabe said, bristling. "Or don't you trust us?"

Ash and Catarina had fallen silent as they listened to the exchange.

"You know we trust you," Jackson remonstrated. "But this is of national interest. I need to be there."

Shadow knew Gabe wanted to keep the numbers down. Jackson's presence, and Catarina's, meant babysitting the non-paranormals.

Gabe groaned. "Harlan? Are you wishing to grace us with your presence, too?"

"You know what?" he drawled, taking in Gabe's resigned expression. "I don't think I will! Being almost killed last time was bad enough. I'm sure I'll keep busy here."

"Thank you!" Gabe said with exaggerated patience.

"In that case," Shadow said, rising to her feet, "I'll pack now and arrange to get back to Cornwall before you leave." She wagged a finger at Gabe. "Make sure you don't leave without me!"

He winked and blew her a kiss, and she swayed her hips as she left the room. That would leave him something to think about.

The ensuing journey to JD's home was uneventful, the time spent talking about the tablet and the photos of the old expeditions. Harlan in particular seemed quite enamoured of the old-fashioned clothing and the romanticism attached to the digs, especially those between the wars. She listened rather than talked, a useful way of extending her knowledge about her new world. She thought she would have liked that time period, if not for the horrendous sexism and racism. One of the many things she didn't have to tolerate in her own world.

When they arrived at JD's, Jackson exited the car with them, but Anna kept them at the front door, eyeing him suspiciously. "JD didn't say *you* were coming."

"I gave him the damn weapon," Jackson said, irate. "And I'm their lift!" He nodded to Shadow and Harlan.

Shadow was both amused and impressed. Jackson had a way of inviting himself into all sorts of things. It was quite a skill. Anna, however, was quite the guard dog, and was clearly undecided about letting him in. Harlan appealed to her on Jackson's behalf. "He's in the PD, Anna, you know that. Come on! He's not staying long."

Anna rolled her eyes and ushered them all in, saying to Harlan, "He's downstairs. You know the way."

She shut the door, and walked towards the back of the house, leaving them all looking at each other, amused.

Harlan lowered his voice. "I don't think she likes us much. Follow me. And don't touch anything, or she'll have something else to moan about."

"I'm a delight," Shadow said as she followed him down the hall and through a heavy wooden door. "There's something clearly wrong with her. Where are you leading us?"

"Back in time," Harlan murmured enigmatically as he led them downstairs into a huge room.

Shadow paused on the threshold, hands on her hips as she took in the space.

Jackson was similarly impressed, muttering, "Bloody hell," beneath his breath as he took in the old-fashioned laboratory.

"Excellent," JD's voice boomed out, startling Shadow. He straightened from behind a series of test tubes and bottles, all bubbling and emitting steam. "You made good time!"

"The traffic was good," Harlan explained as he headed to his side. "You've had success, then?"

"Reasonably!" He wiggled his hand. "My dear." He beamed at Shadow. "Thank you so much for coming." It was the most cheerful she had ever seen JD, which made her instantly suspicious, but JD called her over. "This way!"

Shadow weaved between the long benches, eyeing the bubbling jars with distrust. The room was warm from the heat of the burners, and in the far wall she spotted a fireplace, the coals glowing, and she was glad she only wore her jeans and t-shirt.

JD was standing in the corner of the room next to a large, round table entirely inlaid with an ornate, geometric grid. It seemed to have interlocking parts, and the many concentric rings of symbols could be moved so that different sections aligned. Unnervingly, it emitted a strange power—a low hum that made the air around it shimmer.

Shadow kept her distance. "What is that?"

"This is my alchemical grid of correspondences." His chest swelled as it always seemed to when he was pleased with himself. "It's complicated and took years—*years*—to perfect."

"Complicated?" Harlan almost stuttered. "It's nuts!"

JD shot him an impatient look. "It most certainly is not *nuts*. It's a highly systematic grid that allows me to move the various parts into almost endless matches. There are rings of planets, metals, angels, cardinal signs, months, days, astrological signs, gemstones, and metals, and many things you would not possibly understand."

There was no doubt about that. Shadow had a headache just looking at it. But there was also no doubt that it was a work of art. Inlaid with an intriguing number of materials, it would have taken decades to complete. Or an army of skilled men. She lifted her eyes to find JD still staring at it with pride and asked, "You made this? All on your own?"

"Of course! It has enabled me to unlock this." JD opened his palm to reveal a small, spherical object in a silver material. "This is a knife."

"It doesn't look like one," Shadow said.

Jackson huffed. "It belonged to Barnaby. He did something to it and nearly stabbed me with it."

Realisation dawned as Shadow remembered being attacked by Black Cronos's soldiers. "But they all seemed to pull weapons out of thin air! I didn't see them holding anything like this."

JD shrugged. "Maybe something was tucked into their clothing or armour. Or maybe there are more weapons we have yet to discover. But I think I know how this one works."

"So soon?" Harlan asked, looking doubtful.

JD snorted. "I used my centuries of experience to analyse this." He placed the silver sphere into the centre of the geometric grid, and the sphere shimmered and morphed into a long, sleek, double-edged blade with a simple hilt.

Harlan gasped. "Holy shit! How did that happen?"

JD puffed his chest out as he preened. "I attuned the correct planetary signatures and correspondences. It took a while, admittedly. I had to play around with a variety before it worked. But..." his face fell as he picked up the knife. Instantly, it reverted to its spherical shape in his palm. "It won't last."

Jackson leaned in. "Interesting. Why not?"

"Because I need to be attuned to it!" JD looked both annoyed and impressed.

"A personalised weapon! Very cool."

"But," Harlan pointed out, "this was Barnaby's and he's human, so how does that work?"

JD rubbed his chin as he placed the knife back on the grid where it immediately changed shape again. "I'm not sure. Perhaps it was designed around his aura, or energy signature."

"So that," Jackson pointed at the grid, his eyebrows beetling together with concentration, "is Barnaby's energy reading?"

"Possibly." He shrugged. "Probably."

Still too many questions, as far as Shadow was concerned. "The superhuman soldiers had lots of enhanced abilities. Does Barnaby?"

Harlan looked at Jackson for confirmation. "He didn't seem to. We overpowered him with reasonable ease…once we got rid of the weapon."

Jackson nodded. "Agreed. The trouble is, we found no weapons from the soldiers. They disappeared with their death, or upon leaving their hands. Infuriating."

Shadow was barely listening as she stared at the sleek blade. "I like that! May I?"

"Be my guest."

Shadow picked it up, but although it held its shape longer for her, within moments it had reverted to the sphere again. "Herne's hairy balls! It's gone!"

JD slapped the bench next to him. "A pox on it! I had hoped that you would be the key."

Disappointed, Shadow still marvelled at the lightness of the sphere. "This is almost weightless. It's incredible!" She looked at JD. "How do we make it work?"

"That is the question! Potentially that particular weapon will never work for us because it's so personalised. Unless perhaps we align you to it, or try to change it to align with you?"

Harlan looked sceptical. "Change Shadow? Isn't that dangerous?"

JD spread his hands wide. "I doubt it. Was Barnaby ill in any way?"

"Not while I was interviewing him," Jackson said.

THIRTEEN 133

"Hmm." JD's fingers drummed on the bench. "It's not a physical change. Nothing as dull as DNA. It's about attuning your body. The more I think on it, the more I feel this is aura-based technology."

Shadow dropped the sphere back on the grid, watching it morph again. "No. I do not wish to have my aura changed." She stared at JD. "My fey magic is part of me. It allows me to shield my weapons, move silently, blend into the landscape when I choose, and makes me fast. I will not risk that. But you can make it fit me."

JD's eyes narrowed. "Have you any weapons hidden now?"

She whipped one of her knives out from the sheath on her thigh, and it popped into view in her hand.

Jackson jumped back. "Bloody hell! Where the fuck did you pull that from?"

She smirked. "I am fey."

Harlan smirked, too. "I love it when you do that!"

"So, the question is," JD said, as he took the knife from her hand, "how do we achieve this. Can you stay?"

"For a day, maybe two, but that's all."

JD beamed. "Excellent. I'll get Anna to make you a room up and then we shall begin in earnest. You two may go," he said dismissively to Harlan and Jackson.

"Can't we watch?" Harlan asked, obviously disappointed.

JD stared at him, a calculating expression in his eyes. "You may stay if you wish to participate. But only you. I cannot focus with too many people around."

Harlan grinned with relief, but Jackson rolled his eyes. "I get it. But will you share your findings?"

JD sniffed. "I'm sure an arrangement can be made."

"Thought so," Jackson grunted. "Come and get your bags then, guys." His eyes swept the room. "And be careful."

FOURTEEN

Ash sat back on his heels and sighed, the tablet's bulk looming above him. His eyes ached and his head buzzed with what felt like a million questions—questions that would not be resolved right now.

It was early on Saturday afternoon, and he and Gabe had been studying the antiquities since breakfast. The room was a fascinating treasure trove, and Ash loved nothing more than wrestling with their secrets. Unfortunately, the tablet was hanging on to some of them.

Ash had taken a few breaks to examine other objects, particularly fascinated with the photos of the digs. Catarina had offered to make copies of the ones they deemed most important. Gabe had also been taking photos to show their brothers. His eyes swept around the room again as he sat on the worn wooden floor, sipping water. The objects found with the tablet had been pieced back together, like the tablet, but the smaller statues were less damaged. *But if Jasper's team hadn't found the city, where had they come from?*

Catarina entered through the huge doors carrying a tray, announcing, "I've brought coffee and cake, if you're interested. My cook has made baklava and Turkish delight."

Ash lifted his head and sniffed, catching the rich smell of honey and nuts, and he quickly rose to his feet. "It smells wonderful."

FOURTEEN

She gave him a beaming smile, and once again Ash was struck by how unexpectedly attractive she was. He'd imagined someone older, stuffier, yet she was vibrant and vivacious—despite her sometimes-brusque manner. "My cook does a wonderful job, but I can't wait to get out there and buy locally."

"You and me both," Gabe admitted as he joined them. His hands were dusty, and a smear of ink streaked his cheek.

Catarina poured their coffee from the silver pot, and Ash smelled cardamom. "Arabic coffee?"

"The best." She handed him a tiny porcelain cup decorated with Arabic designs. "I hope it measures up."

Ash took a sip and sighed with pleasure. "Excellent. We make it at home sometimes. My brother particularly likes it when he smokes the hookah."

"Your brother?" She eyed them both curiously. "Just the one?"

Gabe laughed. "There are seven of us. It's quite the houseful."

"And Shadow?" she asked.

"Yes, her too. Not related, obviously," Gabe added hurriedly.

"I should hope not." Catarina had an impish grin on her face. "Your relationship would be scandalous. But I'm curious," she added, her smile slipping. "You, Ash, are Greek, and Gabe, you're not, so why call yourself brothers?"

Ash answered that easily. "We are good friends...very good. So we might not be blood brothers, but our past experiences bind us."

She pulled a stool from under the bench and sat down, and Ash and Gabe followed suit. "I understand," she said, sipping her aromatic drink. "Experiences I had in the desert meant we bonded closely—and argued intensely sometimes, too."

"Don't get me started," Gabe muttered, prompting a laugh from both of them.

Catarina proffered the sweets. "Please take one. I hope they don't disappoint."

"They certainly don't," Ash said, savouring the rich taste of the baklava. He asked something that had been bugging him all morning. "Will you be bringing security with you? A bodyguard? Or a secretary?"

Catarina looked appalled. "Absolutely not! I am not royalty, and can't abide being followed around by anyone. The size of the estate demands we have staff, but that's all. No, I travel alone. Besides," her eyes ran over them, "with you two with me, I doubt I'll need security. Are your brothers of the same build?"

Ash nodded. "They are."

She nibbled on a Turkish delight, the icing sugar dusting her chin, and she absently brushed it off. "I'd like to pay for the hotel."

"It's all sorted," Gabe told her. "Save your money."

"No. This is my way of thanking you for bringing me along." She cast her eyes to the floor briefly. "I know that what I ask is an imposition, but I've always had the feeling that the dig was unfinished business."

Gabe's eyes narrowed. "You're holding out on something."

"Not me, my husband." She studied them again, searching their faces as if wondering whether to trust them. And then she shook her head, brushing a lock of hair from her cheek. "Why is this city so important? You haven't really said."

Ash noted the stubborn lift of her jaw and her intense stare. She was too intelligent to fob off. And she was being incredibly generous and helpful. He turned to Gabe, who had fallen silent. "We may as well tell her. She'll know soon enough."

He reached for another slice of baklava. "Go on, then."

He turned back to Catarina to find her watching him avidly. "You know the myths about the Igigi and the Anunnaki, I presume?"

"Of course! I've read on them extensively. This find prompted my curiosity."

"Do you believe the Igigi are supernatural beings?"

"I believe that many thought them to be, but that myth has transformed them from powerful men and women into something else. Like the Egyptians, the images aren't real. They're art!"

"But what if they *were* real, a hybrid mix of human and beast, their bodies hidden within the city—and within them are secrets to their supernatural abilities? That is what Black Cronos believes."

Her face was pale, her coffee forgotten. "And you?"

"We believe it, too. The city—and their bodies—could hide many secrets. Secrets Toto wishes to exploit."

Catarina fell silent for a long time before she answered, but when she did, she seemed resolute. "I'm taking you to see my husband."

Gabe surveyed the man in the bed and suppressed a shudder. To end up like this would be a terrible fate.

He'd seen photos of Hugo Edevane when he was a tall, imposing man with a thick sweep of blond hair and a piercing gaze. But now he was shrunken, weak, and his right cheek and lip dropped from the effects of the stroke. *Fate was sometimes a cruel mistress*. He hoped his father's angelic status and their ability to heal meant that this never happened to him.

And the room he resided in didn't fare much better. It was elegant—high ceilings, beautiful mouldings—but it was filled with medical paraphernalia, and it smelled of age and impending death. *Surely*, Gabe thought, *he couldn't have long left*. He looked as if he were hanging onto life by a thread.

Catarina hovered by the head of the bed, where Hugo was propped up on multiple pillows. "Hugo, these are the men I was telling you about."

Gabe shook the earl's hand, wondering just how he should address him. He opted for a brusque, "Good to meet you, your lordship."

The earl's eyes were keen, but his grip was weak, as was his voice. "Forget that," he rasped, his voice thick and tricky to understand because of his stroke. "Call me Hugo."

Once the introductions were made, he and Ash settled in a seat. Hugo tried to speak and then wheezed, which set him off in a fit of coughing. Finally, he said, "You seek the city of the Igigi—Enamtila."

Gabe jolted with surprise. "You know its name?" He looked at Ash, confused, but he appeared just as baffled. "How?"

"I'll come to that. Tell me why you're looking for it."

Gabe was glad he was getting to the point. He'd wondered if they would have to spend hours waffling about nothing, but guessed that was impossible for Hugo now. Even sustaining a short conversation was an effort. "It's vitally important that we find it before anyone else."

"I'd suggest you don't go, but you look like men who are not easily swayed."

"We're not."

"Even if I tell you that finding it might kill you?"

"Why would it kill us? It's just ruins, isn't it? And," Gabe added, curious to see Hugo's response, "you found only remnants...not the city itself."

Hugo stared at Gabe and Ash, a flicker of fear behind his eyes. "I know what my wife has told me, but I want to hear it from you. Why the sudden interest in a place that has been lost for millennia?"

Ash answered. "Because of what the Igigi were. Supernatural hybrid creatures created by the Anunnaki. Some say they have the blood of the Gods. Someone wants to exploit that, and that would be a disaster."

Hugo wiped away a tear from his watering eyes, a result of the stroke. "How would they do such a thing? That would seem impossible."

"Alchemy and magic," Gabe answered bluntly. "It may sound improbable, but it isn't."

Hugo didn't laugh or scoff. "You will stop it?"

Ash nodded. "If we can. We have resources."

Hugo fell silent for a moment, sagging against his pillows, but Gabe was sure there was more to come. He looked haunted, and eaten by indecision.

Gabe leaned forward, arms on his knees. "Something happened, didn't it? You actually found the city."

Hugo sighed, closing his eyes briefly. "We found the entrance. That's where the tablet and statues were. Although, we didn't know it was the entrance at the time. It was a shallow cave, high in the hills, and very remote. Everything was in pieces, and we didn't realise at first, obviously, what we'd found." He paused to get his breath. "But then when we understood what the tablet said, we set up camp and started to explore in earnest. We were there for weeks. After an unexpected storm, the rain changed everything. The cave flooded, streams and waterfalls were everywhere. It was...bewildering. But it triggered a rockfall, revealing a ziggurat built into the rock, doors set within it. The name *Enamtila* was carved above them. When the water subsided, we managed to open them, but something happened, something terrible..."

Gabe exchanged a worried glance with Ash, but Catarina's attention was fixed on her husband, her hand resting on his shoulder.

Hugo gasped, "I need water."

Catarina held a glass to his lips, and Hugo took a few sips, clearly agitated. Gabe didn't dare speak, unwilling to rush him or put him off.

Finally, he continued. "Something came out of the rock, and three men were killed. Crushed. Thrown like dolls. Another four disappeared. It was as if the rock just swallowed them. It was mayhem, and we ran."

"*Something*?" Ash asked, not taking his eyes off Hugo. "What did it look like?"

"It was a blur of wings and a beak. Monstrous. Like a demon come to life. All shadows and feathers. I thought I was hallucinating. I was a boy at the time—in my teens, gawky and awkward—and I'm ashamed to say I ran and didn't look back. We were falling over ourselves to get out. I remember pulling my father behind me."

Gabe could imagine it. A figure from myth manifesting out of the darkness to maim and kill. Sheer terror would have sent them running. He asked, "How many escaped?"

"Barely half of us. Me, my father, the archaeologist, three assistants, and half a dozen locals. The rest were lost. Sealed inside the cave."

Gabe glanced at Ash, finding that he looked as puzzled as he was, and Gabe asked, "Sealed? Like in a rockfall?"

Hugo shook his head, his eyes clouded with confusion. "No, nothing so straightforward. It just seemed to seal itself. I don't know how, but it just did. By then, the locals had fled, leaving our small English group and half a dozen camels and horses on our own. Despite what happened, we were determined to leave nothing behind. The objects that are now downstairs in the hall were already out of the cave, being examined in our camp. We packed up what we could and left, too. And we never went back."

"But," Ash said, edging forward in his seat, "do you have a location? Can you point it out on a map?"

"I tried to block it from my mind, and we swore never to speak of it again. My father even destroyed one of the maps. We blamed the deaths on the flood. But I think I can remember it."

"Good," Gabe said, relieved. "We'll bring you a map, and you can show us where to go."

Hugo looked bleak. "Are you sure you want to?"

"We have no choice."

FOURTEEN

As soon as Jackson returned to the division's headquarters, he headed to Waylen's office, pleased to find him at his desk.

He didn't bother with pleasantries. "We had success. We found the original tablet—which is lucky, because the photos we found only showed half of it."

Waylen eased back in his seat, hands folded across his chest. "You're sure it's the right one?"

"Absolutely. Ash translated what he could, but says some of it is cryptic. However, it seems his initial thoughts were right. It describes a history of the Igigi, and the founding of a city. It even talks of the Watchers who they hid from."

Waylen's face broke into a broad grin. "Brilliant. Then we have to get out there. Have you made any arrangements yet?"

Jackson shook his head. "Gabe wants Nahum to arrange it, and that's fair enough. We have given the lead to them. I'll check in with them later."

"What do you think? Is it really likely that the city is intact?"

"It's hard to know. I've been thinking on it all the way here, and it honestly seems impossible. I mean, we're talking three or four thousand years ago, at least!"

"But they were supernatural. They may have had magic that preserved it."

Jackson grunted a half laugh, not sure if Waylen was clutching at straws. "Maybe. But it's not just the Igigi, is it? It's Black Cronos. They may well have more information than we think. The thought of another battle with them..." he trailed off as he remembered the fight at the Dark Star Temple. *That was bad enough.*

"Walk with me," Waylen said, rising to his feet. "Let's get a drink. You look like you need one."

"Ha! You mean *you* need one!" Jackson knew Waylen too well. Come late afternoon, especially on a weekend when he was putting in extra hours, he wanted a beer or a whiskey. The PD had its own well-stocked staff area filled with tea, coffee, soft drinks, and alcohol, as well as food.

They strode down the empty corridors, and Jackson reflected on how odd he always found this place when most of the staff weren't around. Like many government departments, most staff worked Monday to Friday, nine to five, except when they had to monitor crisis situations, which was rare for them. Jackson hadn't been lying to the others. This was not a huge department, and they only had a handful of staff, including a small security team. It really was a division meant to watch, monitor, and report. Their current circumstances were very different to the normal way of things.

Jackson was updating him on the countess as they walked, who he had to admit he found very interesting, when a distant boom echoed down the corridor, shaking everything. They managed to keep their balance, until another boom threw them to their knees.

"Fuck it!" Waylen yelled. "We're under attack!"

Waylen leapt to his feet and ran down the corridor as fast as his limp would allow him, Jackson on his heels, knowing exactly where they were running to.

The cells.

"Have we still got Stefan?" Jackson asked, wishing he had some kind of weapon on him.

"Due to be moved on Monday."

They arrived at the steps leading down to the small cell block, the whole place swirling with dust. Neither hesitated, Jackson pulling his t-shirt over his mouth and nose as he descended.

It had to be Black Cronos. The only two prisoners they had belonged to their organisation. *But how had they got in?* They were several levels below the street.

FOURTEEN

They reached the bottom of the stairs and a thickly-barred gate controlled by a keypad. Just as Waylen was about to punch the number in, Jackson threw his hand out to stop him. The dust made visibility poor, which worked both ways. It would be hard to spot them, but hard to spot the enemy, too. And Waylen had not experienced Black Cronos like he had.

Jackson held a finger to his lips and for a moment, they listened. There were no shouts or footsteps to indicate anyone immediately beyond the gate, so Waylen entered the number on the pad and carefully opened it.

This part of the corridor was where the interview rooms were. The cells were at the far end, beyond another gate and a guard room normally staffed by two men—fully armed and well trained. They crept down the dust-filled corridor in a half crouch, eyes darting everywhere. Another series of smaller explosions sounded up ahead of them, and both dropped to the floor, Jackson's cheek pressed into the cool tiles covered in chunks of plaster.

After pausing for a beat, they were both back on their feet, heading to the guard room. It was central, secured with bulletproof glass that could see the cells and both parts of the corridor, a door on either side, with security screens mounted on the walls. But the far door was blown off and the glass was shattered. Waylen punched in the key code to the door on their side and Jackson pushed ahead, immediately stumbling over a body. *One dead guard, his chest blown open. Shit.* Waylen grabbed his gun, by far the better marksmen of the two because of his military background. Keeping their heads down, they checked the monitors lining the wall. None were working, the screens black.

Heart pounding, Jackson looked through the shattered doorway into the dust-filled corridor and spotted a cell door blown off its hinges. He and Waylen edged onwards, finding every cell empty—including the ones holding Stefan and Barnaby.

There was a second entrance to this level. Another barred gate and a set of stairs that led to a labyrinthine corridor and exited in a disused Tube station. From there a set of steps went to the street. At the base of the blown-out gate was the second dead guard.

"Damn it! I hate these bastards," Waylen said, checking the man's pulse before handing the second gun to Jackson. "They've gone through the station. I'm going to try to stop them."

He had barely finished his sentence before he was pounding up the stairs, but his speed was already impacted by his injured leg. Fearing it was a suicide mission, but not wanting to abandon his boss, Jackson ran after him, quickly overtaking him.

Jackson had only been in this part of the headquarters once, when he was being shown around, and he found the place equally fascinating and disturbing. There were many abandoned Tube stations in London, closed years before usually because of a lack of use, and several tours could take you around them—but not this one. This was strictly out of bounds. The MI5 building had other access points to it. One thing was certain: Black Cronos did their research.

Footsteps echoed off the bare stone walls as they ran to the station, and rounding a corner, a volley of shots ricocheted off the walls. Jackson and Waylen shot back as they dived for cover.

The station was in sight through another destroyed doorway, the rounded tile walls beyond gleaming in the flashes of torchlight. Jackson just had time to see a muscled soldier hurl what looked like a bomb at them before he ran from view.

Jackson grabbed Waylen's collar and hauled him backwards just as another explosion ripped through the passageway, blowing them off their feet.

FIFTEEN

Harlan watched JD place Shadow's fey blade in the centre of the grid, and with amazement, looked on as it shimmered and disappeared.

Shadow looked horrified. "What have you done to it?"

JD clapped his hands together, applauding himself. "I have found the correspondences that your blade attunes to. Your fey magic."

"But where has it gone?" She looked agitated, and in seconds her second blade was in her hands, as if she would threaten JD.

Blithely unconcerned, he said, "Nowhere. It's still there." He reached forward, seemingly grasping at nothing, and lifted the blade out. It immediately became visible again.

Harlan whistled. "Holy shit. That's a neat trick."

"No trick, you imbecile! Alchemy and magic!"

Harlan bristled. JD had very little patience, especially with Harlan, who he seemed to have decided was a borderline moron. Remaining polite, but through gritted teeth, he said, "I guess I didn't expect fey magic to have correspondences."

"Everything connects in this world—*everything*! We share the same vibrations, energies, and connections, except our combinations are different. Shadow's world is still of this one, it's just that her energies work differently to ours."

"I can honestly say," Shadow said, whipping her blade from JD's fingers, "that I have never heard it explained like that before. I don't like my magic reduced to *energies*."

JD shrugged, utterly unconcerned. "Like it or not, that's what they are. You should be pleased. It means I can now attune our unusual weapon to you. I think."

"How?" Harlan asked, genuinely curious.

"You couldn't possibly understand."

That was most likely true. "Well, what about my energies?"

"Later! This one first. Now shoo, both of you. I have more work to do. And don't wander the garden perimeter—I've activated it!"

JD had already turned his back on them, bending once more over his grid, and resisting the urge to grab one of Shadow's blades and plunge it into his back, Harlan turned away and strode across the lab, cursing under his breath.

"That damn, infuriating man!"

Shadow matched his stride, amused. "You let him get under your skin."

"He's crawled under it and taken residence, like a goddamn tick. Doesn't he drive you insane?" he asked as they arrived on the main floor and headed to the sitting room that led to the gardens.

"I find him more amusing than annoying, but I get it." Shadow headed for the drinks cabinet that Anna had shown them earlier, and pulled a bottle of gin out, along with tonic from the small fridge concealed within it. "Want one?"

"Yes, please. And make it strong!"

Harlan walked to the French doors that were wide open, allowing access to a broad, stone-flagged patio area. It was early on Saturday evening, and it was the first time he'd been out of the lab for hours. JD had laden them both with gemstones and metals, read their auras, recorded their astrological signs, and done all sorts of weird things he couldn't make heads or tails of. It felt like they'd been in the lab for days rather than one afternoon.

Before they'd started, Anna had shown them to their bedrooms to leave their bags and freshen up, pointed out where they could sit and relax, and then left them to it. Harlan wondered how she spent her time. Probably cleaning and cooking, plus pandering to JD's whims. If they could be left alone for the evening, that would suit Harlan just fine.

He took a deep breath of cool evening air and tried to relax, grateful to have Shadow push a glass into his hand, saying, "Bottoms up!"

"Cheers." He dropped into a chair and placed his feet on the chair opposite, Shadow doing the same, and he studied the garden with appreciation. "It's quite the place JD has made for himself."

She sipped her drink and nodded. "The advantage of more than the average lifespan to plan for things."

"The same as you." He looked at her graceful profile as she stared across the emerald lawns and flower beds. She'd relaxed her glamour, and her fey beauty was quite breathtaking.

She turned, her violet eyes sparkling. "I guess that's true, but I've never put down roots in one place for such a long time. I've always kept moving."

"Your life of crime, you mean?" he teased her, remembering her sometimes questionable past. *And to be honest, questionable present.*

"Exactly."

"But now? Especially now that you and Gabe..."

She raised an eyebrow. "If you think I'm the marrying kind who's likely to have a dozen kids, then you don't know me at all!"

He threw his head back, laughing. "Oh, I know that. Neither am I!"

She chinked her glass against his. "Excellent. But would I like a base to call home?" She looked around at JD's house. "Maybe. Not this big, though. Besides, the farmhouse suits us for now. We have plenty of space."

"This place has its charms," Harlan admitted. "But the city life works for me right now." He felt rather than heard his phone buzz in his pocket, and realised being in the lab had probably interfered with his signal. "Hold on. My phone's ringing."

"So is mine," Shadow said, pulling it from her pocket with a frown.

Harlan stood and walked to the end of the patio to give her some privacy. "Hey, Jackson—"

But he couldn't say anything else, because Jackson cut in. "Bloody Black Cronos has broken into the division's headquarters. Stefan and Barnaby have escaped!"

"*What*?" Harlan sank down onto the paving in a patch of sunlight. "When?"

"This afternoon, just after I got there. Waylen and I tried to stop it, but almost got blown up in the process. Well, actually, we did get blown up."

"What? Are you all right?"

"My ears are ringing, I'm a bit bruised, and I might have a concussion. I've certainly got a horrendous headache. Waylen has a broken arm, and he's aggravated his old leg wound. We were lucky, though. We could have been buried alive. The guards weren't so lucky. Two were killed in the prison area, and another two at ground level."

Harlan could imagine only too clearly the scale of destruction that Black Cronos could achieve. "Shit. Sorry to hear that, but I'm glad you're okay."

"We're pissed off more than anything. Well, that's an understatement. Waylen is furious." He went on to explain how they'd broken in, and Harlan closed his eyes in weariness. He thought the PD would be infallible. *Clearly not.*

"What about the labs?"

"Not touched. They weren't accessible from the cells. But we're on the move now that we've been compromised. Waylen is sorting out a new location."

"Really? How do you relocate an entire division?"

"We have our means, and it helps that we're small. But that brings me to my next problem."

Harlan groaned. "Your concussion."

"'Fraid so. I can't fly."

"Please don't tell me I have to go to Turkey. I'd be a hindrance!"

"You wouldn't be, but no. We still want you to stay here and keep an eye on JD, especially now that Black Cronos is on the move again. I don't know what protection JD has got at his place, but it's probably wise to increase it. And you be careful, too."

"I'll move into the hotel again if I have to, but we'll be here tonight. He said something about activating the garden perimeter—whatever that means—so hopefully we'll be safe."

"Okay. I'm going to try to sleep, although that'll probably be impossible. I'm still in the hospital. Stay safe, Harlan."

Harlan headed back to his seat after ending the call, finding Shadow watching him. "Everything okay?"

"No." He updated her on his news.

"JD might be a target," Shadow mused. "He'll be the biggest threat to Black Cronos—you know, as far as being able to match their achievements."

"Maybe. I'll warn him later. What was your call about?"

"Flights. We leave tomorrow—early. Gabe is coming to get me."

"So soon?"

Shadow nodded, idly playing with her knife in one hand, her drink in the other. "We have a much clearer idea of what we're up against, and where we're going. And it's a long flight, with multiple stops."

Harlan drained his drink and stared at the deepening twilight, worried for all of his friends, and wondering what might happen later. He stood and rattled his glass. "Time for another drink, and then you can tell me everything."

Niel was still brooding about Zee's comments on his love life, but couldn't deny he might have a point. Not that he was willing to concede that yet. *If ever.* But right now, he had other things to worry about, like the Igigi. And the very attractive woman Ash had brought home with him.

Catarina Edevane was an undeniable beauty, and vivacious and witty as well. When Ash had returned a few hours earlier and made the introductions, she had fit in with his brothers straight away. She had arrived with an overnight bag and dressed in old fatigues, a t-shirt, and sweatshirt, the exact opposite of what he'd expected of a countess. When he told her that, she had laughingly explained that it was her dig clothing, and her pack contained much of the same. Now, however, she was in bed, proclaiming tiredness and the wish to be ready for the early flight.

Gabe was collecting Shadow from JD's home, and they were expected back very soon.

Niel studied his brothers, who were readying weapons and preparing their packs in the living room that looked currently more like a war zone. They had decided everyone except Eli would travel to Turkey, Gabe thinking the more of them there, the better—although, he hadn't fully explained why on the phone. No doubt he'd update them when he arrived later. Ash hadn't discussed anything, saying it was better to talk when they were all together. It also wasn't surprising that Gabe wanted Zee to join them. He had faced the Igigi before, unlike Barak and Ash. Fortunately, Zee was happy to help, and Alex, the witch who owned The Wayward Son where Zee worked, had been willing to give him the time off.

He addressed Nahum. "I presume we can take all of our weapons because we're on a PD-approved flight?"

Nahum nodded as he straightened from a crouch on the floor, his bag at his feet. "Yep. We have special passes, and the airport is expecting us. We'll keep the weapons together, like last time. You're in charge of them, okay?"

"Suits me." Niel strode over to the weapons and started to check them off against the list he'd already made before filling the bags. "How long is the flight?"

"Long! Because of a couple of stops, it will take nearly twelve hours. We fly to Batman, it's the closest airport to Mardin. I've got some big vehicles booked."

Zee had been listening, and shocked, he repeated, "Twelve hours!"

Nahum laughed. "You heard me. Plenty of reading time."

"Or film time!" Barak added as he zipped up his bag. "I don't need to remind myself about the Igigi. I remember them all too well!"

"But you didn't fight them," Niel said, puzzled.

"I met them, though." Barak sat on the corner of the sofa. "I travelled to Bad-tibira once and saw the Igigi at work. They were memorable."

Niel said its English name. "The Fortress of the Smiths. I remember it well. The clang of metal rang across the town's bazaars."

"I went in search of weapons to furnish my men. Back when I still commanded an army." Barak laughed. "I spent a small fortune there, even when I bartered for a good price."

"For what battle?"

"Against the angels, of course. My father waged a war upon one in particular—Dantanian. They hated each other. I can't even remember why. It was bloody, as these things are."

Niel remembered those types of battles only too well. All of his brothers had been amongst the strongest Nephilim, commanding armies of other Nephilim, as they waged war upon the enemies of the Fallen, or upon each other. But that was in the early days, before they had learned to refuse. "How did you find the Igigi?"

"Sullen, for the most part. Not surprising, really. They toiled long hours."

Zee spoke up. "And vented their frustration on us when they rebelled."

"Not just us," Nahum said. "Everyone."

"Is there anything else I can do?" Barak asked, changing the subject. "I've finished my packing. My weapons are with Niel."

Nahum nodded and headed to the corner of the room. "Check the camping equipment with me. There are half a dozen tents, sleeping bags, cooking instruments, and packs of dried food. I don't expect we'll be camping for long…if at all."

For the next few minutes, they were preoccupied with checking everything, except for Ash, who was studying the tablet's inscriptions again. Zee helped Niel, unfazed by his belligerent attitude about Lilith the day before. That was not entirely surprising. Zee brushed things off with ease, which made it hard for Niel to remain angry with him. They were so preoccupied that when Gabe and Shadow swung through the door, they took everyone by surprise.

Gabe had his familiar brooding look on his face, which meant trouble. He dropped his bag on the floor, and studied his brothers' activities, hands on his hips. "Are we prepared?"

"Pretty much," Nahum said. "Just double-checking our equipment."

Gabe's eyes narrowed. "Tents?"

"The works." Nahum folded his arms across his chest. "You look shattered. Both of you."

Shadow sprawled on the sofa, declaring, "Being stuck in a car for hours is surprisingly exhausting."

"You should try driving!" Gabe shot back.

She just grunted at him, and Niel suppressed a grin. It was a bone of contention that Shadow hadn't yet learned to drive. And also surprising. She was so headstrong normally, and so independent, that no one could work out why. And she wasn't averse to technology, either. Niel had come to the conclusion that it was low on her priority list, and had decided he was going to motivate her at some point in the near future.

"The drive didn't help," Gabe conceded as he dropped into an armchair, "but I've got a headache just thinking about what we found. Have you told them?" he asked Ash.

"No. I thought it would be easier if we were all together."

Gabe scanned the room. "Where's Catarina?"

"In bed."

"And Estelle?"

Barak answered, "She'll meet us at the airport. And Shadow, El dropped your armour off. It seems that Dante fixed it, just in time."

Shadow, still reclined, gave him a thumbs up, but Gabe sighed with relief. "Good. We'll need Estelle. With luck she can hide our tents in the desert with a spell. And we'll need her help with whatever comes out of that cave."

"What the hell does that mean?" Barak asked, the tents at his feet forgotten.

"It means," Ash said, the papers slack in his hands, "that the Earl of Breconshire told us the true story of what had happened on that dig. It seems that the Igigi are still very much alive."

SIXTEEN

The heat of the desert was a shock after England's weather, even at night, and Shadow angled the air conditioning in the car to point at her face.

"Oi! You're not the only one who wants the cold air," Niel pointed out, leaning over to slap her hands away and wrestle the vents in his direction.

She glared at him and slapped his hand back, restraining herself from pulling out her blades. "There are plenty of other vents! And besides, you keep saying how fantastic it is to experience proper heat!"

He glared back at her. "I may be a little unused to it, after all this time."

"Children, please," Ash scolded from the driver's seat. "Will you both shut up? It's been a long flight, and we're all tired."

Gabe was in the passenger seat, and he twisted around to stare at Shadow, amusement dancing in his eyes. "Darling, please don't upset Niel. And don't bicker in front of the guests."

Shadow switched her attention to Gabe, her eyes narrowing. When he called her *darling*, it was always with a slow drawl, aimed to provoke her, and it worked. His grin spread as he observed her building annoyance, and she decided she would have her revenge in private.

Catarina was sitting next to the window, and she tittered as she watched their exchange. "Please don't hold back on my account. Family dramas are always entertaining!"

Unwilling to be labelled a drama queen, Shadow decided to call Niel one instead. "It's his fault. He's like a fey prince without his retinue. All pouty and cross."

Catarina did a double-take. "*Fey?*"

Shadow winced. "Old family saying, that's all. Folklore nonsense."

Niel snorted, his lips twisting into a grin. "You're always full of nonsense."

Shadow decided to ignore him, and focussed instead on the view beyond him, through the window. It was Sunday evening, and they had left the city lights of Batman far behind, following a road through the desert and passing small towns and villages on the way. The surrounding landscape was pitch black beyond the settlements, but from what she'd seen in photos, it was filled with rocky terraces, scoured by wind and time.

This area, like several in Turkey, was known for the villages, monasteries, and buildings carved into rockfaces and deep into the hills. A useful way to stay out of the desert heat, and to keep warm in the winter months. "So, the Igigi," she said, voicing her curiosity, "would have been one of the first people to build their city underground here?"

"Potentially, yes," Catarina answered. She turned away from the view to look at Shadow, her expression almost invisible in the dim interior, but the gleam in her eyes was unmistakable. "It's *fascinating*, isn't it?"

"It will be if it doesn't get us killed." Shadow liked Catarina; her sense of adventure was similar to her own. "Are you sure you want to be with us?"

"Absolutely. I need this. It reminds me of the digs in my youth. Unfortunately, as my husband got older, we haven't been on one for many years. I miss it."

"You're an enthusiastic amateur, I presume?"

"I am. But I've picked things up along the way, and I've always liked to be involved as much as possible. Of course, babies got in the way, too."

Niel leaned around Shadow, who was seated in the middle. "They're older now?"

"Of course. Young adults, leading their own lives. Parents have to be careful, you know, not to lose themselves. Or else, when they leave the nest, you have nothing left. You're like a hollowed-out shell."

Niel just grunted, "Very true," and leaned back to stare out of the window again.

Once again, Shadow wondered if the Nephilim had fathered children. It was the one conversation that hadn't come up, especially between her and Gabe. All three Nephilim had fallen silent at that. *Perhaps it was time to ask Gabe. Later.*

Lights appeared ahead of them, illuminating buildings layered upon each other on a hillside, and Ash said, "That's Mardin, where our hotel is. I must admit, I'm glad we opted for this for the first couple of nights."

Gabe nodded his agreement. "Yes, scoping out the area in the daylight will be best to begin with."

They threaded through the outskirts of the town, Nahum and the others in the car behind them, and Shadow studied the streets and buildings, captivated. This was nothing like England or France, and she couldn't wait to explore.

Ash finally pulled into the carpark of a hotel in the old town, Nahum parking next to him, and within seconds they had all exited the vehicles, breathing in the city scents and warm night air. But right now, Shadow was more interested in Gabe and his brothers' reactions to the scenery. This was a type of homecoming for them, and it showed on their faces.

SIXTEEN 157

They had purposefully picked a boutique hotel in a traditional building, and all of them fell silent as they studied it and their surroundings. The smell of food and spices filled the air, and yellow lights blazed against the walls.

Zee took a deep breath and smiled. "This feels like home. I like it."

The tension seemed to seep away and the others nodded and grinned, Niel slapping Zee on his shoulder. "That it does, brother. Come on, let's check in, and then I vote we explore our surroundings. Now that I'm here, I've livened up. And I'm hungry. Airplane food just doesn't cut it."

Barak agreed and patted his flat, muscled stomach. "No, it does not." He winked at Estelle's amused face. "You're not too tired, Estelle?"

Estelle was dressed casually in jeans and a t-shirt, and Shadow was pleased to see she had shed her pinched expression, instead looking as curious as the rest of them. "I am, but I'm hungry, too. And I think I'm too excited to sleep."

"Excellent." He shouldered some bags and headed to the hotel door. "Time to check in."

Harlan yawned and checked his watch, not surprised to see how late it was. It felt like he'd spent days in this subterranean dungeon, instead of just Sunday.

"JD, you must be exhausted, and I know I am. Perhaps we should continue this in the morning?"

They were in JD's laboratory, JD hunched over his grid as he moved specific sections and noted reactions in a small notebook. A knife was in the centre of the grid again, this time a small silver dagger. Every now and again he grunted, clearly frustrated, and for a moment he ignored

Harlan. He had measured Harlan's correspondences earlier, based on the endless questions he'd asked yesterday, and was now trying to align the two together.

JD finally said, "I suppose you're right."

"I know I am. We've been doing this for hours, and getting nowhere."

He glared at him. "Not true! I've made steady progress. It may seem tedious to you, but this is about fine-tuning correspondences and energies, and it all takes time."

"Yeah, but this is what you do. It's mumbo jumbo to me! Why am I even sitting here? I'm not doing anything!"

"Because having the subject close may help. Your energy will resonate and complement the grid."

Harlan closed his eyes, pressing his palms into his eyelids. "If you say so." When he opened his eyes, JD was looking at him, lips pursed. "What?"

"You have no curiosity about this? Unbelievable!"

"Not true! I am curious. It's fascinating in many ways, but I don't really get it. It's all starting to blur." Harlan took a breath, fearing they were about to argue again, and he couldn't afford for that to happen. "You are a genius, and I am not. I'm very good at my job, but not this."

JD sniffed. "Yes, I suppose you are."

Harlan stiffened, suspicious that JD was about to follow that grudging compliment with an insult, because that was what usually happened. Instead, however, there was a large boom from outside, and the whole room shook.

"What the hell was that?" Harlan asked leaping to his feet. And then he realised. "Black Cronos are here." The threat of imminent death had him whirling around and running to the door. "JD, my shotgun is in my room. Do you have any weapons down here?"

"Calm down, you nincompoop! Didn't you listen earlier? This place is secure!"

Harlan skidded to a halt and looked at JD strutting across the room. "But this is Black Cronos! They probably want their weapon back, or your research or something!"

"They can want it all they like, but they won't get it." A pompous grin spread across his face. "Come with me, and you'll see what I mean."

JD led the way to the main floor of the house, where Anna stood in the hall wearing her dressing gown and a worried expression. "JD! Did you hear that?"

"I'd be deaf, my dear, not to hear that. Go back to bed, and don't worry."

Another explosion rocked the house, and a flash of red light illuminated the hall. With surprise, Harlan saw all the occult symbols carved into the wood and plaster flare into life.

JD pointed at them. "See? That's what is supposed to happen. They'll never get in."

Having seen Black Cronos fight several times, Harlan wasn't so sure.

Neither was Anna. She clutched her robe to her throat. "Don't worry? We have never been attacked like this before!"

"Anna! This idiot doubts me enough, don't you start," he grumbled, striding down to the corridor, and then up the stairs to the attic room. He called over his shoulder, "If you insist on worrying and staying up, bring us some whiskey and bourbon!"

Anna scowled and scurried to the kitchen, and Harlan bounded after JD, wondering what the wily old devil had up his sleeve. As they entered the huge attic space with the long glass wall, another flare of light flashed across the grounds, and Harlan closed his eyes and averted his gaze. "Holy shit! What are they doing?"

"Trying to get past my protection. Fools."

JD hurried to a door in the panelling, and swinging it open, revealed another set of stairs winding upward. When they reached the top,

Harlan gasped. They were in a room perched on the roof, the upper half of which had glass all the way around like a lighthouse, offering a 360-degree view of the gardens and surrounding countryside. Underneath the glass were panelled walls and a workstation that glittered with buttons, electronics, and monitors.

Harlan's mouth fell open as he looked at what appeared to be a high tech, state of the art defence system. "What the actual..."

JD's chest swelled. "Impressive, isn't it? I designed it myself."

"But this looks so modern! I didn't think you did modern."

"Always you underestimate me!"

"Not true! I said only minutes ago that you were a bloody genius!"

"Exactly! Should I so choose, I could be employed by any tech company in the world. I am not only a mathematical genius, but I am a master of advanced physics, chemistry, pharmaceuticals, and this century I learned all about electronics. But I do not wish to work for corporations and tech companies. The pleasure of being centuries of years old is that you accumulate knowledge and wealth, and I can do what I bloody well please. Of course, my particular brilliance is the way I blend everything with alchemy."

Harlan watched dumbfounded as JD manipulated buttons and brought up images from his security cameras of the grounds. "Well, I get that, but didn't expect *this*!"

"Of course," JD rumbled on, "I didn't pursue human experimentation and weapons, because frankly, there are boundaries. I am being forced to adjust my thinking on that!"

Alarmed though Harlan was about that statement, he couldn't ask anything else, because JD was pointing to figures on the screen by the main gate. One man lay unmoving on the ground, possibly dead, and another was trying to disable the gate controls. "Look at him! Pestilent bugbear! Watch what happens now."

SIXTEEN

As the huge man took apart the intercom, a red light emanated from it, surging outwards and touching the soldier. The man instantly dissolved and disappeared.

"Holy shit!" Harlan exclaimed. "What happened?"

"Mars happened."

"*What*?" JD ignored him and looked across to the other screens, where a team of soldiers had scaled JD's tall stone-walled boundary and were in the grounds. "Er, JD, they're inside!"

"Exactly where I want them. Keep watching."

Harlan's mouth went dry as he watched the soldiers advance. Half a dozen in total, they passed through the shrubbery to the edge of the lawn. As they spread out into a line and stepped on the grass, a shimmering grid of red lights appeared, strung across the lawn's edge. In a split-second, it exploded, a boom rocked the grounds, and the soldiers vanished.

Harlan's mouth fell open, and he blinked to see properly. "Mars again?"

"With a little Saturn thrown in."

As they stared at the other screens, seeing another two groups of soldiers get incinerated by the powerful grids, JD folded his arms across his chest and sighed. "Excellent. That actually worked better than I thought."

A noise behind him startled Harlan, but it was only Anna with their drinks. She left the tray on the side, well away from any controls, and cast JD a reproving glance. "Is it over?"

He focussed on her with a bright smile, suddenly aware of her presence. When he spoke his impatience disappeared, his voice gentle instead. "I think so, but we'll stay up here a while longer to be sure. Honestly, go to bed now. You have nothing to fear."

She nodded, and with a final anxious glance outside, hurried down the stairs again.

Harlan picked his glass up and handed JD another, pleased to see that Anna had brought the bottles, too. *Good.* This one wouldn't even touch the sides. He knocked the first shot back and topped his glass up before scanning the garden again. His adrenalin had spiked, and his hands were shaking. He took some deep breaths to calm himself down.

The grounds were dark again, a more consuming blackness than before after the flare of lights around the perimeter faded. He studied JD's profile as his gaze swept the camera feeds. "So, this is what you meant earlier, when you told me and Shadow not to wander the grounds."

JD nodded. "Yes. After France, I've been activating my protection all day. I only used to bother at night, but we are private here, and Toto's men don't follow the normal rules. I only deactivate the grids when the gardener is here."

"And you harness the power of the planets?"

"I always have. After the planetary parade I charged my crystals, realigned some, and strengthened the grids. I must admit, it works even better than I thought."

Harlan realised he had underestimated JD. He knew he was a genius, of course, but even so, he hadn't expected this. "That was pretty impressive. How does it work? The basics, I mean."

For once, JD didn't adopt a patronising tone. "It's a system made up of a variety of crystals of various sizes, with different properties and correspondences, all interconnected and placed carefully on their correct alignment. A select few can be..." He struggled to find the right word, eventually saying, "*Muffled* best describes it. That's what turns the system off. When I want it to work, I *un-muffle* them."

A sudden flare in the corner of the grounds made them look up, and another group of soldiers dissolved in a different grid.

Worried, Harlan asked, "Could they overload the system and disable it?"

"No. It's not like electricity. The charge will last a very long time. And the crystals are buried deep beneath the earth. It's taken me a great many years to perfect."

"Perhaps you should offer this system to the PD. It would protect them from further attack."

"Perhaps. But if I'm honest," JD cocked his head at Harlan, "I tend not to offer things I fear could be misused."

"You don't trust them?"

"I don't trust the system, although Waylen and his team seem trustworthy enough." JD settled on a chair, and Harlan followed suit. "In my many years of experience, I have found that it doesn't pay to be too trusting." He shifted his gaze from the grounds to Harlan, his expression filled with disappointment. "I have been betrayed again and again, by friends, kings and queens, governments... At least enemies are predictable. You think I'm abrupt. Abrasive—"

"You are."

"You would be too if you'd experienced what I have. Immortality brings great advantages, but it has also taught me that, generally, people are petty and greedy. Generationally that never changes. It's depressing."

Harlan suddenly felt his animosity melting away as he regarded JD's usually hidden vulnerability. "I guess when you've lived through countless wars and conflicts, it can become difficult."

"Wars are one thing, but inept governments, selfish behaviour, the willingness to exploit others for personal gain—it's all very wearing." JD gestured to his house and grounds. "That's why, when it all becomes too much, I withdraw here."

"But there are positives, right?"

"Of course. I have visited many interesting places, and met many brilliant people. And of course, the chance to study—*really study*—life's great mysteries. And the knowledge—and this seems odd, I know," he said, cocking his head at Harlan, "the knowledge that I will never know everything is actually thrilling. I truly believe we will never unlock every secret of the universe."

Harlan sipped his drink. "You're right. That is odd, coming from you. Especially considering the events in The Temple of the Trinity." Harlan wondered if he should bring it up, considering they were conversing in a way they never had before, but decided to anyway. After all, JD had been obsessed with finding The Book of Raziel and the knowledge it could offer him.

"Ah, that!" JD nodded and topped up his drink. "I did not acquit myself well then. There are some things that grip you so completely, you can lose yourself. That was certainly one of them. Looking back now, I think I had a lucky escape."

"I'm glad to hear you say that, because, quite honestly, you really pissed me off. The Nephilim and Shadow, too."

JD's finger worried at his lower lip as he studied the monitors again. "The angels get in your head, you know. They worm their way in there, overwhelming your will. That is their true power." He closed his eyes briefly, and then fixed Harlan with his steely-eyed stare again. "I have stepped away from that for now. There are other things to pursue. Like Toto."

Harlan guessed that was as much an apology as he would get, and JD's excuse made sense. Angels were paranormal creatures like anything else, possessing powers he couldn't imagine. He decided to move on, too. "How is your research into an antidote to Black Cronos's powers going?"

"Badly. I am frustrated at my lack of progress, and in my eagerness to start, I think I'm going in the wrong direction. I began in completely the wrong place."

"But you said it was early days."

"Even so, you get a feeling for how things are going, and I'm sure I'm on the wrong path. They always seem one step ahead, too, which makes me wonder who is really behind them."

"You mean, other than Toto?"

"Toto is a visible figurehead, and undoubtedly clever, but there are far more involved in their experiments than just him."

"But surely their set up will be like The Order of the Midnight Sun? A group of Senior Adepts who drive it all, with Toto as the Grand Master?"

"I agree that their organisation will have a similar structure. After all, we mustn't forget that Black Cronos had the same beginnings as the order. But more and more, I truly believe that someone of a great age is behind it all."

"You mean someone *immortal*? Like you?" The idea seemed shocking to Harlan, but the more he thought about it, the more it seemed not only possible, but probable. "Another ancient alchemist."

JD nodded and tapped his glass, his expression distant. "Yes. It's crossed my mind before, but I have dismissed the idea several times. I tell myself that I would know, surely. I have known many great alchemists in my time, all brilliant men, and I've always doubted that I could be the only one to have mastered immortality. But I thought I would run into them...recognise them." He shrugged. "But why would I? I have purposefully hidden, reinvented myself, changed my name. I'm JD now, but I have completely changed my name before. And if someone was manipulating human matter, they would not want to advertise it. They could even have been an original member of Black Cronos, or they could have joined later on."

Harlan felt a horrible stirring of certainty at JD's words. *Of course that made sense. Why should JD be the only alchemist to have cracked immortality?* "Do you have some idea of who it could be?"

"Oh yes." JD fixed his acute amber eyes on Harlan, all speculation gone. "I have considered various men and women, and ended up dismissing them all, except for one. The *Comte de Saint-Germain*."

SEVENTEEN

Gabe lay on his back, staring up at the vaulted stone ceiling above his head, listening to the sounds of the city.

Memories resurfaced that he thought he'd long forgotten. Snatches of conversations, walking through the bazaars and markets, long, decadent meals, languorous lovemaking in the heat of the afternoon, and the juicy, sweet taste of fresh figs as they burst against his tongue.

Shadow stirred beside him and wriggled closer, her hand on his chest, her leg wrapped over his. "You're awake," she murmured.

"My mind is too busy to sleep."

"And your stomach is too full of food. You ate like a horse."

He laughed and kissed the top of her head as he pulled her closer. "I always do."

"Not at midnight. And not like that!"

She was right. They had wandered the streets around their hotel, drinking in the sights, sounds, and smells, eventually stopping at a small restaurant where they crowded around a table beneath vines in a courtyard. They had ordered a feast: kisir, saksuka, koftes, a variety of kebabs, gozleme, and many others. The table had been piled high.

Gabe had tasted spices and flavours he hadn't experienced in years, and even though they cooked all sorts of food at home, it hadn't been like this. And now his gut was protesting.

"Are you glad we came?" she asked.

"Of course. I'm glad we're staying here, too. It's good to be in a more traditional place—even if it is only a semblance of the dwellings in our time."

"I know what you mean. The traditional has a feel that the modern does not." She propped herself on her elbow, and drew his chin towards her so that she could look at him properly. A faint light came through the curtains stirring lazily on the night breeze. "When children were mentioned earlier, you all fell silent. I feel we've avoided the subject, but I would like to know. Did you have children?"

A familiar ache filled his chest as he took a deep breath and sighed it out again. Even in this light, Shadow's violet eyes glowed. "I had one, and she died too young."

"I'm sorry. How young?"

"She was three years old." She was so small, and her death served to prove what the angels had promised. He sighed again, knowing he must explain it to Shadow. "We, the Nephilim, were not meant to have children. Our women did not fall pregnant, and if they somehow did, our children did not live for long. I and many others thought we could prove them wrong. But they were right all along."

"Why didn't you tell me?"

"Because it was a long time ago now. It's history."

"It's *your* history. That's important to me."

He bent his head to kiss her, savouring her soft lips and warm curves. "You're very beautiful, Shadow. I'm a lucky man."

"You are. But stop changing the subject." She rolled on top of him, legs straddling his body and elbows propped on his chest as she gazed into his eyes. "Tell me about her. And your wife."

Images flooded his mind again, and the words seemed to dry in his throat as he recalled his daughter's honey blonde locks and almond eyes, just like his wife. "I'm not sure I want to. I quite like them buried in the past. To talk about them makes it more painful."

"Because you loved them so much?"

"Yes. Also, the fact that I wasn't around as much as I should have been. I waged war when I should have been home, and I took them for granted. I wonder if they thought I didn't love them as much as I did, and that they died thinking I didn't care."

"Gabe! Don't taunt yourself with useless recriminations. I'm sure that's not the case!"

"Then why do I feel so guilty?"

She cupped his face with her hands. "Because you're a good man. Share their stories with me. I'm with you now, connected to you, as I've never been with any other man. I want that connection to be even deeper."

Desire stirred within him at those words, but he knew he wasn't the only man she had loved. "You have been with other men."

"But not like this, Gabe Malouf." She patted his heart. "This beats within me now, too. You have done something truly unexpected to me."

He caught her hands in his. His connection with Shadow had been immediate, and they had fought their growing desire for weeks before they had both finally relented to the inevitable. But Shadow rarely opened up like this, for all of the love she showered on him in bed. She kept a little piece of herself apart—until now.

"Is that right?" His voice was husky, even to his own ears.

"I won't lie about that."

He flipped her over, lying astride her, his desire now too strong to ignore. "Then I'll tell you. Later," he said, nuzzling her neck. "You have woken up another type of appetite that needs feeding now."

SEVENTEEN 169

Jackson downed another couple of Paracetamol, massaged his head where he could feel the lump from where he'd hit the floor, and then frowned at Waylen's new office.

"This should work out fine, once the boxes are unpacked. I'm just amazed we're in another building already!"

Waylen grunted from behind the desk and then straightened, his arm in a sling, discomfort etched across his face. "We couldn't afford to delay. When you're compromised, you have to move fast."

"I get that. It's more the fact that there's a place to go!"

Layla Gould, the PD's doctor, was in the room with them, and she gave a dry laugh. "We've always got bolt holes and back-up places. We've just never really had to use them before—except, of course, during the World Wars. This was set up in the early twentieth century, and is the place we used then." Despite the late night and dusty surroundings, Layla was still dressed in expensive clothing and wearing elegant heels. Jackson often wondered if she spent every night at flash functions and posh restaurants. She must have caught his curious glance, because she explained, "I was at a gallery opening when I got the call. My husband is an investor." She marched to his side. "Let's check you out again." She whipped a small torch from her bag and peered into his eyes.

Jackson blinked. "Am I alive?"

"Barely. You are both very bloody lucky. I'm sorry I couldn't get here earlier." She turned to Waylen. "Where's Russell?"

"Supervising the lab move. It's a bloody nightmare." Waylen slumped in his chair. "This mess will put us back weeks."

Russell Blake was the Assistant Director of the PD, and Waylen's right-hand man. He was in his fifties, had a background in science, and oversaw the lab. They were salvaging as much as they could, but it would take time.

Jackson grunted. "Better than months. So," he said, staring at his surroundings, "early twentieth century? That explains the dust and Art Nouveau décor."

"The electricity is up to date, though, and internet connections were put in a few years ago," Waylen explained. "Beautiful furniture though, right?"

Layla stroked one of the designs on the back of the door in typical Art Nouveau style. "It's stunning. My husband would love to see this place."

"Stunning is one word," Jackson admitted. "*Unexpected* is another. Weren't these back-up places meant to be utilitarian?"

"It depends on the director and how much power he had, and when this was requisitioned, he had a lot!" Waylen told him.

They were in another subterranean series of rooms situated under Hyde Park, not far from the Serpentine, the famous lake in its centre, and also close to Kensington Palace. The winding series of brick and wood-lined passages connected to the palace at one point, but was now separated from it by a series of blast doors. In fact, all of the entrances were sealed by blast doors and anterooms, which meant these offices were far harder to get to. *They would have had to be during the wars*, Jackson reckoned. And then another thought struck him; it was highly likely that his grandfather would have worked down here at some point.

More curious because of it, Jackson studied the room again, and then stepped into the corridor, noting several doors that opened off it. The place was designed with great detail. Fine mouldings, polished finishes—although dusty now—jewel-like Art Nouveau window designs set between offices and corridors. Half a dozen staff were carrying boxes as they set up their new workspaces. The whole department had been activated to come in and help. Jackson shook his head. It was hard to believe they were so far underground.

SEVENTEEN

Entering Waylen's office again, Jackson addressed the director, startling him as he emptied a box. "Who was the man who achieved all this?"

Layla snorted. "Woman, actually! A member of the aristocracy."

"Aristocracy? A royal?"

She smiled impishly, the grin taking years off her face. "Oh, yes! We had an auspicious benefactor. Princess Louise. The fourth daughter of Queen Victoria."

"You're kidding? I didn't know that!"

"She lived in Kensington Palace for years, and when her mother died, it freed her to pursue other things. Like this. She was quite the feminist, you know." Layla laughed. "I adore her. Anyway, this isn't getting my rooms sorted. I'd better get on. And you, Jackson, should get home. Rest is the best thing after a head injury."

She left, leaving the scent of floral perfume in her wake, and with a sigh, Jackson had to acknowledge she was right. He'd left the hospital that morning, disobeying doctors' orders, and had helped Waylen and the other staff make the emergency move. Now his head was pounding, and the Paracetamol wasn't touching it.

"I think she's right," he admitted to Waylen. "You should go home, too."

Waylen finished plugging in his computer and sighed. "My arm is throbbing, but I'll finish this first." He studied Jackson with narrowed eyes. "But you look like shit. Go home and sleep late. But come back tomorrow. I'll have a room for you."

"Seriously?" Jackson had only ever been a regular visitor before.

"The way this thing is going with Black Cronos, we'll need you around more than ever. Any objections?"

"None whatsoever. Thanks, Waylen."

And with a spring in his step, despite his headache, Jackson went home.

Harlan helped himself to another liberal glass of bourbon, cast an anxious glance out of the windows, settled back in his chair, and asked, "The Comte *who*?"

JD also surveyed his grounds before answering. "The *Comte de Saint-Germain*—or the Count of St Germain, as we say in English. You've seriously never heard of him?"

"Actually," Harlan mused, thinking on the name, "it does ring a bell. An alchemist, you say?"

"One of the most famous. Or should I say infamous?" JD's head dropped forward in contemplation, almost on his chest as he sank deeper into his chair. "I met him during his lifetime, by which I mean his legitimate one, several times over a close period of years. That was in the mid-1700s. I was of course *dead* by then, and going by a completely different name, and I certainly didn't reveal who I was to him. But he already had a reputation and was extremely influential. However, rumours—that he encouraged—suggested he was already over three hundred years old, even then. And then people bumped into him after years of not seeing him, and remarked on how he hadn't aged. Of course," he looked at Harlan, "I studiously avoided him after a while. I didn't want him to be aware of how I didn't age, either. And of course, I moved around a lot—careful to avoid such rumours myself. But he courted it. Despite his undoubted brilliance, I thought he was a charlatan. But now..."

Harlan shook his head, confused. "Why a charlatan? You achieved immortality. Did you really think he couldn't?"

"You think I'm arrogant about my achievements, that I believe no one else could do what I have? No. That's not it. It's the fact that he toyed with people about it. What foolish nonsense! It's almost childlike. Attention-seeking. If anyone had proved it, his life would be forfeit!"

"You think that about your own?"

"Of course! I don't wish to be kidnapped for my knowledge, or to be studied like a lab rat."

"What's changed your mind about the count?"

"Things he was talking about back then—immortality, remaining youthful, his ability to manipulate gemstones and jewels. His links to secret societies that persisted up to the nineteenth century—I have read on him extensively over the years. And then of course Black Cronos appeared. Or rather," he corrected himself, "they became more visible."

"From what I recall, we first interacted with them in the late 1800s."

"Yes, although those early meetings were sporadic. Just after I formed The Orphic Guild."

"A coincidence?"

"Perhaps. But at that time there was a resurgence of groups interested in esoteric studies. The Order of the Midnight Sun stepped out of the shadows then, and others formed—The Hermetic Order of the Golden Dawn and the Freemasons, among others. And spiritualism in general was on the rise."

Harlan leaned forward, eyes fixed on JD. "But why him?"

JD met his stare. "I think I saw him—fleetingly. And I think he saw me. I went to a talk hosted by The London Geographic Society of all places, and he was there, too—on the other side of the room. He asked a question, and I couldn't believe my eyes. His clothes were different, obviously, and his hairstyle—no longer one of those ridiculous wigs that fashion forced us to wear. But it was him. His voice..."

"You didn't stop to meet him?" Harlan thought that meeting someone else who had mastered immortality would surely be a good thing. It would lessen the feelings of loneliness.

JD shook his head vigorously. "No. There was something about him. A dangerous edge. It was always there. I sensed it when I first met him."

Harlan considered his next words carefully, and then said them anyway. "You know, you also have one of those. Your willingness to sacrifice things and people...your analytical mind. It makes you cold."

JD shrugged. "Maybe. Anyway, I have nothing but that sight of him and my intuition to go on, but I'd put money on it. He is Black Cronos's Grand Master."

EIGHTEEN

Early on Monday morning, Nahum pulled the car off the dusty road that was surrounded by desert, and turned to Barak, who was in the passenger seat. He had Catarina's map stretched across his lap, heavily marked, with his finger on the spot identified by the earl.

Nahum asked, "Are we close?"

"According to this we are, and the GPS agrees."

They had entered the coordinates of the dig into the car's navigational system, but Catarina had warned them that they weren't exact. Although the earl couldn't remember the specific location now, they were a lot closer than they would have been only days before.

Ash leaned forward, wedged between Niel and Estelle. "Are we close enough to set the tents up?"

"A little further," Barak answered, staring ahead into the wild terrain. "There are still more people around than I would like."

Estelle leaned forward, too. "Don't forget that I can veil us in a protection spell."

"Nevertheless, I would still like us to be more off the beaten track," Nahum mused, looking through the windscreen and lowering his sunglasses back over his eyes.

The directions had led them deeper into the desert, the rocky terraces folding around them like a rumpled blanket. He tried to marry it with his recollections of the past, but it had been so long ago that it was virtually impossible. It used to be greener, and so much was missing. And of course, so much was new.

He looked to the south. "Do you remember the ziggurats towering above the city walls? The gardens within the cities? They were spectacular."

"I remember the paved roads," Niel said. "They were so flat, so perfect. And there were canals and rivers."

"It wasn't this dry then?" Estelle asked, wonder in her voice.

"Not at all." Ash's hand swept across the horizon. "You could see patches of greenery among the desert sand, far more than there is now."

"And what about Mardin?" Estelle asked, looking comfortable in the heat. Her hair was pulled back into a ponytail to keep her neck cool, and she wore a t-shirt that showed off her toned arms. "That's an ancient city."

Nahum twisted in his seat to look at her more easily. "The layout is familiar, but even so, most of the buildings are new compared to our time...even the really ancient ones. It has a familiar feel, though."

Barak tapped the driving wheel. "Come, brother. Let's get on so I can stretch my legs."

Niel grunted. "I second that!"

Nahum nodded, and checking that the road was clear he accelerated again, following the twisting asphalt that shimmered in the heat. Barak directed him on to a narrow track that led up into the hills, leaving the main road far behind. They rose higher, snaking along the contours of the terraces, passing hollows in the rock, until they finally reached the end of the path.

"Shit. It doesn't go any further," Nahum said, driving off the road and onto hard, packed earth and sand. "Are we close?"

"Hard to say," Barak said, frowning. "I think beyond this terrace, but I'm not sure."

Niel was already opening the door. "Then we need to explore on foot."

They were already high above the plane, and yet terraced rockfaces, pitted with dark crevices and cave entrances, still rose around them, casting their surroundings in deep shadow. It was deserted, too. They clambered out, and once out of the air-conditioned car, the heat felt like an oven.

Barak stretched his arms above him as he studied the landscape. "This could be a good place to camp, but I'd prefer to be out of view of the road."

Ash nodded. "I agree. Why don't you and Estelle check out beyond the ridge, and we'll investigate here?"

"Sounds good. Estelle, are you ready?"

"Sure." She swung a small pack over her back and fell into step next to Barak, heading towards the rift in the rock.

Nahum turned to Ash and Niel, disgruntled. "Look at this place! It's riddled with hollows and caves. I know we've narrowed it down, but it's still going to be hard to find."

"But we're high up," Ash said, his eyes gleaming. "And therefore, the many folds in these terraces could mean multiple entrances. The Igigi wouldn't box themselves in."

"Look around!" Nahum swung his arm wide, and despite his sunglasses, shaded the top of them as he stared around him. "Look at how ridged the whole landscape is. On first impression, it all looks the same. And down the valley there are monasteries set into these hills. We could find remnants of many old dwellings, but be in the completely wrong place!"

"Have faith in the map," Niel said, "and in the directions we were given."

Niel seemed to have forgotten his argument with Zee the other night, although he seemed not as upbeat as he usually was. Nahum hoped that being out here would do him good.

"While I don't want to come across Black Cronos," Nahum admitted, scanning the road they'd just driven up, "at least seeing them here will mean we're in the right place."

"Do you think we can risk flying?" Ash asked, almost a plea in his voice.

Nahum knew why. To glide along the desert thermals would be fantastic. "As long as we don't fly too high, we'll be fine."

He pulled his t-shirt off and flung it in the car, and then extended his wings. The rush of pleasure gave him a surge of adrenalin, and he soared upwards, catching the current. If they achieved nothing else this morning, at least he'd have flown in the sunlight. Something he hadn't done for a very long time.

The market sellers' voices assaulted Shadow's ears as she browsed the stalls in the bazaar, but she was enjoying every moment.

Mardin reminded her of the cities of the Djinn in the Realm of Fire; the rich yellow stone of the buildings gleaming in the sun, the desert stretching around it in all directions, the pungent scent of spices, and the overwhelming heat. It all triggered her senses. And what was even better was how excited Gabe was to be here.

He had eventually fallen asleep after his disturbed night, and she watched him now, aware of the grief he carried still, and wishing she could ease it more. Knowing about his child made her want to protect him. *Or at least his heart*. He was huge; he certainly didn't need her physical protection. But their talk seemed to have helped. A soft smile had played about his lips all morning, and he bartered now with obvious pleasure. She couldn't understand a word he was saying, but he seemed at ease here, as did Zee. He was a short distance away with

Catarina, browsing the spices for their cooking—at Niel's insistence, while he explored with Nahum.

Shadow couldn't lose herself entirely to the moment, though. She kept a wary eye out for signs of Toto and The Silencer of Souls. If they weren't already here, they would be soon. The paperwork they had found in their bags meant they were targeting this area, too. With luck, Nahum and the others would have found a promising spot to set up camp. Shadow just hoped they wouldn't be camped out for weeks.

Gabe finished his bartering and placed the small selection of pots into his backpack before shouldering it again, and walking on to the next stalls. "Excellent find. We'll take some fresh food with us, as well. It will last a few days at least, so we don't have to survive on that reconstituted stuff." His nose wrinkled as he said it, and she laughed.

"Dried food isn't great, but it's better than nothing. Although, we won't be that far from the town anyway, will we?"

"An hour or so, maybe more. It's hard to say. I guess one of us could always come back for supplies if we need to." He echoed her own sentiment. "Hopefully we'll be there hours, rather than days."

"You're looking forward to this, aren't you?"

"The camping? Yes. The Igigi, no."

They caught up with Zee and Catarina, and Zee gestured to the bags they carried. "We managed to get a good price for these blankets, so we won't freeze at night."

Shadow was unconvinced. "Are you sure we'll need them at all? We've got sleeping bags."

"The desert is always cold at night, especially higher up, where we'll be," Catarina explained. "My husband said they had camped well above the plains."

"Fair enough," Shadow said, reaching forward to take a bag from Catarina. "Are we done here?"

"Except for some meat and a few treats," Gabe said, leading them towards the food section of the market. "Time for some authentic Turkish delight, I think. And then we'll be ready for coffee."

Fifteen minutes later they were seated at a table on the pavement in front of a small café, shaded by a colourful umbrella, with the smell of cardamom coffee wafting around them. Gabe opened the box of Turkish delight and passed them around, and Shadow selected the pistachio flavour. "Perfect, thank you."

"So, what now?" Catarina asked, lifting her hair to allow her neck to cool as she glanced down the crowded street.

"We load the car up and join the others in the hills," Gabe said. He leaned back in his chair, facing the street, so he could see their surroundings with ease. "I'll feel safer when we're away from prying eyes."

"You think they're here?" Catarina asked.

"If not now," Zee said, "then they'll be here soon. There's too much at stake to wait." He smiled at her. "You did well to hide the maps."

"I wish I could have hidden the tablet, too."

"Herne's flaming bollocks!" Shadow exclaimed, her hands already on her knives. "I think I've just seen The Silencer of Souls."

"The *who*?" Catarina asked, alarmed, her head whipping around at the same time as the others.

Zee quickly explained, "The woman with Toto."

"That's her name?" Catarina shrank in her chair. "She sounds deadly."

"She is," Shadow murmured, not taking her eyes off the deadly woman. "So far, we haven't been seen. She's at the far end of the street. She must have come out of one of the little lanes."

Gabe downed his coffee and threw the box of sweets into his pack. "Then we'll leave right now."

"You go," Shadow said, standing. "She's heading away from us. I'm going to follow her."

EIGHTEEN

"No! There's no need," Gabe said, his brow creasing with worry. He had a tendency to do that lately. Ever since they'd become a couple. It was protective, caring, and also seriously annoying. "If she hasn't seen us, then we're in no danger."

Shadow stood her ground. "But knowing where they are and who she's with will help us. And she won't see me. You know she won't."

Gabe huffed and stared at Zee for support, but Zee just shrugged. "She's right. An idea of their numbers will be useful. But don't be long, Shadow. We'll pack up and be out of here within the hour."

Shadow nodded, checked her watch, and then left them, slipping through the crowd with ease as she engaged her fey magic. It wasn't as effective in towns, but it worked well enough, and unless the soul-sucker was a very good actress, Shadow remained convinced they hadn't been seen. The crowd of other café patrons had hidden them well.

Shadow reached the end of the street, momentarily puzzled. They were in the old town, halfway down the hill that Mardin was built on, and the warren of streets was both fascinating and baffling. She hadn't seen her quarry cross the road, so Shadow headed right, and was rewarded a few moments later when she caught sight of her threading through the locals and tourists, before taking a left turn. Shadow hurried after her, The Silencer of Souls leading her deeper and higher into the old town, past ancient buildings, places of worship, hotels, restaurants, and cafés. The number of people around thinned out, but the lanes wound frequently as they staggered upwards, steps mixed with gently sloping rises, and it was easy to stay out of sight. Although Shadow was on alert for any other Black Cronos members—they had a dead-eyed look to them that she'd come to recognise—she spotted no one else.

Finally, the woman slowed and turned into a building, and after waiting a few moments before getting closer, Shadow realised she had entered a traditionally designed boutique hotel, similar in style to their own. A narrow lane, barely more than a footpath, ran along the side, leading up steps and to more streets behind it, and Shadow realised she could climb onto a wall to see into the hotel courtyard that was undoubtedly at the rear.

She raced down it, vaulted onto ledges, and found a spot against a wall in deep shadow, hidden from the morning sun. She settled into place, drawing her fey magic around her, and concentrated on the scene below: a fountain in the centre of a stone-flagged courtyard, with potted plants scattered amongst tables. But voices from above caught her attention. A wide balcony with fretted stonework overlooked the area, the door thrown wide open. A flash of white-blond hair appeared out of the gloom of the room. Shadow was almost at eye level and she froze, trying to sink into the wall. As she focussed, The Silencer of Souls came into view, and someone was next to her. Stefan Hope-Robbins had joined them.

Barak emerged from the narrow gully that ran between a ridge of terraced rock, and found himself in a flat area surrounded on all sides by craggy rockfaces, all except for a break to their right offering a view of the desert below.

The wind dropped and he turned his face to the sun, saying, "I like this place. This would suit us well for a campsite. The top is wide enough to allow in a good amount of sunlight, and sheltered enough to protect us from the winds."

"I agree," Estelle said, already striding to the gap to look on the desert below. "The drop from here is sheer, so easy to defend, too."

He walked to her side, feeling the air cool as he plunged into shadow. But beyond, the glare of the sun on the golden sand was enough to make him pull his sunglasses firmly over his eyes. "Stunning, isn't it?"

"It has an unusual beauty. Harsh, but I like it."

"It becomes addictive after a while. It looks like nothing could live out there, but it teems with life." He smiled down at her. She was above average height for a woman, but still barely reached his chest. Her hair was still in a ponytail, and he saw the sweat glistening on her skin. A tan was already developing, and she seemed to be more relaxed than ever. "This place suits you, Estelle. You look beautiful."

Her hand brushed across her cheek, sweeping an errant hair away, suddenly self-conscious. "Thank you. You look...beautiful isn't the word. *Magnificent*." She laughed and sighed out, "Yes, that's right."

Barak hadn't kissed her yet, but he figured there was no time like the present. They were alone, in a place of stark beauty, and she seemed to be more relaxed with him than ever before. He turned to face her and pulled her into him, her arms resting on his chest. He didn't speak. He didn't need to. She looked up at him, her gaze wary but promising, and cupping his hand around the back of her head, he leaned in to gently kiss her. She sank against him, responding fully, and their kiss grew deeper, until they broke away, both breathless.

"Well," he said, when his voice steadied, "that was worth waiting for."

A smile lit her face, but she was already pulling away. "Yes, it mostly certainly was. But we should probably find the others and set up the camp."

He pulled her back to him. "We should, but they can wait a few minutes more." The arrival of loud, noisy brothers would ensure no more intimacy for a while, so he'd get it while he could.

Nineteen

Jackson was feeling much better after a good night's sleep, so it was with a sense of excitement that he returned to The Retreat—on first impressions a ridiculous name, considering what the corridors beneath Kensington Gardens housed. It sounded like a spa.

But the more he thought on it, he decided that the name probably suited it well. After the attack on their previous headquarters, and with Black Cronos on the offensive, they needed a place of safety, especially one finished with Art Nouveau décor.

He made his way to Lancaster Gate Tube Station, and then walked to the Serpentine South Gallery, which housed one of the entrances to The Retreat. Opening a shabby looking door at the rear using the key Waylen had given him, he entered a dusty room with an abandoned filing cabinet, desk, and chair that clearly no one had used in years. Another sturdy door made of oak with iron bands was at the back of the room, and a shiny new intercom with a camera had been fitted next to it. He was relieved to see the door looked robust, and although a discreet entrance, that security was already in place. He buzzed through with his name, smiled at the camera, and in seconds the door clicked open smoothly, allowing him into an antechamber and a set of stairs leading downwards. At the bottom was a reception and security area, manned by two familiar armed security personnel.

NINETEEN

After signing in and checking him for weapons, he was allowed through to the corridor leading to the heart of The Retreat, and this time, more alert than he'd been the day before, Jackson took his time to examine his surroundings. The winding corridor, lined with polished wood and brick, had decorative Art Nouveau embellishments, with age-appropriate light fittings. A light layer of dust coated everything, but he could already see a couple of cleaners at work, and the smell of polish and disinfectant hung in the air.

A murmur of voices came from an office, and recognising them, Jackson knocked the partially open door and stuck his head inside. There were at most a dozen people in the Paranormal Division, including Waylen, Blake, and Layla. The two people in this office were analysts who monitored paranormal events across the United Kingdom, and the rest were lab staff or security.

"Hey, guys," he said, greeting Petra and Austin.

Both seemed ridiculously young to be in this type of job, but he had to acknowledge that they were efficient and organised, and had qualifications bursting out of them. He estimated both to be in their late twenties. Petra was a petite woman of West Indian descent, with a sharp sense of humour and a cackling laugh, and Austin was a skinny man from somewhere in the Midlands. Both bonded over music that was incomprehensible to Jackson. While Petra oversaw England and Wales, Austin monitored all paranormal activity in Northern Ireland and Scotland.

"Hey, Jackson," Austin said, turning from the huge white board they had mounted on the wall. "Are you okay after the attack?"

"Well, my headache has settled after a good night's sleep." He perched on the corner of a desk. "You two are lucky you weren't there."

"You two are lucky you weren't killed," Petra pointed out. She had been reading from a piece of paper in her hands, and she placed it on the desk. "I was always told this job was monitoring and surveillance only. They lied."

Jackson tried to reassure her. Both of them, actually. They looked equally tetchy. "Not true. This *was* unusual, and we should never have kept Hope-Robbins and Armstrong at the headquarters for so long. We won't make that mistake again." He hadn't talked to Waylen about it, but was sure he'd agree—although, they had obtained information from Barnaby that they might not have otherwise learned. "In fact, I don't think this place even has cells. And this location is secure, and somewhere unexpected."

Austin laughed. "Yeah, I guess so. I feel like I'm working in a museum. Waylen reckons this is long term, too."

"It makes sense. Why try and find another place, when with a few upgrades, you get to work here? It's classy!" He gestured at the whiteboard where they recorded their current cases of interest. "I see you've brought that with you, too. Anything fun going on?"

Austin grinned and tapped the huge map of the United Kingdom pinned to the wall. "Rumours of Selkie sightings in Scotland. Right at the top."

"Selkies! For real?" Selkies were seals who were rumoured to be able to take to the land and turn into women. Some fishermen had been lured into taking selkie wives. "Are they dangerous?"

Austin shook his head. "No. Far from it. They have a gentle, almost solemn quality to them—or so the legends say. But the fact that the locals are talking about it is unusual. The police are monitoring it, just in case it means something more unsettling."

Jackson was confused. "Like what?"

"That's the question, isn't it?"

"And I am monitoring," Petra said, shaking her paper, "a pack of shifters in Cumbria. There are reports of shifter border wars. Hopefully it won't blow up, and they usually manage themselves, but the last thing we want is for the human population to be dragged into it."

"Nothing in London?" Jackson asked.

NINETEEN

"There's always something in London! But nothing we need to worry about—other than the attack on us, of course."

"I better let you get on," Jackson said, standing and heading to the door. "Have you heard, though, that I'll be around more often?"

Austin smiled. "The boss told us. It makes sense, considering how often you're here at the moment. Welcome aboard."

When Jackson finally arrived at Waylen's office, he saw that it looked far more organised than Waylen did. Day-old stubble covered his jaw, and his hair was ruffled, but he was at least wearing a fresh shirt.

"Did you even go home?" Jackson asked by way of greeting.

Waylen looked up from his computer, startled, and then laughed. "Yes, but I appreciate that it doesn't look like I have. It was a late finish and an early morning." He gestured to a door on the far side of the room. "Fortunately, I have a private bathroom. Perhaps I should take a break for a shave."

"Don't bother on my account." Jackson nodded at the computer. "You're online already, then?"

He nodded. "As the director, it's my job to keep our back-up rooms and plans operational." He grimaced as he looked around at a few errant cobwebs. "That doesn't apply to cleaning, but we're getting there."

"It's not an easy task to uproot a whole department, so I'm impressed. But I'm also intrigued," Jackson said, voicing what he'd been musing on overnight. "You're offering me a room, but I sense there are conditions attached."

"You're right. Follow me." Waylen walked out to the corridor, his limp more pronounced than usual, and led him down a small side passage before opening a door. "This is your office. You're the head of the investigation into Black Cronos as of now. Well, you will be if you accept."

Jackson barely took in the room, staring instead at Waylen, who leaned against the doorframe watching him with a hopeful expression. "Seriously? Don't you already do that?"

"I oversee everything, including the lab. I kept an eye on Black Cronos, but it was never an issue, because they barely made waves. Now, with them actively causing problems, I need someone monitoring them, and considering your recent involvement, you're the best candidate."

Jackson had been expecting to have greater involvement with Black Cronos, but not this. "An official role, then?"

"Yes. Are you interested?"

"Of course I'm interested! Especially considering what happened with my grandfather. How will this work?"

"Let's talk inside," Waylen said, striding into the room and dusting off a chair before sitting.

Jackson followed him, taking a seat opposite. "I report to you, obviously."

"Of course. I thought your role could dovetail with Petra and Austin. Anything that sounds suspiciously like Black Cronos comes to you, and you can follow it up. Keep a database—much like they do now for paranormal issues. I'll be honest, most of Black Cronos's stuff hasn't been looked at properly in years, just because they've kept a low profile. I'm planning to share everything we have, and you can see if you can join the dots."

"In case we've missed something."

"We've definitely missed stuff. It's time to look at everything with fresh eyes, historical as well as what's happening now."

Jackson thought of Harlan. "I can see if The Orphic Guild has more information they haven't shared yet, too."

"Excellent. Any source is good. You're Harlan's main contact now, too."

NINETEEN

"And what about Gabe and Shadow's group? They're in Turkey now. What if they need extraction teams for bodies or relics? I have no idea how to organise that."

"That's my job. I liaise with other departments for all of that. Same as we use government morgues for the bodies that Layla oversees. You just let me know what you need—and that includes logistics, like flights."

Jackson nodded, relieved to be focussing on the things he liked. "And what about my other job? Hunting for occult objects. Can I keep that up?"

"If you have time—which I doubt you will right now." Waylen laughed at Jackson's perplexed face that he obviously hadn't hidden very well. "Don't worry. You will again, I'm sure, in the future. We just happen to be having an intense period right now."

"Tell me about it!"

Waylen stood, prompting Jackson to stand, too, and they shook hands. "I'm glad you've accepted, Jackson. I'll organise the contract and send you the files we have. Some stuff is on the computer already, but you'll have to add the rest."

"That's fine. I can't wait."

And Jackson meant it. The slow-burning vengeance that he always carried over his missing grandfather and his team ignited with a sudden fury, and he was determined to find every single scrap of evidence he could.

The team had made good time out of the city, and Gabe studied their secure camp, deciding that for now, they were in the best place possible.

The tents had been set up in a circle, a firepit already constructed in the middle. The weapons had been distributed, and Estelle had cast a protection spell over the camp and their cars that they'd left at the side of the road. Zee and Barak were currently perched high on the rocky terraces, hidden within shadowy clefts to watch their surroundings.

"Good job," he said to his brothers. "And with Estelle's protection spell, I'm satisfied that Black Cronos won't find us."

"Ominous news about Stefan Hope-Robbins, though," Nahum said, his eyes roving over the rocks surrounding them before settling on Gabe again. "He's obviously very important to them if he's out here."

"It doesn't change the risks for us. I'm more worried about their soldiers than him, and Shadow didn't see how many they have with them."

"And you're sure no one followed you out of the city?"

Gabe shook his head. "No. We kept a close eye on the road, and we certainly weren't followed up this track. I guess we should take advantage and start searching for the lost city. Do we think it's in one of these terraces?"

Ash cut in, a puzzled expression on his face as he looked up from the map. "I'm not sure. We're close, but I doubt this is it. It doesn't look like the photos, but nothing I've spotted so far actually does."

The old, grainy photographs were on Catarina's lap, and she started to sift through them before passing them around the group. "Unfortunately," she said, "these rocky terraces are all so similar."

"We need landmarks," Niel said. "Odd shapes that might be more obvious from above than on the ground, perhaps."

Catarina frowned. "Do we have a plane at our disposal?"

Niel froze, as did his other brothers, but Shadow laughed. "Ah. You didn't think that one through, Niel!"

Gabe grunted with annoyance, but most of his brothers laughed too, a resigned expression on their faces as Niel said, "There's probably something about us we need to share."

This was always inevitable, and despite Gabe's initial wishes to keep their abilities a secret, it was clear that in this business it was going to prove difficult. Especially when wayward countesses insisted on coming with them. He knew he should have put his foot down.

Catarina looked at the group clustered around the firepit, a question in her eyes, as well as wariness, and Gabe realised she was probably now acutely aware of the fact that she didn't know any of them, not really, and the one person she did, Harlan, was not there.

"Well?" she asked, almost withdrawing back into her camp chair.

Gabe tried to reassure her. "It's nothing alarming. You are safe with us."

"That's good to know, because you're worrying me now!"

Estelle's expression was mischievous. "Perhaps you should show her, Niel." She turned to Catarina. "It's really quite something."

Niel shook his head as if to rebuke her, but Gabe knew he was looking forward to it. All the Nephilim loved to spread their wings, and they all loved the looks it got them, too. It stoked their egos, and Gabe couldn't deny it. He knew he loved nothing better than Shadow's admiring glances, and her hands digging deep in his feathers, especially when they were... He mentally dismissed those images, already feeling his stirrings of desire at the memory.

Niel pulled his t-shirt over his head, revealing his impressively muscled physique and more of his unusual tattoos, and stepping away from the group, his wings appeared out of nowhere. He spread them wide, turning slowly. "Sorry if it shocks you!"

Catarina gasped, and leapt to her feet, knocking the chair back as she did so. "*Shock*? Oh, my God!"

Niel's grin widened. "Not a God. Just a Nephilim."

In seconds, Catarina wobbled and her face turned a deathly white, and Ash, who was closest, reacted first, catching her before she fell.

"Oops," Niel said, looking stricken. "I didn't mean to make her faint!"

"Bloody preening pillock," Ash muttered as he lifted her effortlessly and carried her to some shade in the tent. "We have to remember that she's human! Not fey, not a witch, or a shifter. She's a countess, and an amateur archaeologist!"

Shadow smirked as she played with one of her knives, turning it over her fingers with lightning speed. "She insisted on coming. These are the consequences. And besides, she'll get over it."

"I agree with you," Estelle said, fireballs erupting into her hands. "Wait until she sees what I get up to."

Shadow narrowed her eyes, and Gabe was relieved when Shadow didn't top it with a boast of her own. The last thing he needed was Estelle and Shadow at loggerheads again.

"Please, Estelle," Gabe remonstrated. "Let's keep it to just one shock at a time. And Niel, put your bloody wings away! Perhaps we need food, too. It feels like hours since breakfast. We can plan our next move once we've studied those photos again."

Niel obliged, pulling his t-shirt on again, but there was an undeniable twinkle in his eye as he grabbed their supplies. "Yes, sir. And I'll cook. Maybe I should offer to take Catarina for a flight, later."

"Just focus on the food, for now!" Gabe told him.

And then Gabe had another thought. If it took Niel's mind off brooding about Lilith, perhaps he should entertain the countess.

TWENTY

Harlan stared with disbelief at the number of books spread across JD's table in his vast library.

"There are this many volumes written about the *Comte de Saint-Germain*? That's nuts!"

"He fascinated thousands of people in his time." JD sniffed, drew himself upright, and pointed to a packed shelf. "Much like myself. There are just as many about my life, you know. Most of them full of poppycock!"

It was mid-morning on Monday, and they had both slept in after their late night and the attack on the grounds. Despite proof of JD's brilliant defence systems, Harlan had found it difficult to relax, and it was only with dawn that he had finally settled into a deep sleep.

Harlan tried to keep the incredulity from his voice and failed. "You buy books about your own life? Why?"

"I like to know what people think. I sometimes review them—under a pseudonym, of course. I can be quite scathing."

"No shit." Harlan could envisage JD reading books about himself, huffing with annoyance and uttering Shakespearean curses as he did so. He decided to change the subject before he said something rude, and picked up the closest book about the count. "Are there any you'd recommend?"

"Not that one. That's a copy of the only book he's ever written—allegedly."

Harlan glanced down at the title and frowned as he read it out loud. "*The Most Holy Trinosophophia of the Comte de Saint-Germain*. What's it about?"

"It's an allegorical account of a spiritual and alchemical initiation." JD sneered. "Not so allegorical, I'm sure."

"I thought he would have published lots of books and papers. Isn't that what you alchemists do?"

"Exactly. And that's why I always thought him to be a charlatan in those respects, despite his brilliance in other ways."

"But that's clever, surely. If he is immortal, and born earlier than he professed to be, publishing anything would destroy his mystique."

"True," JD said, picking up another couple of volumes. "But for background on him and his life, and some of his letters, I'd recommend these two books. But see what you think. Others may appeal."

"You said that no one knows his true nationality?"

"No. He was deliberately vague about his origins, although he later said he was the son of Francis Racoczi the second, Prince of Transylvania, born in 1690." JD shrugged. "But others thought he was Italian or French, or even Polish. Some asserted that he had been around since the time of Jesus." He snorted. "I don't believe that for a second!"

Harlan thought he'd misheard. "*Jesus*? You're kidding!"

"No. That's what I mean! He courted rumours back then. Encouraged them. Deliberately misled people and laid false trails. I honestly took him for a colossal fake. I've certainly come across others." Harlan wondered if he was referring to Edward Kelley, the man who JD had worked closely with, and who had scryed and contacted angels for him. Books now suggested he had fooled JD for years, but Harlan wasn't about to bring that up. JD gestured to the books and the library. "Make yourself at home. I'll need you again in an hour or so to finetune that knife. I feel I'm close to a breakthrough."

"You're going back to the lab?"

He nodded. "I'll make sure Anna brings you some lunch."

"Okay, but JD, I need to get back to London tonight. I know this is important, which is why I stayed, but I've got cases to follow up. And I need to let Jackson know about your thoughts on the count."

"Ah, yes, you should." He worried his lower lip as he stared into the distance. "Let's chat later, before you go. I may have some ideas of where we should look."

He swept through the door, closing it softly behind him. Harlan picked the books up and settled into a comfortable armchair in a patch of sunlight under the window. As much as Harlan was looking forward to curling up in JD's extensive library and reading up on an interesting character, he couldn't ignore his other work. But he had to admit that working closely with JD this weekend had gone a long way to rebuilding their relationship. He wouldn't call them friends, but at least JD was civil now, and Harlan felt he understood him better.

But if they could find the count, which sounded fairly impossible at this stage, what was next?

Nahum stood atop the highest point of the rock terraces that surrounded their camp, studying the contours of the land in the setting sun, and then frowned again at the photos in his hand.

"We're in the wrong place," he said to Zee, who stood at his side.

"You sure? I thought the GPS and map suggested we were close."

"Not close enough. The Earl of Breconshire—Jasper—deliberately destroyed the most detailed map." He sighed. "I didn't find anything below us, did you?"

"Not a thing. Most caves are shallow or narrow, more like clefts. I sensed nothing."

"Do you expect to?" Nahum asked, puzzled.

Zee shrugged. "Maybe. The Igigi were powerful creatures, with their own kind of magic. It makes me think we should feel something, even after all this time."

"Perhaps we will." Nahum lifted his head, inhaling the scent of the desert that the wind carried to him. "Dusk comes soon, and then we can fly higher. Maybe it's a good thing not to be camped too close, considering what happened to the earl's team."

"You think something might emerge from the city?"

"Don't you?" Nahum said, remembering what they'd been told of the earl's story. "It sounded like he was genuinely terrified. I don't know what came out of that cave, but it certainly wasn't friendly."

"Perhaps the Igigi set up some kind of defence system," Zee mused. "Something automated. They were clever at building things."

Nahum pocketed the photos as he thought on Zee's suggestion. "Automatons, perhaps? But the earl said the rock came to life. None of it makes sense!"

As they were speaking the sun plunged below the horizon, leaving a smear of blazing light in the west, before it began to fade. Immediately, the heat ebbed away, too.

"Let's wait here until it's dark enough, and then we'll re-join the team," Zee said. "And let's hope Catarina has recovered from the shock."

Ash stoked the fire, setting the flames blazing again before lifting the pot from the chain they had used to suspend it. The water in it was hot, and he made a cup of tea for the countess, adding plenty of sugar too, and then made one for himself.

They were the only ones in the camp, the others having separated to investigate their surroundings. All of them thought it best to offer the countess some space to get over her shock. Her faint hadn't lasted long, but when she came around, she had stared at Ash and asked, "Have you got wings, too?"

He nodded, keeping as much distance between them as possible in the small tent so as not to scare her. "All of us do, except for Shadow and Estelle."

"They're...normal?"

Ash had winced. "Er, not exactly. But let's talk more later."

He had left her to gather her thoughts, and she finally emerged from the tent when the camp had fallen quiet. Now she sat opposite Ash in silent contemplation, staring into the flames.

"Catarina, have some tea. It's good for shock. Or so the many English people I know keep telling me."

Catarina finally relaxed and smiled. "It's the mundaneness of it, I think."

"I prefer other drinks myself, but I'll drink tea with you."

"Let me guess. Ouzo?"

"Mastika, actually, but it has been a while since I tasted it."

She took the cup from his outstretched hand, sipped it, and then sighed. "I feel a fool."

"Why? It's not every day you see a Nephilim. Well, six of us, actually."

"Where are the others?"

"Giving you space. And searching for the entrance to the city, of course."

She looked him straight in the eye. "The Nephilim are supposed to be myth."

"So are the Igigi, but we're out here looking for them."

"You're supposed to be violent, too."

"We have been," Ash confessed. And then thinking of their recent exploits said, "Well, we still are, but only when we need to be. We certainly don't attack those weaker than us." He smiled. "That includes you."

"I'm glad to hear that!"

"I can take you back to the hotel if you'd prefer." She had shrunk back into her chair again, flinching at every noise.

"I had considered it, but then again, when I asked to come here—"

"Demanded, actually," Ash reminded her, amused.

She pursed her lips. "I guess that's true. Anyway, it was because I craved a distraction from my husband's illness and the small world that my life has become. I'm certainly getting that, aren't I?" Without waiting for him to answer, she said, "And besides, you're right. I came looking for the mythical Igigi. If you exist, then so must they."

Ash laughed. "I can confirm that they *did* exist, but whether they still do is another matter. We arrived here by unusual means." He gave her a brief description of their recent history.

She shook her head. "All my life I have devoured these myths and legends. I feel like I'm in a storybook now. Look where we are! In a desert, around a campfire, and a handsome Nephilim is watching over me." She met his eyes over the fire. "Now I know why you look like a Greek God."

"You can blame our angel fathers for our looks. They bestowed a certain amount of divinity upon us."

"Then they did the world a favour."

Ash's eyebrows shot up. It seemed the countess was flirting. *Fine*. He could cope with that.

"I'm hoping that means that you want to stay?"

"Yes. I've got over my shock...more or less. You'll just have to forgive me if I stare a lot." She sipped her tea again, and Ash wasn't sure if it was that or the firelight that had restored the colour to her cheeks. "I have another question. You said Shadow and Estelle were not quite human?"

"Correct. Shadow is fey, and Estelle is a witch."

"Ah! Okay. A fey and a witch. I feel suddenly inadequate."

"Don't." Ash leaned forward. "You know your husband better than anyone, and these maps and papers. You've studied them for years. Potentially, you'll find the cave quicker than us. We're close."

"I hope I can. But I admit, I'm scared."

"You'd be a fool not to be. Now," he said stirring and moving to the cooking supplies, "I promised I'd cook, and if I don't, I'll be in trouble. We all have big appetites."

Catarina smiled, threw the dregs of her tea into the fire, and stood, too. "In that case, I must help. And later, if we search again, I insist on going, too."

When Niel arrived back in the camp, he was relieved to see Catarina relaxed and chatty.

He'd stayed away from the camp for a long time, feeling guilty for scaring her—even though it was unintentional. *Ash calling him a preening pillock hadn't helped*. Although, he had enjoyed seeing Catarina's wide-eyed appreciation of his physique before she fainted.

It smelled like the meal was ready, some kind of spicy meat stew that was simmering over the fire. If they didn't find the cave in the next day or so, they'd be out of fresh food and resorting to reconstituted dried meals, and he wasn't looking forward to that.

"Niel!" Barak said, spotting him as he stepped out of the shadows. "We thought we'd lost you. We're about to eat."

The team was gathered around the fire in small groups, talking quietly. Nobody looked particularly excited, so he thought that like him, they hadn't found the cave yet.

"I thought I'd give Catarina some space," he said, looking at her with what he hoped was a contrite expression on his face. "I'm sorry. I didn't think you'd faint."

"Neither did I!" she shot back. "It's not as if I'm a giddy schoolgirl! Don't worry, I'm fine now."

"Good. Let's hope Ash isn't going to poison us."

Ash glared at him. "I think you know I can cook quite well. And besides, Catarina helped me!"

"That should be no recommendation," she confessed. "I'm not that good a cook. I just did as I was told."

Niel grunted. "Well, it smells good, and I'm starving."

"Then let's dig in," Barak said, handing out bowls.

The meal was informal, with everyone helping themselves, and tearing off hunks of bread to mop up the spicy sauce.

While they ate, Gabe asked, "Has anyone got any leads on the city?"

Everyone shook their heads.

"I've seen something," Niel confessed, not wishing to alarm Catarina in particular. "I watched a convoy of cars on the road, heading into the desert. A little further south from here. I didn't want to get too close, but it could be Toto. They were in their usual black vans, and some off-roaders, too."

"Why the hell didn't you mention this sooner?" Gabe asked, annoyed.

"I've been here five minutes, Gabe. And besides, that's another reason I'm late. I watched them set up their camp. But I was high up, so I couldn't see details."

Shadow's eyes narrowed. "Then take me there. I can get closer and listen."

Gabe glared at her, their familiar dance already starting. "Are you mad? If it's them, their soldiers will be everywhere!"

"I am fey! They will not see me, as long as that big idiot drops me far enough away so we're not spotted."

Niel bristled with annoyance. "*Idiot*? I spotted them, didn't I? And I have wings that a certain someone does not!"

Shadow poked her tongue at him before addressing Gabe. "Besides, what if they're in the right place and we're not? We need to stop them—tonight. And if not, we need to resume our own search. We can't afford to wait."

Ash asked, "How far south, Niel?"

He shrugged. "Five kilometres or so? Beyond another large ridge of rock."

"How many soldiers?" Zee asked.

"At least a dozen, probably more."

Barak turned to Gabe. "Could we try and take them out? That would eliminate the risk from the start."

Gabe shook his head. "No. Let's stay well out of their way. With luck, they won't find the city or us. We only attack if we need to."

Niel had a feeling he would say that. "That's fine for now, Gabe, but if we find the city, I don't want to get hemmed in by them. If the Igigi are alive and aggressive, we could end up trapped between two powerful groups."

Gabe nodded. "I know. We'll assess as we go, and in the meantime," he sighed deeply and looked at Shadow, "be careful. Observe only!"

She gave him her biggest smile. "Of course. I'll thank you properly later."

Gabe smirked while Niel feigned vomiting. "If you mention anything about your sex life while I'm flying you there, I'll drop you, understand?"

Shadow didn't answer, instead giving him the finger, and he silently counted to ten.

TWENTY-ONE

It was getting late by the time Jackson finished organising his new office and the seemingly endless files to his satisfaction.

He was pleased with his room. It had an old-world grandeur about it, with its sweeping lines and old-fashioned lamps. The cleaners had come through mid-afternoon, and now the woodwork was gleaming in the soft lamplight. A decorative window inlaid with an ornate stained-glass design was set into the wall dividing the room from the passage, and through it he saw the light from the corridor. The occasional silhouette passed by on the way to the kitchen and communal room that was at the end of the corridor, but it was impossible to see who it was.

It was because of this window that he forgot he was so far underground, despite the fact that it didn't show a view of any sort. It relieved the monotony of the wood panelling and made him feel less shut in. His phone worked, his computer worked, and he found a couple of comfortable chairs and a low table to go in the corner of the room, salvaged from a storeroom that contained all sorts of interesting pieces of furniture. Waylen had given him free reign, a benefit of being on a small team in a place able to accommodate more. It made him wonder if the Paranormal Division had been bigger at one point, or if Princess Louise just had grand aspirations.

TWENTY-ONE

Jackson checked his watch, and with a shock realised it was time to meet Harlan. In five minutes, he was outside Serpentine South and making his way to the now dark entrance where he saw Harlan leaning against a wall, dressed casually in jeans, boots, and a leather jacket.

"You survived your time with JD, then?" he asked Harlan by way of a greeting, his eyes sweeping over him. "You don't look like a man at the end of your tether."

Harlan laughed. "There were trying moments, no doubt about that. And it's fair to say I have a new appreciation of his talents. But first, tell me why we're outside Serpentine South at eight at night. You said we were going to your headquarters."

Jackson realised he was looking forward to this. "We are. This is the main entrance for our new place. Come and see."

He led the way back to the deserted office, through security, and along the passage to his private office, pleased to see Harlan was as impressed as he was with the PD's new headquarters.

Harlan shook his head. "It never fails to amaze me what's hidden beneath London."

"I know! Kensington Gardens, of all places. I think Waylen is still here, somewhere, and Blake and the science techs are still organising the labs. This forced move will put us back days, if not weeks. It's infuriating."

Harlan wrestled with his leather messenger bag. "I brought you a present. A couple, actually." He handed Jackson a bottle wrapped in paper. "A housewarming present to suit your fancy new office. I'm hoping you have glasses."

"Hardly fancy," he said, pleased to see a bottle of good quality whiskey. "Thanks, Harlan. Just what I need."

Harlan's gaze swept the room. "Art Nouveau? Are you kidding me? This place is fantastic." He fished in his bag. "Here's present number two—although it's a loan, really. A book for you to read."

Harlan placed it on the low table and took a seat, and Jackson joined him once he fished around in a cupboard for cups. "Forgive me. I've yet to find the cut glass and decanters."

"I'll cope."

Jackson cracked the lid and poured them a couple of fingers, raising it in a toast. It wasn't until it was blazing a warm trail down his throat that he realised how thirsty he was. And hungry. He reached forward for the book and frowned. "*The Comte de Saint-Germain*. Why are you giving me this?"

Harlan brushed his hand through his thick dark hair, a crease settling on his brow. "Have you heard of him?"

"I have, actually. He's a very interesting figure." Jackson placed his glass down and flicked through the book. It was well thumbed, a few pages marked with sticky notes, and pencilled scribbles filled the margins.

"JD thinks he's Black Cronos's Grand Master."

He fumbled the book with shock. "*What*? Are you kidding?"

"No. And the more I read today, the more I think JD is right. You know he was rumoured to be immortal in his own lifetime?"

"Sure. He's one of the most fascinating historical characters I know of. He influenced royalty, amassed loads of money, was an amazing musician, spoke multiple languages..." He trailed off, studying Harlan's serious expression. "Black Cronos?"

Harlan outlined JD's reasoning. "And it makes sense. If JD has achieved immortality, why couldn't the count? He may even be older than JD, if those rumours are correct. The many encounters with him that people have recorded all suggest he was *really* odd, and he disappeared for years on end. When he did turn up again, he hadn't aged a day. His great age could well explain how he has made his soldiers so advanced. JD is having trouble wrapping his head around what they've achieved, and that's saying something."

Jackson picked his glass up again and leaned back in his chair, rubbing his face, perplexed. "I don't know whether to think that's great news or terrible. But, if you're right, then we have something to build on." He glanced at the stack of boxes on the floor. "It also means I have a new focus for those."

"JD has a few suggestions where he thinks he may have a base, too. Places in Europe."

"Like where?"

"France, where he spent many years as the advisor and friend of King Louis XV. Or, because Spanish and Portuguese were his most fluent languages, JD suggests that maybe there's a base in one of those countries. He's still compiling a list of possible places."

"Wow. Okay, so much to think on." Jackson's excitement about his new role bubbled up again, mixed with some trepidation. "If it is him, he's a formidable opponent."

"We have formidable friends."

"True. How did JD get on with the weapon?"

"He's made some progress, but he thinks he started it all wrong and is going back to basics." Harlan huffed. "I'm going back in a couple of days. I'll get his list then, too. But for now," Harlan stood, draining his glass as he did, "I need food, and so do you. Come on, let's find a pub."

Shadow landed with Niel a short distance away from Black Cronos's camp, which, like theirs, was encompassed by rocky terraces, and although she enjoyed flying, Shadow was relieved to have the hard earth beneath her feet again.

It was odd flying with Niel, as Shadow had only ever flown with Gabe before, and it was clear that Gabe wasn't that thrilled about it from the warning glance he gave Niel before they set off. His arms felt odd around her, and although she was good friends with Niel, despite their bickering, it felt oddly intimate. Not that Niel did anything except carry her. They flew high overhead for a short while, dipping down lower and lower in a wide circle before landing on a ridge just beyond their camp, in a fold that was out of their view. The camp was comprised of half a dozen off-road vehicles, several large tents, and many soldiers.

"You're right, Niel, that definitely looks like them," she admitted, adjusting her armour breastplate that Dante had fixed.

"Shadow, please be careful. Don't get too close. There were at least a dozen soldiers there, and they may have different abilities to what we've seen before."

Shadow bristled at his advice. He was looming over her, his tree trunk arms resting on his hips. "I'm not an idiot."

"I know. You're highly skilled, but so are they. Don't get too close. I'll hover overhead to keep an eye on you."

She nodded, all too aware that her cockiness could sometimes get her into trouble. "I'll head back here when I'm done. Maybe an hour, max."

"And if you're in trouble, I'll join in. I have your back, sister."

Shadow shot him a grateful smile as she pulled her fey magic around her and melted into the desert night. The stars glittered overhead, the swathe of the Milky Way cutting a path across the sky as she headed up the rocky incline, the uneven ground not an obstacle even in the dark. The air was cool now, but she barely noticed she was so intent on her quarry.

As she reached the top of the ridge, she slowed down, and slid flat on her stomach until the camp was laid out below her. The terrace sloped sharply downward, a tumble of rock and hollows with the occasional stunted bush clinging to life. One wrong move and she would set off a rockfall, but she had to get closer.

Easing to a crouch, she edged her way down, flitting from hollow to hollow. She could see soldiers below her guarding the way that led to the road. Unfortunately, a couple were studying the sky overhead, crossbows in their hands. She thanked the Gods that Niel had flown high. It seemed they were expecting company. In total, there were at least half a dozen men and women, all dressed in familiar black clothing with protective armour, some carrying their unusual weaponry. In the centre of the camp was a large fire, and a pavilion-style tent had been erected, which seemed to be a meeting space. As she dropped lower, she could see a table inside it, covered with paperwork. Stefan and Toto were deep in conversation, heads bent over what looked like a map. The Silencer of Souls was nowhere in sight. Other large tents had been set up as a type of barracks, and a couple of soldiers were gathered around a fire.

What was of more interest was a generator and the cables plugged into it. They led into a narrow cleft in the rock, and from deep within it was a gleam of light. *Had they found the city, after all? And was that where the other soldiers were? She could see fewer than Niel's estimated numbers.*

Shadow assessed the camp again. While the centre was lit with torch light, flames flaring in the night breeze, the outskirts, particularly under the rockface were in darkness, and no one was outside the break in the rock. She needed to get in there. Edging higher, and careful not to alert the guards, she stuck to the rocky terraces, clinging like a limpet, and made her way around the camp until she was much closer to the cleft. Dropping onto the ground, and making sure she hadn't been seen, she crept inside.

The cleft was long and narrow, a pale light glowing at the far end, showing up the rough, uneven walls and sandy floor, and the entrance to a cave. The banging of metal on rock drummed around her. She would have to be careful. When she reached the end, she could be spotted. However, when she finally made it to the cave, she found the dozen or so soldiers at the far end, working under the lights to break down a section of rock. The Silencer of Souls seemed to be supervising them.

But why there?

Shadow kept to the dark edges, finally scrambling up to a secure perch with a good view of the action. The soldiers were battering at what appeared to be a gate carved into the wall of rock. It was huge, and covered in carvings of the now familiar shapes of the Igigi. Stone pillars on either side had places for torches, and now that she was higher, she could see that the ground had a series of channels in it.

But the longer she watched, the more puzzled she became. For a start, she couldn't understand why they weren't using their explosive devices to blast through the rock. *Maybe they were worried about causing too much damage and bringing down the roof on their heads.* The other problem was that she had studied the grainy photos that Catarina had brought with her, and this cave looked nothing like that one. *This was another entrance, and Black Cronos had beaten them to it.* Even worse, there was nothing she could do to stop them. There were far too many to take on. Her priority was to get back and tell the others.

Shadow was on her way back to the cave's mouth when the roar of breaking rock signalled their success in smashing through the stone gate. Rock dust filled the air, and she pulled her jacket over her nose in an effort not to sneeze.

The Silencer of Souls broke away from the main group, a triumphant smile on her face, and headed to the exit, no doubt to tell the others. There was no way Shadow could get there before her, but she could follow her, and might even be able to kill her before she reached the camp.

Shadow followed her into the narrow cleft, knives drawn, and quickened her pace. She was within knifing distance when the woman dropped, rolled, and threw a weapon at Shadow. With lightning-quick reflexes, Shadow dodged and struck back, but her opponent threw herself at Shadow, and in the narrow, confined space, Shadow had nowhere to go.

Ash circled another section of the terraced rock, trying to discern landmarks, whilst keeping a tight grip on Catarina. Not that he needed to worry. She was clinging to his arms so tightly he thought they might go numb.

"Are you okay?" he asked her.

"Fine." She sounded breathless, but from what he could see of her face, she looked elated. "This is amazing. And terrifying. I feel like Lois Lane with Superman."

He laughed. "Christopher Reeve. I saw that one. Please don't freak out like she did."

"I'm keeping it together...just."

"Focus on the search. That will take your mind off it."

She snorted in a very unladylike manner. "Like that would help!"

She wriggled back against his chest, and Ash realised this was the closest he'd been to any woman in a long time. *Or a man, for that matter.* Ash was relaxed about his lovers. He was drawn to the person, not the gender. But it was a shock for him to think of Catarina in that respect, and he blamed it on his hormones and the heat of the desert.

"I'm serious," he said, his lips close to her ear, pleased to see a blush spread across her cheeks.

"You need to drop down lower—to the right."

He did as she instructed, gliding down so they were above the next ridged valley, and it was the change of angle that triggered his memory. And for Catarina, too.

"I see it! That spur. It looks familiar."

Ash dropped lower, the shallow valley below the spur closing in, until with the lightest of landing, they were on the ground. Catarina took a moment to release herself from his hold. Her eyes were wide as she studied the odd angle of the space, and the sheer wall of rock to one side.

"Ash! This looks like the photos!"

She fumbled in her pocket and found the envelope they were contained in. Her fingers shook as she pulled them free, and Ash shined a pocket torch on them, comparing the photos to their surroundings. There was no doubt the scene was incredibly similar.

"I agree. That area in particular looks the same. That, however, does not." He pointed to the sheer rock that looked strangely smooth compared to the rest of the terrace.

"That's because it was the entrance before!" She jabbed the image of the cave's entrance. "Wait." She dropped to her knees and spread the images out, marrying them together by overlapping, and the broad expanse of the rocky terrace suddenly came together.

"Herne's bollocks, you're right. It's the same place."

Her eyes danced with excitement. "My husband said the cave sealed itself. A rockfall, perhaps?"

"That's not a rockfall. Not a natural one, anyway." Tentatively, he walked to the sheer face, Catarina next to him, and ran his fingers across the surface. "It's too smooth. Sculpted."

"By the Igigi?"

"I presume so. It's further to the east than we thought, though. We're at least two miles out."

"More remote. Is there even a road here?"

"There must be if your husband's team came here, but we'll check when we fly again."

Her shoulders dropped and she sighed as she looked up at him. "They didn't come by car. They arrived by camel. There probably is no road here!"

"Fuck it!" Ash groaned as he realised their mistake. He'd been trying to marry the directions to a road. Now he felt like a complete idiot. "But still, we followed the map as best we could."

"No matter. We've found it now, I'm sure."

"Let's check a few more photos, just to make sure. If we're going to uproot the camp, I want to make sure we're right this time."

Besides, he liked being alone with the countess under the Milky Way, with nothing but the soft susurrus of shifting sand and the wind through the rocks. Taking another few minutes alone would be no hardship. And from the long look she gave him as she turned back to the photos, he had a feeling she felt the same.

TWENTY-TWO

Niel watched Black Cronos's camp from above, looking for any sign that Shadow had been spotted.

She had long since disappeared from his view, and although he loved his own strength and speed, he wished he had even half of her stealth. He hunkered down on a rock, folding his wings away, and now that he was closer, he could see the men with their crossbows trained on the s ky.

He considered his options, wondering if he could take some of their soldiers out, but it was too risky alone, especially with Shadow down there. The soldiers guarding the rough track that led to the paved road were all within sight and sound of each other, so it was impossible to pick them off.

A jeering shout below broke his concentration. With horror he saw The Silencer of Souls emerge from the cleft, her arm wrapped firmly around Shadow, who looked almost insensible as she was dragged into the camp. Stefan and Toto emerged from beneath the main tent to close in on them, and all the guards turned to watch, including the ones with the crossbows.

Niel seized his chance. He jumped from the outstretched rock, his wings close to his side as he dived downwards, sword in one outstretched hand.

It seemed Shadow had seized her moment, too. As soon as she cleared the cleft, she broke free of her captor and threw her knives at Toto and Stefan. As Stefan scrambled for cover, Toto fell awkwardly. Shadow didn't stop, pulling her swords and whirling them as she faced The Silencer of Souls.

Niel changed direction. He attacked the two closest guards with his sword, knocking them off their feet and inflicting deep cuts, before swooping on one of the soldiers with a crossbow. He shot a bolt at Niel, but it went wide, and Niel landed on him, flattening him to the ground. He grabbed the crossbow from his outstretched hands, whirled around, and using the stolen weapon, took out the other soldier armed with the crossbow, satisfied to see the bolt pierce his throat.

The camp was now in chaos. Toto had collapsed on the ground, and Stefan was at his side, while Shadow danced out of reach of The Silencer of Souls and the remaining guards. Her swords were a blur of motion, and despite everyone's best attempts, they couldn't get close.

Niel charged across the ground, pulling his axe free and smashing one of the main tent poles as he passed it. It collapsed onto the ground, half enveloping Stefan and adding to the confusion. Shadow ran to his side, and wrapping one free arm around her, he launched into the air again.

"Fuck me, Shadow!" he yelled as they ascended. "What happened?"

"That bitch happened, of course."

"I thought you were unconscious," he told her.

She twisted to look at him, a wicked grin on her face. "That's what she thought, too. But I have news. Bad news. They've found another entrance. I'll explain when we land."

Niel nodded, and soon they were back at their own campsite. But for some reason, everyone was packing up.

"What's going on?" he asked as he landed and released Shadow from his hold.

Ash grimaced. "We're in the wrong place, but we're sure we've found the entrance now. We're a mile or two out."

Gabe dropped the half-packed tent he was holding and hurried to their side, his eyes hard as they raked over them both. "What happened? Why are you carrying a crossbow?"

Shadow shrugged coolly. "I had an incident."

Gabe folded his arms across his chest. "An *incident*?" This time when he looked them over, he was more worried. "Are you injured?"

"I am fey! Of course not."

Estelle snorted as she joined them, the rest of their team circling around. "You're not immune, Shadow. Your chest injury proved that the other day."

She shot her an impatient look. "I was caught off-guard then. Today I had my revenge."

Gabe's voice was almost a growl. "How?"

"Niel was right. Black Cronos has set up camp a few miles south in a secluded valley, accessed only by a rough track. Toto and Stefan were distracted by paperwork, and the soldiers were busy watching the track that led to the valley. A narrow cleft in the rockface led to a cave, and I was able to sneak in. Many more soldiers were in the cave, including that bloody woman." She paused, perplexed. "There was a huge stone gate set into the rock wall. It was richly carved with images of the Igigi, stone pillars on either side. To me it looked ornamental. But they had a team with machinery and tools, and as I was there, they broke into it—put a hole right through the door. It was thick, too. At least a couple of feet."

The group looked uneasily at each other, and Zee asked, "What was on the other side?"

"I was too far away to see anything other than darkness, but it must be a way into the city." She turned to Catarina. "The photos didn't look like the cave your father-in-law found. Perhaps they discovered a rear entrance? Or a side gate?"

Catarina's eyes clouded with confusion. "Does it matter, as long as we have a way in, too? Are you sure they've found the Igigi's city? It could be something else entirely."

"The carvings on the gate were like those on the stone tablet," Shadow said. "I'm sure."

"And besides," Nahum said, "two cities or underground complexes would just be nuts. They have to be the same."

Gabe huffed with annoyance. "Agreed. The only thing that matters is that they're getting into the city and we're not." He looked at Shadow and Niel, his earlier reticence gone. "What if we follow them in and finish this now? How many soldiers are there?"

"A couple of dozen?" Shadow suggested with a shrug. "I think we're already too late. But I wounded Toto. One of my knives found its mark."

Ash cut into the conversation. "While it's annoying that they have found their own way in somehow, we have Jasper's entrance, and we need to use it. Let's get moving. The four wheel drives should make it to the new camp, even though there's no track to speak of. I'll fly and lead the way, okay?"

There was a chorus of agreement, and as everyone disbursed, Gabe grabbed Niel and pulled him aside. "Do me a favour. Follow us to the new place, and then circle back and check on Toto's camp. If we can enter from their side too, we can trap them between us."

"While I like your reasoning, Gabe, I need to warn you that the other entrance is a good few miles away. That means the city beneath us is huge. I don't think us splitting up is a good idea."

Gabe's eyes took on a faraway expression as he considered his options, and he reluctantly nodded. "Point taken, but check anyway. We can't be too careful."

Gabe studied the smooth stone wall, Nahum beside him, and grunted with frustration.

"I think Ash has gone mad!"

Nahum patted his shoulder. "Sorry Gabe, but I think he's right. The photos marry up. How we get in there is another matter."

The sun was rising, casting a rosy, pink glow over their new campsite, which they had set up quickly. After a cursory examination of the area, Gabe had instructed the others to get some sleep. It had been a long night, and he wanted to make sure they were fresh when they entered the city.

If they entered the city.

He glared at the wall again, frowning at its smooth, unyielding surface. "How in Herne's hairy bollocks did they achieve this?"

"The Igigi always had their own magic, gifted by the Gods. That's why they were such great builders. And that's why we have a witch with us."

Gabe tore his gaze from the rock and stared at Nahum, his brother's blue eyes looking even bluer against his bronzed skin. Even just a couple of days in the desert had deepened his tan. "You think she can open this up?"

"I spoke to her before she went to sleep. She has a few ideas, but she looked beat."

Gabe knew Estelle's magic was powerful, and hoped she could find a way through. He voiced his other concern next. "How did Black Cronos find another entrance? We thought we'd be ahead of them, and now they're already inside!"

"They must have found another source. But we have an advantage they don't. We know the Igigi."

"Which is no advantage at all if they're dead. For all we know, they've got a map of the place and are raiding their dead bones right now."

"Or they've been buried in a rockslide or caught in a weird Igigi trap and are all dead themselves." Nahum looked amused. "We focus on our end, not theirs."

Gabe grunted again, knowing he was being unreasonable. But frankly, he wouldn't feel happy until they were in there. "The other thing we need to decide is whether we leave someone outside on guard. What if Black Cronos finds this place and follow us in?"

"Look around. We're well off the road here, and hidden from view. We barely got the off-road vehicles here. And they haven't got wings."

"True." Gabe groaned as he ran his hands through his hair, already gritty with sand and sweat. He'd forgotten how the desert invaded all clothes and belongings. "Do you miss this?"

"The desert?" Nahum asked, startled.

"The whole place. The food, the heat, the culture..."

Nahum shrugged. "Yes and no. That was one life, this is another. And we're here now. We can travel whenever we want—and planes make it much easier now!"

Gabe nodded. "True. I guess it's just weird being back. I thought it would feel like I was coming home, but instead I just feel unsettled. So much has changed."

"And so much hasn't. We chased them across these deserts before. Well, to the south, at least. Until these hills swallowed them."

Gabe met Nahum's bright blue eyes. "The Igigi can't possibly still be alive, can they?"

"My head says no, but my heart..." Nahum shook his head and sighed. "I actually hope they are."

A shadow fell over them as they talked, and in seconds Niel landed next to them, his snowy wings streaked pink and gold by the early morning sun.

"You're pushing your luck with the light," Gabe told him.

Niel just grinned. "Someone will think I'm a big bird of prey. And the light is still dim."

"You are a big bird of prey," Nahum said, laughing. "What did you see?"

"A dozen guards protecting the entrance, and more inside. Reinforcements have arrived. I watched them go in, all armed with their strange weaponry." Niel clenched his jaw, clearly uncomfortable with what he'd seen. "They have something big planned. If we were to attack them now, I'm not sure we'd survive. We're outnumbered—especially in the open. Our only option is to stop them inside, when hopefully we'll have stealth on our side. And there's no sign of Toto or Stefan, or that bitch, either."

Niel was obviously still furious about their encounter in Scotland, which was completely understandable. Gabe was, too. "Damn it. Part of me hoped we could finish this now, but I knew it wouldn't be that straightforward. Let's ignore them for now and focus on this."

"That's presuming we can get in, and that our entrance will connect with theirs at some point," Nahum argued. "If there's been a rockfall, we're screwed anyway."

"Let's try to be positive," Gabe said. "They were excellent builders. Let's hope whatever they built is still intact, even if they are long gone."

"Have you slept while I've been gone?" Niel asked him, changing the subject.

Gabe considered his gritty eyes and befuddled brain. "No. But I'll be fine. You two should sleep, though, while we have the chance."

Nahum shook his head, directing Gabe to the tent he was sharing with Shadow. "Nope. We all need a few hours' sleep. We're under Estelle's protection spell, so we'll be safe."

"That's true," Niel nodded in agreement. "We're invisible from above. If I didn't know where you were, I wouldn't have had a clue."

"Good." Nahum was already yawning. "And besides, only Herne knows what we'll face in there. We need all the rest we can get."

Gabe reluctantly had to admit he was right, so with a final glance around the camp to make sure all was in order, he ducked into the tent he shared with Shadow. Shedding only his boots, he curled in alongside her, and it seemed he'd only laid his head down for seconds before he was asleep.

Unfortunately, his sleep wasn't dreamless. Images of the Igigi and their prolonged battles dogged his thoughts. The clash of weapons, the long days spent under a searing hot sun, the weary game of cat and mouse, and the traps and ambushes that accompanied the sure and certain knowledge that they weren't going to be successful. And even more, that they shouldn't be. And then there was the memory of a conversation with his father.

"Why are we doing this?" he demanded after a particularly hard campaign in which nothing tangible had been achieved. "You rebelled against your God! Why not let them?"

His father, all flashing eyes full of dark malice, said, "Because we have new partners now, and we have sworn to help the Anunnaki. I personally promised help."

Gabe virtually spat at him. "And yet, you aren't! I am. I have had enough. This ends now."

His father, Remiel, an archangel who was once known as 'God's Thunder' before he fell with Lucifer, was prouder and more headstrong than most. He towered over Gabe, almost blinding in his brilliance.

"It ends when I say it will."

"Then do it yourself!"

Gabe turned his back on Remiel, making to leave the cave where their encounter had taken place. But instead, he found himself pinned in place by his father's power—and his threats. "Any independence you think you have will cease if you fail to do this. And that includes your life with your beautiful wife."

Gabe's blood ran cold as he turned to face his father. "You don't need to threaten her."

"It seems I do. You have a place on Earth for one reason—and that is because I willed it."

Gabe glared at him. "You don't even know why you're here anymore! You argued with your God in the bid for independence, fled your former home, and now resent everything about the place that is your new home! You mourn your loss of privilege, and you flounder in chaos."

Remiel leaned in close. "Don't test me, Gabreel. You still have a home left to return to. Isn't the loss of your child enough?"

Gabe felt such a white-hot rage at those words that he could barely speak, but it was quickly followed by terror at what else he may lose. So, he left the cave carved from the curling dunes and returned to his team—defeated and furious. But the following weeks achieved nothing until even Remiel and the other Fallen angels who had sided with the Anunnaki had been forced to admit defeat.

And then a voice pierced Gabe's dreams that was not a memory at all.

"*You failed before, Gabreel. Do not fail again.*"

Seconds later Gabe woke up, sweat pouring off him, and he shot up in bed, instinctively reaching for his sword, only to find that the tent was empty and Shadow was still sleeping at his side.

But there was no mistaking the voice. It belonged to his father.

Remiel.

It was with relief when Harlan entered his own office at The Orphic Guild on Tuesday morning, happy to be settling back into his normal routine.

There were a couple of cases he needed to focus on, and once he'd made coffee, he accessed the files and evaluated where he'd gotten up to. However, his peace was short-lived when his phone rang, and he cursed when he saw who the caller was.

"Maggie!" he groaned, sounding like he was dreading their conversation, but secretly loving the battle of wits he endured with her. "What crap have you called with now?"

"You're a cheeky fucker, Harlan! You constantly call me with shit that *I* have to mop up! And besides, I could be asking you to dinner."

He tried not to laugh at her caustic tone. "Are you? I'm not sure we're that well suited."

"I know we're bloody not, you smooth American bugger! No, I'm ringing about a body."

Harlan had never been called *smooth* before and wasn't sure he liked it. *However...* "A body? Why are you calling *me*? I swear I haven't murdered anyone."

"It's Barnaby bloody Armstrong. Someone spotted him floating in the Thames this morning."

"*What*?" All of the playfulness left his voice, and he sagged into his chair. "You're kidding."

"I don't kid about death, you moron." Her voice softened. "Sorry, I know you knew him. You arrested him, didn't you, for the PD?"

Harlan fumbled for his coffee, feeling suddenly nauseous. "Yes, with Jackson, only a few nights ago. But Black Cronos broke him out when they raided the old headquarters on Saturday. Did he drown?"

"No. He was already dead, a look of abject horror on his face. No obvious wounds, but remarkably like Blaze. Ring a bell?"

"The Silencer of Souls."

"Most likely. But it's not his death I'm ringing about. It's what we found in the autopsy."

"You've done that already? When did you find him?"

"Yesterday afternoon. There was a small key in his stomach."

Harlan thought he was hearing things. "A *what*?"

"A key, to a bank deposit box. And what's in it will interest you."

"He swallowed a key?"

"Well, he didn't bloody use surgery to get it in there!"

"Sorry, I'm in shock." He kept seeing Barnaby's resigned look when he finally stopped struggling, and couldn't help but feel he was responsible for his death. "What was in the box?"

"Notes on old stories about a buried city."

"Really? Because we already found stuff in his room on that. Did it mention the Igigi?"

"Something like that. But there were also notes about a bloke called Count Bellemare. Lists of places and names. It means nothing to me, but I thought you and Jackson might be interested."

Harlan's pulse quickened at the mention of a count. "Are you sure it wasn't the Count of St Germain?"

"No. Definitely Bellemare. You can collect them if you want. I've taken copies for my own records, but I know you're looking into Black Cronos." She snorted. "Frankly, I'm too busy to deal with that crap right now."

Harlan was already standing and grabbing his jacket. "Yes, please. I'll come get them right now."

TWENTY-THREE

Estelle laid her hands on the smooth rock, sending her awareness out and feeling for space beyond it.

She was aware of the team watching her, but blocked their attention out. Earth magic wasn't her strength, but this was a relatively simple thing to do. Witches responded strongly to natural energies, and the earth vibrated with it. In the desert, it felt much the same as anywhere. At the moment all she could feel was solid, unyielding rock, but as she walked along the rockface, her touch detecting the imperfections in the surface, she felt a change. She stopped, pressing both hands against the rock and closed her eyes. Beyond the initial thickness loomed a huge space.

Relieved, because despite her natural faith in her abilities she was keen to impress the Nephilim and cement her place in the team, she turned to face them. "This is the spot. Beyond the rock is a cave."

Gabe was at her side in seconds, and she lifted her head to look up at him as he asked, "Did you detect any magic?"

"None...not yet, anyway. Do you want me to open it up?"

"Do you think you can?" Barak asked, approaching behind them. "What if we set off a rockfall?" His beautiful, dark eyes settled on Estelle's face. "We don't want you buried under it."

Estelle felt the now familiar flutter settle in her stomach. His look felt like a caress, and ever since their kiss yesterday, she wanted more of him—his lips, his hands... Now, however, was not the time to indulge in daydreams. She forced her voice to be steady. "If I focus on a small spot using a targeted blast, it should be relatively safe. Of course, I'll stand back, too. We all should." She looked at the rock and frowned as another idea struck her. "In fact, I should be able to carve a doorway if I use fire, too. That would strengthen the surrounding rock like a lintel."

Gabe rubbed his already thick stubble, looking at Estelle with doubt-filled eyes. And something else. He appeared more rattled than he normally did. "Is that possible?"

"Have a little faith," she said, sounding more confident than she felt.

She ushered everyone back and then sent out a pulse of magic. It was a blend of power as well as fire, designed to melt the rock and then fuse it. She cast a spell used to move obstacles, and doubled her intention. Instead of blasting the rock in a display of strength that would no doubt have caused a rockfall, she used her magic like a laser beam, and very soon a small hole appeared in the rock. Manipulating her power across a larger area, the hole grew bigger and bigger.

She couldn't help grinning with her success. The rock seemed to melt away, and in a few minutes, a doorway opened into the space beyond.

Whoops erupted from the team behind her, and she turned, still grinning, pleased to see looks of incredulity on everyone's faces. *Especially Shadow's.* "Impressed?"

"Very!" Nahum said, slapping her on the shoulder as he reached her side. "Wow. That was like watching a sculptor."

Shadow sniffed. "Not bad, I admit."

"Could you do better?" she asked, cocking an eyebrow, unable to resist baiting her. Shadow's presence was a constant thorn in her side, but one she had to tolerate. It didn't help that Shadow was a devastatingly efficient killer and tracker, and breathtakingly beautiful in an ethereal way.

Shadow shrugged and pouted, and Estelle smirked as she hurried after the others. Gabe had his sword in one hand and a torch in the other, already peering into the dark space.

"Wait!" Estelle said, pulling him back. "Let me throw some witch-lights in."

In seconds, half a dozen witch-lights were bobbing around the cave beyond, but Gabe quickly thrust her out of the way. "Let me go first."

Estelle's first instinct was to whip his legs out from under him. *Bloody Nephilim*. They were a force unto themselves, so full of ego.

Nahum followed Gabe, Niel and Ash on their heels, but Barak and Zee hung back. Shadow caught her tight expression as she joined her at the entrance.

"They're very annoying sometimes," Shadow told her. "I take my revenge by beating them at sword-fighting."

Zee must have heard her comment and laughed. Estelle didn't know Zee as well as the others. He was as tall and broad-shouldered as his brothers, with dark, almost black hair that had a slight curl to it. Like many of the other Nephilim he looked Middle Eastern, and had an angular face that seemed even more so now that his hair was pulled back into a high ponytail. His dark eyes currently flashed with humour as he teased Shadow.

"Sometimes, Princess," Zee said, tweaking her hair.

"*All* the time!" she shot back, swatting his hand away. "Have you beat me yet?"

Zee smirked. "I'm biding my time. Ladies, after you!" He extended his arm into the dark space, encompassing Catarina in his statement.

Despite Zee's teasing, Catarina looked nervous. She gestured at the newly formed doorway. "Is that safe?"

"As safe as anything more conventionally engineered," Estelle assured her, and shouldering her pack, she walked into the cave beyond. However, she paused next to Gabe and his brothers just inside the threshold, shocked at what lay beyond. "By the Gods…"

Her words trailed off as she took in the large cave and what appeared to be a ziggurat carved into the far wall. A steep ramp led to an entrance halfway up. Huge double doors that looked enormous even from here awaited them, with cuneiform writing carved above them. Its shape stood out in sharp relief from the rockface, the witch-lights also highlighting the carved faces and figures in the rock.

In seconds the others had shuffled in, and they all looked as shocked as Estelle felt.

Catarina took in a sharp breath next to her. "This is what my husband saw! We've actually found it."

"And those are from the rockfall." Ash pointed to the rocks scattered over the ground, some still on the ziggurat itself.

Estelle didn't take her eyes off the huge stone structure. "It's breathtaking. I can't believe what I'm seeing."

"It *is* impressive," Shadow admitted. "But why build such an ornate entrance if you don't want anyone to see it?"

Nahum gave Shadow a sharp, appraising glance. "That's an interesting question, but maybe it's just because they could."

"Or because they want to invite someone in…and then trap them," Gabe grunted.

Barak stood next to Estelle, his presence radiating towards her, impossible to ignore. "Keep your spells at the ready, Estelle. I don't like this." The muscles in his arm flexed as he gripped his sword. "The Igigi were swift and deadly when they attacked. And big."

"Bigger than you?" Catarina asked, wide-eyed.

"Much. And some of them had wings."

"But brother," Zee said, readying his crossbow as he studied the cave, "they were not naturally aggressive. Don't forget that. Only pursuit and slavery did that to them."

"Where are the bodies?" Niel asked. He swung around to look at Catarina. "Your husband said men were killed, right? Their bones should be here."

Catarina stuttered, her hand grasping her backpack. "I don't know. Perhaps his memory was confused, and they dragged some out?"

"No," Gabe said with certainty. "He said that they fled and the walls turned to rivers of rock. There are no rivers of rock here."

"But that," Zee said, pointing to a broad stone channel cut into the floor, "looks like a dry canal. It runs from the base of the ziggurat face to down there." He pointed to a dark hole low down on the opposite cave wall where it met the floor.

A chill ran through Estelle and she shivered, wondering what dark place the old canal led to.

Barak noticed her reaction and said, "They built waterways for kings and gods. Their expertise was like no other. Their cities were green."

"Like the Hanging Gardens of Babylon?"

"Absolutely. Stories like that have survived for a reason. No one who saw it could forget it." He pointed to the face of the ziggurat. "Each level of the ziggurat is set back from the level below, and every ledge would be filled with plants. Water channels ran everywhere...they looked magnificent."

Estelle had seen images and she knew what he meant, but before she could ask anything else, Gabe was already moving on.

"Okay," Gabe said, scanning the cave. "So there's the sort of half-ziggurat, and what looks like an entrance in it, the empty canal, and not much else. No sign of bodies, rockfalls, or old digs. But this is the place, and the ziggurat is our way in."

"Or down there," Zee suggested, looking at where the watercourse reached the hole in the rock.

Gabe looked incredulous. "Let's leave that as a last resort." He addressed Estelle. "Are your protection spells still over the camp?"

She tried not to take offense at his question. "All secure. And I can protect this entrance, too."

"And have we got all of our gear?"

There was a chorus of murmured agreement and nods. All of the Nephilim were heavily loaded, not only with weapons, but with food and basic supplies too, and the women had smaller packs. They had discussed the plans over a hasty breakfast, and while nobody wanted to be underground for too long, they wanted to prepare for every eventuality.

"Good." Gabe took a deep breath. "Then let's see if we can get farther than your husband did, Catarina. Barak, Zee, Shadow, and Estelle, keep to the rear and watch for attack from behind. But all of you—stay close."

And with that, he led them towards the steps leading to the ziggurat's entrance.

Jackson sank back into his chair, all elation at his new office and role leaching out of him as he absorbed Harlan's news.

"Barnaby is dead? Fuck me." He rubbed his hands across his jaw and closed his eyes, envisaging their last conversation. "Poor bugger. He said his life was forfeit, and to be honest, I didn't quite believe it. And now he's dead." When he opened his eyes, he found Harlan looking as guilty as he felt. "If we hadn't arrested him..."

"I've been wrestling with this news all morning, but this is not our fault. He got himself into this, and there was a price to pay."

"I know you're right, but I still feel like shit."

"But," Harlan said, leaning forward and slapping his messenger bag on Jackson's crowded desk, "he was hiding things. Things we now have."

Jackson perked up and leaned forward, eyeing the bag. "Like what?"

"Information about the Igigi and Count Bellamarre."

"Who?"

"Count Bellamarre is another name that the *Comte de Saint-Germain* used—one of his many pseudonyms."

"You're shitting me! Barnaby was researching him?"

Harlan started to pull papers out of his bag, a mix of loose sheets, notebooks, and old files. "Looks like it. Maybe he thought he could use it as a type of insurance, maybe blackmail. Or perhaps he was just curious."

"Considering how he was only too happy to betray The Order of the Midnight Sun, it wouldn't surprise me if he had something similar planned for Black Cronos. Sneaky shit." That news lifted a weight from Jackson's shoulders. "Now I don't feel quite so guilty that he's dead. How did you find out all this?"

"Maggie Milne phoned me. They discovered a safety deposit key stuck in his gut, and by checking his bank details worked out where it was for." Harlan grimaced. "They found it in the autopsy. God knows when he swallowed it."

Jackson groaned as he recalled the night they caught him. "He was fussing at that side table in his living room, remember? When he offered us a drink? Perhaps he suspected what was coming and swallowed it then."

"Oh, yeah! When he had his gin and tonic." Harlan huffed. "Some special agents we are, when we didn't even notice that."

"I was too busy checking out his room, and you were hovering by the door. It's not that surprising. Anyway, what's he written?"

Harlan spread the papers out, pushing them towards Jackson, but grabbing one file. "He has made lists on properties once associated with the count and his pseudonyms. I think he fixed on the name Bellamarre in particular, because of the name of the email address he used." Harlan's eyebrows rose, and his lips twisted into a rueful smile. "Beautiful Mother. *Bella Marre* in Spanish."

Jackson groaned, feeling like an idiot. "Of course! I thought the address was weird, but presumed it was just meant to mislead." He shuffled through some of the notes written in a crabbed hand. "This supports JD's idea."

"Unless this name is someone's idea of a gigantic hoax. A tease."

"Perhaps. What kind of properties are in there?"

"All sort of places. Castles and palaces, old townhouses, even manor homes across Europe—all the way to Romania. There are loads of them! But," Harlan pointed out, "we could cross-reference them with JD's suggestions."

Jackson leaned back, hands behind his head as he considered their options. "So potentially, one of these addresses could be a base for Black Cronos."

"Or multiple bases."

"This is brilliant! This could lead us right to the heart of their operation. And what about the Igigi? What's he got on them?"

Harlan huffed. "Some garbled notes on another historical find in Turkey when it was part of the Ottoman Empire. I started reading it and it gave me a headache, but I think it refers to a city beneath the sands. I have no idea whether it refers to the same place, or somewhere different."

"Can you spare a few hours to help?" Jackson was starting to feel overwhelmed again as he took in the enormity of the tasks ahead.

Fortunately, Harlan took pity on him and shed his jacket, placing it on the chair behind him. "I can give you a couple of hours—as long as you have lots of coffee on hand, and promise me lunch."

"Deal."

Ash paused in front of the huge stone doors built in the middle of the ziggurat, feeling a heady rush of euphoria as old memories resurfaced.

It seemed odd, but he had forgotten how imposing these buildings were. The doors in front of him were massive, towering four times his height, carved reliefs of Igigi making decorative panels. The walls stretched away on either side, and the top was lost in darkness that the witch-lights didn't penetrate. Behind him, the ramp carved out of the rock fell to the cave floor below.

He laid his hand on the rock, noting the seam where the two doors met in the middle, and he turned to Shadow. "Were these like the doors that Black Cronos broke through?"

"They were smaller, less ornate, but essentially the same." Her face wrinkled with annoyance. "They completely shattered it. I hate wanton destruction."

Niel grunted with annoyance. "Unless we can find a way of opening them, we'll be doing the same."

"Through those?" Zee asked, incredulous. "These will be several feet thick. There's no way we'll smash through them!"

Ash hastened to calm his brothers. "I'm sure we can work it out. There must be some kind of mechanism. They invented hydraulics and the wheel, after all."

"True," Barak said, heading to the far side of the left-hand door and peering upwards. "If I remember correctly, they used a series of wheels to open doors and move walls."

"That's true, brother!" Nahum shed his pack and t-shirt, extending his wings as he spoke. "The mechanisms were high on the walls."

In seconds both were flying upwards, examining the sheer walls of the ziggurat, while the others shuffled nervously below, wary of any sign of movement.

Catarina surveyed the cave, her expression one of disbelief. "I find it hard to believe this is where my husband was. Any sign of the dig has been erased."

Ash exchanged a cautious glance with Gabe as he said, "If anything, this suggests that at least some of them are still alive. Perhaps they moved the bodies."

"But if so," Gabe whispered, "where are they now?"

A muffled shout from above had them all looking up, weapons drawn. All Ash could see was the deeper shadows of his brothers' beating wings as they conferred together, and then Nahum landed next to them.

"We found a narrow gap in the rock above on either side of the doors. We can see a glimpse of cogs beyond. We're going in."

Gabe nodded, his hand clutching his sword. "Be careful!"

For what seemed like endless minutes nothing happened, and then a slow, grinding noise rumbled across the cave as the seam started to inch apart.

Catarina's breath caught and she stumbled back a pace. "They've done it!"

Ash squeezed her shoulder in reassurance, but grinned at his brothers. "After all these years, we've finally found them."

"But will we live to regret it?" Gabe turned and cautioned the others. "Let's take our time heading in. There could be traps."

The doors inched slowly open, the grind of the cogs mixing with the scraping of sand and gravel beneath the doors. Estelle once again threw witch-lights inside, and as soon as they were able to edge through the opening, their pale light revealed the broad hall that lay ahead.

Torches lined the walls, and as they stepped inside, the torches flared into life, throwing the hall into leaping firelight and shadow.

Gabe whipped around to stare at Estelle. "Was that you?"

She shook her head, her eyes wary. "No."

Gabe swallowed and gripped his sword even tighter. "A trick?"

"Or a mechanism?" Niel countered. "But if so, someone must maintain it."

"Herne's hairy balls," Ash whispered, ignoring their whispered questions. The hall was imposing, reliefs of the Igigi carved into panels that ran along either side of the room. The roof was high, the cog mechanism on a platform towering above them. Nahum and Barak flew overhead, acting as guards above them, while the others shuffled forward below.

"Another doorway," Shadow said pointing ahead to a pair of burnished copper doors at the far end of the hall.

"From what I recall of the normal structure of these buildings," Zee said, "there will be a series of anterooms before we reach the large, central chamber. But this is not a normal ziggurat, so I may be wrong."

"Exactly," Niel agreed. "Beyond there could be the city proper."

A flare of excitement flashed through Ash's body as he said, "Only one way to find out."

But they had advanced barely halfway down the hall when a strange, clanking noise had them whirling around, weapons raised. But there was nothing they could do as a huge metal gate dropped from a recess in the roof, sealing the entrance and trapping them inside.

When Harlan finally arrived back in his office, it was late afternoon. He had barely had time to make himself coffee when there was an irate knock on his door and Mason burst in.

"Here you are! You've been gone for hours!"

"I've been working!" Harlan responded, just as annoyed. Obviously, he wasn't about to disclose that he'd been helping Jackson. Besides, he had managed to devote a few hours to one of his latest cases. "Is something wrong?"

Mason was as elegantly dressed as always, but his crankiness gave him an air of dishevelment, which was at odds with his normally smooth manner. "I want to know if there's been any progress in finding Black Cronos!"

Harlan looked at him, perplexed. "We have leads, but that's all. It's going to take time finding them. They've taken the word *covert* to a whole new level."

"That's what JD said." Mason stalked across the office to stare out of the window. "It's not good enough."

Harlan pushed his irritation aside. For some reason, Mason thought he was some kind of super sleuth, and he realised Smythe's death was still weighing heavily on him. Instead, he said, "You're talking to JD now?"

"Yes. He phoned me. He's been trying to reach you, too. He wants you to return to Mortlake."

Harlan checked his phone, baffled, and realised he'd missed several calls that must have come through while he was at The Retreat. "Perhaps he's made headway with the weapon."

Mason rounded on him. "What weapon?"

"He's trying to replicate Black Cronos's weapons. I thought I told you. He's tried a few angles, but when I left him yesterday, he thought he'd found the best way."

"You're *helping* him?" Mason looked outraged. "You're supposed to be stopping him!"

Harlan took a deep breath and exhaled slowly, then walked to his espresso machine and started to prepare coffee. Yelling at Mason wasn't going to solve anything, and he needed to regain his composure. "You asked me to keep an eye on him. This is one way to do that. Besides, this might help us work out the whole superhuman thing—which, by the way, he has no interest in doing to himself!"

Mason calmed down. "That's good, I suppose."

"Better than good. We need to understand what they're doing. The Nephilim found weird super-dogs in Scotland. Who knows what else they're experimenting with! Did JD tell you that his estate had been attacked?"

"No!" Mason folded his arms across his chest. "When?"

"Sunday night. Want one?" He gestured to the coffee, but Mason shook his head. "It was serious. If JD hadn't installed such excellent defences, we'd have been killed. I suspect they're tracking down their stolen items. And it seems they want to develop superhumans with wings." He quickly updated Mason on the hunt for the Igigi, and what Gabe's team was doing.

Mason's eyes narrowed. "Why track down ancient beings who most likely don't exist when they could just capture a Nephilim? They have superhuman strength and wings, don't they? And are the sons of the Fallen." His face wrinkled with distaste. "As disgusting as their methods are, surely analysing a Nephilim would have greater value."

A chill swept over Harlan. "I hadn't even considered that. But to be honest, they're so formidable and have killed so many of Black Cronos's soldiers that surely they would avoid that idea completely."

"They're formidable as a group, but split up they're more vulnerable. How many have gone to Turkey?"

"All except for Eli." Harlan fumbled for his phone, worried for Eli's safety, and then he recalled what Gabe had told him. "The witches set up protection over the farmhouse weeks ago. He should be safe, but I'll call him anyway."

"I'll leave you to it." But halfway across the room, Mason stopped. "We haven't got any of their *'items'* here, have we? Are we in danger?"

"No. Nothing except the records we've always had. And I have bad news. Barnaby Armstrong is dead. He was the order's mole."

Mason seemed to deflate a little more. "I knew Barnaby. Not well, but... That's terrible news. What a fool, to get himself involved with such things."

"And Mason, I may have to go to JD's tonight—"

Mason cut in, "That's fine. Do what you have to do. Anything that helps find them is fine by me."

TWENTY-FOUR

Shadow stood before another set of burnished doors, this time made from a variety of metals in a complex design, wishing the others would hurry up.

Despite their best efforts, they were unable to open the gate that had trapped them inside. The mechanism that triggered its release was hidden from view, and they had unwillingly conceded that they needed to proceed. At least they knew there was another way out—admittedly through Black Cronos. They had just spent the last ten minutes walking through another long hall decorated with carved panels depicting the Igigi's flight from the Anunnaki. The carvings were elaborate and stunningly intact, and recorded a more detailed version of the founding of their city than what had been displayed on the tablet.

Shadow was the least overawed of all of them. Catarina, Estelle, and the Nephilim had lingered, virtually speechless as they studied the images and the story. The Nephilims' wonder had been compounded by the fact that they were mentioned frequently, as were the Fallen, and she watched them wrestle with their emotions as they drank it all in.

Gabe was especially shaken. When she had woken earlier after a short but heavy sleep, it was to find Gabe wide awake, staring at the roof of the tent, a sheen of sweat on his brow that had nothing to do with the heat. His eyes held shock and anger, and it was with much effort that she had finally persuaded him to tell her what was wrong.

Remiel.

Neither could decide what that meant. *Was Gabe's father watching their every move? And if so, why hadn't he physically appeared?*

They had decided not to tell the others, but Gabe was clearly distracted, and she was sure the others had noticed, especially Nahum. Perhaps they had put it down to finding the city. For all of their wishes and expectations, it had surprised everyone. But now time was marching on, and Black Cronos was already ahead of them.

"Guys!" she shouted. "We need to get on! We can come back to this later."

While they tarried, she studied the doors. There was no sign of any cog mechanism, and she laid her hand on one of them and pushed. As if on oiled hinges, it swung open easily, and gripping both swords, she stepped into the blackness beyond.

The torch light from behind her illuminated a short distance ahead. She had stepped onto a broad balcony, but below was a black void that even her keen eyesight couldn't penetrate. On either side, a fretted stonework balcony stretched into darkness, and she sensed huge space ahead of her.

Sheathing one sword, she pulled her battery-powered torch out, but the beam barely pierced the dark. By this time the team had lined up next to her, and Estelle's witch-lights revealed that they were overlooking a vast city carved out of the rock, and in front of them a broad sweep of steps led down into its heart.

Catarina found her voice first. "Oh, my God. This is enormous. This is far more than I was expecting!"

"This surpasses anything they built for the Anunnaki," Ash murmured. "I wonder if they managed to get light into here somehow?"

TWENTY-FOUR

The city comprised of a variety of buildings, some of which were huge, while others were smaller dwellings. Holes in the distant cave walls suggested other tunnels or even houses built into the rock itself. The buildings staggered downwards like an inverted pyramid to a flat section at the bottom. Something glassy was reflected in the witch-lights, and Shadow realised it was a series of waterways at the bottom. In addition to the buildings were enormous, carved statues—all half man, half beast, with the heads of eagles, wolves, bears, and other animals.

Barak pointed to the opposite side of the city. "There are tunnels to the rear. Perhaps they lead to other parts of the city." He turned to the others, a question in his eyes. "They must have buried their dead down here, so it may even be a burial ground."

Gabe nodded. "It makes sense that it would be beyond the city proper." He turned to Nahum and Barak, who still had their wings extended. "Fly over the city, and we'll progress on foot for now."

But as they approached the top step, torchlights flared again, illuminating the perimeter of the city, and a few spots below.

"Fuck it," Niel muttered, swinging his torch. "Things like this don't work after hundreds of years without something maintaining them. We're walking into a trap."

Ash shook his head. "I'm not so sure. They designed ingenious systems of lights and hydraulics…" But he stopped speaking, instead staring beyond Niel.

Shadow stepped to his side, wondering what he was looking at, but instead was distracted by a statue at the top of the stairs that seemed to shift in the firelight. She blinked to clear her eyes, thinking it was a trick of the light.

But it was no trick, and gripping her swords, she yelled, "The statues are coming to life!"

"They aren't bloody statues!" Gabe yelled back, lining up next to her. "It's the Igigi!"

As another huge gate dropped behind them, trapping them inside, the Igigi moved with lightning speed. He lifted the long spears in his hands and lunged at Gabe and Shadow. Both leapt out the way, weapons raised to defend rather than attack. But other Igigi where appearing out of the darkness, their immense shadows advancing before them as they hunted down the Nephilim.

Catarina screamed, and Shadow felt rather than saw the effects of Estelle's magic as she repelled another attack. But Shadow could only concentrate on her own battle. She had seen many odd creatures in her life in the Otherworld, but there was no doubt that the Igigi advancing on her was *very* odd. It was easily eight feet tall, with the body of a man but the head of a wolf. Its skin was of burnished gold and its eyes gleaned like silver.

Its movements were so swift that Shadow barely had time to react. She needed to up her game. She drew on her fey magic, normally shielded from the others, and instantly felt her speed and perception increase. But Gabe had insisted they not kill the Igigi if they encountered them, and she kept his words in mind while she ducked and defended. *If only the Igigi knew that.*

Several Igigi were advancing on either side, and the team was trapped within the narrow confines of the balcony. Shadow had the feeling that the Igigi had purposefully waited to lure them into the city's gates before attacking.

As her opponent's spear came within millimetres of plunging into her stomach, she leapt over the balustrade and onto the rooftops below. Fortunately, the first was only a few feet beneath the balcony. The city, as she had noticed earlier, staggered downwards to the flat centre below, and she leapt from rooftop to rooftop, hoping that the Nephilim were protecting Catarina. She certainly couldn't get close to her. But she had achieved some breathing space from her attacker, because she was far nimbler than it was. She was now several levels down, trying to decide how to evade the creature and return to her team.

But then the wolf-headed Igigi bellowed and followed her onto the rooftops.

Gabe was battling his own Igigi as they almost fell down the broad set of steps. Nahum was flying overhead, and she saw him swoop down to collect Catarina, but her rescue was short-lived. An eagle-headed Igigi with enormous wings soared through the cavernous space and attacked Nahum, forcing him to veer away dramatically.

Ash, Zee, and Niel were all fighting back-to-back as half a dozen Igigi surrounded them, and Estelle, like Shadow, had dropped onto the rooftops, protecting herself with blasts of magic. Barak was nowhere to be seen.

A sudden movement from above made Shadow throw herself on the flat rooftop, face-up, and with horror she saw an eagle-headed Igigi swoop down on her. She had just enough time to roll into a gap between buildings, and found herself on the street level, dwarfed by the huge stone edifices. A warren of lanes—much like the lanes in old Mardin—spread out in a web around her.

She raced through them, trying to find a way back to the stairs, and heard Gabe yell something unintelligible in what she presumed was the Sumerian language. She followed his voice, but found the path blocked by another Igigi, its silver eyes watching her dispassionately.

Barak was high above the city in the cavernous recess of the roof, which was as beautifully finished as the rest of the city. Niches had been cut in the walls, and while many were empty, others were not.

Three Igigi emerged from their perches, their enormous wingspan buffeting the air as they advanced on Barak, weapons drawn. They came at him from all sides, but he dropped like a stone, plunging from their advance to find airspace below. His smaller size gave him greater agility, and he was thankful that he was born to fight, whereas they were not. But they were still quick and strong.

He glanced below, noting his brothers similarly embattled, and was relieved to see that Estelle was managing to defend herself. *But how long could this last, for any one of them?* They desperately didn't want to kill the Igigi, but wounding them was inevitable in their effort to get away.

Suddenly he was grabbed from behind, his wings half crushed between the steely grip of his attacker, and he yelled in Sumerian, "Stop fighting! We're here to help!"

"You should have thought of that before you invaded our home, Nephilim!"

Barak brought his fist up and smashed behind his shoulder, smacking his opponent in the face. But he didn't lose his grip, and they plunged towards the water at the base of the city.

Estelle was casting several spells, but they all seemed to bounce off the advancing Igigi like they were wearing some kind of spell-resistant armour.

She grunted with frustration, presuming it was their supernatural abilities that offered them protection. At least the blasts of power were keeping them off-guard. *Just*. Like Shadow, she scrambled across the rooftops, but nowhere near as agilely. Wishing she had Caspian's mastery of air magic, she kept running and slipping, her hands now starting to bleed as they caught on the jagged edges of tiles and rock.

This was a nightmare. And they were being driven further and further into the city. She couldn't be sure, but she had the horrible feeling they were not planning to kill them, but capture them, and that couldn't be for any good purpose.

As two Igigi advanced on her she realised she needed an ally, and unfortunately, Shadow was it. She clambered to where she had last seen her, and then dropped from the roof into the street below, shrouding herself in a shadow spell as she raced down the lane. Little light illuminated down here, and by the time the Igigi pursing her had reached where she had been, she'd be long gone and invisible.

Drawn by Gabe's voice, she rounded the corner to see Shadow up ahead, her path blocked by a wolf-headed Igigi wielding a spear in one hand, and a curved sword in the other. Estelle took a moment to study the strange being. His thighs were thick with corded muscles, as were his arms. He wore ornately engraved armour—breastplate, arm and leg guards—and a long cloth with embroidered edges was wrapped around his waist. Everything about him reminded Estelle of Anubis. He advanced on Shadow, looking impregnable, his bulk blocking the way ahead.

Shadow was backing up, but wasn't running, no doubt assessing her options. Estelle decided to help, aiming a spell at the section of wall next to the Igigi. The stone blocks exploded, blasting the creature backwards. Estelle hurled a ball of energy at him, forcing him back further.

Estelle hissed, "Shadow, over here!"

Shadow spun around, eyes narrowed, and ran to her voice, Estelle lifting her cloaking spell for the briefest of moments. "Was that your handywork?" she whispered. "Great timing."

"I know. I'm a witch." Estelle decided to answer as cockily as Shadow did. As the thundering of footsteps sounded overhead, Estelle draped them both in her shadow spell and turned. "This way."

Niel yelled at his brothers, "We need to join the others—take to the air!"

Zee grunted as he ducked and rolled. "All very well, brother, but that's not so easy right now!"

Niel swung his axe, trying to get the Igigi surrounding them to back off rather than hurt them, but that was not easy, either. "Any ideas, Ash?"

"A time machine?"

"Not funny." Niel arched backwards to avoid the brutal thrust of a spear, and swung his axe up, shattering the spearhead and earning him time and space. He glanced around him in the brief seconds of respite he had before another attack, and noticed something odd. "There are no others coming. They're either hiding, or this is it." He brought his sword up to form a cross with his axe and repelled another attack.

"A final guard, you mean?" Ash said, panting heavily now.

"Exactly. If we can get through this…"

"Gabe is on the stairs," Zee said. "We need to get to him. If we strike as one coordinated force now, we'll make enough room to escape. Let's extend our wings together—one powerful thrust will send them all back."

As they fought to give themselves enough space, Ash yelled, "Now!"

Nahum clutched Catarina to his side, noticing she felt like a wounded bird fluttering in his hands.

He was shaking her around like a rag doll, and knew he had to get her onto the ground, but he couldn't leave her. She was far too vulnerable, and he wasn't sure where the safest place was. He'd managed to fend off one attack, but noticed they were being herded to the city centre—a large square surrounded by canals.

In fact, he realised as he studied the area, *down there were no other Igigi at all*. No one was emerging from the buildings or streets. The whole place was deserted, like a ghost city. *But was it a trap?* He had a sudden idea.

"Catarina, are you okay?"

She was breathless when she answered. "Hardly, but I'll survive—thanks to you."

"I'm going to check the tunnel at the back. Hold tight."

She managed a grunting laugh. "Like I'd let go!"

He soared to the tunnel, grateful that he seemed to have passed by undetected, for now. The tunnel entrance was huge and once he arrived there, he could see passages leading off it. It was a maze down there. He strained to hear anything, but the noise of the fight in the city behind him smothered any other sounds. And if Black Cronos was down there, they weren't close...yet.

They needed a truce, but right now, Nahum wasn't sure they were going to get it.

Gabe gripped his sword and backed down the steps, aware of other Igigi advancing on him.

Scanning the area, he estimated there were at least twenty Igigi of various types moving in on them from around the city, and several more overhead. He was furious with himself. Although they had debated their existence, he had seriously doubted that they were really alive, and now they were under attack and struggling.

His first appeal had been ignored, so he tried again, speaking in their language once more. "Stop fighting us. You are under attack by another group, and we are here to help you!"

The snake-headed Igigi he was fighting laughed. "You have never helped us before, Nephilim. It is because of you we are here."

"Not true!" he shot back. "It is because of your rebellion against the Anunnaki that you are here. We had our own orders to follow."

While the Igigi wasn't actively attacking him, he kept advancing, and Gabe kept retreating down the broad stairs. A blast of falling rubble came from his right, indicating that the other Igigi had not stopped fighting, and he saw Ash, Zee, and Niel all take to the air as they forced their attackers back. Within moments, all of them landed behind him.

A flurry of wings from above had him ducking, but it was Nahum and Barak, both swooping down, with Nahum clutching Catarina tightly in one arm, his sword in the other. But Shadow and Estelle were nowhere in sight. The only clue to their whereabouts were the few Igigi fanning out across the rooftops, and he hoped they were hiding somewhere. Winged Igigi landed on the steps behind them, and Gabe realised they were surrounded.

He turned to the others, sheathing his sword and shouting, "Put your weapons away!" Niel hesitated, a mutinous expression on his face, and he added, "Niel—do it!"

Glaring at him, Niel did as he asked, but his fingers hovered over the butt of his axe—just in case.

"See!" He appealed to his opponent, extending his empty hands and gesturing to the others. "We wish you no harm. We're here to help!"

The snake-headed Igigi didn't answer, instead stepping back to make way for an enormous Igigi who landed with surprising grace for his size. He was winged and had the head of a hawk. His shoulders were huge, his wings much bigger than Gabe's own, and he cocked his head, a steely glint in his eye.

"You should be dead, Nephilim. How are you here?"

"A quirk of fate." He decided to be honest in the hope that it earned him some trust. "We died in the flood, and had a second chance when a portal allowed us to come back here. Only my six brothers and I returned."

His eyes narrowed. "Only seven from all the hundreds? Then you've fared even worse than us. Your name?"

"Gabreel of the House of Remiel. Greetings from my house to yours." He straightened up, throwing his shoulders back and drawing himself up to his full height. He often tried not to look imposing. He knew his height and build were threatening. But this was an Igigi, and trying to shrink away from who he was would do none of them any favours. "And your name?"

"Gishkim, named after my ancestor, the great Hawk Igigi who led the rebellion and the flight to independence."

Gabe nodded as the memories flashed through his mind. "I remember your ancestor. He was powerful and wise. I apologise for this intrusion, and seek permission to be in your city."

Gishkim's mouth twisted into a smile. "Gabreel, son of Remiel. You are mentioned in our stories. You and your men pursued us for weeks. Many of our dead fell at your hands."

"And many of mine at yours. We were different men in those days. They were the years when our fathers had more sway—before we sought our own independence."

"I know something of this. Scraps of news filtered down to our city when we dared venture to the surface. Before the flood that killed you." He glanced around him. "A flood that almost killed us, too."

Gabe nodded. "We had expected you to be dead." *In fact, how the hell had they survived down here without sunlight for all these years?* It seemed impossible.

Ignoring Gabe's confusion, he said, "So, you have come to raid our city."

"No! We have come to help defend you against an attack from a mutual enemy."

"Even though you thought us dead?" Gishkim looked amused. "The dead don't need defending."

"It's complicated. You are under attack right now. Your back gate has been blown wide open, and men are—"

Gishkim cut him short. "We know. Others have gone to intercept them. They will not get far—like you." He shook his head, a sneer starting on his lips. "Always so superior, Nephilim. You forget we have strengths, too."

"But those are no normal men," Gabe said, his eyes not leaving Gishkim's golden ones. "They carry odd weapons and unusual powers."

"And you are the sons of the Fallen, and yet we have captured you." He gestured to the Igigi who surrounded them, spears and swords drawn. "But your team is different. Two humans, and someone from beyond our world." He glanced around, perturbed. "She is missing, as is one of the humans. Where are they?"

"I have no idea. Hiding, I suspect, in fear for their lives." Gabe just hoped they weren't injured, or about to do something catastrophic. He fought back his impatience. "But you don't understand. It's not your riches the others want. It's *you*!"

A distant explosion rocked through the city, and everyone swung around to look towards where the tunnels led further underground. Gabe closed his eyes briefly. *Please let that not be Estelle and Shadow.*

Gishkim immediately dispatched half a dozen Igigi, and then gestured to the Nephilim. "You're coming with us."

TWENTY-FIVE

Harlan watched JD's deft hands as he placed the small metal ball in the centre of his complex grid, and then adjusted the outer circles.

"I was going about it all wrong," JD told him, his lips pressing into a thin line. "I was trying to change the properties that the metal already has, when I should have just started afresh using the base metal."

"Okay," Harlan drawled, wondering what he was going on about. "That means what, exactly?"

JD pointed to the rows of bubbling jars that were connected by a series of tubes. "The metal is put into its base state, and then its alchemical correspondences are refined and adjusted—to you, the planets, all of it. Then I put it into a mould to make the weapon and fix those properties, and then reduce it again." He gave Harlan a wolfish grin. "I won't bore you with the details."

"Good. It's already gibberish."

"Watch." He turned the final circle, and the copper ball in the centre morphed into a copper blade. "Pick it up."

Harlan eyed it warily and then glanced at JD, who looked like an excited child. Taking a deep breath, Harlan picked it up, holding the blade on his outstretched hand as if it might bite. A strange tingling sensation started in his palm and flowed up his arm, and he almost dropped it. "What the fuck! It's doing something to me!"

"Wait!" JD instructed. "Let it settle."

Harlan glared at his arm and the dagger, willing nothing else to happen. He liked his arm just the way it was. "What now?"

"What now? You are an utter nincompoop! Look! It isn't changing."

"Oh!" Harlan suddenly realised what he meant. "It's holding its shape."

"Because it's attuned to you." JD took the blade from Harlan's palm and it changed shape again. "See? It won't hold its shape for me. No matter what I do, it will never be a weapon." He placed it back on Harlan's hand again, watching with glee as it changed shape once more.

"But Black Cronos can change their weapons' shape seemingly at will. From nothing to weapon and back again instantly. How do I do that?"

JD stared at him expectantly. "Have you *tried* changing it by will?"

"Like with my mind?" Harlan looked at him like he'd gone crazy, but JD continue to stare at him, so he focussed on the blade, willing it to change shape as he clenched his hand. "I feel like a dick. Nothing is happening."

JD's shoulders slumped again. "One step at a time. I haven't worked that bit out yet." He studied Harlan with narrowed eyes. "Maybe it's because you haven't been enhanced yet. It's attuned to you, but maybe there should be something more…"

"Oh, no!" Harlan dropped the weapon on the bench like it burned his hand and stepped away. "You are not changing me! I am not turning into one of those creatures. No way!"

"You aren't even slightly tempted? You could fight with the Nephilim on equal terms."

"I don't give a crap about that." Harlan stared at JD, horrified. "Those men and women were cold—their eyes dead. And that Silencer of Souls..." He trailed off, his horror at her memory already making his skin crawl. "They're unnatural! We don't know what it does to their mind—their soul! No way. And besides, you said they were aberrations! Have you changed your mind?"

JD looked sheepish. "No, but I thought it might be possible to just do a mild enhancement. I am intrigued about it all."

Harlan changed tack. "How are you getting on with finding an antidote?"

"I'm not. I don't know nearly enough to start doing that. My enthusiasm got the better of me the other day."

Harlan felt sorry for him. It must be frustrating to be so clever and yet not know anything about the supernatural enhancements. Another thought struck Harlan. "Barnaby Armstrong, The Order of the Midnight Sun's secretary and Inner Adept, wasn't enhanced. He was just a regular guy in bad clothes."

"Hmm, food for thought."

JD's eyes still gleamed with intrigue, and Harlan stepped back again. The only comfort he had was that he was younger, bigger, and much stronger than JD—just in case he tried to restrain him in some way.

As if he'd read his mind, JD rolled his eyes. "Calm down. I'm not about to do anything to you. I'm just frustrated. It's clever. Ingenious, even."

"You're clever, too. You'll work it out—just not by using me as a guinea pig. By the way, Barnaby was researching the *Comte de Saint-Germain*."

"Really? Interesting." JD sat on a stool, staring intently at Harlan. "Did he say why?"

Harlan grimaced. "He's dead, so no."

"Dead? Not another one! This is worrying. They seem to have abandoned their low-key activities completely."

"Well, to be fair, we don't *know* they killed him, but it's the most likely answer. Killed by The Silencer of Souls, we think."

"Her again..."

"Maggie Milne found some papers in his bank deposit box. But everything points to him maybe preparing to blackmail them, or even just safeguard his future. That didn't work, obviously."

"And what were his findings on the count?"

"We're still going through his notes, but he assembled a list of places associated with him. We thought we could cross-reference it with your ideas." He pulled a copy of the list from his messenger bag that lay on the bench and passed it to JD.

JD grunted as he read, huffing occasionally. "There are some addresses in here I've not heard of, but a few I have. There are a couple in England."

"I know. We thought we should start with those."

"He didn't like England. Had a bad experience here, apparently. However, he did carry out secret missions in England for King Louis XV of France. He was very close to him for years."

Harlan shrugged. "Whether he liked the place or not, those addresses are still worth investigating."

"Of course. He would likely do whatever would confound people." JD's face wrinkled with distaste. "Odd little man." Harlan tried not to smile as JD uttered the phrase they all used to describe him, but JD hadn't noticed and was already continuing. "How are you going to investigate them?"

"Do the basics first, like checking ownership records to see if anything odd is going on, and then some covert surveillance."

JD nodded and walked over to inspect the potions bubbling in jars. Harlan shouldered his bag, ready to leave as JD said, "I suggest you be careful. If his defence systems are anything like mine, you'd be dead before you even knew what was happening." JD shot him a speculative look. "Where are Gabe and Shadow?"

"Still in Turkey...I think. I haven't heard from them." A knot of worry tightened in his gut. "They were chasing down the lead on the Igigi and their hidden city."

"The Igigi!" JD's eyebrows shot up. "You didn't mention them."

"That's what they found beneath Arklet Abbey. We think Black Cronos is looking to find Igigi bones or something of the sort. Something else to experiment on." Surprised, he added, "You've heard of them, then?"

"Of course. Sumerian slaves to the Anunnaki." JD cocked his head on one side and tapped his lips thoughtfully. "Did you know they were the first recorded civilisation to have used crystals in magic?"

"No. Do you think it's relevant?"

"I don't know. But remember, the count liked his crystals, too." He turned away, inspecting his alembic jars again. "Something to consider, perhaps."

Harlan had been preoccupied with the weapon and the count's old haunts, and had pushed the Igigi to the back of his mind, but now he decided that they warranted further investigation. It was time to leave.

"I'll be in touch, JD," he said, taking one last look at the alchemical grid before weaving through the benches.

"If you change your mind on taking our experiments a little further, let me know."

"I can assure you, I will not."

And with JD's dubious offer ringing in his ears, Harlan hurried to the stairs, eager to leave what he was beginning to think of as JD's dungeon.

Nahum sat on the stone floor of the confined room they'd been placed in and watched Gabe pace relentlessly. It wasn't a cell, but it was secure.

The walls were constructed of huge blocks of stone, all expertly fitted together with barely a seam visible, and the roof was made of vaulted wood and lined with sheets of metal. There were no windows, and the only way in or out was through a thick, iron-barred, wooden door. But there were decorative reliefs on the walls painted in rich colours, huge designs that stretched from floor to ceiling.

Ash was talking quietly with Zee and Catarina, and Niel and Barak were investigating every single part of the room, trying to find a way to escape it.

Nahum suspected they were in a records room of some kind, although why it should be so secure, he wasn't sure. Frankly, he was too distracted right now to take any real notice of the space. Their weapons had been taken from them, and Gabe had shot them all a warning look to comply with instructions. Nahum knew he was determined to prove they were allies, but that wasn't really working right now.

"We have to find a way out of here," Niel said, abandoning his search and pounding the door with his fist.

"Not like that, you idiot," Nahum said wearily. "Save your strength. The fact that we're not dead yet bodes well. I think they want to check out our story."

"Or hunt down Estelle and Shadow and use them for leverage."

Nahum snorted. "They clearly don't know them, do they? I just hope those two haven't killed each other."

A spark gleamed in Niel's eyes. "Want to wager who would win in a fight? I think I'd go with Shadow."

Barak clearly felt he needed to defend his almost-girlfriend. "Estelle can hold her own!"

"I can barely hold my own against Shadow," Gabe pointed out. "I'd rather hope they're working together."

TWENTY-FIVE

"Do you think the explosion was them?" Ash asked, ending his conversation with Zee and Catarina.

"I doubt it." Nahum leaned back against the wall, trying to get comfortable. "It was too far down that tunnel. There's no way they could have got there so quickly. It had to have been Black Cronos."

Catarina's eyes were wide. "They're using explosives?"

"We warned you," Ash told her as he turned away to study the carved panels. "They're relentless. I just wish the Igigi would let us help. Perhaps Shadow and Estelle are trying to get us out right now."

"With three Igigi outside?" Zee said, looking doubtful. "Unlikely. Besides, it would undermine our offer of help if we broke out. We need Gishkim to know that he needs us."

"Unless Black Cronos gets to him first," Barak pointed out. "And then it won't be him coming through that door. It will be *them*."

Shadow sat on the rooftop closest to the tunnel entrance, Estelle next to her. Both were veiled in the invisibility spell, and Shadow enhanced it with her own fey magic.

They had lost their pursuers a good ten minutes ago, and had watched Gabe and the others get locked in a building in the narrow streets at the rear of the city, close to the cavern walls.

"Gabe would not thank us for breaking him out," Shadow murmured to Estelle. "He wants to do this the right way. It's important to him."

"It would be tricky with guards posted on the door," Estelle said, "but it's doable. What worries me more is what's happening down there."

For the last few minutes, they had seen the Igigi running or flying down the tunnel, and so far, no one had returned. "If Black Cronos overrun them and end up here, we're all in trouble. I think we should go and see what's happening."

"And leave the others locked up?" Estelle's scorn dripped from her words. "They'll be furious!"

"Missing your boyfriend already?" Shadow countered, unable to keep the sarcasm from her voice.

There was a momentary pause, and then Estelle answered, her voice like ice. "He is not my boyfriend."

"Well, he should be," Shadow pointed out, miffed on Barak's behalf, even though he had never uttered one word of reproach about Estelle. But Shadow could see how he looked at her. "He won't wait forever."

"He doesn't need to wait forever! I'm just...sorting things out in my head. Besides, you and Gabe waited long enough!"

"We had business concerns."

"Bullshit. You were as worried about messing things up as I am. Anyway, this is not the time for us to be talking about our love lives—or lack of."

"There's no *lack* of on my behalf, I can assure you."

"Shadow, you are the most irritating woman. I don't know why I even rescued you!"

"*Rescued*? I didn't need rescuing!" Shadow clenched her blades. "You are infuriating."

Another blast echoed down the tunnel, this time carrying dust and shouts, and as awful as that was, Shadow was very grateful for the distraction.

"Come on. We've waited too long. They need our help," she said, slipping off the roof and landing softly on the ground.

"And the others?" Estelle asked, landing next to her.

"We can come back, if needed. And besides, Gishkim is no fool. He'll come for Gabe if he needs help. And if he doesn't, we'll have to talk him into it."

TWENTY-FIVE

As the sound of the second explosion died away, Barak pounded on the door. "Let us out! We can help!"

He didn't advertise the fact that the main part of his worry was Estelle, although he knew his brothers sensed it. When silence greeted him, he pounded again. "We're sitting ducks in here! Let us out!"

"It sounded closer that time," Zee said, his usually calm demeanour now ruffled. "What the hell is happening out there?"

Ash turned away from the decorative panels he was studying with Catarina. "I just hope it's the dead they're raiding, and Black Cronos is not trying to capture the Igigi."

"We can't afford for either of those scenarios to happen, but I wouldn't put anything past Black Cronos, or..." Gabe paused, anger written all over his face.

"Or *who*?" Barak asked, finally stopping his banging on the door.

Gabe raked his hands through his hair. "I had a dream last night. Except, I don't think it was a dream, not really."

Nahum cast a puzzled glance at the others. "You're not making any sense, Gabe. What do you mean?"

Gabe was looking at the floor, but then he finally looked up at them. "I heard from my father last night. He said I was to finish the job—as in, kill the Igigi."

A stunned silence followed, but Ash found his voice first. "It had to be a dream, Gabe. It's just being here again that brought it all back."

"No. It was no dream. It was him. His voice passed through me, just like it always did. Like a blade." He wiped sweat from his brow. "I hoped we'd left them all behind. Have any of you heard anything from your fathers? Nahum?"

Everyone shook their heads, Barak included, and Nahum rose to his feet to grip Gabe's shoulder. "Why would our father contact you and not me?"

"I don't know! But I'm sure it wasn't just a dream. He sounded too angry."

"Dreams can feel like that," Barak pointed out. "Ever since my injury and that strange healing, I've had dreams of my father. They've woken me in a cold sweat sometimes, too." *More times than he'd care to admit, actually.* Barak, like his brothers, enjoyed his freedom in this intriguing new world, and had no wish for a battle of wills with his father again.

Gabe met Barak's eyes, fear and anger in his own. "I'm not wrong. And I'm damn sure not going to be a slave to that again. I'd rather die first."

"Woah!" Niel intervened. "There'll be no dying. They couldn't control us in the end back then, and I'm certain they can't do it now."

"And we've been here for months," Zee added, "and haven't heard a thing. Only Niel had that encounter with Chassan, and that led to nothing. And found those weapons, of course..."

Niel grunted with annoyance. "I still haven't worked out why they were there! Why put our weapons in Raziel's own temple? It doesn't make sense."

"Guys," Catarina said, breaking into their conversation, "let's focus on where we are now. There seem to be other stories on these panels...stories from after the battle."

"She's right," Ash said, turning to study them again. "These are stories about the building of their city. Look at the images of falling water, and what seems to be a light source coming from above."

They all stepped closer to examine the panels, and Barak said, "I flew to the roof of the cave earlier. Like the ceiling here, the roof is vaulted and lined with various metals, but I didn't have time to examine it properly before I was attacked. There might be some kind of light up there—something covered up right now."

"And," Zee added, "there are plenty of canals going through the city. There's no running water now, though."

Catarina pointed at the far panels. "But look—there are images of fields and irrigation systems. Rivers and lakes. Did they live above ground for a while?"

"Unlikely," Gabe said, obviously puzzled as he studied the carvings. "And look at the edges. The curve suggests a cave wall again."

Gabe was right. The edges of the panel did suggest a curve, which meant the fields and irrigation were underground.

"Seeing as you can't grow food in darkness," Barak said, "what in Herne's horns did they use for light?"

A baffled silence followed the question, until Ash directed them to another panel. "This depicts a battle in the city with creatures with wings—and it wasn't us! We never found this place!"

"This image right here," Catarina said, pointing, "depicts a body of water, and look at the huge waves that tower over the mountains. Could it be a flood? *The Flood*?"

"You're right," Barak said with certainty as he studied the expert carvings. "It has to be. The city survived it...no doubt a tribute to their engineering."

Nahum's eyes narrowed. "But the fight with the winged men occurs after that panel—after the flood. We were all dead then. And like Ash said, we never found this city."

"So, who are they fighting with?" Niel asked. "Did Nephilim survive?"

"Oh shit," Gabe groaned. "Our fathers. They must have resumed the battle after the flood. Perhaps the flood was meant to kill the Igigi, too."

Zee huffed, hands on hips. "Our fathers doing their own dirty work? Unlikely."

"Unless they were compelled to," Ash said thoughtfully. "Our God—and I use the term *our* loosely—wasn't the only God, obviously. The Anunnaki were Gods too, and while some Gods have numerous titles depending on who worships them, there were many others, all of whom had their own powers, whims, and fancies. Myths across the world talk about a giant flood. We have always harboured the belief that our God caused the flood, but what if the Gods worked together to make this happen...a chance to start again? The Igigi rebelled against their masters, just like we did. We died, they didn't."

Barak stared at Ash, disturbed at the scale of what he suggested. "You're suggesting it was a clean-up job? So why aren't the Igigi all dead?"

Nahum's eyes gleamed. "Because the Fallen are fallible. They always were. That's why they fell in the first place. The Igigi found a way to beat them, or to..." he faltered, searching for words.

Catarina finished his sentence. "To render them powerless. They removed them as a threat, somehow."

A commotion outside the door interrupted their conversation, and they turned quickly, prepared to fight.

Gishkim threw the door open, sending it crashing against the wall as he burst inside, eyes blazing with fury. "Our attackers are trying to capture us, and are desecrating the City of the Dead! Why?"

Gabe stepped up to him. "I told you. To study you and recreate you, and they'll do it any way they can. And I fear the bones of your ancestors won't be enough. It's your magic that intrigues them—your mix of brains and physicality, animal and human. They will put you in cages and study you. Is that what you want?"

Gishkim growled. "No! Does your offer of help still stand?"

"Of course it does!"

"Then follow me—except for you." He pointed at Catarina, and then at the wolf-headed Igigi behind him. "You will stay here under Urbarra's guard."

TWENTY-FIVE

Catarina stepped back, eyes widening with fear, but Ash placed a reassuring hand on her arm. "It's for the best. We'll see you soon." But as he passed Urbarra on the way out of the room, he glared at him. "If you hurt her in any way, you'll answer to me."

Barak nodded his own reassurance at Catarina, suddenly aware of her fragility. He followed his brothers, but paused on the threshold, staring into Urbarra's cold eyes, and decided to back up Ash's threat with his own. "You'll answer to all of us."

TWENTY-SIX

Shadow raced down the main tunnel leading out of the city as fast as she could, while still allowing Estelle to keep up.

She was tempted to just abandon her, preferring to fight on her own, but although Estelle had plenty of magic to deal with whatever might come next, Shadow couldn't quite bring herself to let her fend for herself. *Damn it. Was she starting to like the woman?*

The tunnel was dark, lit only by the occasional flaring torch on the wall. They passed several smaller side-tunnels all of them in total darkness, but the commotion was coming from ahead. They raced around a bend and into a cloud of dust and smoke.

Shadow slowed, pulling her shirt over her mouth and nose. A section of the roof had fallen down, a mix of rubble and huge blocks of stone. She warily looked up, spotting gaping holes in the ceiling, but the solid rock beyond the stone blocks remained intact—for now.

She could sense Estelle next to her rather than see her, and said, "They're trying to seal the passage."

"We'd better get inside then before they succeed," Estelle answered, already moving forward.

In another few feet the dust cleared, revealing a series of interconnected caves ahead of them, filled with ziggurats of various sizes and designs, and Shadow presumed they were towering memorials to the dead. The tunnel emerged onto a colonnaded walkway partway up the cave wall, another just above it, reminding Shadow of cloisters. A place for reflection, perhaps, but these seemed deserted right now.

Fire provided the only light, from the torches placed on the walls to huge metal braziers casting grotesque shadows on the ground. Off to the side was another tunnel, at the entrance of which Shadow saw the bright, white-blond hair of Toto and a few soldiers. But within the burial city a fierce battle was raging. Shadow estimated two dozen Igigi were fighting Black Cronos soldiers, some in groups, others alone. A couple of Igigi were flying overhead, but the soldiers were trying to pick them off with crossbow bolts. Fortunately, the Igigi had their own longbows, but it meant the air zinged with arrows, adding to the hazards. Already there were unmoving bodies from both parties littering the ground.

Shadow pulled both her swords free—the Empusa's and the Dragonium one—and twirled them with lightning speed. She grinned at Estelle, eager to get into the fight. "May your aim be accurate, and kills be swift. Hunt well, Estelle."

Estelle returned her grin with her own tight-lipped one. "Hunt well, Shadow." She surveyed the cave with narrowed eyes, and targeting the biggest group of soldiers, launched fireball after fireball at them.

Shadow vaulted down the steps, rounded the first ziggurat, and immediately saw three soldiers battling a snake-headed Igigi. He staggered back under the onslaught, a deep cut along one heavily muscled arm, and Shadow saw his eyes glaze as he stumbled backwards.

Poisoned blades. It had to be. Much like the poisoned bolt that struck Barak.

Unseen by the soldiers who were already closing in, one of them carrying a long pole with prongs at the end, she gleefully attacked them from behind whilst cloaked in her fey magic. She stabbed one in the back, dragging her sword across him and virtually slicing him in two, decapitated the other, and as the third whipped around, alarmed, she cut his throat. In seconds, all three lay dead at her feet, and the Igigi was swaying, eyes dazed.

Shadow pointed to the dark entrance of the closest ziggurat. "You've been poisoned. Get yourself in there and hide."

She had no idea if he could understand, and she hadn't got time to hang around and find out. Gesturing once more she ran onward, her blood singing to be back in battle. This is what she was born for, and when her time came, this is how she wanted to die. But now was not that time.

Today she would take her revenge on The Silencer of Souls.

Estelle was using her shadow spell periodically, casting it on and off as she needed to like a cloak. It was no longer useful whilst hurling fireballs and spells at the battle below, but when she ran from place to place, it masked her movements, causing confusion for her pursuers.

She was already drawing the ire of the Black Cronos soldiers armed with crossbows, and she ran along the walkway, sheltering behind the thick stone columns before taking pot shots.

A soldier with a crossbow was racing up the stairs to Estelle's level, leaving her vulnerable on that side. With a well-aimed blast, Estelle took out the balustrade, hurling the stone into the soldier. The collision threw her attacker onto the ziggurat below, and she landed in a mangled heap.

Estelle ran to the left, casting her shadow spell around her again before sheltering behind a column. She edged around it, pleased to see half a dozen soldiers running to intercept her, and immediately ran in the opposite direction. She paused behind another column, this time much closer to the entrance of the tunnel where Toto watched the battle, his expression tight. She suspected the bulky area on his shoulder was a dressing over the injury that Shadow had inflicted. He certainly seemed to hold it awkwardly. A guard looked in her direction, and regardless of her spell, she ducked behind the pillar.

Estelle took a deep breath, trying to calm her racing heart, while thinking of a spell for Toto that would be both insidious and unexpected. *A spell to heat the blood would do it.* She rounded the column, the words already forming on her lips, her intent sure. But Toto had vanished, and in fury she used it on a nearby soldier instead. He roared and fell to his knees. The others whirled around, one aiming a strange weapon at her. A blast of energy struck the column next to her, the stone shattering, and she dived to the floor.

Bollocks.

Gabe and his brothers flew down the tunnel to the City of the Dead, emerging through the dust of the explosions to see the fight raging below.

Gabe's first thoughts flew to Shadow. *Where was she?* He scanned the area, but it was too dark beyond the pools of firelight, and he knew she'd be using her fey magic to conceal herself. He next wondered where all the Igigi were coming from. The city they had left was in darkness, deserted. But before he could reason through it, a bloodcurdling cry made him wheel in the air, just in time to avoid a long spear hurled from the darkness below.

Their arrival had drawn attention.

Gishkim was already shooting arrows at Black Cronos's soldiers, but many of the Igigi were struggling with the onslaught. Black Cronos were using their unusual weapons with devastating efficiency—particularly those weapons that emitted the powerful blasts that had wounded Shadow and buried Ash and Niel under a pile of rubble in Scotland.

Fortunately, the Igigi had their own armour, but it was clear that the strength of the attack was taking them by surprise.

Niel and Nahum were already assisting in a skirmish, but Zee had flown high and was using the crossbow to pin Black Cronos down. Barak wheeled to the right to join Estelle on one of the balconies, while Ash was on the ground fighting in one-to-one combat. Gabe was about to fly down to assist an Igigi below when he saw movement at the base of one of the ziggurats in the next cave, well beyond the main fight. Another muffled boom and a flash of light erupted from the spot, and he realised Black Cronos was trying to get into one of the ziggurats.

He changed direction, flying high enough to keep out of range of the crossbows, and as soon as he was close, swooped down on the Black Cronos soldiers at the ziggurat's entrance.

Gabe decapitated one before he even knew what was happening. He grabbed another by the collar, smashing him into the wall of the ziggurat, and followed it up with a thrust of his sword. The third he pinned to the wall with one wing, leaving his feet dangling off the ground. Gabe whipped his dagger from his belt, throwing it with deadly accuracy. He struck the soldier's throat, and blood splattered everywhere, including across Gabe's face and wings. Gabe dropped the man to the ground, grimacing at the feel of the hot, sticky blood on him.

Up close, Gabe saw a hole blasted through the ziggurat's thick door. *Shit.* More soldiers were inside, no doubt hunting for remains. *Grave robbers.* Gabe's fury erupted. As he advanced, a soldier emerged from the hole, others behind her. She raised her hand and blasted him using a strange device.

The power threw him backwards, and he crashed into the next building, momentarily stunned. *Bollocks.* Gabe groaned as he staggered to his feet. His chest ached and his head throbbed, and just as he was about to throw himself at her, she raised her hand, pointing the strange device at him again. He could see the power pulsing in her palm, and the malevolent gleam in her eye as she levelled it at him. His armour was already smoking, and he wasn't sure he could survive another hit that powerful.

His first preference was always to attack, but he had no choice now. The distance between them was too great. He dived behind an ornate wall that surrounded the closest ziggurat. As he landed behind it, another blast took out a chunk of it, showering him in rubble. He used his wings as a shield, but the bombardment continued.

He was pinned down, with nowhere to go.

Niel gritted his teeth as he threw off the soldier who had tackled him to the ground, his knife millimetres from Niel's ribs.

Damn Black Cronos. They were like a virus. They just kept coming, and he was sick of them. He rolled quickly, swinging his axe down with a thud, but missed as the soldier rolled away. Fortunately, Nahum's throwing knife embedded in his throat, blood spurting everywhere as he collapsed on the ground.

Niel grunted as he stood, pulling the knife free and swiping at the next soldier who raced at him. He sliced through his throat, and he too fell quickly. With no one else in sight—not alive, at least—he took a deep breath and wiped the sweat from his face, cursing loudly.

He wiped Nahum's blade on his fatigues to clean it, then passed it to him, saying, "Holy shit, brother. They must have got reinforcements. There are far more Black Cronos soldiers here than I saw outside."

"After their failed attack on the farmhouse and in France, they're taking no chances." Nahum was also covered in blood and sweat, and he nudged the nearest dead soldier with his feet. "This one did this." He gestured to the top of his left arm, and Niel saw a deep cut, saturated with blood. Fortunately, it was already congealing. "I'm lucky it wasn't worse, but it stings like a bitch. Come on. Let's help the others."

They were in a narrow alley between ziggurats, but the sounds of shouts and clanging of metal indicated many fights were still raging across the cave. And then a deeper clang sounded—something much heavier and bigger.

Something horribly ominous.

"What the hell was that?" Niel asked, alarmed.

"Nothing good. Let's get moving."

As soon as Barak entered the City of the Dead, he searched for Estelle, his heart in his throat. There were already many dead and wounded, and he was relieved not to see her body on the ground. He immediately lifted his gaze, spotting her emerge from under a pile of rubble on the first level balcony. She had barely regained her feet when she hurled a mix of fireballs and curses at the soldiers racing up the stairs.

Her well-aimed magic took out the first couple, knocking them over the stairs and taking some other soldiers out behind them. But a group was advancing on her other side too, and she would struggle to deal with both. Barak swooped in low, winging his way along the outside of the balcony, before deftly folding his wings and leaping over the rail to land behind them.

His approach was so swift, they had barely time to turn before he threw the first one over the rail to a crunching death below, and then plunged his sword into the next. The third soldier, however, was ready for him.

TWENTY-SIX

The next few seconds were a furious clash of blades, each grunting in the other's face, and his opponent was easily as big as Barak was. But up close, especially in the light of the smoking torches, Barak saw that his skin had a coppery sheen, just like his eyes.

Barak's blade cut the skin on his forearm, but the wound was dry, leaking no blood at all. *Fuck it*. As if sensing his frustration, the soldier smirked, incensing Barak even more. After several more clashes with neither gaining an advantage over the other, Barak had enough. He turned so that his back was to the wall, flung open his wings, and used them to propel himself and the solider he gripped through the stone balustrade. The swiftness of the move caught his opponent by surprise, and with an enormous crack, they both tumbled over the edge. Barak immediately released his opponent, watching his flailing limbs as he plummeted to the ground and landed in a mangled heap. In seconds Barak was back on the balcony, winded and covered in cuts and grazes.

Estelle raced to his side, her eyes scanning him. "Are you okay?"

"Just about. Are you?" He looked beyond her shoulder, but the way was clear—although, the stairs were smashed. "You've got rid of them all."

She smiled, but her eyes were wary. "It was tricky. They're so quick." She turned to survey the tunnel Black Cronos had arrived through. "We need to cut them off before any more arrive."

A new clanging noise resounded through the chamber, and Barak groaned. "What now?"

The immediate area in front of them was deserted, the view blocked by a row of ziggurats, but a flare of fire in the distance drew their attention, as did another loud clang.

Barak turned to Estelle, "I'm going to look."

"Take me with you!" She grabbed his arm, her hand warm and soft on his muscled forearm.

"There are men with crossbows, it's too dangerous."

"I think most are gone. They were the first that the Igigi and Zee targeted—and me, too. Besides," she wiggled her fingers, "I'll be an extra weapon for you."

He hesitated for a second, but he didn't like leaving her alone either, knowing she would make her own way to the noise. "All right. But you have the use of one hand only. You'll need the other to hold on tight." He swept her into his arms, facing her forward, and gripping her securely, leapt off the edge. He heard her sharp intake of breath and said, "Sorry. I was hoping to make our first flight together a little less dramatic."

"I can cope with drama, but maybe—"

Her words were lost as they swooped over the next ziggurats and saw the havoc below. Most of the fighting was taking place in the centre of the first cave, and dozens of Igigi and Black Cronos were engaged in battle. Barak spotted Niel and Nahum in the middle of it all, but the most horrifying sight were the three huge cages at the edge—traps for prisoners. Black Cronos soldiers were poised beside them, ready to haul them away. One of them had a motionless Igigi trapped inside, and the second contained Ash.

Zee was perched high above the City of the Dead. The roof here wasn't as well finished as in the other cave, and deep crevices provided places to wedge himself and watch, his crossbow trained below.

He had taken out the Black Cronos soldiers with crossbows, appreciating more than ever the advantage his wings gave him, and was now trying to pick off the soldiers whilst avoiding the Igigi. Not far from him, another Igigi was watching too, longbow cocked and ready. Eagle-headed and eagle-eyed, he was a good shot, but the skirmishes below were now making life tricky. And then the cages appeared, dragged in from the far tunnel.

They should have expected this. If Black Cronos wanted Igigi to experiment on, they needed to capture some alive. For some reason, Zee imagined them extracting the Igigi bound and trussed. But of course, that would always have been hard. They were huge, muscled, and built for endurance. Logically, a cage was the only way. Perhaps they had brought them here in sections after assessing the way in first. But equally, how would they get them out of the desert? Unless a large truck had arrived, and Niel hadn't mentioned that. Or…a helicopter? Something big enough for transport. *And that meant Black Cronos was far better connected and well-resourced than they knew.*

With horror, Zee saw a motionless Igigi being hauled out of the crowd of Black Cronos soldiers and thrown into a cage, the door clanging shut behind it. And with even greater horror, Ash's motionless body was thrown into the next cage.

No…

Immediately, soldiers began hauling the cages out, swiftly rolling them on hidden wheels, and Zee's initial shock turned to ice cold rage. He looked across to the Igigi, and with an unspoken agreement, they dropped from their secure perches and made a beeline for the cages as they disappeared into the tunnel.

Ash was groggy and confused, feeling only a cold floor beneath him and the sensation of moving. He filtered through his memories, trying to recall what had just happened.

Mid-fight, just as he thought he was getting the upper hand with a silver-eyed soldier with whirling blades, something hit him from behind, sending him sprawling. A jolt of pain made his body convulse, and his jaw clenched so hard he thought it would break. And then he'd passed out.

As he dragged himself upright, his vision finally clearing, he saw that he was in a cage being escorted by several soldiers, a couple carrying a long stick with electrodes on the end. Ash had done enough reading to know what that was. It wasn't any weird Black Cronos weaponry. It was a standard cattle prod. He'd been electrocuted. One soldier looked across at him, waving the prod menacingly. His intent was clear: one wrong move and he would use it again.

Ash kept very still. He had no wish to repeat that experience, and he had no weapons. Instead, he focussed on his surroundings.

They were moving at pace up a long, flat tunnel, an escort of soldiers in front and behind. Ahead was another cage with an Igigi trapped inside. The tunnel was broad and high-roofed, but rudimentary compared to the one they'd passed through earlier. Ash could only console himself that it would surely be long, and they'd have to haul them up a slope or steps to get to the surface. They'd be more distracted then, and would possibly be manhandling the cage awkwardly.

Ash settled into the middle of the cage, calmly gathering himself. That would be the moment he'd have to strike. And he hoped his brothers would be there to assist him.

TWENTY-SEVEN

Shadow had spent the last few minutes silently stalking and killing several Black Cronos members.

Shadow liked stealth kills. They were clean and efficient. While she enjoyed combat, there was nothing more satisfying than killing someone who was completely unsuspecting, but thoroughly deserving. And Black Cronos absolutely was. They were thugs. Bred for destruction, and utterly psychopathic. And she had a grudge. After their bruising encounter under Arklet Abbey, she now had a score to settle. They all did. As soon as she could, she planned to head outside, following Black Cronos's way in, and take out as many soldiers there as she could.

However, ten minutes earlier, she saw Gabe pass swiftly overhead. She'd kept her eye on him ever since he entered the cavern, and she was glad Gishkim had finally seen sense. But then she realised Gabe had not returned. And even worse, The Silencer of Souls was heading to the next cave, in the same direction as Gabe. Dressed all in black, her eyes impassive, she had skirted around the fighting, prowling like a panther, and carrying a wooden box with a handle.

Interesting.

Shadow followed her. Once or twice the woman turned, her eyes narrowed, but Shadow froze, certain her fey magic would keep her protected. She moved on, and so did Shadow.

As they reached the next cave, Shadow realised what was happening. Well away from the fighting, one of the ziggurats had been broken into. A couple of Black Cronos members were already carrying boxes out. *Remains, or something else? Relics or weapons, perhaps?* Typical graverobbers would covet funereal tokens that might accompany the dead, but not Black Cronos. Relics had no relevance to them unless they were magical. It had to be bones...or the dust of them, at least.

Shadow increased her pace, hoping to attack The Silencer of Souls before she reached the others. Unfortunately, the woman increased her pace too, and she headed into the tomb before Shadow could reach her. Seconds later, she emerged with Toto, both drawing away to talk privately. Frustrated, Shadow hung back in the darkest shadows, watching them. Toto's arm was in a sling, but he looked otherwise well, and she cursed her wayward shot. But something had disturbed both of them, and with the bark of a command at the Black Cronos soldiers, he walked away with The Silencer of Souls, threading through the ziggurats to the next cave, their pace quickening with every step.

Shadow's eyes narrowed. *What else was going on here?* Frozen with indecision, she debated her options, but decided that following them was more important than what was happening here. Just as she was about to leave, a blast directed at a corner of the next ziggurat commanded her attention, three soldiers closing in as they fired again and again. That could mean only one thing.

Gabe.

Her suspicions were confirmed moments later when she saw an outstretched wing flash above the wall and a chunk of rock sail over it, landing with a thunk among the advancing soldiers. Several more followed, scattering the soldiers.

This was her chance.

She ran in, grabbed the closest one from behind, and drew her blade across the soldier's throat. She fell at Shadow's feet, blood bubbling out of the wound. The remaining two soldiers were distracted by the bombardment of stone, and she swiftly killed the next. By then she was in Gabe's range too, and danced out of the way of an incoming block of stone, as did the soldier. Unseen, she ran up behind her, driving her blade up into her ribcage before cutting her throat with the other b lade.

It had all happened so quickly, and the other soldiers were so pre-occupied with the boxes of bones, that the exchange went unseen by anyone else. Shadow scrambled up the stone wall and vaulted over the top, hissing, "Gabe! It's me!"

"Shadow!" A broad grin split his face as he pulled her into his arms and kissed her. "I was worried about you."

She pulled back, smiling. "I've been having lots of fun. Your immediate attackers are dead now. But," her smile disappeared, "that bitch has arrived and taken Toto somewhere." She waved vaguely toward the other cave. "Something else is going on here. And they're stealing bones!"

"I know. They pinned me down before I could do anything." He ran a dusty hand across his face, smearing dirt along it. "Fuck it. How big is the group by the next ziggurat now?"

"Just a few. We can take them together. And then we need to find that bitch."

Gabe grabbed his weapons. "Good. Let's do this."

Nahum hung in the air, Niel next to him, watching a caged Ash and an Igigi vanish into the tunnel, soldiers surrounding them.

"Right, brother," he said, turning to Niel. "Ash and the Igigi are our priority. The others are withdrawing, now that they have what they want."

"Trying to," Niel corrected. "The Igigi aren't letting them go so easily."

"But they can't get close, either. That final line is holding them off." Nahum's jaw clenched. "We'd fare better in flight—especially now that we have the crossbows."

"But they have their explosive handheld devices. However," Niel shrugged, his huge shoulders shifting upwards, "what's life without a little danger?"

Nahum considered their best approach, and then spotted Zee alongside Barak who was holding Estelle. He whistled, and in seconds they were all hovering together, Estelle looking flushed. "You saw that Ash was captured?" Nahum asked.

Zee nodded, his eyes fixed on the tunnel's entrance. "We need to follow them. Now."

"But where's Gabe?" Barak asked. "I haven't seen him in a while."

"Right there." Niel pointed to where the huge, dark-winged shape of Gabe was flying towards them, Shadow in his arms. Moments later he had joined them, and Niel said, "You had us worried for a moment."

Gabe grimaced. "I got pinned down, but we took out a group in the next cave stealing remains. They're all dead."

"And I killed a lot on my way," Shadow added.

Nahum nodded. "Good. But we have bigger problems now. They've captured Ash and an Igigi. They're heading out, and we have to stop them."

Gabe paled, cursing under his breath. "And the rest of the Igigi?"

"Some dead, but others are still battling down below," Barak said. "But Black Cronos are holding them off. We need a plan."

"Right. And Shadow says Toto is on the move, too." Gabe assessed the situation quickly. "Gishkim is fighting with his men. We need to help them. If we get rid of the rear guard, we can get close to Ash. Whatever happens, they *cannot* take them."

"And there's Toto." Niel pointed to where a unit of soldiers were stealthily moving up the stairs, Toto and The Silencer of Souls in the middle of them. "They're heading to the main city."

"What can possibly be of interest to them there?" Zee asked, confused. "It's deserted. There's just Catarina and Urbarra left there."

Nahum grunted with annoyance. "Something has been bugging me since we arrived. The city is deserted, and their City of the Dead is huge. That means their main population is somewhere else. That must be where they're going." The others looked shocked. "You know it makes sense. There are a *lot* of soldiers here. And the panel in the room we were locked in shows irrigation systems and a light source. There has to be another city."

"But how do they know where to go?" Estelle asked. Her hands, Nahum noted, were gripping Barak's arms so tightly that her knuckles were white.

"The same way they knew about the other entrance. Old intel."

"I don't give a shit about the details right now," Gabe huffed. "Zee, Barak, Estelle, Nahum—you chase down Ash and the Igigi. We," he nodded at Niel and Shadow, who rested easily in his arms as if she'd done it her whole life, "will stop Toto, and join you as soon as possible. If you can, get a message to Gishkim, so he knows the plan."

Nahum met his brother's determined gaze, knowing failure was not an option. Nahum would rather die than let Ash be taken prisoner. All of them would. "Don't worry, Gabe. We won't fail."

And with a nod at the others, they wheeled around to begin another assault on Black Cronos.

Harlan was glad to get back to the peace and quiet of his own flat after what felt like a whirlwind few days.

He turned the lights on and threw the windows open to allow the cool night breeze to banish the stuffiness of his home. It carried the sounds and smells of London up to him. He made a beeline to the shower, feeling like he needed to wash off days of accumulated dirt and stress, and when he was finished, he grabbed a beer and headed to his study.

Ever since he'd left JD, he'd been thinking about the Igigi and what else they may offer Black Cronos. But logically, there'd be nothing to find in their city except bones and ruins. He'd tried to contact the Nephilim and Shadow several times, and then Catarina, but no one answered. He wasn't sure if that was good or bad. If they'd found the city and were underground, there would be no signal. *But if Black Cronos had found them...*

He shook off his worry and started to research the Igigi. He hadn't got very far before there was a knock on the door. Startled, he checked the time. It was late. Almost ten. He grabbed the baseball bat he'd taken to keeping close—like that would stop Black Cronos from killing him—and headed to his front door to peer through the spyhole. With relief, he saw only Olivia.

"Goddamn it! I thought you were Black Cronos!" he said, ushering her in.

"Like they'd knock!" Olivia looked like she'd been out to dinner. She was wearing one of her elegant dresses and high heeled shoes, and she smirked as she looked at his bat. "How very American."

"Funny," he said, leading her down the hall to the study. "It could make a big dent in someone's head if I was attacked."

"And a big dent in yours if they wrestled it off you."

"I'm disappointed that you have no faith in me. I work out!"

"And they're superhumans." She cocked an eyebrow at him. "Are you still worried they'll come for you?"

He shrugged. "Not really, I guess, or I'd be back at the Mandarin Oriental. I'm not big enough to bother them right now, which is fine by me." He nodded at the computer screen. "I am, however, looking into their latest interest. What are you doing here, anyway? All dressed up and nowhere to go?"

"I had dinner with a potential client who needed reassuring about our abilities, and now I'm checking in on you. I was worried, and I admit, I'm nosy."

He laughed. "I'll get you a drink and fill you in. Wine, gin, beer, coffee?"

"A beer is just fine with me," she said, shrugging off her light jacket and grabbing a chair.

When he returned to the study, Olivia was scrolling through his web searches, and she looked at him, puzzled. "You're still looking into the Sumerian stuff?"

It had been days since he'd last spoken to Olivia, and he'd forgotten that he told her about the tablet. "Yes. We found the original tablet in Wales. It has taken Gabe and the others to Turkey."

"*What*? I didn't know that!"

"They're looking for the city. And might have found it, too."

"It would be a wreck, right?"

"That's the thing. We don't know. And I haven't heard from them for days, which makes me worry."

"Because you think Black Cronos is there, too?"

"Yes. We're even more sure now that they want whatever they can find to experiment on." Harlan glanced at the computer screen again. "The other worrying thing is JD's theory on who's behind it all. The *Comte de Saint-Germain*."

"Oh, I've heard of him." Olivia leaned back in the chair, drank her beer, and regarded Harlan silently for a moment. "That's a hell of a theory. And the Igigi, too. Bloody hell, Harlan, I know we live and work in the strange world of the occult, but this is stretching things, even for us. A hidden city beneath the desert, and another immortal alchemist!"

"If John Dee did it, why couldn't someone else? And we know there are many old civilisations out there that have vanished with time. Look at what they're finding in South America with Lidar. And Cambodia! Evidence of ancient civilisations—extensive cities—lost beneath the jungle. Why shouldn't there be one underneath the desert?" He couldn't help but feel disappointed with Olivia. "We went to the Temple of the Trinity. I can't believe you doubt it."

"Well, that's true. And your encounter with a Minotaur in a Mithraic Chamber."

He closed his eyes at the memory. "That was horrific."

Olivia sighed. "I'm being unfair, but I'm just trying to stay grounded here. You're right, odd discoveries are made all the time. I wonder what else the Igigi could offer Black Cronos?"

"Isn't their superhuman status enough?"

"Maybe. They're the subject of many conspiracy theories."

He sipped his beer and sat next to her. "I must admit, they are not something I was that familiar with until this week. It's not really my field."

"Mine either, but I love a good conspiracy theory. They are rumoured to be aliens."

Harlan snorted, almost inhaling his beer. "You're kidding."

"Nope." She pointed at the article on the screen. "Most people who work in this field focus purely on the evidence of the Mesopotamian empire, of which the Sumerians were a part of. It was only in the last century that we found so much evidence of their existence. Studies suggest that there are seven main Sumerian Gods, called the Anunnaki. All of them lived in Heaven, and had entire cities dedicated to them. City states. Their idols were revered and treated as the living embodiment of the Gods. Their servants, the ones who built their cities, were the Igigi. However, some people—pseudoscientists—suggest they were ancient astronauts who came to Earth to spread their knowledge." She smirked. "Fun!"

"I think we should stick to the facts. JD said the Sumerians were one of the first recorded people to have used crystals in magic. And The *Comte de Saint-Germain loved* his crystals."

"So, the Igigi are part of Sumerian culture who used lots of magic based on crystals...crystals with Otherworldly powers, perhaps. Amazing builders, too. They invented so many things."

"I was chatting with Jackson about it," Harlan said, nodding. "In theory, there are many things about them that could interest Black Cronos. And that doesn't bode well for Gabe. I just hope they're okay."

Gabe turned his back on the others, trusting that they would do the best they could. Now, he focussed on Toto's group.

"I guess you want to be on the ground, Shadow?"

"Of course. That woman is mine."

"Oh no, sister," Niel put in swiftly. "After that debacle under the abbey, she's *mine*."

Shadow gave him a twisted grin. "We'll just have to see who wins, won't we?"

Gabe inwardly groaned. There was always so much competition between them all. "Just don't forget the others while you're vying to kill her. I'm going after Toto."

Black Cronos were only a few steps away from the broad balcony that led to the tunnel. Gabe arrowed his wings and dropped quickly, swooping above the soldiers in a rush of silent speed and accuracy. "Take a few out before I drop you?" he asked, mouth to Shadow's ear.

"Of course."

Angling low, arms gripped around her waist to support her and her feet braced on his, she was able to hold both swords. As they swept above their enemies' heads, her blades despatched two without them even realising that they were coming from above. He released Shadow from his grip and she landed gracefully, blades whirling. Niel dropped in the centre of the pack, using his wings to sweep the soldiers away. They crashed into walls, and some flew over the side of the stairs, landing in a crumpled heap below.

Toto spun around, hand raised, and Gabe had just enough time to see the flash of the weapon in his palm. He dived out of the way, and the mighty blast of power surged past him, taking out a chunk of one of the huge pillars that supported the upper balcony. Rubble blasted everywhere, sending everyone diving for cover, and Gabe wrapped his wings around himself, using them as a shield.

An ominous crack emitted from the pillar as it started to crumble, and huge fault lines appeared in the balcony overhead. Everyone looked up, the soldiers scattering. Niel and Shadow barrelled through them, racing to get into the tunnel before the balcony collapsed. Gabe was closest, and he vaulted through the opening. Toto and The Silencer of Souls were racing ahead, a handful of soldiers with them, just as a huge fall of rock descended.

A chunk of stone crashed into his back, sending him sprawling. *Fuck, fuck fuck.*

Gabe was sick of being blasted by rocks and covered in dust. His eyes stung, everything ached, and he couldn't stop coughing. But Niel and Shadow had made it through, and in seconds they were all on their feet and running after them.

And then Gabe had another thought. "Urbarra!" he yelled at the others. "We need to alert him!"

"Not me," Shadow yelled back. "I'm not letting her out of my sight." She pointed to the fleeing Silencer of Souls, who ducked down a side corridor with Toto and the others.

"And not me either," Niel argued, glaring at Shadow. "I have a score to settle."

"Fine," Gabe ground out through clenched teeth. "As far as I can see, they're all trapped anyway. It's just a matter of time. I'll get him." And besides, Urbarra might have a quicker route—plus, he needed to make sure Catarina was okay.

Leaving the others to pursue Toto, Gabe flew through the tunnel and into the city, landing outside the stone building where Catarina was being... *Protected?* He hoped so.

Urbarra was standing sentry, a spear in one hand, and a sword in the other. His eyes swept across Gabe's grubby appearance. "What's happened?"

"They're retreating—finally, but with a captured Igigi and one of my brothers. Don't worry!" He held his hand up as Urbarra's eyes filled with rage. "We're chasing them down, but..." He quickly told him about Toto, and Urbarra's growl made Gabe's hair stand on end. He started to move, eyes on the far tunnel, but Gabe stepped in front of him. "Am I right in thinking you have another city?"

He froze, eyes hardening. "What do you know about that?"

"It's a reasonable guess. Am I right?"

"Yes. It's a big one, and well protected, but even so..."

Catarina's voice disturbed them as she hammered on the door. "Urbarra! It's the light source! It has to be what they want."

He turned and flung the door open, glaring at her. "What do you know about the light source?"

Catarina looked none the worse for her captivity. "I've been studying your records—your history. You stole some kind of gemstone that powered your city. Gave it light. Am I right?"

Urbarra hesitated, and then nodded. "Yes. Our ancestors stole it from the Anunnaki. It's what has enabled us to live here for so long. The Stone of Utu."

Gabe could barely believe his ears. "Are you fucking kidding me? You stole *that*?" His shock was so huge, he felt as if the earth had shifted beneath his feet. The Stone of Utu was renowned through the Sumerian world. There had always been rumours about the Anunnaki Gods. That they wielded the powers of the universe, brought from the skies. He had never seen it, and they certainly hadn't advertised its loss. *And no wonder.* It would have weakened them in their subjects' eyes. A revelation struck him. "That's the *real* reason we had to find you. And our fathers searched for you."

Urbarra nodded. "There were six other stones, one for each God, but we only took one. Its power could be devastating in the wrong hands. And it would mean the end of us. We would die, and our city would collapse."

"Is there another way to get there? Niel and Shadow are following them, but they need help."

Urbarra nodded. "Follow me."

Catarina forced her way out of the room, glaring at Gabe. "You are *not* leaving me behind!"

He was too anxious to get moving to argue. "Then you'd better stay close."

Barak raced down the tunnel after the fleeing Black Cronos soldiers, with his brothers, Estelle, and the Igigi keeping pace alongside.

After a combined assault on the remaining Black Cronos soldiers in the City of the Dead, the stragglers ran, but they had a head start, and were annoyingly quick. Partway down the tunnel, as it started to twist and turn, they hunkered down and began blasting them again, holding them back.

With every passing minute, Ash and the captured Igigi were getting further away. Barak's worry about his brother rocketed, and he could see the rising panic in his brothers' eyes, too.

But Gishkim remained calm. "We have another route. This place is riddled with tunnels that we created many years ago for just such a scenario." He barked an order, separating his team into two groups, the other led by Dumuzi, a jackal-headed Igigi who seemed to be his second in command. "Dumuzi, you stay here. Continue the attack and make them think they're blocking us. We'll head down here." He gestured to a side passage as he addressed the Nephilim and Estelle. "This will bring us out into the main cave." A ferocious scowl split his face in two. "They'll regret ever coming here."

Barak looked at Estelle while his brothers followed Gishkim's team who were already setting a fast pace. So far, she hadn't complained once. "Are you coming with us?" He hated to lose sight of her, but she was making no move to follow them.

She shook her head. "I'll stay here. I think I'll be of more use—and I won't slow you down." Her hand cupped his cheek as she held his gaze. "Be careful."

He kissed her palm, feeling the innate strength beneath her femininity. "And you. I like..." he gestured between them, "whatever this is."

She smiled, and it lit up her face, making his heart jump. "So do I. Be safe, Barak."

He kissed her palm once more, and then ran to join the others, holding the promise in her eyes close to his heart.

TWENTY-EIGHT

Niel couldn't believe his eyes as the enormous vista of another underground city opened up before him.

"Herne's hairy bollocks! How is this even possible?"

Even Shadow, who pretended never to be impressed by anything, pulled up short. "I have no idea. Where is the light coming from? And the heat?"

They had progressed down a roughly carved tunnel that ended at a thick wooden door, and passing through it, now stood on a stone platform high above a verdant valley. Streams and rivers flowed through fields and forests, and clusters of buildings were spread throughout, the main city appearing in the distance. Igigi moved in the fields below them and along the lanes, and following the main road, Niel spotted a huge gate set into the wall directly below them. But ahead of them was a series of stone walkways set beneath the metal-covered dome of the cavern—a mixture of silver, bronze, copper, and gold. Ahead, set into the roof, a light source blazed, and that's where Toto and The Silencer of Souls were heading.

Niel pointed. "The gate down there must be the main entrance."

Shadow nodded. "Accessed by another tunnel, somewhere below this one. This is a kind of service access. How have they found it?"

Niel shook his head. "They've obviously either found a better source than us, or have some impressive technology. But," he stared at the handful of soldiers ahead who were facing them on the huge stone walkways, weapons drawn, "we need to get rid of them to get to Toto and that bitch."

"The light source looks like it would be too big to take."

"They always do their homework, Shadow. They must be sure they can get it. That's why she's carrying a box." Niel grimaced. "There are four guards left. I'm going to fly around them, draw their fire, and take out who I can. The roof is high enough that I can get above the walkways. I'm going to make this quick."

Without waiting to hear her response, he dropped off the ledge, plummeting to the ground until he was a good way beneath them before extending his wings. He then swept up, circling fast and rolling quickly, so his wings shielded him. He felt a few blasts come close, ruffling his feathers, but he kept going, his speed and momentum too much for them to counter. As the first soldiers came into view, he levelled out, opened his wings, and headed right for them. He took two out immediately, sweeping them off the walkway to plunge to their deaths. The other two scattered, and he swung back around. They had both flattened themselves against the walkway, and keeping low, he grabbed one mid-flight, and dropped him over the side, his scream resonating through the chamber.

Shadow had used Niel's distraction to run in, and she tackled the next soldier, coming perilously close to the edge as they rolled together. Just as Niel was swooping around, she kicked out, sending the last soldier plummeting over the edge.

"Nice job, sister," he said, landing next to her. "Ready for the next two?" Toto and The Silencer of Souls were still running towards the light source, but had pulled further ahead now. He opened his arms. "I can give you a lift."

Shadow didn't hesitate. "Let's go."

Ash braced himself against the bars of his cage as Black Cronos carried it up the steep slope to the surface.

Despite their strength, they were breathless, and it was no wonder. The cages were heavy and hard to manhandle over the rough ground. This tunnel was nowhere near as finished as the one they had entered through, and he could hear grumblings and mutterings amongst his captors, especially about Stefan Hope-Robbins.

Good. With luck, infighting might break out.

He'd overheard them saying that Stefan was waiting on the surface with a team to take them away. Ash had anxiously watched behind him, and had become increasingly more despondent that his brothers weren't in sight. But it wasn't over yet, and he was now much more rested than his captors.

Fresh air swept over him as a huge gateway appeared ahead, a hole blown in it, and he realised they'd reached the gate that Shadow had seen. He hadn't got much time left. He'd have to make his move. Now.

Suddenly, a strange rushing and roaring sensation filled his ears, and he realised the breeze felt damp. *What the hell?* And then he realised what it was. *Water, a lot of it, somewhere up ahead.*

Zee was tucked safely in a narrow tunnel high above the cave floor, watching the Black Cronos soldiers emerge from the hole in the gate below and head across the cave to the narrow cleft in the rock that was the exit. He was eager to attack them, and annoyed that Gishkim had urged them to wait.

Nahum was barely reining in his patience, especially when he saw the first cage appear, and his hand tightened on his throwing knives. Barak was equally impatient, but Gishkim ignored them, he and his team instead focussing on manipulating a mechanism set into the wall—a system of cogs and gears.

When a roaring noise filled his ears, Zee immediately knew why. Water gushed out of an opening in the cave high above the gate, sluicing down into the dry canal below. Gishkim and the Igigi had opened the ancient water channels. At first, he'd thought there was only one, but within a few seconds, another three around the cave started to release water, again all several metres above the ground.

Water churned out, the noise deafening, as the waterfalls plunged below. The canals were instantly full of water, and then they started to overflow.

There were no attempts at heroics from Black Cronos soldiers now. They ran, water sloshing around their feet, a couple already losing their footing and getting washed away.

Gishkim gave them a feral grin and pointed to the cleft. "I suggest you leave through there if you wish to reach the others outside. I will go, too. I need to teach these trespassers a lesson."

Zee shook his head. "We need to get Ash out. And your Igigi."

"And you will," Gishkim said calmly. "While the rest of them drown."

Barak cricked his neck, eyes already on the exit. A few men had already entered it, but the water was overwhelming the others. "I'll come with you, Gishkim. Brothers, join us soon."

Gishkim and Barak soared across the cave, a couple of Igigi with them, while Nahum and Zee headed to the area just beyond the gate, the handful of remaining Igigi scrambling down behind them.

Confusion reigned as the water churned. The main current swept to a hole in the far wall, carrying many soldiers with it as the water level rapidly rose. The cages, both of which were now out of the tunnel and half submerged, had soldiers clinging to them like life rafts.

Zee swooped down on them, no longer needing his crossbow. The soldiers were sitting ducks.

Ash had never been so relieved to see his brothers, or the mass of water that was flooding the cave, carrying the soldiers with it.

They had been caught completely off-guard. But although Zee was flinging the other guards into the rushing current, the bastard with the cattle prod was still grimly hanging on, and determined to use it on Ash.

He couldn't use it on the cage because he'd electrocute himself, but he prodded wildly through the bars, trying to hit Ash. But the action made him unbalanced, especially now that the current was tearing at him, and he only had one hand free to hold on.

In a perfectly-timed move, Ash snatched the cattle prod from his grasp and used the blunt end to hit the soldier in the face repeatedly. His eyes rolled back, and Ash grabbed him before he could let go. He threw the prod out of the cage, and wrapping his arm around the man's throat, pinned him to the bars.

"Zee! He has the keys."

"On it, brother," Zee yelled, dropping another soldier into the swirling water before joining him. He searched his pockets, and quickly pulled a key free. "Got it. You can let him go now."

"Good," Ash grunted, watching the soldier fall into the water with a splash.

Zee inserted the key into the lock, threw open the door, and extending a hand, pulled Ash out of the cage and onto its roof. "You had me worried."

"I'd like to say I had complete faith in you, but I was getting worried, too." Ash sighed heavily, repressing a shudder. "I was desperately trying not to think of what horrible experiments I might have been subjected to. I would rather have died first." He turned to the trapped Igigi, Nahum clinging to his cage as he tried to wrench open the door. "Let's help Nahum. Hopefully the key works on that cage, too."

Nahum was drenched, the water still rising rapidly, as the amount pouring into the cave was far more than could drain away quickly. He eyed the key with relief. Fortunately, it worked on the second lock, and once they released the Igigi, he clambered onto the cage's roof, too.

The Igigi growled with relief. "I never thought I would owe the Nephilim my life."

"If I'm honest," Nahum admitted, "I never thought I'd be saving it. But your brothers have a lot to do with it. This water, for instance."

"We have built fail safes throughout our world. We can never risk losing it to enemies."

World.

That word struck Ash as odd, but now wasn't the time to ask any more questions, as the Igigi gave a series of piercing whistles that were swiftly answered by others. Immediately, the torrent issuing from the walls started to slow. The Igigi must have closed the mechanism again. The cave began to empty, as waist-high water flowed through the hole in the wall and into the darkness beyond, and continued to pour through the crevice to the outside world. For a few moments more they held on to the cages that had wedged into the narrow canal base, waiting for the current to slow, as the captured Igigi couldn't fly.

Ash looked back to the gate, which led to the city complex. "Where are the others?"

"Tackling other issues," Nahum said, looking worried, "but Estelle should be..."

He didn't need to say anything else. A few lights in the distance heralded the arrival of the others, and soon Estelle emerged through the gate with the other Igigi, grim-faced and covered in dirt.

She sighed with relief at the sight of them, the group sloshing through the remaining water toward the cage. "Thank the Gods. We've killed the rest of them. Where's Barak?"

"Out there," Zee said, already headed to the cleft. "Let's join him."

Ash jumped to the floor, stretching his cramped limbs and flexing his wings before following him. He was looking forward to exacting more revenge on Black Cronos.

Gabe studied the mechanism in the centre of space, mouth dropping open as he examined the unbelievable engineering that was around him.

It had taken what seemed to be an age to reach this place, its entrance hidden in the rear of one of the other buildings, and Gabe wondered what other features this old city hid. Urbarra had barely explained anything while on the move, and Gabe had focussed only on keeping up with him, and making sure Catarina was keeping up with *both* of them. Fortunately, she had, seemingly undaunted by their strange surroundings.

The passage had sloped upwards on a gentle gradient, the occasional side path leading off it, but Urbarra had ignored them, guiding them steadily onwards until stopping at a central space with all manner of mechanisms that disappeared into darkness on either side. It was like they had arrived in the space above a stage. Standing still, Gabe felt the hum of the machinery beneath his feet, and saw a track set in the floor that disappeared into the gloom on either side; they were at the top of a rise, the ground falling away beyond them.

TWENTY-EIGHT

It seemed Catarina was equally shocked. "What is this place?"

"I have no idea, Catarina," he said, baffled, but translated the question to Urbarra.

He smiled in response, his wolf's grin unnerving in the dim light. "There's a reason Gishkim left me to watch Catarina. I'm one of the Igigi who maintains this—it is how the Stone of Utu passes overhead, lighting our world below."

Gabe gaped. "Like the sun?"

"Yes. It disappears at the end of every cycle to simulate night, passing backwards and forwards across the sky. Essentially, the roof of the cavern is covered in metal to add to the brightness. I'm about to speed that up. It will trigger a warning."

As Gabe translated for Catarina, Urbarra manipulated a control panel, and an enormous clang resounded around them, as if coming from deep within the core of the cavern. Immediately the humming beneath Gabe's feet increased, and Urbarra nodded, satisfied. "The Stone of Utu will now head towards its night time resting place. If our attackers are seeking it, it will soon be far from their reach."

Gabe felt suddenly out of his depth. "How did you achieve this?"

"We have been here for thousands of years. Our building skills were already superior to most. We have had time to perfect them for our needs." Urbarra positioned himself above a large hatch set into the floor. "This opens to a shaft, which leads to the maintenance platforms below. That's where the tunnel the others took will lead."

"What's going on?" Catarina interrupted. "I don't understand."

"Sorry," Gabe said, forgetting that he'd been speaking ancient Sumerian, and he quickly summarised what they were doing. "And below the platforms?"

"Our world. We will be high, as if in the Heavens."

Gabe nodded. *Good*. He would go through it and find The Silencer of Souls and Toto—and with luck, kill them both...if they weren't dead already.

Shadow ignored the nausea that Niel's erratic flight was causing, focussing only on her objective.

The Silencer of Souls and Toto were both taking pot shots at them, but they were mainly focussed on their goal. The light source.

Shadow had to turn her face away, the dazzle was so bright, but their enemies had come prepared, both now strapping darkened goggles on the faces as they ran.

"Why the hell didn't I bring sunglasses with me?" Niel groaned as he dodged another blast.

"Because no one told us about a bloody great crystal," Shadow pointed out.

"I don't think I can get us any closer."

"Niel, I swear to the Gods, I shall cut your balls off if you don't drop me close enough."

"Wait! Something's happening. The light..."

He trailed off and Shadow squinted at the source, wondering what he was talking about. But he was right. The light was dimming, just as Toto and the woman were reaching the platform below it.

"Get us closer!" Shadow yelled, readying her weapons.

By now the light was dimming rapidly, night settling over the city, and Niel arrowed in on the spot. As soon as he was above the walkway, he dropped her.

She landed like a cat on all fours, quickly bounding upwards and racing towards The Silencer of Souls, who was distracted by the disappearing crystal. Shadow didn't hesitate, and she tackled her to the floor, simultaneously raising her knife to stab her. But rather than The Silencer of Souls pushing Shadow off, she grabbed her head and pulled her close, raising her lips eagerly to hers.

TWENTY-EIGHT

The momentum was unexpected, and Shadow toppled forward, her knife clattering to the floor as she lost her balance. But she had just enough strength to slide to the side, those deadly lips missing her own by inches.

As Shadow scrambled to grapple her opponent, they both ended up rolling over and over again, and the next thing she knew, they'd plunged over the side and were freefalling.

Barak thrust his sword forward, plunging it through the shoulder of a Black Cronos soldier who was heavyset with dull grey eyes.

The force of Barak's thrust was so great that it pinned him to the rock behind him. Barak restrained his other arm, and swiftly slit his throat with his dagger. As the man slumped forward, he pulled his sword free, scowling at the blade that was now pock-marked and scarred from the fight.

Warily he spun around, weapon raised, but there was no one left to fight.

All of the Black Cronos soldiers lay dead, half a dozen Igigi lying next to them. The survivors stood, winded and panting, some bent double from their exertions. Zee and Ash, both wounded from what Barak could see, were with a group of Igigi, some of whom were bleeding heavily, all looking at the sky. Another cluster of Igigi were searching through the dead bodies, no doubt checking that they really were dead, Estelle with them. But Barak couldn't see Nahum.

He looked skyward, wondering if he was flying, but then a groan drew his attention, and Barak spun around. From the midst of a few fallen dead soldiers, a figure moved. Barak flung the dead bodies aside, revealing Nahum beneath them, eyes glazed with pain.

He quickly assessed his injuries, and saw a knife sticking out from under his ribcage.

"Nahum! You've been stabbed. Don't move."

"I couldn't move if I wanted to, brother." His breaths were fast and shallow, sweat covering his face. He fumbled for the knife, his hands slick with blood and shaking.

"Don't touch it!" Barak warned, moving his hand gently away. "We're best leaving it in place right now." He shouted to the Igigi. "We need help! Have you a healer in the city?"

The shout summoned everyone, and they crowded around. Ash and Zee shoved them aside so they could get closer. Ash looked at Barak, panic in his eyes. "He's lost a lot of blood. We have to stabilise him to give him the best chance of recovery."

Estelle pushed him aside. "I can help, but we need to get him inside. Somewhere warm."

Gishkim was hanging back, watching, but now he said, "We have an infirmary, in our main city. I can take you there. In fact," his lips pursed as he took in the number of wounded, "we all need to go, apart from a few we'll leave behind to seal the entrance. I'll fly Nahum there myself. It will be quicker."

Estelle was kneeling by Nahum's side, murmuring a spell as her hand cradled over his wound.

Barak nodded and stood, allowing Gishkim to get close, and then turned to his brothers. "Has anyone escaped?"

Zee dragged his gaze away from Nahum, pointing to a distant shape in the sky. "See the lights? A helicopter took off while we were fighting—with Stefan Hope-Robbins in it, I suspect." He gestured around him. "He doesn't seem to be here."

For a moment, Barak focussed on the retreating helicopter, trying to calculate if he could reach it, but Zee squeezed his shoulder. "I've already considered it. We wouldn't get to it in time. They're gone."

"Shit," Barak huffed. "What about Toto and that bitch?"

TWENTY-EIGHT

"Still inside, I suspect. But whether they're dead or alive..."

He trailed off as Gishkim lifted Nahum effortlessly, his huge muscles rippling beneath his burnished skin. He barked out a few orders, and the Igigi who were well drew back, nodding at the command, while the others prepared to move.

It seemed it was time to leave.

As soon as the hatch was open, revealing the shaft beneath, Gabe saw a ladder attached to its side, and he leapt in front of Urbarra.

"I'm going down. Take care of Catarina."

Urbarra scowled. "I'm no babysitter. I'm going, too."

But Gabe didn't stop to argue, instead starting his descent. He had no idea where Shadow and Niel were, but he had to find out.

The shaft wasn't that long, but the light he could see below was rapidly dimming, no doubt due to the disappearing Stone of Utu. Even in the shaft he could feel the rumbling of the mechanism. As the ladder cleared the shaft, he could see the platform below, and he jumped down the last few feet, extending his wings as he did so. His gaze swept the area, taking in everything possible in the rapidly dying light.

A short distance away, Toto was firing his weapon at Niel, who was sheltering behind a column of rock. It seemed even Toto wasn't stupid enough to hit the column and risk the structure that was keeping him alive. *Although*, Gabe thought, puzzled, *where on Earth did he think he could go?* There was no escape, and defeat was inevitable.

And where was Shadow?

Niel bellowed at him, reading his mind. "Shadow has fallen off the platform with that bitch! Go get her!"

Gabe suddenly realised what was happening. Toto was pinning Niel down deliberately.

Gabe soared over the edge, heart in his mouth. *How long ago had it happened?*

A vast darkness spread below him, but lights were visible in the distance. His breath was coming quickly as his panic escalated, and he yelled, "Shadow!"

An answering shout came from beneath him, and he finally spotted two tumbling figures below.

He dived down, wings close to his side, knowing exactly how to angle them to get the most speed. Their fall was swift, but their tumbling bodies weren't as quick as his descent. It seemed to take a horribly long time to reach them though, and the ground below was getting closer. Buildings were becoming more detailed, and he could discern rivers and fields. But there was no time to wonder at the view.

Shadow and The Silencer of Souls were locked together, limbs wrapped around each other. Gabe could see Shadow desperately trying to keep the woman's face from her own, but they were inches apart. Neither seemed to have any weapons anymore.

As soon as he was close enough, Gabe grasped The Silencer of Souls by her hair with one hand, and her jacket with the other. As soon as she realised Gabe had caught her, she twisted around, grabbing him with a claw-like hand and releasing Shadow.

But Shadow wasn't letting go that easily either, wrapping her legs around the woman's waist and falling backward, like a crazy trapeze act.

Gabe had by now stopped their descent and they hung in the air, his wings outstretched, a maniacal grin on his face. He had the upper hand, and the woman knew it. Even in the dark he could see her wide-eyed expression, her pupils almost black. She was trying to twist towards him, her fingers clutching at his face. But her angle was all wrong, her back towards him, and Shadow's weight at her waist was keeping her pinned in position.

Still clutching her hair, Gabe freed his other hand, drawing his dagger from its scabbard and placing it beneath her chin. She scrabbled at him, her look of malice draining from her face, her strength no match for his own. Gabe could still feel the coldness of her lips from their last encounter, the horrible weakness she'd caused him, and he stared her down.

"Time's up, bitch."

For the first time in all their encounters, she spoke, her voice only a harsh whisper. "There are more like me. They will come for you."

"Then I'll kill them, too."

Gabe plunged his knife into her throat, and she fell limp in his arms, her blood spurting over him. Shadow scrambled over her body and clung to Gabe, and when he was sure she was secure, he dropped the woman's corpse, watching her fall to a field below. He swallowed when he realised how close they were to the ground. If he'd been there a few seconds later, Shadow would have been dead, too.

"Damn you, Gabreel Malouf! I wanted to kill her myself!" Shadow's legs were wrapped around his waist, her face inches from his, her expression furious.

"Oh, I'm sorry! I thought I just saved your life! Or can *you* fly now?"

She scowled, words battling to get out, but in the end all she managed was, "Bollocks!"

"That's my girl. Shall we go and check on Niel now?" It wasn't really a question, and he was already wheeling in the air, his wings beating as he climbed back to the distant platforms beneath the metallic sky. "Toto had him pinned down with that damn blasting weapon of theirs."

But by the time they arrived on the platform, Gabe flying in low and quick just in case of attack, it was all over.

Niel and Urbarra were standing over Toto's dead body, and even Catarina had arrived. She stood in the centre of the platform beneath the shaft, terrified to move as she took in the city below. Gabe landed softly, Shadow unwound herself to stand on her own two feet.

Niel sighed with relief. "I always knew you'd be hard to get rid of, Shadow. I trust The Silencer is dead?"

"Of course. But not by my hands." She scowled at Gabe. "He did it."

Gabe gave a mock bow, feeling a huge surge of relief that these two people who had been haunting his dreams for weeks were now gone. "And now Toto is dead, too."

"Courtesy of Urbarra," Niel said.

Urbarra gave a wolf-smile, his blade bloody in his hand. "It was my pleasure."

"Look at him," Gabe said, eyeing the dead man with distaste. "He looks pathetically small in death, and yet he was a force of nature in life." He sighed. "It's a shame we couldn't take him back for questioning."

"He would never have talked," Niel said. "In fact, once you went for Shadow, he became ever more reckless."

Gabe knew Niel was right. Toto would have been determined to take his secrets to the grave, but what did his loss mean for Black Cronos and their alchemical experiments?

Urbarra's question pulled him from his thoughts. "Will any more attack here?"

Gabe shrugged, uncertain, but it was Niel who answered. "They were the only group heading this way, so it's unlikely, but we can do a final sweep to make sure."

Urbarra nodded, relieved. "Good, and once that's done, I'll take you to the city. Hopefully we'll get some news on the others."

TWENTY-NINE

Shadow accepted the wine that was offered her, sipping it gratefully as she took in their strange surroundings.

A few hours had passed since they killed Toto and The Silencer of Souls, and the other Nephilim and Igigi who had battled outside the city had joined them. They had been offered use of the public baths, a system of hot and cool pools and saunas. Their injuries were dressed, their filthy clothes, stained with blood, sweat, and dirt, had been sent to be cleaned, and they were now wearing the clothing of the Igigi. It was, admittedly, a little large. More importantly, Nahum was resting in the infirmary, his condition now stable, and Zee was keeping him company.

And now they were all seated under the stars—fake, of course—at a long wooden table, surrounded by vines that scrambled across a wooden pergola. A stone building was behind them, a hum of noise coming from the Igigi inside as they finished preparing the food. Gishkim and Urbarra were seated with them, as well as a handful of other Igigi, females included. It was, without a doubt, very surreal. The Igigi's voices sounded all too human, and yet their appearance, with their animal heads, was anything but. At least Shadow was used to satyrs and the oddness of the fey, some of whom were very different in appearance, but Catarina, for all her composure, still looked utterly shocked. Estelle seemed more at ease, but Shadow suspected that was out of sheer bloody-mindedness. She sat opposite Shadow, next to Barak, chatting to him while studying everyone intently.

The Igigi wore the traditional clothes she'd seen on the old stone carvings, although considerably more ornate and decorative, and made of fine silks and linens in gloriously rich colours. Shadow felt like she was in one of those carvings now. And the Nephilim looked...well, seeing them in their finery made her view them in a whole new light. They always exuded power and authority, especially together, but in traditional clothing, she knew exactly how they would have looked in their time. *No wonder they were kings and princes.* Their skin, like her own, was oiled and perfumed, their hair freshly washed and styled, and they were certainly at ease, chatting to the Igigi.

Shadow was sitting next to Gabe, and she turned to him, struggling to understand their conversation. "Can you translate? How does this place exist?"

Gabe looked guilty as he stopped listening to an exchange between Ash and Gishkim. "Sorry, Shadow. And you, Catarina." She sat on his other side, eyes wide. "Excellent questions, and one we've just asked, too. I'll tell him to slow down so I can translate properly." Gabe turned to Gishkim who nodded at his words before starting again, this time more slowly as Gabe repeated everything after him. "He says that they had to flee from the Anunnaki, because despite their strength and size, their labours were killing them. And they'd had enough of working so hard for such little reward. The Anunnaki would never have agreed to let them leave, and so they rebelled. But what we didn't know was that they had the Stone of Utu."

Catarina interjected, "One of the seven Gods?"

"Exactly. Utu represented the sun, and was believed to have a sun chariot. His sister was called Inanna, and was the Queen of Heaven."

Catarina nodded, clearly excited, her voice low as she said, "Also called Ishtar."

"Exactly. Each of the seven Gods had a city dedicated to them, and the Sumerians were the first to use crystals in magic. Each God had one that mirrored its own powers." Gabe paused as he listened to Gishkim again. "They knew that if they were to succeed, they must hide deep underground, but to survive long term they needed a source of light—their own sun. So, they stole Utu's crystal."

Shadow nodded. "The stone they now use above. It's huge, surely?"

Gabe shook his head. "Not really. They looked like large eggs, highly polished, beautifully finished, about so big." He held his hands approximately twelve inches apart. "But the power they contained was enormous. And if you could use magic, as many of them did, you could manipulate that."

"The Igigi can do magic?"

"Some can—of a sort. Manipulation of the basic elements of air, water, fire, and earth. Not quite how Estelle can." He shushed them again, listening to Gishkim before continuing. "The city they built above, the old one, was their first, but they soon realised that wouldn't be sufficient. Once they explored the cave system here, they found this one. Most of it is natural. The rest they mined, connecting it to the next."

Estelle leaned across the table and said, "But the fields and irrigation systems, that seems impossible to maintain."

Gabe rapidly translated her question for the Igigi. It was another who answered this time, not Gishkim. A woman with the head of a hawk, while the human part of her body was clearly feminine. It was...odd.

Barak translated next. "They have magi, who we call magicians. Rock was transformed to earth, seeds are collected and replanted, and the water system down here is controlled to make irrigation possible. When we leave," Barak explained, "they will destroy all the tunnels to the surface. She warns us that they will never be found again. They no longer have use of the outside world, and never will again. When we have eaten our fill, offered in thanks for our help in defending their city, they will escort us to the surface. Despite our aid today, we are cautioned that if we ever try to find them again, we will die. Whatever we need to find out, we need to ask now. We'll never have another chance."

"There is something you should discuss," Shadow said, hating the fact that she was bringing up the subject, but knew she had to anyway. "You need to ask about your fathers."

Estelle met her eyes and nodded. "Yes, you're right. They do."

Shadow was surprised, but glad of her support. Gabe and Barak, however, groaned in unison.

"The last thing I want to talk about is bloody Remiel," Gabe complained.

Shadow glared at both of them. "You have to. It could be important for your lives right now!"

With a look of resignation, Gabe attracted Gishkim's attention and asked the question, and the separate conversations that had been taking place all around the table ground to a halt. Gishkim, however, looked amused when he answered, and Gabe's shoulders dropped as he leaned back in his chair.

"Well?" Shadow demanded, irate.

Gabe had a sparkle in his eye when he translated. "After the flood, the Igigi left their underground city, wondering if they could live in the desert again, seeing as the area had been wiped clean. The cities they had built were destroyed, the Sumerian Gods had retreated, and they were prepared to build afresh. But unfortunately, all that did was advertise their survival, and the Fallen came looking for them. However," Gabe smiled, "the Stone of Utu saved them. Utu is not only the God of the sun, he is also the God of justice. They used it against the Fallen, weakening their powers in this world. It stopped them taking human form completely. They couldn't march on Earth or breed with women, and their powers were blunted."

"Which means," Shadow said, "that they have no hold over you either, right?"

Gabe looked at his brothers. "That's how I interpret it. What about you?"

Niel snorted. "Sounds too good to be true, but it would explain a lot."

"Maybe," Ash suggested, "they're licking their wounds and trying to find a way back. I can't imagine they'd just accept it."

"Sounds like they had to," Barak said, amused. "But you're right, they wouldn't like to be defeated. However, it still leaves them with plenty to fight about amongst themselves. I reckon our return is insignificant, in general. You hearing Remiel, Gabe, was a desperate attempt at persuading you to help him."

"Which means," Shadow said, nudging Gabe gently, "that the next time he appears in your head, you can tell him to get lost."

Gabe's tension finally ebbed away, and he reached for his drink. "I can guarantee that I most certainly will."

With that promise ringing in their ears, the arrival of steaming plates of spiced meats and vegetables halted their conversation, and heralded the end of their stay.

Jackson emptied out the final box of papers, dust flying everywhere, and coughed, waving his hand around in a futile attempt to clear the air.

He had been in his office since six that morning, eager to get the place in shape, but that meant clearing the last few boxes of Black Cronos information. Thank the Gods, it was the final one. He was already over it.

"You all right, old man?" Harlan asked, poking his head around the door.

Harlan looked fresh, clean, and undeniably American. There was something horribly energetic about him, from his well-cut hair to his excellent tan, which he seemed to maintain despite the English weather. His expensive leather jacket oozed style as it sat on his impressive shoulders—a result of endless sessions at the gym, no doubt. And yet despite all of that, he had this roguish attractiveness that made Jackson feel like a scarecrow. Let's face it. He actually looked like a scarecrow. He wore the same thing day in and day out. He consoled himself that he had his own charm, and grinned at Harlan as if he hadn't just had such uncharitable thoughts about his good friend.

"I will be when all of this crap is out of the way," he answered. Jackson threw the old box on the floor in a fit of pique, and then checked his watch. It wasn't even nine o'clock yet. "You're up early. Everything okay?"

"Yes, I have very good news. I heard from Gabe earlier. They found the Igigi, killed a lot of Black Cronos soldiers, and in an added bonus, took out Toto and The Silencer of Souls, too."

"*What*? Are you kidding? Damn it! Couldn't we have caught one of them?" And then he realised what Harlan had said. "And what do you mean, found the Igigi? Their city, you mean?"

Harlan wiggled his hand. "Kind of. What I tell you stays between us."

Jackson groaned. Harlan seemed to be taking this cloak and dagger stuff very seriously. "We're in the top-secret Paranormal Division. Of course I'll keep it a secret."

"I mean it. No memos to Waylen, nothing documented. Only the bare essentials." Harlan raised an eyebrow, looking insufferably pleased with himself.

"He's my boss."

"And what he won't know won't kill him. It's important."

TWENTY-NINE

Jackson wasn't at all sure that he liked where this was going, but he nodded anyway. "Go on."

"The Igigi are alive and well, and living deep under the desert in a massive cave system. It seems Black Cronos had alternate intel that led them there. And it wasn't just their bones or bodies they wanted." He held a hand up, forestalling questions. "It seems that several hundred years ago desert nomads found their caves, and they were accepted as friends because of the fact that they avoided the cities and lived in the desert. The story of their friendship was passed down in the tribe and eventually recorded, long after that friendship had ceased to exist. That's what Barnaby found and passed on to Toto. That's what was in the papers in the bank deposit box. A name is mentioned in there, too. Another traveller that the nomads met. A Count Soltikoff." Harlan's mouth twitched in a smile.

"Oh, shit. One of the pseudonyms of the count."

"Exactly. He never visited the city, but obviously has known of its existence for years. This adds weight to our argument that he's behind Black Cronos. And Barnaby was starting to realise it, too."

Jackson stood abruptly and headed to the drink supplies and the kettle plugged in on a sideboard, switching it on. He needed tea. *Strong, sweet tea*. "It's really him."

"Unless he's got descendants. But that's unlikely."

"I've tried to pretend it wasn't real, but this is another bit of evidence. I guess it's good. Something to work on."

Harlan's face fell. "There's bad news, though. Stefan was there, but he escaped in a helicopter. We have no idea where he is. And before she died, The Silencer said there were more like her. She said they would come after us, and it wasn't over yet."

Jackson squeezed his tea bag until it was very strong, and put another spoonful of sugar in his mug just to cheer himself up. "Want one?"

Harlan looked alarmed. "Not if you're going to try and give me diabetes! Black coffee would be better."

"It's instant."

"Forget it. I'll stick to water."

Jackson sat down again, sipping his steaming drink. "Well, that settles it. We need to narrow down addresses. Having failed here, who knows what he might have planned next. Have you got any leads yet?"

"You're kidding, right? There's a mass of stuff to wade through. There are a couple of English addresses, but JD already reckons they're a dud. What about you?"

Jackson shook his head. "Not yet. I've only just emptied all the boxes. I'll begin cataloguing it all later. It's going to take a long time."

"And," Harlan shuffled in his seat, making himself more comfortable, "I have an interesting case myself. It could prove tricky."

"Fair enough." As much as Jackson wanted Harlan helping him all the time, he knew he had to keep The Orphic Guild happy. "You'd better warn Gabe and the others that they might have some stakeouts coming up."

Gabe let the cool night breeze wash over him, grateful to experience fresh air and natural night sounds again.

They had been escorted from the depths of the Igigi city to the surface a few hours earlier. Their camp was undisturbed and still protected by Estelle's spell, and their vehicles were intact. The shock of the late afternoon sun seemed to scald his eyeballs, despite the cleverness of the Igigi's light source, which had risen as they were preparing to leave.

The Igigi had kindly taken them on a brief tour of their world, an exhibition of pride and achievement, but then they had been ushered out, and Gabe knew there were many parts of it they would never get to see.

They hadn't lingered in the desert, in a hurry to get back to Mardin, and once there, they had checked back into the hotel and slept for hours. Their group had been quiet on their return, subdued even, but the good news was that Nahum was better—sort of—and they were now sitting in a rooftop restaurant not far from their hotel, their food ordered and with drinks in front of them.

"Cheer up," Nahum said to him, a hand on the site of his wound as he grimaced. "At least you weren't stabbed."

"Not as badly as you, but I'm still covered in cuts," he said, glancing down at the bandages that were wrapped around his arms. They were on his legs too, but at least those weren't visible. He'd hoped that in this new life they might not be fighting so much. *Perhaps this trip would be an anomaly.*

Niel snorted. "The whole lot of us look terrible. It's a miracle they let us in here. Well, apart from Catarina, who looks undamaged and very respectable. And you, Estelle. You escaped with only a few bruises."

He was right. They were all bruised and bandaged to varying degrees, each one making the odd wince when they moved. The restaurant staff had raised quizzical eyebrows, but their politeness and fluent Turkish saw them admitted anyway.

"My ribs ache," Estelle admitted, "from where I struck a wall, but the baths and sauna helped."

Catarina laughed as she looked down at herself. "Physically I might look fine, but I have mental scars. When we arrived here a few days ago, I had no idea that we would actually find..." she faltered. "*Them.*"

"You wanted an adventure," Shadow pointed out.

"I did. And I have plenty to share with my husband. I can assure you, their secret is safe with him." A look of uncertainty crossed her face, and Gabe knew she was wondering how long he'd have left.

"Well," Shadow huffed, "I came closer to death than I have in a long time. Something I do not wish to repeat."

Gabe squeezed her hand. While Shadow hadn't said much about her fall with The Silencer of Souls, he knew she was shaken by it. She really had been moments from death, and Gabe's heart faltered at the thought of it. But he teased her regardless, and Niel. "So much for you two arguing about who would kill her." He winked, watching Niel scowl. "It was left to me to do the honours. By the sound of her final threat, though, there are more of them like her."

"I would imagine," Ash said, "that there are a lot more of all of them. They certainly arrived with reinforcements after you two saw them." He nodded at Niel and Shadow. "And they have a helicopter."

"Private, no doubt," Zee said, signalling for more beer to the waiter. "And that means they have lots of money."

"But they're not infallible," Estelle argued. She leaned forward on the table, her hand fiddling with the napkin. "They underestimated the Igigi, despite the old records they found from the nomads. Or maybe because of them. They were friends, and assumed the Igigi were weak. And that man who heard their story…what was his name? Count Soltikoff, right?"

"The man we believe to be the *Comte de Saint-Germain*. Sounds arrogant to me," Barak said. "Just like Black Cronos. It's their Achilles heel. And the Anunnaki, for that matter."

And their fathers' Achilles heel, too, Gabe thought, and from the speculative looks around the table, his brothers thought it too, although no one wanted to say it.

He addressed Estelle next. "The last few days haven't put you off working with us, then?"

"Not at all." She glanced up at Barak, a smile on her lips. "I'm finding it a welcome challenge after dealing with boardroom antics."

Gabe felt rather than saw Shadow's resigned shuffle in her chair but ignored it, thinking he'd enjoy taking her mind off it later. "You held your own, Estelle. You're a welcome addition to the team." She beamed with pleasure, her resting bitch face vanishing. But to be honest, he hadn't seen it for a few weeks anyway. *The Barak effect.* "But I have a feeling we'll be splitting up our efforts in future."

"Why is that?" Shadow prompted.

"Harlan and Jackson need our help to search for the *Comte de Saint-Germain*, and Harlan also thinks he may need help on his next case."

Nahum held his hand up, and then winced as it pulled his side. "I'll help Harlan. I'm over Black Cronos and bloody alchemists. Damn secret societies. I'm up for a good, old-fashioned relic hunt." A grin split his face. "I might get to avoid old tombs and underground cities, too."

"You're kidding, right?" Zee said, amused. "I'm sure there'll be plenty more tombs. Any idea what Harlan wants us for?"

Gabe shook his head. "Not a clue. He said it would be a nice surprise when we got home."

Catarina was leaning on the table, listening avidly to every word. "I envy you your freedom. Your life sounds fun. When my husband passes, because I know it won't be long, I shall travel again."

Ash smiled at her. "That sounds like a good idea. You're far too young to give up on life completely. Besides, you're travelling now. Enjoy it while you're here."

"We all should," Barak said, reaching for his beer. "Let's stay a while longer, soak up the sun, and let our wounds heal before we go home." He gave Estelle a long look that she returned. "I'd like to show Estelle the sights, and I'd like to explore the place, too. I was worried that being here would be unsettling, but it's not so bad."

"I agree," Niel said, his expression resolute. "If anything, it's banished a few ghosts."

Gabe wondered if he meant Lilith, but he certainly wasn't going to ask. Instead, he raised his glass in a toast. "I think we all need to banish a few ghosts. Let's drink to that."

Thanks for reading *Hunter's Dawn*. Please make an author happy and leave a review here.

This book is a spin-off of my White Haven Witches series. The first book is called *Buried Magic,* and you can buy it here. The tenth book in that series is called *Stormcrossed Magic*, and is out in August 2022. Get it here.

If you enjoyed this book and would like to read more of my stories, please subscribe to my newsletter at www.tjgreen.nz. You will get two free short stories, *Excalibur Rises* and *Jack's Encounter,* and will also receive free character sheets of all the main White Haven witches.

By staying on my mailing list you'll receive free excerpts of my new books, as well as short stories, news of giveaways, and a chance to join my launch team. I'll also be sharing information about other books in this genre you might enjoy. Read on for a list of my other books.

AUTHOR'S NOTE

Thanks for reading *Hunter's Dawn*, the fourth book in the White Haven Hunters series. I thought it would be fun to explore more of the Nephilim's past, and the Paranormal Division with Jackson also seemed to take on a life of their own.

You can be sure that Black Cronos will continue to appear, along with their mysterious Grand Master, but there'll be more fun occult hunts with Harlan, too. I'm planning on writing another White Haven Hunters book later this year.

The Sumerian civilisation really was lost for years, and there is so much speculation about the Igigi and the Anunnaki. If you're interested in reading more, head to my website, where I have blogs on the backgrounds to all my books: https:/tjgreen.nz

I am still planning on writing a few short story prequels—for Shadow, certainly, and hopefully Harlan and Gabe, too.

If you enjoy audiobooks, *Spirit of the Fallen*, White Haven Hunters #1, and *Shadow's Edge*, White Haven Hunters #2, are both available now, and *Dark Star* is imminent. Links are on my website: https://tjgreen.nz/

If you'd like a chance to get involved in my books and join my fabulous Facebook group, just answer the question and I'll let you in:

https://www.facebook.com/groups/696140834516292

Thanks to my fabulous cover designer, Fiona Jayde Media, and to Missed Period Editing.

I owe a big thanks to Jason, my partner, who has been incredibly supportive throughout my career, and is a beta reader. Thanks also to Terri and my mother, my other two beta readers. You're all awesome.

Finally, thank you to my launch team, who give valuable feedback on typos and are happy to review on release. It's lovely to hear from them—you know who you are! You're amazing! I also love hearing from all of my readers, so I welcome you to get in touch.

If you'd like to read a bit more background on my stories, please head to my website—www.tjgreen.nz—where I blog about the research I've done, among other things. I have another series set in Cornwall about witches, called White Haven Witches, so if you enjoy myths and magic, you'll love that, too. It's an adult series, not YA.

If you'd like to read more of my writing, please join my mailing list. You can get a free short story called *Jack's Encounter*, describing how Jack met Fahey—a longer version of the prologue in *Call of the King*, my YA Arthurian series—by subscribing to my newsletter. You'll also get a FREE copy of *Excalibur Rises*, a short story prequel to *Rise of the King*.

Additionally, you will receive free character sheets on all of my main characters in White Haven Witches—exclusive to my email list!

By staying on my mailing list, you'll receive free excerpts of my new books, as well as short stories and news of giveaways. I'll also be sharing information about other books in this genre you might enjoy. Finally, I welcome you to join my readers' group for even more great content, called TJ's Inner Circle, on Facebook. Please answer the questions to join! https://business.facebook.com/groups/696140834516292/

Give me my FREE short stories!

https://tjgreen.nz/landing/

About the Author

I write books about magic, mystery, myths, and general mayhem, and they're action-packed!

My primary series is adult urban fantasy, called White Haven Witches. There's lots of magic, action, and a little bit of romance.

My YA series, Rise of the King, is about a teen named Tom and his discovery that he is a descendant of King Arthur. It's a fun-filled, clean read with a new twist on the Arthurian tales.

I've got loads of ideas for future books in all of my series, including spin-offs, novellas, and short stories, so if you'd like to be kept up to date, subscribe to my newsletter. You'll get free short stories, character sheets, and other fun stuff. Interested? Subscribe here.

I was born in England, in the Black Country, but moved to New Zealand 16 years ago. England is great, but I'm over the traffic! And then recently I made another big move to Portugal! I live in the Algarve with my partner, Jase, and my cats, Sacha and Leia. When I'm not busy writing I read lots, indulge in gardening and shopping, and I love yoga.

Confession time! I'm a Star Trek geek—old and new—and love urban fantasy and detective shows. My secret passion is *Columbo*! My favourite Star Trek film is *The Wrath of Khan*, the original! Other top films for me are *Predator*, the original, and *Aliens*.

In a previous life, I was a singer in a band, and used to do some acting with a theatre company. On occasion, a few friends and I like to make short films, which begs the question, where are the book trailers? I'm thinking on it...

For more on me, check out a couple of my blog posts. I'm an old grunge queen, so you can read about my love of that here. For more random news, read this.

Why magic and mystery?

I've always loved the weird, the wonderful, and the inexplicable. My favourite stories are those of magic and mystery, set on the edges of the known, particularly tales of folklore, faerie, and legend—all the narratives that try to explain our reality.

The King Arthur stories are fascinating because they sit between reality and myth. They encompass real life concerns, but also cross boundaries with the world of faerie—or the Otherworld, as I call it. There are green knights, witches, wizards, and dragons, and that's what I find particularly fascinating. They are stories that have intrigued people for generations, and like many others, I'm adding my own interpretation.

I also love witches and magic, hence my additional series set in beautiful Cornwall. There are witches, missing grimoires, supernatural threats, and ghosts, and as the series progresses, even weirder stuff happens.

Have a poke around in my blog posts, and you'll find all sorts of articles about my series and my characters, and quite a few book reviews.

If you'd like to follow me on social media, you'll find me here:

Facebook,
Twitter

Pinterest, Instagram, TikTok, BookBub.

OTHER TITLES BY TJ GREEN

Rise of the King Series

A Young Adult series about a teen called Tom who's summoned to wake King Arthur. It's a fun adventure about King Arthur in the Otherworld!

Call of the King #1

King Arthur is destined to return, and Tom is destined to wake him.

When sixteen-year-old Tom's grandfather mysteriously disappears, Tom stops at nothing to find him, even when that means crossing to a mysterious and unknown world.

When he gets there, Tom discovers that everything he thought he knew about himself and his life was wrong. Vivian, the Lady of the Lake, has been watching over him and manipulating his life since his birth. And now she needs his help.

The Silver Tower #2

Merlin disappeared over a thousand years ago. Now they risk everything to find him.

Vivian needs King Arthur's help. Nimue, a powerful witch and priestess who lives on Avalon, has disappeared.

King Arthur, Tom, and his friends set off across the Other to find her, following Nimue's trail. Nimue seems to have a quest of her own, one she's deliberately hiding. Arthur is convinced it's about Merlin, and he's determined to find him.

The Cursed Sword #3

An ancient sword. A dark secret. A new enemy.

Tom loves his new life in the Otherworld. He lives with Arthur in New Camelot, and Arthur is hosting a tournament. Eager to test his sword-fighting skills, Tom is competing.

But while the games are being played, his friends are attacked and everything he loves is threatened. Tom has to find the intruder before anyone else gets hurt.

Tom's sword seems to be the focus of these attacks. Their investigations uncover its dark history and a terrible betrayal that a family has kept secret for generations.

White Haven Witches Series

Witches, secrets, myth and folklore, set on the Cornish coast!

Buried Magic #1

Love witchy fiction? Welcome to White Haven, where secrets are deadly.

Avery, a witch who lives on the Cornish coast, discovers that her past holds more secrets than she ever imagined in this spellbinding mystery. For years witches have lived in quirky White Haven, all with an age-old connection to the town's magical roots, but Avery has been reluctant to join a coven, preferring to work alone.

However, when she inherits a rune-covered box and an intriguing letter, Avery learns that their history is darker than she realised. And when the handsome Alex Bonneville tells her he's been having ominous premonitions, they know that trouble is coming.

Magic Unbound #2

OTHER TITLES BY TJ GREEN

Avery and the other witches are now being hunted, and they know someone is betraying them.

The question is, who?

One thing is certain.

They have to find their missing grimoires before their attackers do, and they have to strike back.

If you love urban fantasy, filled with magic and a twist of romance, you'll love Magic Unbound.

<u>Magic Unleashed #3</u>

Old magic, new enemies. The danger never stops in White Haven.

Avery and the White Haven witches have finally found their grimoires and defeated the Favershams, but their troubles are only just beginning.

Something escaped from the spirit world when they battled beneath All Souls Church, and now it wants to stay, unleashing violence across Cornwall.

On top of that, the power they released when they reclaimed their magic is attracting powerful creatures from the deep, creatures that need men to survive.

<u>All Hallows' Magic #4</u>

When Samhain arrives, worlds collide.

A Shifter family arrives in White Haven, one of them close to death. Avery offers them sanctuary, only to find their pursuers are close behind, intent on retribution. In an effort to help them, Avery and Alex are dragged into a fight they didn't want but must see through.

As if that weren't enough trouble, strange signs begin to appear at Old Haven Church. Avery realises that an unknown witch has wicked plans for Samhain, and is determined to breach the veils between worlds.

Avery and her friends scramble to discover who the mysterious newcomer is, all while being attacked, one by one.

Undying Magic #5
Winter grips White Haven, bringing death in its wake.

It's close to the winter solstice when Newton reports that dead bodies have been found, drained of their blood.

Then people start disappearing, and Genevieve calls a coven meeting. What they hear chills their blood.

This has happened before, and it's going to get worse. The witches have to face their toughest challenge yet—vampires.

Crossroads Magic #6
When Myths become real, danger stalks White Haven.

The Crossroads Circus has a reputation for bringing myths to life, but it also seems that where the circus goes, death follows. When the circus sets up on the castle grounds, Newton asks Avery and the witches to investigate.

This proves trickier than they expected when an unexpected encounter finds Avery bound to a power she can't control.

Strange magic is making the myths a little too real.

Crown of Magic #7
Passions run deep at Beltane—too deep.

With the Beltane Festival approaching, the preparations in White Haven are in full swing, but when emotions soar out of control, the witches suspect more than just high spirits.

As part of the celebrations, a local theatre group is rehearsing *Tristan and Isolde*, but it seems Beltane magic is affecting the cast, and all sorts of old myths are brought to the surface.

The May Queen brings desire, fertility, and the promise of renewal, but love can also be dark and dangerous.

Vengeful Magic #8
When lost treasure is discovered, supernatural creatures unleash violence across Cornwall.

Midsummer is approaching and Avery, Alex, and the White Haven witches, are making plans to celebrate Litha, but everything stops when paranormal activities cause havoc.

Smuggler's gold is found that dates back centuries, and a strange chain of events is set in motion; Newton needs magical help.

The witches find they are pitted against a deadly enemy, and they need the Cornwall Coven. But not all are happy to help - a few members have never accepted White Haven, and their enmity puts everyone in danger.

Some things are meant to stay buried...

Chaos Magic #9

The rules have changed.

Reeling from the events that revealed other witches were behind the attack on Reuben and Caspian, the White Haven witches don't know who to trust.

The search for those who betrayed them tests their resources and their abilities, and as the fallout shatters alliances, they draw on their friends for support.

But it's not easy. The path they follow is dark and twisted and leads them in directions they can't predict.

Knowing who to trust is the only thing that may save them.

Grab the ninth book in the White Haven Witches series now, but be warned, nothing is as it seems...

Printed in Great Britain
by Amazon